CENTRAL

Enchantments

Kathryn Harrison

Enchantments

· · · ·

A Novel

FOURTH ESTATE • *London*

First published in Great Britain by
Fourth Estate
An imprint of HarperCollins*Publishers*
77–85 Fulham Palace Road,
London W6 8JB
www.4thestate.co.uk

1 3 5 7 9 10 8 6 4 2

A catalogue record for this book is
available from the British Library

HB ISBN 978-0-00-747256-7
TPB ISBN 978-0-00-745606-2

Book design by Simon M. Sullivan
Printed in Great Britain by
Clays Ltd, St Ives plc

MIX
Paper from
responsible sources
FSC
www.fsc.org   FSC C007454

FSC™ is a non-profit international organisation established to promote
the responsible management of the world's forests. Products carrying the
FSC label are independently certified to assure consumers that they come
from forests that are managed to meet the social, economic and
ecological needs of present and future generations,
and other controlled sources.

Find out more about HarperCollins and the environment at
www.harpercollins.co.uk/green

For Joyce

The eyes those silent tongues of love.

—CERVANTES

Contents

· · · · ·

The Hole in the Ice

· · · · ·

*B*EHOLD: IN THE BEGINNING there was everything, just as there is now. The giant slap of a thunderclap and, *bang,* it's raining talking snakes.

A greater light to rule the day, a lesser light to rule the night, swarming water and restless air. A man goes down on two knees, a woman opens her thighs, and both hold their breath to listen. Imagining God's footsteps could be heard in the cool of the day. But God walks silently along the bank of the muddy river that flows out of the Garden, the river that divides and becomes many: Usa, Kolva, Yug, Onega. Narva, Obsha, Luga, Okhta. Volycha, Sestra, Uver, Oyat. Volga, Kama, Neva, Ob.

From the windows of the house that was my childhood home, I heard a river running. The Tura hurried past our village to join the Tobol, and the Tobol joined the Irtysh, and the Irtysh joined the Ob, and the Great Ob carried our cries and emptied them into the Kara Sea, which, being frozen, preserved them like flies in amber.

"Go on," Alyosha said whenever I fell silent. "Please, Masha, I like to hear your voice."

And I did; I told him about my father, about me, about Siberia. I told him stories my father told us when we were children. I did whatever I could to distract him.

. . .

THE DAY THEY PULLED FATHER'S BODY out from under the ice, the first day of the new year, 1917, my sister, Varya, and I became wards of Tsar Nikolay Alexandrovich Romanov and were moved, under imperial guard, from the apartment at 64 Gorokhovaya Street to the Alexander Palace in Tsarskoe Selo, the royal family's private village outside the capital. Eighteen years old, I hardly felt I needed a new set of parents, even if they were a tsar and tsarina. But every week brought more strikes and increasing violence to St. Petersburg. Revolution, anarchy, marshal law: we didn't know what to dread, only that we were accelerating—hurtling—toward it, whatever it was. And, as the tsar's officers pointed out, having summoned Varya and me from our beds before dawn, banging at the door with the butts of their rifles, anyone with a name as inflammatory as Rasputin would be an idiot to try to leave St. Petersburg unaided and without protection. As long as the Romanovs remained in power, they represented our only possibility of escaping Russia before it was too late to get out.

But first: my father. For without Grigory Yefimovich Rasputin, the end of the Romanovs is no different from that of the Hapsburgs or the Ottomans or any other of the great dynasties that collapsed at the beginning of the century.

Word traveled quickly, more quickly than it would had any other man's body been dragged from the river. After I signed a paper confirming that the deceased was indeed my father, missing by then for three days, the police escort was to return Varya and me to Gorokhovaya Street to gather our clothes and what few things we cared to keep. But before we could climb back into the sledge it was surrounded by a mob. A crowd of people had come running to where we'd stood minutes before, on the frozen river. They came from their homes with bowls and jugs and cast-iron kettles—anything that could hold water. Some ran pouring wine and vodka, even perfume, into the gutters as they hurried to the Neva to fill their newly emptied bottles. I saw a samovar so big it required three men to carry it, and I saw an old woman lugging a chamber pot. Now, that would have made Father laugh until he hooted and howled and dried his eyes with the heels of his hands— the idea of a withered crone ladling his ghost into her chamber pot.

The crowd surged onto the river like a wave and swept all the officials away from the hole in the ice, the one out of which the police had dragged my father, beaten and bloodied, his right hand raised as if making the sign of the cross. People thronged the hole. They fell on their knees, praying and weeping. The common people, the people my father loved, all along they understood what the intelligentsia were too blind to see. They wanted the water that touched my father as he was dying, the water into which his soul had passed, through which it had swum.

Thousands of people, tens of thousands—the officials lost count as they continued to arrive—came to the Neva that day and the next and the one after that. They came and they came and they wouldn't stop coming, from all parts of the city and from the outlying towns and provinces. They came over the Urals, from Siberia. Nothing could stop them, not blizzards, not cavalry soldiers. Squadrons of Cossacks on horseback took aim and fired into the crowds, and their nervous mounts reared up and came down plunging, their shoes striking sparks from the paving stones, pale pricks in the freezing gloom.

For all the horses I'd ridden in my life, I'd never seen any as spirited as these. Towering black giants, not one of them less than twenty hands high, they weren't shying at the noise and chaos—no, that was what they wanted, an orgy of movement and sound. The dark luster of each animal's coat; the volatile quiver of its flesh as it responded to its rider's intent, not to his hands, which were busy with a firearm, but to his will, which commanded the horse's body as if it were his own; the nostrils flared wide at the smell of gunpowder; the shrill whinnying and the sharp gleam of each hoof: in an instant, the sight and sound and smell of them had, like a whetted blade, pared away the rind of shock that left me, in the wake of my father's disappearance, insensible to every feeling.

I watched, struck still with wonder, as the air around the horses changed color, like iron held over a flame, stealing its heat. The officer who had his gloved fingers wrapped tightly around the top of my arm gave it a shake, as if to dispel what he must have assumed was my fear. But all it was was my succumbing to them, allowing their desire to possess me to the point that I wanted it too— the crumple and yield of bodies under hooves. Then the clamor around me ceased, all the clatter and cries and sharp cracks converged into words only I could hear, and my father's voice spoke my name. *Masha,* he said, *be comforted,* and though I wasn't faint, I fell back so the officer had to support my weight. At last something had caught and cut me, made me gasp. Until that moment, I was afraid I'd lost not only my father but myself as well.

THE CROWD THINNED, eventually it did, but not before opportunists had set up shop along the riverbank, selling empty jars and bottles to anyone who hadn't brought one, as well as hawking bread, cheese, pomegranates, kvass and vodka by the glass, cider dipped from a pot hanging over a fire. Day and night, pilgrims stepped around and over stiffening corpses as they walked past the armed soldiers and onto the river, the gray ice of its surface slick with freezing fresh blood. They slipped and scrambled and pushed one another aside to reach the hole in the ice, because the water my father touched he made powerful. For the rest of that terrible winter, the last of the Romanovs' rule, St. Petersburg shuddered under one riot after another, and her citizens' blood remained on the ice under the Petrovsky Bridge.

At noon one February day, nearly two months after my father was murdered, I returned to that bridge and stared at the stain below. I'd come back to the city to sign our furniture over to an auctioneer, so the apartment could be rented. "We could chop up his bed into splinters and sell them as relics," Varya said as I was leaving on my errand, and I gave her a look. For all I knew, she might have been serious, but I, not Varya, was the one responsible for settling my father's estate, what little there was of it.

How, after cyanide had failed, and bullets as well, after someone had broken his poor head with a brick or a cudgel, had Father's assassins at last succeeded in killing him? They dropped him from where I was standing, perhaps. Dropped him over the guardrail and watched as the force of his body's impact shattered the river's frozen surface, gravity, which holds planets and moons and even the golden sun in its thrall, no longer innocent but an accessory to murder. Or they brought axes. They walked onto the river, bold as brass, dragging Father behind them, his hands and feet bound. Was he conscious? Did he have to watch his murderers hack at the ice to open a door to his drowning? The ringleader was a man he'd mistaken for a friend. Invited to his home, Father had come willingly and drunk the poison he was served.

The Petrovsky Bridge was bewitched, people began to say, and they avoided its narrow pedestrian walkway whenever possible, certainly at night, when traffic subsided and moans rose up from under its span. There must be a natural explanation for water making such noises as it flows beneath a frozen surface, but no one was interested in natural explanations, not that winter. And there were more curious phenomena, impossible to account for. In the attempt to wash the blood away, to remove the unwanted reminder of my dead father's continued hold over his disciples, cauldron after cauldron of boiling water had been poured over the frozen blood. Tinder was collected, saturated in gasoline, and set to burn on the ice. But the stain refused to fade. As if to accuse the assassins, it darkened and spread, and even reasonable people grew to fear a place where a holy man had been martyred.

Looking down from the bridge, I could see where blood had pooled and feet had tramped and bodies been dragged through the congealing red slick of it, each boot print and smear recorded on the river's surface. The hole in the ice never froze back over that winter. Too many people visited the spot, refilled their bottles from its bottomless font, rinsed their crucifixes, and kneeled to pray. The same pilgrims, some of them, left crosses and candles. The wind blew, it whistled and shrieked, but it knew to leave the crosses standing, the candles' flames burning, and the soup in its bowl. Someone had remembered Father's favorite meal and brought him a deep dish of thick cod soup, which steamed day and night through one blizzard after another, surrounded by a ring of water where it had melted the ice. Others brought boots, a gift traditionally presented to an itinerant healer, and there was a cask of Madeira, bottles of kvass, too many ikons to count, a heaped tangle of prayer cords, and silk stoles, such as priests wear, in gold, purple, red, in every color. Prayers, quite a lot of these, copied onto paper and, if the petitioner lacked the requisite faith, held down with rocks. But the wind let them be, rocks or no rocks. Crutches and canes and unraveled bandages, all testifying that, dead as he was, Father Grigory continued to heal those who came to him. No thief was fool enough to take any of the gifts his petitioners left, not even something as valuable as a pair of stout boots.

If only Father had remained that humble man, walking from one town to the next, he might have avoided so early a death. Forty-seven. With a constitution like his he should have lived to be a hundred.

A Red Ribbon

· · • · ·

HE JOURNEY BY TRAIN from St. Petersburg to Tsarskoe Selo, sixteen miles to the south, wasn't nearly long enough for me to gather my wits. It was, at least, a slow sixteen miles, as the track had to be cleared of snow every day, several times a day, in midwinter. I told myself, on boarding, that I would use the time to write my mother a letter saying what I could not, for reasons of economy, fit in a telegram. But I never even opened my satchel to find pen and paper. Once I'd settled myself in one of the imperial train's velvet-upholstered seats, I sank immediately into a haze that left me balanced like a napping cat between unconsciousness and the hair-trigger alertness that allows it to spring out of sleep and onto a mouse. Scenery unfurled, splendid and sparkling, the last of the slanting midwinter sunlight flaring off mirrors it found in the ice. Varya, two years younger than I, slept sideways in her red velvet seat, her legs tucked under her and her hands caught between her cheek and the back of her seat in an attitude of prayer. Unbound, her dark hair fell around her shoulders like a cloak. Twice the train slowed, stopped, and, after whatever obstruction had blocked our way was cleared from the tracks, started up again.

It was dusk when we reached Tsarskoe Selo. A detail of cavalry officers greeted us at the station, and once Varya and I had disembarked, holding tight to our bags in defiance of a footman's attempt to carry them, the mounted police escorted us to a carriage bearing the gold imperial crest. Flanked on either side by a moving wall of horses and men, for a moment I felt my sister and I had been arrested rather than adopted, and I hesitated before climbing into the conveyance.

"What is it?" Varya whispered as she sat next to me.

"Nothing," I said. "It isn't anything." As the carriage started rolling, we each slid to one side of the seat, looking out the window at what we'd last seen in late summer, when it was lushly green rather than white. The sun had set, the moon was rising. The carriage lamps turned everything they touched pale yellow, and behind every yellow thing lay its purple shadow. As we approached the Alexander Palace, I saw that only the imperial family's private wing was illuminated—lit from top to bottom. From a distance it looked like a lantern left standing in the snow. But then it grew suddenly big, and we stepped out of the carriage and into a world we'd visited infrequently, and never without our father. Apart from Father we had no connection to the tsar and his family.

The trip from the foyer to the suite of bedrooms (to which a butler, housekeeper, and finally a chambermaid delivered us) involved a surprising number of double doors. Each set opened silently before us, obedient to its pair of liveried, white-gloved porters, and swung silently shut. With every threshold I crossed, with every set of doors that closed behind me, I felt that much more sleepy, as if walking ever deeper into a hypnotizing spell. By the time a lady-in-waiting had emptied our suitcases and hung up our clothes— I could not convince her, as I had the footman, that we could do for ourselves—I was on my back on my bed, asleep on the counterpane, my shoes still on my feet and my hands folded like a dead girl's over my heart.

I might have remained there until the next morning without moving so much as a finger, but within an hour of our arrival the tsarina had summoned me to her mauve boudoir, a room infamous throughout the continent for a color scheme so unconditional that lilacs were the only flower admitted.

"Why not both of us?" Varya said, following me to the sink, where I splashed my face with water to wake myself up. I lifted my shoulders in a shrug and went out after the page, tucking my blouse into my skirt as best I could while hurrying behind him.

I had no answers for Varya. I had no idea of what was going to happen next—it seemed like anything could, in this new, father-less world—and no power to protect her, supposing she'd allow such a thing. My sister and I were close in years but little else. Not that either of us wished the other ill, but the time Varya spent in Petersburg changed her from a shy, self-conscious girl to a secre-tive, dishonest one. From the day she arrived in the city, my sis-ter found it hard to endure exposure to so many staring eyes, and she never developed a tolerance to our providing fodder, as the daughters of the Mad Monk Rasputin, for schoolgirl gossip and taunts. From the beginning I understood it was our father's power that inspired slander—if a person is conspicuous, people will say anything about him. And what point was there in taking issue with fate? Father's persecution and martyrdom had been foretold.

Still, our growing steadily apart was as much my fault as Varya's. She wasn't one to talk about what bothered her, and I shirked my duty as her older sister, avoiding the chore of slowly coaxing her unhappiness out of her head and into my lap, where I'd have to respond to what I couldn't repair. For, once Father had decided on a thing, there was no changing his mind, and, though he remained faithful to his peasant ways, he had been set on pleasing our mother by having her daughters educated as she was, in a proper girls' school. We had to stay with Father in St. Petersburg, and Varya would remain enrolled whether she hated it or not.

I don't know how long my sister had made a practice of lying before I noticed that the lies she told seemed oddly useless. They didn't get her out of trouble or get anyone else into it; they weren't malicious. Instead, Varya's lies seemed peculiarly lacking in consequence. I'd ask her, for example, if she'd enjoyed a concert I knew she'd planned to attend, and she'd tell me she hadn't gone after all. Then I'd bump into an acquaintance with whom she'd spoken during the concert's intermission. Had she been pursuing some clandestine business, it would have been the other way around: she'd have said she attended the concert to excuse an absence for a different cause, the one she wanted to hide. But if each lie alone seemed to serve no purpose, the habit of telling them amounted to camouflage. For as long as one lie went undiscovered, my sister was protected by the façade it presented, and many of them together created a kind of psychic fortress in which to hide, maybe even a new identity, a life whose terms she dictated and kept separate from Father's and mine. It also formed, perhaps only incidentally, a barrier between the two of us. On those occasions I challenged Varya, she'd change the topic or, like a politician, answer another, different question, one I hadn't asked. She slipped away as quickly as a wet bar of soap.

I almost didn't see the tsarina when I entered her darkened boudoir, having been given a nudge by the lady-in-waiting when I hesitated on the threshold. She was lying on a chaise longue, and the boudoir was as rumored: the chaise was upholstered in a slippery-looking mauve chintz, the floral-patterned carpets were all shades of mauve, as were the walls, tablecloths, bellpull, curtains, and the blanket pulled up over her knees. Even her lips were mauve, and her fingertips too. I'd heard it said the tsarina had had scarlet fever as a child, and the disease damaged the valves of her heart.

"You poor, dear, brave, wonderful girl," she said in answer to my curtsy. "The apple of your dear father's eye. You cannot imagine how he praised you to me, how proud he was. 'Don't be fooled by her size,' he'd say, 'my little Masha is destined for great and astonishing things. The good Lord has shown me the crowds that will gather for only a look at her.' " She paused, her eyes searching mine. "I am so sorry we—you—have lost him. Poor child, you look thoroughly worn out. I'll ring for tea, shall I?"

"I don't—" I said. "I hardly know what to think."

"Of course you don't. How could you at a time like this? Did you know how your father spoke of you, my dear? Did he tell you about your future?"

"Only a little," I said, and she frowned, faintly.

"Ah. I'd hoped that with you he had been . . ." She paused, perhaps searching for a word she wanted. " . . . more forthcoming."

"I . . . I'm afraid I'm not sure what you mean."

"Did he say anything about it? Your future?"

"No," I said. "It sounds as if he may have told you more than he did me."

"Ah." The tsarina put a finger before her lips, as if cautioning me to keep a secret. "We—you—will have to be patient, then," she said after a moment. "We will have to wait and see."

I smiled in response to the tsarina's smile, finding it hard to keep up my end of the conversation. In truth, I couldn't think of any but one thing, my mind prodding and poking, tonguelike, at the absence of my father, pressing up against what was no longer there and trying to measure the loss. I didn't want to contemplate his murder every minute, but I couldn't stop adding up the days and hours leading to his disappearance as if it were an equation I could rework to arrive at a different answer, the one in which I'd had the foresight to prevent Father's leaving the apartment that night. From my father's death to my portion of responsibility for his death to Varya's and my future, one fixation ceded to the next; there was our mother's safety to worry over, and the dangers of travel versus those of remaining in Russia—

"You and your sister will live here, at Tsarskoe Selo. It was your father's wish."

"Thank you, your—"

"Please," the tsarina said, and she shook her finger as though at a naughty child. "No titles. And no more curtsies either."

I nodded. My head seemed to bob up and down on its own. Without falling back on prescribed formalities, I had little to say, and my eyes strayed to the books on the tsarina's shelves and the paintings on her wall. History, mostly of the Orthodox Church, theology, and landscapes of mauve rivers and mauve forests and fields, mauve haystacks and mauve mountains. Suddenly, then, the overhead light went on and I saw that the tsarina had risen from her pillows. Sitting up straight as a fence post, her hand still on the switch plate, she was breathing rapidly and her eyes were frantic and bright, almost glittering. I wondered if she was suffering an attack of some kind, and I was on the point of calling for help when she reached out and seized my hand.

"I know it's in you," she said. Her hand wasn't, like her words, feverish but as cold as though she had one foot in her grave. Other than suppressing a shudder, I didn't respond to her assertion. Cryptic as it was, I could pretend I didn't understand her meaning, and I remained silent under her stare. The voluble self I knew seemed to have parted company with me, and I felt as though I were inhabited by a stranger, her expression blank, seamless as an egg.

"That's why he made Nikolay Alexandrovich your guardian, yours and your sister's." The tsarina's eyes didn't focus on my face so much as they approached it as they would the lid of a box. I could feel her looking for a place to pry me open and peer inside. "Your father wouldn't have left Alyosha without having planned for his future. He sent you to us. He wanted you near the tsarevich, to keep him from harm. To heal him when he is ill and to comfort him. He sent you here for Alyosha. For Alyosha and for Russia as well."

So I wasn't beyond being shocked anew, as that declaration had my mouth open before I had anything to say. It was rumored the tsarevich had been a terror as a little boy, spoiled by a family and servants who couldn't bear to deny a sick child whatever he asked, as long as it couldn't harm him. At table he'd taken food from others' plates, kicked and cried whenever he was disciplined. The risk that he might do himself injury while thrashing about was so great that soon even the hint of a tantrum's approach guaranteed his demands would be satisfied immediately. Even were he no longer inclined to such tricks, he would still be accustomed to getting what he wanted.

"How do you know he didn't send Varya?" I asked, surprising myself with my own impertinence, but the tsarina laughed. At least I hadn't been so forward as to suggest my father might have put his daughters in the care of the tsar to protect us rather than the tsarevich.

"You know, Matryona Grigorievna—Masha—that it is you who takes after your father. And I'm not speaking of your blue eyes and black hair." She squeezed my fingers with sudden strength. "You know I am right."

"Yes," I said. It seemed rude not to agree. I'd thought to claim my portion of the Neva's water, but then I asked myself what it could give me that I didn't already have. The tsarina was right, I did take after my father, if not in the one way she hoped.

The color of the tsarina's lips was the same, exactly the same, as that of the cushion behind her head. I wondered why she didn't trouble to rouge them and then asked myself why I was dwelling on so trivial a matter. Alexandra Fyodorovna. I'd never before thought of the tsarina as an ordinary woman, with a name like other women have, lying on a chair with a little table at her side and on it a crumpled handkerchief and a plain glass of water, half drunk, next to a small, worn Orthodox prayer book. The book had a red ribbon between its pages, to keep a reader's place, and the ribbon's unraveling at the end caught and for a moment held my eye. Alexandra Fyodorovna was the same as any other woman, the same and no different, and her health was poor; she was frightened for the safety of her son. I could feel her anxiety, even see its shadow pass across her features, as though a cloud had come between her and the light from overhead.

"What is it, my daughter?" she said, as if she'd perceived the shift in my understanding of her. "Do you mind if I call you my daughter?"

"No. You may, of course, call me what you please." No matter what came out of my mouth, it sounded different from the way I'd meant it to. Either it was overly familiar or courteous to the point of seeming insincere.

"Wouldn't you prefer to sit down?" Alexandra Fyodorovna said. "You're pale."

A telephone call away, that's all Father had been. The tsarina's driver would have left to fetch my father before she picked up the receiver to summon him, and Father would be delivered to the Alexander Palace in less than an hour. But now he was dead, no longer at her side to provide her strength, and the tsarina's weak heart was beginning to fail. She'd always had bad spells, as I knew from my father, a month or more of breathlessness that kept her confined to bed, but I never imagined anyone could look as haggard as she did now. The continuing strain of the war against Germany; the food shortages; the strikes and the rioting; the long days she spent nursing moribund soldiers in one of the Red Cross's makeshift hospitals (for she was always greedy for good works, for opportunities to sacrifice herself in the name of God and country): all of these had taken their toll on the woman my father and every other Russian peasant had learned to call Little Mother—*Mamochka.*

Mamochka, Father always said when he bent to kiss her jeweled white hand. I never heard him call her by any other name.

"How, then," I said to the tsarina, "shall I address you?"

"In any way that you are comfortable, Masha. We are a family now, the Romanovs and the daughters of Father Grigory. Your father himself has ordained it. We no longer stand on ceremony. We are equals."

This seemed unlikely—ridiculous. Still, I nodded and smiled politely.

BUT ALEXANDRA FYODOROVNA WAS RIGHT. Or, if she wasn't right on the first day of 1917, she would be by the ides of March, when Tsar Nikolay was forced to surrender his throne, a blow she'd receive with the grace and fortitude expected of her station and that would complete the job of ruining her health irrevocably. Of course, the abdication of Nikolay II, emperor and autocrat of all the Russias, was a shock not only to us but to all the world, the kind of warning that ought to have been delivered by the Four Horsemen of the Apocalypse rather than a plain little military detail, for life as we knew it was over and Armageddon begun.

As for the tsarina, once she'd fulfilled the obligations of the wife of a deposed ruler (which was mostly, as far as I could tell, finding and burning whatever might be misconstrued as evidence of her husband's having exploited the proletariat for the advancement of decadent, royalist agendas, should he be tried), she took to her bed once and for all, too distraught to tend to her own children, her four strapping daughters and Alyosha, the long awaited, greatly desired, and gravely ill son she bore for tsar and emperor, for Russia. The boy on whom so many hopes had been laid.

Lucky for me, to whom it fell—as good as by decree—to comfort Alyosha and keep him amused when he was confined to bed, it turned out the tsarevich was intoxicated by every detail of a country person's simple life. He asked to hear about my father as a boy and what it was people did to amuse themselves in faraway Siberia. I could tell he pictured it all wrong, imagining everything east of the Urals to be a kind of uncharted territory without a single modern convenience—no train, no telegraph or telephone, no electricity or indoor plumbing. All of us squatting in yurts, stitching up hides into trousers and tunics, and wearing underclothes made of yarn from off our spinning wheels. Riding wild Tartar ponies and murdering, raping, and pillaging one another as a matter of course with our blackened frostbitten ears and fingers falling off. The kind of life a rich and pampered boy might think wild and romantic.

"Like Temujin!" he said, delighted with the idea.

"Who?"

"The Khan Temujin. Genghis Khan. Don't you know anything, Masha?"

"A lot more than you do. Just not every detail about every last uncivilized warmonger. And, no, it was not like that. Fewer people and buildings, more flowers and less soot, that's what it was."

But Alyosha was no different from the rest of the Petersburg aristocrats who took one look at my father's ill-kempt beard and threadbare tunic and confused him with Jesus. I told Alyosha no one back home ever had to worry about amusing themselves, as every member of a country family had to work all day to keep bread on the table. But to a bedridden prince, this, too, sounded like fun.

Of course, I had to tell Alyosha about Baba Yaga, for what proper Russian leaves childhood behind without learning about Baba Yaga and her hut? Somehow he'd got to the grand age of thirteen without having heard of her.

I told him Baba Yaga lived in the forest in a hut that danced on the legs of a chicken, sliding sideways through the trees and shadows, and I recited the magic words to speak at its door. *Little hut, little hut, turn your back to the forest, your front to me.*

"A new one," Alyosha would say when I asked him what story to tell, and I did, more times than I can count. I made them up from bits and pieces of other tales, from what I knew and what I didn't know I knew. Usually, the words flew out of my mouth before I had a chance to think them through, entertaining me as well. Alyosha—Tsarevich Alexei Nikolayevich Romanov—was a big boy, tall and sturdy for his age. But when he was ill, feverish and in pain, he liked to be babied. When he was ill you couldn't imagine the boy he was when he was well, a boy whose nickname was Sunbeam; that was how easy it was for him to make others smile. But Sunbeam had inherited the English disease from Queen Victoria, his mother's grandmother, an illness carried by females and suffered by males, a torture whose name was never spoken, not even by court physicians. Especially not by court physicians. The threat to the tsarevich's life inspired fear so intense that to say its name aloud was dangerous and would have been unlawful had anyone been given leave to set the word down in ink. If the people were to learn that the crown prince—the future tsar and heir to the world's greatest autocracy, ruler-to-be of two hundred million souls—could bleed to death from a tumble down the stairs or a bump on the nose, Russia's ebbing faith in her government would drain away all the more quickly, hurrying the collapse of three centuries of Romanov rule and of tsarism itself.

Hemophilia: for all it was spoken, the word might as well have not been invented.

House Arrest

· · • · ·

EBRUARY 1917 BROUGHT TEMPERATURES so low a thousand locomotive boilers froze and burst, each stranding as many as fifty cars. And not one of the few trains left running could enter Petersburg; every track leading into the capital had been buried in drifts. The laborers who would otherwise have dug them out were dying at the front, a line that moved over the continent as fire does through the dry grass of the steppes, leaving smoke and ruin in its wake. No flour was delivered to the city, no butter, and no sugar. Without coal, lights dimmed and flickered. Newspapers went unpublished. The letters I wrote and mailed to my mother never reached her. The telegraph office was closed. Actors performed to empty houses, as did musicians and ballerinas. And vodka poured from water faucets and ran in the gutters—it must have, for never has there been, neither before nor after, such uniformity of drunkenness. Inebriated bands of looters broke into bakeries and smashed storefronts to make off with bread, while a few doors down the Nevsky Prospekt the windows of Fabergé remained intact, crusts suddenly more valuable than cabochons.

Corpses piled up in the streets. Every so often, the wagon from the potter's field would stop; then two men jumped down and picked up one body after another. The first man took the corpse by the hands, the second grabbed the feet, and together they swung it onto the growing heap. When they'd collected all they could, they drove the bodies to a pit, dropped them in, poured on the quicklime, and went back to the streets for more. It looked as if St. Petersburg was dying as she had been born, thousands of unknown and uncounted workers dumped in communal graves.

"How strange and claustrophobic it must be for the dead who haven't a private grave or even a coffin. I'm sure such things are as important to the dead as to the living."

"What peculiar things you say, Masha."

"I can't not think of them, poor things, all heaped together on top of one another, having to molder next to strangers, the dust of one life mingling with that of another. And very lonely, as no one can come calling on a person without a headstone."

"There's no point in thinking of them at all, as they are dead and you didn't know them."

"I know you consider yourself very clever, your highness, but not all thoughts are undertaken with a purpose. They just arrive, that's all."

"I wish you wouldn't say that."

"What?"

"'Your highness.'"

"I'm sorry, Alyosha," I said, and I begged his pardon, as I'd had to do on several occasions since the day we were left in the schoolroom to get to know each other, an introduction postponed by my falling ill with quite the worst flu I've ever had. My head was aching when I left the tsarina in her boudoir, my eyes dry and hot. As soon as I was delivered to my room, I crawled under the counterpane in my street clothes and fell into a restless sleep from which I woke before dawn, worrying over Father's body, which the coroner had promised to release by noon, and his burial, for which arrangements had yet to be made.

There was no point trying to rest. I bathed, dressed, and secured permission to return to the capital, and by the time I made my way back to bed, I'd missed another and another night's rest and, thoroughly spent, succumbed to a fever that climbed and broke, climbed and broke, a hundred times it seemed, before I was well enough to sit up against my pillows with a tray on my lap.

"You'd better eat something," Varya observed from the chair by the window, where she was buffing her fingernails in the wan winter light. "You look like a ghost."

I felt like one too, when I made my way to the water closet, my head spinning with the effort of walking a few yards. Too faint to stand and put my hair to rights before the mirror, I took the brush back to bed with me, where I found I wasn't any more equal to the effort of sitting up for as long as it would take to untangle so many snarls.

"What are you staring at like that?" Varya asked.

"Nothing. I was just trying to sort out the date." And to separate the nightmares I'd dreamed from the one I was living.

"The ninth."

"Of January? That's impossible."

"Ask Doctor Botkin. He should know—he's been in to see you every day."

"The admiral? The one with the gold buttons?"

"He's not an admiral. He's a physician."

He looked like an admiral, though, with a navy-blue military coat trimmed with enough gold braid to inspire nautical fever dreams, and he wore so much cologne it made me sneeze, which he interpreted as evidence of continued infection, keeping me to my bed for a full week more and quarantined to my room for another one after that. It was February before I made the tsarevich's acquaintance, stepping into our friendship on a more querulous note than I might have had the tsarina not saddled me with a responsibility I knew I couldn't meet.

"You have the reputation of being a rather difficult person," I said, aborting a curtsy and offering him my hand. I didn't mean to say it—the words just popped out of my mouth.

"Really?" he said, squeezing my fingers hard, as if to assert his station. "Who told you that?"

"I don't know. Someone must have, but I don't remember who."

"It wasn't your father, was it?"

"No," I said. "A girl at school, most likely. Father never criticized." Alyosha said nothing. He was more handsome a boy than I'd gathered from photographs, with dark hair and gray eyes. "Do you know why I'm here?" I asked, finding myself annoyed by his good looks and by his height, which allowed him to look down his straight nose at me. "Here at Tsarskoe Selo?"

"Because my father wished it."

"Yes, I suppose that is true, in that nothing happens outside your father's wishes." I wondered suddenly—but only after the words left my mouth—if the tsarina had meant me to keep our conversation in confidence. "My understanding is that Father believed Varya and I would be safer here than anywhere else he might send us in his absence. Your mother imagines I will be able to do for you what he did," I said. "That I can cure you."

"Does she?" the tsarevich said. He studied me from where he was standing, leaning against one of the schoolroom desks. There were five, one for each of the Romanov children.

"She told me she did. She seems to believe Father bequeathed me to your family for the purpose of preserving your health."

The tsarevich nodded. "That sounds like Mother."

"You seem quite well to me," I observed.

"I am at the moment," he said. "It won't last though. It never does." His expression was one of resignation, but he didn't feel sorry for himself. I could see that much.

"Well, then," I said, "I suppose I will be tested when the time comes, and we will discover if I'm of any use to you."

Alyosha smiled, his eyes on my face.

"What are you looking at?" I asked him.

"Nothing. Your father called you his 'little magpie.' I was wondering why."

"A pet name, that's all." One inspired by my talking too much when excited. "Like a bird in a tree," Father used to say. But I didn't explain this to the tsarevich. I was still holding tight to whatever I could that was left of my father, guarding it jealously and keeping it for my own. It wasn't fair to blame Alyosha, and I didn't. Still, I had to push the thought away: if it weren't for his everlasting illness, my father would never have been murdered.

"You'll have to . . ." he said, "I mean, I hope you will forgive my mother. She is . . . I'm afraid she can be a little unreasonable. I've caused her so much worry, you see. It's made her nervous. And she . . . she believes . . ." Spots of color appeared on his cheeks.

"What does she believe?"

"In the grace of God," he said after a moment.

"And you?"

"I believe in history," the tsarevich said, with a gravitas I wasn't ready to accept as genuine, coming from a boy who wasn't quite fourteen. I hadn't yet learned—witnessed—how life had taught him fatalism.

"And what about the future? Do you believe in it too?" I wish I'd only thought the words, but I said them aloud, with a tart tone in my voice.

BULLETINS ARRIVED AT TSARSKOE SELO; the tsar was apprised of each new disaster, but weeks passed and he did nothing—nothing of a political nature. He marched through the woods, he swam in the saltwater natatorium, he hunted, and he rode his horse, until, on March 10, he made the mistake that cost him his crown—well, not *the* mistake, as there already had been too many to count, but the last and most egregious one. He ordered that the capital be returned to its former state of relative calm, no matter what was required. To accomplish this, his police tore around the city in armored cars; his Cossacks galloped along the avenues, cracking whips and brandishing bayonets; his soldiers fired Chauchats imported from France that spat out 240 bullets every minute. But not only was it too late, order no longer possible; the actions he took against the rioting citizens inspired the Bolsheviks to organize themselves and prepare to challenge his authority.

"How much does my father understand of revolution? Anything?" Alyosha wanted to know. "Can it be a concept he refutes, one he finds heretical, the way Pope Urban the Eighth insisted the sun revolved around the earth and called Galileo a heretic?"

"I should think you know him better than I," I said, answering what was probably a rhetorical question. We were in the schoolroom, occupied with our separate studies—Alyosha's directed by his tutor, whose head was bent over the second volume of Gibbon's *Decline and Fall* while Alyosha force-marched himself through the first. I was rereading *Jane Eyre,* in English instead of Russian, allowing me to call it a scholarly occupation rather than the pleasure—the escape—it was. Varya was with the Romanov girls, learning the correct way to put stalks in a vase, a lesson I'd dodged as Admiral–Dr. Botkin, having detected a wheeze while listening to my back with his stethoscope, wouldn't allow me to walk through the cold to the greenhouses.

Tsar Nikolay didn't talk about politics. He had four uncles filled with opinions and would have been, by everyone's account, happy to hand them the empire. He wanted only to be allowed his exercise and to travel to his army's headquarters in Mogilev, where he could sleep, eat, and march among his soldiers. As far as I could tell, he spent more time with his army than he did with his family, and I'd heard it said he would have had trouble deciding between the life of a soldier and that of a farmer, had he escaped his heritage.

But, as all the world knows, he did not escape, and on March 21, 1917, General Kornilov, who had lately presided over the Petersburg garrison, arrived at the Alexander Palace to inform the tsarina that, as there wasn't any empire left, she and her family were under arrest. The former tsar, his abdication extracted from him as he traveled in his imperial train, had yet to return home from Mogilev to Tsarskoe Selo because the railway workers had received the news of the tsar's having been toppled as an invitation to stop service for all Romanovs and their retainers.

"Go down. See what's happening," Alyosha said, after Kornilov had been announced. He got up from where he was sitting with his bodyguard Derevenko, playing yet another game of dominoes, a game I hated and refused to join. Alyosha had two bodyguards, Derevenko and Nagorny, both of whom appeared to dote on their charge and were gentle in spite of their military demeanor. Each had previously been a naval officer; now they took turns supervising all the tsarevich did, to make sure no harm came to him, and carrying him in their arms when, inevitably, it did.

Alyosha gave me a push toward the stairs, and I pushed him back, just a little bit, because I hated that kind of thing in boys, especially in princes, who ought to know better than to boss people about, if only because they got all they wanted anyway. After slipping downstairs, I hurried to the drawing room's double doors, which were left open into the corridor, one widely enough that I could hide myself behind it, my back to the wall. Even Father admitted that his little magpie had a talent for silence and for making herself as invisible as a scullery maid.

I watched through the crack as Alexandra Fyodorovna received

Kornilov. By now, nearly a week after her husband's abdication, she'd moved on from destroying official correspondence to incinerating private letters, diaries, telephone messages, bills from the wine merchant and from the purveyor of caviar and truffles, even the former tsar's game book, in which was recorded every boar, buck, and bird he'd dispatched with his shotgun—any scrap of information that might fall into the hands of some malevolent someone bent on slandering her poor blameless Nikolay. The drawing room's fire had burned all night, its flames licking, cracking, and smacking as it consumed leaf after leaf of creamy stationery bearing the gold-embossed Romanov crest. The flue must have needed adjusting. The ceiling over the hearth was blackened with soot.

"Abridging history, I see," Kornilov said, sniffing at the smoke-tinged atmosphere. He was a good-humored-looking man, with ears that stood out like handles from his shorn head and a mustache so robust it obscured his lips. The tsarina rose from where she had been sitting among emptied boxes. Her mauve-lipped pallor continued to unnerve me. On the cushion next to hers was a small bundle of billets-doux to her from her husband. This was all that remained of what had been thousands of letters to tens of recipients, her grandmother, Queen Victoria, foremost among them.

Already I'd overheard servants talking among themselves about plans for the tsarina and her children to join Tsar Nikolay at Murmansk, the seaport on Kola Bay, where they'd find a ship to board for a journey west toward asylum. Because even if England's George V, the tsar's own first cousin, wouldn't have them, surely somewhere would. America or Australia or whatever other continent invited thieves and outcasts and exiled dreams.

But what of Varya and myself? I didn't know whether we would be considered a part of the Romanov family and treated as such, or taken by the new regime's police to be questioned about Father, or liberated with the rest of Russia and discharged into the chaos of Petersburg to make our way home to Siberia, and I didn't know which would be worse or if we had any choice in the matter. And timing—there was timing to consider. I'd intended, before the tsar left for Mogilev, to approach and speak with him, to find out what he knew, or could control, of our fate, but each time I'd succumbed to my fear of taking up the topic at exactly the wrong moment. Though they'd encouraged us to befriend their children and, to all appearances, welcomed us into their lives, the tsar and tsarina were like two people poised on the crest of a breaking tidal wave, surveying the landscape against which they would be dashed. Each time I marched myself, like a responsible older sister, down the corridor to the tsar's study, rehearsing my little speech in my head, I ended up turning right where I should have turned left, grabbing my coat, shoving my feet into Wellingtons, and stealing away as fast as I could to the one place I knew I'd find comfort.

Just the smell of them and the sound of their breathing and all the other noises I knew so well: their soft whickering, the swish of a tail after a fly, and the accompanying stamp of a hoof. Just to press my face into the soft flesh of their necks, run my fingers over the ridge of velvet nostrils, feel the gust of their warm breath hit my face, my neck and chest. I would have petitioned to live in the stable had the idea not struck me as one my hosts would find preposterous.

Peering through the crack at Kornilov, I wished I'd had the nerve to approach the tsar while there was still time to act, before Kornilov and his soldiers came for us. But I hadn't, and perhaps because it was simpler to contemplate their fate, I found myself worrying about the horses before the people. What would happen to the old ones, long retired from the harness? I hoped the groom would think to end their lives mercifully before soldiers took over the stables. And the others, who were fit for work, accustomed as they were to tranquil bridle paths and the affection of all who cared for them, what would happen to such animals were they commandeered by the gathering Red Army and forced into the pandemonium of civil war?

There was one horse I particularly liked, Gypsy, a black mare compact enough that a bareback rider—the only kind I knew to be—was comfortable straddling her withers. She shared a loose box with Vanka, an aged donkey the Cinzelli Brothers' Circus had presented as a gift to the tsarevich and his sisters after a private performance at Tsarsko Selo. As Botkin had forbidden me to ride as well as walk in the cold, I spent hours sitting in the hay, long enough that I'd seen Vanka do what she was famous for doing. Occasionally, the donkey entered a sort of fugue state in which she believed she was before an audience and, without any warning, ran through a repertoire of tricks that included running backward. The first time this happened, Alyosha told me, the tsarina had nearly fainted as the donkey swiftly (demonically, it seemed to Alyosha's mother) approached him, the muscles of her hindquarters pumping energetically. What would the nervous tsarina assume but that the animal was rabid?

"I'm surprised she didn't order that Vanka be destroyed," I said to Alyosha.

"Oh, she did. Of course she did. But Father showed her how Vanka wasn't afraid to drink water from a bucket, and she had to admit the donkey was only confused."

"I don't think she's confused," I said. "She's happy remembering when she was performing, that's all."

The tsarina's voice was too low for me to hear her from behind the door, but Kornilov's wasn't. Although he characterized our arrest as precautionary, intended to protect us from the predation of revolutionary soldiers, he asked the tsarina to summon the palace guard and household staff so he could announce that their responsibility to the Romanovs had come to an end. Those who wanted to remain in the deposed tsar's service, Kornilov explained, would be held under arrest with his family, confined to one wing of the palace, no longer free to come and go.

Poor Gypsy. She was too small to be a cavalry horse. I imagined myself running to the stable before the Red Guard arrived, opening the doors to all the stalls, and shooing their occupants toward the woods, but the only likely outcome of that was getting myself shot. And it wouldn't save the horses—even if they left, they'd come straight back. Tsarskoe Selo was the only home they knew.

"What of Varya and me?" I asked the tsarina when Kornilov left the room to address the servants. I was so alarmed by this new turn of events, and by then comfortable enough with the tsarina, that I didn't bother to conceal or even excuse my eavesdropping. As soon as Kornilov was out of sight, I rushed out from behind the door like a child and burst into the parlor. The tsarina looked at me and smiled, as might a hostess to a guest she didn't know, a vague, perfunctory expression that betrayed no emotion.

"I've spoken with Nikolay Alexandrovich," she answered, her tone almost serene. "He is confident he can negotiate on your behalf. There are officials who remain faithful to his wishes even if they can no longer be called commands. And remember, Masha, you are a Rasputin. You are God's chosen, safe in his providence." I nodded, as I had when she'd said the same thing a week earlier, after we learned the tsar had stepped down.

"May I send my mother word that Varya and I are all right?"

"Of course. You must send her a telegram. I'll call Fredericks— he'll help you. It's all God's will, Masha. You know that. Nothing comes to pass that isn't. How could it?"

As I reported to Alyosha when I went back upstairs, only a few loyal and mostly ancient retainers were staying in the Romanovs' service: two valets, half a dozen chambermaids, ten footmen, the kitchen staff, the butler, and old Count Fredericks, an unlikely source of help of any kind.

The Old Guard and the New

· · · · ·

Master Emeritus of Court Life, Count Vladimir Fredericks might well have been relieved by the contraction of his demesne. Disoriented by the imminence of a revolution that had declared his worldview not only myopic but also corrupt, for weeks the count had been continually lost in the palace corridors. Sent bearing a message from the tsarina to her confidante, Anna Vyrubova, the count would nod briskly, click his shiny heels, and return to the tsarina's suite some hours later, his mouth and mustache quivering in anxious confusion and the message still on his salver, envelope unopened.

"Why, Count . . ." the tsarina would begin, but then she'd trail off and smile. "How debonair you're looking, dear Vladimir! No wonder poor Anna didn't read my little note. She must have been overcome with shyness when she saw your new waistcoat. Exquisite! It is new, isn't it?" The count, who at ninety was at least as vain as he had been at twenty, looked down at his waistcoat (which was certainly not new despite his freshened appreciation) and forgot the shame occasioned by the failure of his errand. No one had the heart to scold him, and he spent his days in perpetual futile perambulation, wandering in and out of one suite of rooms after another until he arrived somewhere he recognized.

It was Count Fredericks who had been in charge of lighting

when, in 1873, five electric lamps were installed on Odesskaya
Street. The count had been following the announcements of the
grim eastward march of progress and was among those who gathered for the lamps' inaugural illumination. A terrible light, poisonous and green, flickered, strobed the crowd of faces, and flooded
their open mouths with something that looked like oil of vitriol. Or
so Fredericks reported to Tsar Nikolay's grandfather, Tsar Alexander II. Electricity, he predicted with obvious relief, was too vulgar to catch on. A year passed, and then another, and soon it was
five, and there was no further mention of electric lamps. Someone
had finally taken down the ones on Odesskaya Street, which had
remained lit only as long as their inaugural performance. Fredericks, considering his position secure, celebrated their removal by
ordering many times the amount of candles he usually did for a
year. But no sooner had the candles been delivered than some in-
fidel greedy industrialist plugged the entire Liteiny Bridge into a
sinister smoke-belching generator, and just like that the Neva was
showered with diamonds. Transformed into a great glittering serpent, the river turned and twisted under the delighted gaze of the
hundreds of technology-mad fools packing the bridge's span, and
the count went back to the Winter Palace and embarked upon an
epic bender. By 1889 the palace had its own direct-current gener-
ating station, and the ever more forceful incursion of vulgarians
denied the count his august position: Bringer of Light to Darkness! For some weeks the count refused to leave his candlelit room
or take any nourishment besides that found in Finnish vodka. As
a gesture of condolence, Fredericks was promoted from Minister
to Master of Court Life, and from that point forward no one ever
had the heart to scold him. There are those people who cannot be
transplanted from one age to the next.

As luck would have it (ours, not his), the count's lack of foresight provided those of us now confined to the palace with limitless candles to burn once the electricity and gas were cut off.

The thing to do about the telegram was to get Varya to ask OTMA for help. OTMA was the name the Romanov sisters made up for themselves as a single entity—that's how close they were to one another. They used the first letter of each of their names and arranged them by birth order: Olga, Tatiana, Maria, Anastasia. While I know they spoke as individuals, I remember them as a Greek chorus, dressed alike in long white gowns and providing a plaintive, sometimes sighing commentary on our plight. Like their mother, the sisters were devout, given to dropping to their knees and praying in concert. Soon after we moved in with the Romanovs, Varya fell in line behind OTMA, clearly happy to have discovered not just one sister whose company she preferred to mine, but a matched set of four. She was suited to life as a princess—even a deposed one was better than nothing—and granted Tatiana the same role her sisters did. Olga, twenty-one, might have been the eldest, but she happily ceded authority to nineteen-year-old Tatiana, the most efficient and pragmatic sister, on whom the younger two, eighteen and sixteen, depended as a kind of governess. Now that they had been abandoned by the servants, she was the only one they had.

OTMA. If the tsarina wanted something done, she didn't summon Count Fredericks. It was OTMA she called to her boudoir.

THE TSARINA DIDN'T RESEMBLE the image her people had formed of her. Despite having been born a German princess, she wasn't a spy with a private phone line to the kaiser; she wasn't my father's mistress; she wasn't a frigid, humorless termagant who drugged Tsar Nikolay into submission so she could meddle in state affairs. If she could be faulted for anything, aside from religiosity, it was her opaqueness. Alexandra Fyodorovna was clever, far more than her husband, and had discovered how to protect herself from psychic penetration by anyone save her immediate family. Deploying an innate impulse toward generosity and never taken by surprise, as she didn't receive guests for whom she hadn't prepared comments, she generally began her delivery of these from yards away, across the room, carried toward her victim on a frothy wave of hyperbolic praise and affection. "How are you? How lovely you look! You're doing your hair a new way! How elegant it is! What a lovely gown, and only you could wear it so well! You've brought the sunshine with you! Really, it's just come out from behind a cloud! You dance more gracefully than anyone I've ever seen. I can't believe you didn't grow up in Paris, speaking French as you do, like a Parisian, it's remarkable." On and on it went, a panegyric that overwhelmed her listener to the point that he or she would hurry to correct so falsely and flabbergastingly positive an impression, but too late: into his or her hands the tsarina would press a little gift, nothing extravagant but still the thoughtful kind of something that inspired a genuinely grateful response. For how was it that the tsarina, busy as a tsarina must be, had remembered one's passion for Jordan almonds or the novels of George Eliot? By the time one realized what had happened, the tsarina had done it again: eluded what she considered capture, leaving nothing more tangible than a fading whiff of Guerlain's Après L'Ondée, the perfume she'd worn every day since the tsar had first given her a bottle, during their courtship.

"As you see," I said to Varya once we'd lived with the Romanovs for a month or so, "there are ways other than lying to protect oneself." My sister looked at me. It had been some time since I'd last questioned her about one of her fibs.

"I have no idea what you're talking about," she said. "And neither do you."

. . .

THAT AFTERNOON IN THE DRAWING ROOM, Alexandra Fyodorovna treated General Kornilov with a warmth and politeness that
confused the man, who kept apologizing and repeating himself,
clearly worried that the now former tsarina was failing to understand the reign of terror he'd been dispatched to introduce. Once
the old guard and staff had defected—this happened with a bewil-
dering and hurtful swiftness—the Alexander Palace was closed to
visitors, its doors not only locked but nailed shut, all but the main
entrance and the one through which food was delivered to the
kitchen. From that point forward, no package would go unopened
or uninspected, no message reach its recipient in an envelope that
remained sealed. OTMA could do nothing to facilitate sending a
telegram or anything else.

Step by step, each action undertaken in the name of guarding
the Romanovs' safety would undermine their influence and separate them from their supporters, of whom there remained many
millions, if not in the city then in the heartland. The peasants—
who would become the proletariat—had never considered the tsar
responsible for their poverty. The tsar was God's anointed, just
as was Christ, and they questioned the actions of neither. If they
suffered, it was because the lot of mankind was to suffer, and if
the men who oversaw their labor were corrupt, well, that was the
devil's doing, not the tsar's. As for Russians who hadn't been loyal
to the tsar, most were riven. They'd worked to end tsarism, they
believed absolutely that it must be brought down, but tsarism was
an idea, not a man, and their satisfaction had its counterweight
of grief. Many who claimed they hated Tsar Nikolay found they
didn't enjoy his mortification.

The new guard was received with no little astonishment by the
Romanovs and their remaining staff, as the soldiers were—it was

clear from their smell as well as their behavior—drunk. They'd stopped in the village shop that sold wine and spirits, terrorized the proprietor with their shouting and gun-waving, and helped themselves to his wares. All through the palace the soldiers went, shouting, cursing, and singing lewd songs, stabbing their bayonets into the upholstery, slicing up paintings and tapestries, and breaking whatever they didn't steal.

It was probably inevitable that Varya and I, as daughters of the infamous Father Grigory, became the objects of coarse and sordid taunts. "Put your mouth on this and heal it," one lout said, backing me into a corner with the front of his trousers unbuttoned and a pistol in hand. My refusal to acknowledge his words made him angry, and he pinned me against the wall. The fumes of his breath should have prepared me for how his tongue would taste. For a moment I thought I was going to be sick, but then my teeth closed down on it, proving what I'd suspected: finishing school had not, by everlastingly underscoring the necessity of a lady mastering her passions, conquered the hot-tempered girl I was. And nothing the health instructor said had warned me that a girl's initiation into sex—my first kiss!—might be so vile. The guard pulled away, bellowing, as shocked by what I'd done as I, who was gagging on his blood and spitting it out of my mouth even as he opened his and showed me the damage to his tongue.

"Stupid slut," he said, or something like it. The injury slurred his speech to the point that I hardly knew what he said.

For a week or more, Varya and I both endured insults and threats, but she was as good as I at acting deaf, dull, and stubborn. The Red Guard were under orders (at that point, anyway) to restrict their once-exalted prisoners without touching their persons, so once the soldiers had corralled all of us onto one floor of the family's private apartments, they no longer could take any liberties requiring privacy. Cramped as we were, there was that to be grateful for.

. . .

DEREVENKO, WHO HAD CARED FOR ALYOSHA for eight years with a devotion that appeared sincere, had either feigned that love or lacked the character to resist what appeared to him as an immediate existential promotion. In the hours before he abandoned the tsarevich, he tested his new agency by sprawling on Alyosha's bed and ordering him about.

"You!" he barked. "Light my cigarette. Polish my boots and shine my buckle. And when you've done that, go to the kitchen and get me something to eat."

In silence, without betraying any resentment, Alyosha did all these things while his sisters and I looked on, none of us daring to protest. Dina, as Alyosha called him, sprayed crumbs over the bedclothes and wiped his greasy fingers on the satin wall covering while the tsarevich went to find the "good big traveling trunk" the sailor asked for.

"That," Derevenko said when Alyosha came back. He pointed at Alyosha's scale model of the family's yacht, *Standart,* on which they sailed the Baltic Sea each fall. "And that. And all of those. Into the trunk with the rest of it." Derevenko watched as Alyosha did as he was told, filling the trunk from his shelves and drawers and closets. The railway cars and sailing ships; the battalions of minuscule soldiers that marched—some of these playthings had been made by Peter Carl Fabergé and were worth inestimable rubles; the clothing the tsarevich wore for court appearances; his ikons and saints' medals; his boots; his hairbrush and comb: whatever the sailor imagined would fetch a good price, especially those things that bore Alyosha's initials or some other proof of their ownership, went into the trunk. When it was filled, he stood from the bed and brushed the crumbs from his shirt onto the floor.

"There it is," he said to the tsarevich. He picked up an ornamental sword, its hilt engraved with the Romanov crest, and used his shirt cuff to polish the ruby set into the pommel. "Severance pay." He threw the sword back onto the pile of plunder and kicked the trunk's lid shut.

Perhaps Alyosha's forbearance had been, as he said when we spoke about it that afternoon, more the result of shock than noblesse oblige, but I saw him differently after Derevenko's departure; I stopped calling him "your highness." If the rumors had been true, if he had once been a child who threw tantrums and behaved shamefully, he was no longer that overweening boy, and it was wrong to tease him as if he were.

No one slept that first night. The tsarina dismantled Tsar Nikolay's dressing room and found where he had saved the letters she'd written him during their courtship, and at three in the morning had set to work burning any that seemed prudent to destroy, as her children looked on. They, as well as Varya, gave the impression of being too stupefied to comment, but I was tantalized by the letters, enough that I insinuated myself into a corner from which I could make out the words of the one the tsarina had been reviewing before she turned to poke the fire. "It's cold, isn't it?" I said to Tatiana, pretending I'd moved to be closer to the hearth, but neither she nor her sisters gave any indication they noticed my trespass, only a replica of their mother's vague smile, which they had perhaps been trained to summon in response to any social awkwardness.

I would never be able to summon the tsarina's face without seeing it as it appeared while she destroyed her own carefully preserved history, letters so passionate I had to remind myself to keep my features composed while I read what I could of them. It was the first time I'd encountered that kind of thing—a love letter. I hadn't known they existed outside of novels, and I wondered if my mother would have written such things to my father if he'd known how to read.

That she might have was strangely fascinating to me. I contemplated the idea the way I did the exhibit of birds of the new world at the zoological garden. Here was plumage the color of which I'd never seen before.

The tsarina read quickly, but I could tell she wasn't skimming the words, she was reading each one, her eyebrows drawn into an anxious V, her lower lip caught between her teeth, and her eyes wholly focused on the work before them, one page after another bearing her excitable penmanship, line after line punctuated by nothing save dashes and exclamation points. In contrast, the tsar's hand was so regular a typewriter might have produced it.

The Tea-Tray Toboggan

· · · · ·

VARYA, OUR BROTHER DIMITRI, and I grew up as Father had done, in that part of Siberia where spirits walk the forests and swim the rivers and apparitions of the Holy Mother are not unheard of. Our flesh-and-blood mother, Praskovia Fedorovna Dubrovina, hailed from Yekaterinburg. A city girl when she arrived, the daughter of a merchant who retired to the country, Mother didn't believe in what she called country superstitions, the kind held by people who lived in a town like Pokrovskoye, little more than the intersection of two roads, one to Tyumen, the other into the wild.

I spent my childhood in Pokrovskoye, knowing nothing of cities, until Father told Mother about the young ladies he met at court and she responded as if to a direction from on high. Providence had arranged a means of securing an education for her daughters, one we could never receive at home, and so I was enrolled in the Steblin–Kamensky Academy for Girls and sent to Father in St. Petersburg, labeled by my mother like a package to be handed from wagon to barge to train. Varya came two years later, when she turned ten. I was excited to be in so grand and important a place, where I could hardly sleep at night for all the carriages and automobiles I heard in the street, their wheels turning over the cobbles. My father might know the future, but I did not, and I welcomed what appeared to be good fortune without wondering the cost.

Some of the girls at the academy were not allowed to speak to us. Their parents thought Grigory Rasputin a charlatan, either that or the devil. Because no one knew what it was that Father did, that it was he who stood between the tsarevich and death, and because Father was so often closeted with Alyosha and his mother while Tsar Nikolay was off waging war, gossip had it that he and the tsarina were lovers, that he and the tsar's daughters were lovers, that he and the tsarina's ugly confidante, Anna Vyrubova, were lovers. What else could explain the frequency of his visits to Tsarskoe Selo? Rasputin had mesmerized all the women around the tsar; the tsarina herself was his puppet; the two of them conspired to lead the tsar to make disastrous decisions. Father Grigory was the Antichrist in disguise, the skin hidden under his tunic bearing occult letters and symbols—Marks of the Beast—and he intended to destroy the motherland. Some days we would walk to school and, alert to such things, I'd see that a new inflammatory drawing had been printed and plastered on one wall after another we were forced to pass. Most were cartoons of Father and the tsarina, usually unclothed and locked together in positions that defied human anatomy if not some scoundrel's filthy imagination.

"Keep your eyes down," I told Varya. "You walk. I'll hold your hand and guide you."

And so we made our way to the academy, with obedient Varya's innocence intact. Varya was like that when she was younger, untroubled by the kind of curiosity that forced me to look at everything, no matter how gruesome or depraved. There was never a month without a rumor, often printed by what pretended to be a reputable newspaper, about my father's demonic control over the fate of Russia. Political power, rather than the tsar's daughters or their mother, was the prize he allegedly sought. The ludicrous nature of such reports had one benefit, in that I never worried any of them might be true. My father might have been a libidinous man who took every opportunity to gratify his desires, but he wasn't so brazenly disrespectful, or such a fool, as to cuckold the tsar.

Even if Varya and I didn't receive so many invitations to teas and birthday parties as did our schoolmates, a city like St. Petersburg offered endless distractions. Window-shopping was a thing we could do all day, wandering up and down the Nevsky Prospekt with Dunia, who had come from Pokrovskoye to keep house for Father, all of us entranced by objects as ordinary as brooms and washboards so long as they were in a bright window. We had to hurry Dunia past the Singer building, though, as she had a helpless attraction to sewing machines and could stand all day staring at the models on display, and heaven help us if there was a demonstration. For Dunia, that was better than Shakespeare.

Being a crown prince has its rewards, of course, but, like most with royal blood, Alyosha paid with his freedom. There was much of the world, almost all of it, he had never seen. What did he know of his own birthplace? Oh, he'd been taken like a tourist to all the sights, the Bronze Horseman and the Alexander Column and the little cottage from which Peter the Great had issued his decrees while he waited for his metropolis to assume proportions befitting his majesty. Alyosha had slept through a ballet at the Mariinsky Theatre; he'd stuffed his fingers in his ears while one or another of Antonina Nezhdanova's arias transformed the same theater's stage lights into a rain of broken glass that fell past the imperial box and, as if it were a planned effect, landed like glittering bits of ice on the proscenium. More than once he'd been allowed to meander among the shops at Gostiny Dvor, as much as a boy accompanied by an imperial guard can meander. In the shining black bombproof carriage presented by Napoleon III to his great-grandfather Alexander II—and what more suitable gift from one tyrant to another?—he'd toured the Nevsky Prospekt and its fine shops filled with pastries and furs and haute couture fashions. With their English governess, he and his sisters had taken tea in a tea shop, just like a more average set of aristocratic siblings, and he'd strolled with their French tutor and repeated after him the word for store (*le magasin*), for window (*la fenêtre*), for police (*les gendarmes*), for cheese (*le fromage*), for horse (*le cheval*). (*Trés bon!* said the tutor.) Under the watch of Derevenko or Nagorny, he'd seen the showrooms of Fabergé. Peter Carl Fabairzhay, who made a fashionable French name of his Russian one and from whose atelier came the jeweled eggs presented by tsars to their tsarinas, each egg worth more than most people's houses. Fabergé, whose hands had strung the tsarina's long ropes of pearls. Aloysha's mother wore her pearls every day.

"They die if you don't," Tatiana had told me.

"What do you mean, die?" I said, having no idea they were alive. The ropes moved as the tsarina walked, swayed and tapped against one another, their clicking distinct from the whisper of her slippered feet on the floor.

"They go gray and their luster disappears. All the light goes out of them."

I nodded, as I always did when Tatiana offered me such splinters of information. They weren't casual asides. She spoke intently, as if bit by bit she was imparting a kind of code that, with practice, I could use to accomplish great things. I liked it. Not for the wisdom she volunteered—it wasn't of a type I considered useful—but for the earnestness in her eyes, which was maternal. I could tell she was edifying me as she did her sisters and Varya, out of a sense of duty.

Alyosha had, like me, watched the sun sink over a slow-flowing summer Neva, a few errant beams spraying off the gilded dome of Saint Isaac's. Whenever it wasn't frozen, the Neva's flat surface reflected sunsets of freakish beauty. Fuchsia-pink clouds streaked with violet and orange were a regular occurrence in a city ringed with factories exhaling smoke. Neighborhoods spewed smoke as well, dark plumes rising from fires in the harbor district's slums, warrens of squalid cells connected by dirty passages so dark they seemed subterranean. Workers, stuporous with exhaustion or drink, or more likely both, dropped their still-burning cigarettes, and whole city blocks discovered the speed with which rotten timbers burst into flame. Across the wide river was the Peter and Paul Fortress, where would-be revolutionaries rotted away in solitary cells infested with rats—at least they did until Alexander II made the mistake of coming out from behind his bombproof carriage door and down its bombproof steps to tread on a grenade. After that, the ministers of his successor, who was Alyosha's grandfather Alexander III, thought it prudent to remove prisoners and the plots they hatched to the old Schlusselburg Fortress, forty miles upstream from Petersburg.

Whenever he was allowed, the tsarevich had stood at his father's side, staring down from the balcony of the Winter Palace at endless bristling ranks of bayonet-bearing soldiers parading below them to collect their tsar's—his father's—blessing before they walked into battle. But that was all Alyosha knew of the city from which, he had been told, he would rule the nation he was to inherit, and for whose future he was being educated.

He'd never seen behind the pink and yellow stuccoed façades of the great avenues, never been to the Haymarket to gasp in wonder at the city's squalid soul, a tide of beggars, drunkards, and whores washing through the aisles of market stalls like debris loosened by one of the Neva's dependably imminent floods, each a guaranteed-to-be-pestilential deluge of cholera germs and candelabra, of corsets, croissants, chapbooks, clocks, chopsticks, and—

"Wouldn't candelabra and clocks be too heavy for water to take away?"

"You'd think so, but I've seen both in the street after it receded. As well as a drowned dog with a diamond collar being undone by a drunk Dutchman dancing by."

"Was that D, then?"

"Yes. Along with doors and dumbwaiters and, um, drawing-room chairs. And dice."

"Now E."

"Egrets. Eggs. Electric lamps. Elastic. Epaulets. Elephants."

"F."

"Fire screens, feather beds, forks, foxes, anything French."

"Such as?"

"French beans. French bulldogs. French toast."

"G."

"Garters, garden gates, greengages, grandmothers, and grand-fathers. Glasses, those for tea and those to look through." George V, I stopped myself from adding to the list. We'd only just learned that the offer of asylum in the United Kingdom had been rescinded now that King George had given his too hasty invitation enough thought to realize what a mistake it might be to expose his disgruntled populace, also suffering the privations of war, to living proof that emperors could be overthrown. We hadn't had even a week to enjoy the fantasy of being freed before it evaporated.

The early months of 1917 were the Romanovs' purgatory, a state somewhere between death and judgment, in which they—we all—entertained hopes of escape from whatever punishment the growing strength and organization of the revolutionaries augured. The possibility of freedom was not much different for us than for souls in purgatory: it would depend upon sacrifices made by those who remained in a world to which we were barred return. Varya and I were never told specifically to avoid the topic of our collective fate, but, living in the home of a tsar, we followed the example of our hosts, and politics wasn't something I discussed with anyone save Alyosha.

One good thing about the Haymarket, I told the tsarevich: whatever was stolen on Monday could be found there on Tuesday, displayed among the wares of merchants offering items from an "estate sale," as their grimy placards announced. Except that the previous owners, generally speaking, weren't dead. Maybe vendors of apples and cheese and sturgeon didn't offer purloined goods—maybe—but the dishes and cutlery, the clocks, andirons, samovars, oil paintings, statuary, and lead-crystal stemware, not to mention the odd harp, taxidermied yak, or leopard-upholstered love seat, had been taken from a sleeping or absent owner. Anyone thorough in canvassing the goods on offer would in time come upon something he recognized. "Look," you might hear someone say, "Aren't those Great-Uncle Vladimir's dueling pistols?" Or, "Didn't that friend of yours, Anna-What's-her-name, have a silver tea set with this exact pattern? I thought she said it was one of a kind." And undoubtedly it had been, but, alas, once blue-white cataracts had dimmed Anna-Whoever-she-was's brown eyes, her groping fingers never guessed that the larcenous servants she trusted had replaced her tableware, her plates and spoons and glasses and bowls, with cheap imitations.

"Why, look over there," Alyosha said, closing his eyes as he did when pretending. "Father's favorite shotgun." He could be the most literal-minded boy, absolutely hemmed in by reality, and the only way he knew how to use his imagination was by closing his eyes to what was in front of them. As for the rest of the family, they seemed well practiced at being blind with their eyes wide open. Either that or they pretended optimism for one another, voicing what they knew were fantasies.

"And your sister Olga's chess set."

"Nagorny's tennis racquet."

"Botkin's diamond studs."

We were so bored locked up at Tsarskoe Selo—and for the tsarevich, every day he was kept in bed was yet another insult added to that of being kept hostage—that Alyosha and I made play of whatever we could and went to any length to invent amusement. Perhaps only they who have endured a similar punishment would understand.

Of course, Alyosha wouldn't have been confined to bed if he hadn't tobogganed down the service stairs on a tea tray. But he did, and the day after he did I overheard Botkin tell Nagorny the swelling was so bad, blood was leaking through the pores of his skin.

I've never encountered so eccentric and tenacious a passion in another family, but the Romanovs, save the tsarina, were, to hear Alyosha tell it (in an attempt to explain his misadventure), the most unreasonable tea-tray riders, in all seasons, under all circumstances. Were the family to pass a tempting hillock of dry grass or sand dune when they traveled together on the imperial train, Tsar Nikolay would order the locomotive be stopped and the cars backed up to the hillock.

"Just an hour," he'd tell the engineer. "Once we're rolling again, we'll make it up easily." And then he and all four girls and Alyosha (if he was well and both his bodyguards were present to run on either side of him, and if the tsarina allowed it) would tear out of the cars with serving trays and dedicate themselves to making as many trips down the slope as they possibly could within the time allotted.

Winters at Tsarskoe Selo, the tsar built a mountain of snow on the park lawn. He shoveled and shoved from all directions, the girls helping with their own smaller shovels, until he and the children agreed it was high enough. Then they all rushed in and out of the palace with kettles of water to pour over the packed snow, until their little Matterhorn developed a slick glazing of ice on one side. Up the snowy side they filed, taking turns shooting down the icy track until they were too tired to stand. Not Alyosha, of course, as mishaps were guaranteed on so hard and fast a surface. All winter long, his sisters' shins were black and blue and covered with lumps under their wool tights, while poor Alyosha sat at a window and watched, or sat outside on a bench and watched, or, when he couldn't stand it anymore, perpetrated some act of tomfoolery like the one that had recently lamed him. I hoped it was tomfoolery. When I looked at the stairs Alyosha had ridden down, I couldn't see how he might have thought to avoid an accident. But if he had hurt himself on purpose, then why? What motive might excuse his courting disaster, plunging into it?

It hurt him horribly, especially when Botkin forced the leg into its brace, but he never complained. Not to me. The only people he showed his tears were his mother and Nagorny, who had been relieving himself when Alyosha snuck away and boarded the tray. When he learned what had happened, the big man wept and wrung his hands. He went before the tsar and tsarina, and on his knees he begged to be allowed to keep his position as Alyosha's protector. As if, trapped as we were under house arrest, there were a queue of applicants waiting for the job.

ONLY THOSE WHO LIVED at Tsarskoe Selo, within the walls of the Romanovs' carefully guarded privacy, could understand how suffocating was the pall of dread that descended in the wake of one of Alyosha's injuries. No one raised a blind or pulled open the drapes; every light was left burning all night. Minutes, hours, days: they had significance only insofar as they tracked the progress of the tsarevich's suffering. Servants walked hurriedly, wordlessly, with downcast eyes. To an unknowing observer it would seem each had a dire piece of business to accomplish, and yet nothing happened when Alyosha was bleeding, nothing of consequence. His sisters played cards, not with one another but each with her own deck, laying out game after game of solitaire. No record on the gramophone, no fingers on the piano keys, no sound other than the ticking of clocks and the whisper of cards being laid down or picked up. And the screams, muted by closed doors and long corridors but still audible, as if the walls themselves were crying out.

The tsar, who couldn't sit still under benign circumstances, launched himself at one unnecessary physical task after another, chopping and riding, marching and drilling, inspecting and cleaning and firing his shotguns, bringing down game that would go uneaten. The tsarina wept desperate, guilty tears for the curse she'd unwittingly bestowed on the son she loved better than herself. She prostrated herself before her hundreds of ikons and begged God's forgiveness. What had she done to deserve such a punishment?

Knee or kidney or big toe: whatever Alyosha had bumped filled with blood that, unable to clot, went on flowing until the hemorrhage created enough pressure to stop itself. Until the blood had no place left to go. The result of an injury could happen quickly, as when larger vessels were involved, or it could manifest itself with insidious slow stealth, hours or even days after he'd tripped and fallen or stumbled accidentally in play, as much as he was allowed to play. Applying ice might slow the bleeding, but in the end the hemorrhage would still cripple the joint or, worse, engorge the organ to the point of rupture. Grave results from something as small as a burst capillary, no thicker than a strand of hair. And no matter how dreadful his pain (and it was bad enough some days that we all prayed he'd faint, and sometimes he did), Alyosha wasn't allowed morphine—a precaution lest the crown prince develop a dependence on opiates.

Not yet eleven when Father told me about this so-called precaution, I understood it as one of the routine cruelties adults commit against children in the stated interest of strengthening their characters while succeeding only in damaging certain individuals beyond repair. Even as a child I knew that to allow such agony to go unassuaged was barbaric, and on those few occasions when I happened to accompany my father on a visit to the Alexander Palace, I was frightened in a way that had nothing to do with shyness—I've never been shy—or the proximity of the demigods we like to make of royalty. I'd gotten it into my head that the Romanovs were a monstrous kind of family, insensible to the suffering of their most vulnerable member. I must have jumbled up what little I knew about them with stories from history books. My years of formal schooling had only just begun, and we'd been instructed to memorize the succession of all the tsars back to Mikhail of *Rus,* the name Mikhail gave the piece of land he'd carved away from the Golden Horde and taken for himself. *Rus.* And he called himself *Tsar,* for Caesar, as it was his intention to make Moscow a new Rome and from it rule his empire.

It's Ivan the Terrible, of course, who seizes hold of a child's imagination, and I fell prey to dark fantasies of his hiding somewhere in the Alexander Palace. Ivan, who suffered seizures of rage and used his scepter to bludgeon the son he loved, only to fall to his knees, howling in anguish, while he rocked the murdered boy and cradled his broken head. Who other than Terrible Ivan could have summoned such noises from a tsarevich?

The first time I heard Alyosha's screaming, I was ten and a half years old and new to city life. Waiting for my father in the blue-and-gold parlor, I went down on the palace floor. Not that I keeled over, I just bent my body into the shape it demanded—folded my legs under me, pressed my face into my knees, and shut my eyes tight. I remained like that for I don't know how long, learning what it means to be scared stiff. I heard footsteps in the corridor, servants passing, but no one inquired about my peculiar position there on the blue-and-gold carpet. Or perhaps no one noticed me. Perhaps whoever glanced inside the parlor mistook me for an ottoman.

I never got used to Alyosha's screams, not ever. When I was eighteen and heard them and remained on my feet, still I folded up inside. On nights I can't sleep for thinking, my attention called back to the past, I hear those screams. Whose decision was it to give him no morphine? Why didn't anyone prevail upon Tsar Nikolay, or the physicians, to revisit the question of drugging the boy, rescuing him from a torture he endured not once but over and over? What loving mother could have borne witness to her child's begging for help, for release, for death even, and not insist he be given whatever it took to alleviate his pain?

I was a coward. Tsarina or no tsarina, I fled at the sight of Alyosha's face gone gray with pain and slick with the perspiration that soaked his hair and the nightshirt no one dared change, because at the touch of anyone's hand his screams grew louder. His eyes were sunken and ringed with black circles, and he had the peculiar and pathetic ability to keep his leg absolutely still while the rest of him writhed. What answer did I have to so grave an injury as this? From the moment Alyosha had driven his knee into the newel post, blood flowed into the joint, until the swelling bent and paralyzed his leg, stretching the skin until it shone and, yes, wept red tears. The blood that no longer circulated died, and its cells broke down and flooded his body with chemicals that drove his temperature up. He vomited from the fever and the pain and screamed when the act of vomiting jarred his leg. So this was what my father had been summoned to treat. I hadn't known such tortures existed. I might have heard the tsarevich scream when I was a child, but I'd seen him only when he was well, from a distance, and whatever Father told me of Alyosha's illness didn't prepare me for what it was—how could it have?

I think I might have stood it if he hadn't screamed so. But I couldn't stay by his side when he screamed, I couldn't. Especially as there was nothing I could do to stop it. Suddenly, my failure to take any of the Neva's water seemed exactly that: a failure. What if it had absorbed some aspect of my father and could have granted Alyosha even a little watered-down relief? Pilgrims had left their canes and bandages around the hole in the river's ice. They believed in it, whatever it was the river carried away and swept into the Gulf of Finland, from which no one could retrieve it. A minute, even less, of Alyosha's screams was all that was required to strip away my enlightened education and reveal me to be as superstitious as an ignorant peasant.

I knew my father had sometimes remained with the tsarevich hour upon hour, but under his hands Alyosha's tortures, and his screams, would have diminished. I'd never known of anyone, not even people with legs crushed by logs or eyes pierced by porcupine quills or appendixes on the verge of bursting, who didn't eventually fall silent under my father's hands.

"So much vital energy wasted on protest," he'd complain, falling into his armchair so I could pull off his boots while Dunia brought him his slippers and a glass of Madeira. "And not one of them able to direct even a fraction of it to any purpose. I have to do it for them." His eyes, at the end of a long day, showed me what other people's pain did to him.

The tsarina stayed and listened to Alyosha's agonies to punish herself. Not that another mother wouldn't have kept vigil by her child, but a different woman might have done it in a spirit other than guilt. Alexandra Fyodorovna behaved as one who had administered a slow poison to her best beloved, immediately regretting her rash and wicked act and remaining with her victim, sometimes even writhing with him in anguish. When I saw this, so eerie and distorted a mirror of Ivan cradling his poor murdered son, I felt a shudder crawl up my neck.

The tsarina never left Alyosha's side without being physically pulled away by Dr. Botkin or her husband. To give Alyosha aspirin for the fever that attended a hemorrhage would make the bleeding even worse, and, without the release of morphine, all Alyosha could do was lie as still as possible, his temperature so high that Botkin had no recourse but to drench him in rubbing alcohol, summoning whimpers more awful than screams for their ability to communicate a kind of exhausted resignation, noises like those I've heard from dogs as they slink, subjugated and beseeching, toward the hand that whips them.

Handsome Alyosha

· · · · ·

HE FIRST TIME Alyosha and I spoke after his accident, we were as awkward with each other as if we hadn't yet met.

"Masha," he said when I hesitated in the doorway of his room. "Aren't you going to come in?"

"Of course I am," I said, and when I got to his bed I asked him how he was feeling.

"Very well, thank you."

I hope I managed to close my open mouth upon hearing so preposterous an answer. He was drawn and pale and every so often visibly braced himself against pain, holding his breath or holding tight to the side of the bed.

"Are you sure?" I asked stupidly, and we looked at each other. He smiled at me then, after we'd done staring.

"Well, I've been better, perhaps," he said, "but I'm on the mend. Botkin said—"

"I'm so sorry, Alyosha," I interrupted. "I wish I . . ."

"Masha. I didn't think you—"

"No, no, I know you didn't. But I'm sorry I can't. Had I known what . . . what . . . I never would have made light of it, not even in jest."

Alyosha shook his head. "I don't remember your making light

of anything," he said. With his cheeks so white, the thick black lashes around each gray eye were that much more striking.

"I'm—I'm terribly sorry, Alyosha. Please forgive me. I was flippant when we—"

"Masha."

"No, listen. All the while you've been ill, I've felt so ashamed. Over and over I heard myself say I supposed I would be tested when the time came and then we'd discover if I was of any use to you. And, of course, I wasn't. Not that I was vain enough to imagine I would be, only that I didn't understand what your mother wanted me to do for you. I didn't imagine a person could go through anything as horrible as . . . as you have. Now that I know, I'm even sorrier to be so useless. I've been hiding in my room, praying she won't summon me."

Alyosha laughed, and winced because it hurt him. "I don't doubt you have," he said.

"Please. I'm talking to you in earnest, Alyosha."

"Stop fretting. I told you, or I tried to. I'm past the crisis, or whatever Botkin calls it. I'll tell Mother I'm sure it's your doing."

"No, no, don't. Don't, Alyosha. Please don't. She knows I'm useless."

He looked at me, his arms crossed over his chest, smiling at my using my hands to beseech him. "At least I've distracted everyone for a bit," he said, "given Mother and Father something else to think about, other than . . ." He trailed off, frowning at me. "You like me now," he said after a minute. "You like me better than you did before. Why?

"It's true, isn't it?" he went on when I was silent. "If it wasn't, you'd have disagreed with me."

"You make it sound as if I didn't like you before."

"Perhaps you didn't. Oh, Masha, don't look so—"

"I never didn't like you. I just . . . now I see how preoccupied with myself I've been, with Father's death. It came between me and . . . and everything. Between me and the rest of life."

Alyosha nodded. "Are you afraid?" he asked after a moment.

"Of what?"

"Of living without him."

"No. Maybe. I don't know what I thought it was before— someone dying. Someone who isn't a stranger but a person you love. Now that I do, it's . . . Nothing's the same. Or it's me that's not the same. No matter what I'm doing, or even if I'm doing nothing, it's like looking at a picture hanging on the wall and seeing it's crooked. In my mind, I keep trying to adjust it, whatever it is, and stepping back to consider. But it's me that's the problem. I'm listing in some way I can't correct." I stopped talking, surprised to have found myself confiding in Alyosha, who nodded slowly as I spoke.

"I think I understand," he said. "As much as I can, anyway. Actually, I probably can't imagine at all what you're suffering. That was a presumptuous thing to say. I just meant I wished I could."

"Could what?"

"Understand. I want to understand. I realized, but not in time to shut up, that I was talking about myself when I asked if you were afraid. Do you know, this is the first time in my life I've had an accident without his coming to my rescue? Now I . . . well, now I know."

"Know what?" I asked.

"What it's like when he isn't here," he said, after I'd given up waiting for any answer at all.

"Oh, Alyosha. I'm so—"

"Please don't tell me you're sorry again."

"But I—"

"It's only Mother who's unreasonable enough to expect you to help. Masha. Masha, please don't," he said.

"It's nothing."

"You're crying."

"No I'm not."

"You look like you're crying."

"Don't you know," I asked, after drying my eyes on my sleeve, "that when someone says she isn't crying, you're not supposed to argue with her?"

BEFORE MY FATHER DIED and I came to live with the Romanovs, most of my visits to the Alexander Palace had been accidental, a matter of my being with Father when he was called to tend to an emergency. Most often I was left in the blue-and-gold parlor, and sometimes a lady-in-waiting offered me a book or a paint box and paper. Once, the children's governess collected and deposited me in the nursery playroom, where I saw something I'd never seen before: a wheeled chair for invalids but made small, for a child. There was a wagon in the playroom too, and a plump little horse covered in real horse hair, with a real mane and wheels where its hooves should be and a saddle big enough to sit on, and I looked at the three things, each with its four wheels, and felt what I couldn't yet identify as pity. I was so overwhelmed by all of what was around me—the riches, the servants, the vast number of rooms—I had no idea what I felt, other than outrage at the wanton wickedness of taking pieces of a real horse to make a plaything. What kind of family would provide a child such a toy? I missed my horses back home—I think I missed them more than I did my mother—but I wouldn't have touched that false steed, not if it had been the last suggestion of an equine specimen on earth.

In truth, I didn't dare touch any of the toys. Not while the screaming continued. The longer it went on, the younger I became, whittled
down from ten to a baby of five or six, prey to morbid imaginings
and sure such sounds could only be the work of malevolent Ivan,
who had bewitched the nursery, stunned and stilled each toy. Any
doll that could lie down and close her eyes had done just that. The
ball and hoop rolled back to their places in the cupboard, and the me-
chanical wonders that entertained the tsarevich—railways and factories, fleets of ships that sailed, battalions of minuscule soldiers that
marched—remained motionless, waiting on the fate of their bedridden owner, a boy who would have traded everything he owned
for the one pleasure denied him, the gift for which he begged every
Christmas and every birthday: a bicycle.

So I gave one to Handsome Alyosha.

"What color is it?" Alyosha wanted to know.

"Red, of course."

"Tell me what it looks like."

"You know what a bicycle looks like."

"I want to know what *his* looks like."

"Handsome Alyosha's bicycle is red," I told Alyosha, "but the
handlebars are chrome."

"Does it have mudguards over the tires?"

"It does."

"Well, why aren't they chrome too?"

"Who said they aren't?"

"Is it a Raleigh or a Triumph?"

"Neither."

"Royal Enfield?"

"No."

"It has to be an English bicycle."

"Says who?"

"I don't like American ones as well as I do English."

"It's not American or English or French or anything else. It's magic. Handsome Alyosha can pedal it on water and above the clouds. He's ridden it through the heavens. Every new moon there's a race around the largest of Saturn's rings, and Handsome Alyosha always wins."

"Who else is in the race? Who comes in second and third?"

"Hermes and Chronos. God of travel and god of time."

"What about Zeus?"

"He watches. The race is meant to entertain him."

"How can it be entertaining if it always turns out the same?"

"Because Zeus and all the others never believe Handsome Alyosha will win. No matter how many times he comes in first, they think it will be different the next time. After all, they're gods. They don't understand how a boy on a red bicycle can win, especially not against Chronos, who can slow the hand of a stopwatch, or Hermes, with his winged sandals."

"Are all the gods there watching?"

"The men, yes, but not all the women. There's a grandstand and clubhouse built on one of Saturn's inside rings, just as at a horse race. Dionysus runs the concession and all he serves is champagne, fois gras, and caviar. Toast points, of course, for the pâté and the caviar. Demeter won't come, because she's always quarreling with her father—he's Chronos. And Artemis hates cycling. She disapproves of everything except bows and arrows. That's as much technological advancement as she tolerates. But Hera and Aphrodite are there, and Athena, of course. Hestia sometimes, but she's a homebody. She never feels she has the right clothes for going to the races."

Sitting by Alyosha's bed, I could invent this kind of nonsense for hours, so Handsome Alyosha never lacked for adventures, but the beginning of his story, the part Alyosha asked for more often than any of the others, was the story of Handsome Alyosha and Baba Yaga.

Handsome Alyosha had a cruel stepfather who made him do all the most menial chores while he and his ugly sons lazed about. But Handsome Alyosha had a secret. Before his real father died, he had called his son to his bedside and from under his pillow he pulled a little soldier doll. *Keep him with you wherever you go, Alyosha,* his real father said, *and never let anyone see him. If you get into trouble, give him a morsel of food and ask his help.*

And so he did. The stepfather thought he could destroy Handsome Alyosha's health and good looks by working him to death in the cold while he and the louts who were his sons warmed themselves by the hearth, but it was the soldier doll who chopped wood and drew water from the well. Since the wicked ones made no effort to help Handsome Alyosha, they never saw how it was that the brave doll hunted and dressed the game he killed. *Be sharp, little sword,* said the doll to his knife, *be swift,* and so it was.

One day, when his useless lazybones stepbrothers allowed the fire to go out, Handsome Alyosha's stepfather sent him to Baba Yaga to fetch a light, and the doll told the boy to be brave and do as he was asked. As long as he kept the doll in his pocket, no witch could harm him. But Handsome Alyosha couldn't help but feel frightened, for, as everyone knows, Baba Yaga eats children. She flies through the night in a mortar, using the pestle as a rudder and a broom to sweep away the traces.

"What traces can she make if she flies?" Alyosha asked.

"Why, the bits of hair and gristle she spits out. The fingernails and the teeth."

Handsome Alyosha could hardly speak for fear when he found that the hut was made of human bones. But, *Little hut, little hut, turn your back to the forest, your front to me,* he said when he reached its door.

Naturally, Baba Yaga didn't give a boy what he asked for until he had performed the usual sorts of terrible tasks witches impose on children. Baba Yaga flew off in her mortar and left Handsome Alyosha behind to kill the thousand snakes in her corncrib and to fill her wood box with tinder gathered on a distant mountaintop, and all the while the hut's frightful scaly legs went on dancing so wildly the furniture flew about the room. But with the help of the soldier doll, Alyosha accomplished his impossible chores easily. He even bridled Baba Yaga's three bewitched horses, red for the sun, white for the day, and black for the night.

How did you! Baba Yaga screamed, when she flew home and found she couldn't punish the boy.

My father's blessing, Handsome Alyosha answered, as he knew this was the one magic Baba Yaga could not overcome. She had to give the boy fire as well as a skull in which to carry it home.

Handsome Alyosha walked through the dark forest without further trouble, holding the skull so its flame-bright eyes shone like headlamps to show him the way through the trees. When he reached his home, the fire leapt out of the skull and burned up the stepfather and stepbrothers as just desserts for their unkindness. Three heaps of ashes, that's all that was left of them.

"And then?" Alyosha would prompt.

And then Handsome Alyosha kept the magic soldier doll in his pocket until the day he died, when he was no longer a poor boy but the tsar of all Russia, an old man who had fought many battles and won many wars and who had nine hundred and ninety-nine great-grandchildren. That's how far his dying father's blessing had taken him and why the story was Alyosha's favorite. Often in danger of being extinguished, the life of Handsome Alyosha was filled with peril and impossible quests, even more so than the real Alyosha's.

I knew I couldn't help him as my father had done, couldn't whisper to the clamoring blood and stop its flow. Couldn't lay a hand on an injury and make it disappear. But I could tell stories, and they were, most of them, true.

The Virgin in the Silver Forest

· · • · ·

"IT HAPPENED IN the Silver Forest."

"The one outside Moscow," Alyosha said.

"Yes, outside of Moscow."

The setting was important. It wasn't any forest but that particular forest of birch and pine.

"Once upon a time, when you were a little boy, you fell down in the park and injured your arm, and your poor frightened mother summoned my father to come to you from Moscow."

"He was there for the opening of an orphanage," Alyosha continued. "Father Grigory's Home for Children."

"Yes." Although it wasn't so much an orphanage as a place for destitute families to leave their children, lest they starve. All the money Father was given as bribes he gave away, often to orphanages, and this one had thanked him by changing its name. I think it was a hard thing for a tsarevich to consider: that loving parents might abandon their children to be fed, clothed, and protected—care they could not themselves provide.

"He missed the opening," I said. "The re-opening, really. He bought a ticket for the first available train to Petersburg."

"And then?" Alyosha said.

"And then," I answered, "as there were hours to fill before its departure, he went for a walk."

After I'd told Alyosha the story of the Virgin in the Silver Forest once or twice, it became something closer to a prayer than a distraction. Were I to omit a detail, Alyosha supplied it. If I changed anything inadvertently, he corrected me. It had to be the same each time, exactly the same.

"Your father didn't like walking in cities," he'd prompt, and I'd say, "No, he didn't. He didn't like it at all."

For Father, a walk meant going beyond the outskirts of Moscow, with its poverty-choked streets. Apart from their taverns, where he could dance with gypsy women, Father found the noise and ugliness of cities offensive. To get to the Silver Forest, he crossed a fallow field. Once inside the trees, sheltered from the wind, he found the woods silent, and he saw how a storm had left everything, every needle and twig, glazed with ice. The sun shone on the trees and reflected off the ice, and every tree around him blazed with light. He couldn't walk without peering through his fingers, his hands held before his face to protect his eyes, and he went forward that way, deeper and deeper into the Silver Forest.

There was no color anywhere, only white snow, white ice, trees frosted white. Not a color so much as a flare of illumination too intense for mortal eyes. He didn't see the Holy Mother until he was in her presence.

The Virgin took the form of a fir tree, all of her sparkling white, with boughs for arms, and in each arm she held one of the lives my father had saved, human lives and those of animals as well.

"Was I there too?"

"Of course. By then Father was a man of forty years, and the tree was as tall as a church spire and laden with souls. Every soul including that of the first creature he'd raised from the dead, a—"

"Little white goat."

"Yes. The Holy Mother had so many arms—boughs—and the light was so intense that Father found himself dazzled, unable to go on looking and equally unable to turn away. To help me understand, he drew a picture of the apparition."

"Can I see the drawing?" Alyosha asked the first time I told the story. "Did you keep it, Masha?"

"I have it among my things. I'll fetch it if you like."

My father was barely able to write. When he tried, the letters came out backward or out of order—a nearly faultless memory hid his lack of education, as he could quote page after page of scripture while pretending to read—but his hand was that of an artist. He'd drawn a crown of sparkling snowflakes over the Holy Mother's head and rooted her feet into a bank of snow, and he made each of the branches that were her arms curve gently outward from her trunk, its outermost twigs like fingers cradling the head of a newborn. One sleeping soul rested along the length of each branch, toes toward the trunk. Some lay on their sides, some on their backs; all had his or her eyes closed.

"Bring a light," Alyosha asked when I came back with the drawing. It was late in the afternoon; the room had fallen into shadows. Alyosha studied each face on each bough, looking for a likeness of himself, I assumed, but I kept this to myself.

"What happened next, Father?" I'd always ask about his walk in the Silver Forest, and he always answered with the same word: "Nothing."

Nothing happened, at least not as things usually do. He'd known he was in the presence of the Virgin, that's all, and his happiness was so intense he neither moved nor dared think his own thoughts for fear she'd leave him, and when she did leave he fell to his knees and wept.

MY FATHER WASN'T BORN with the power to heal. He described himself as an indolent second son, who neither expected nor wanted to inherit the family farm. Even when he wasn't busy causing the usual adolescent mischief, he didn't make himself useful. He never could think about working when there was a girl in sight, and both he and his older brother, Mischa, looked forward to Mischa receiving all their father's property.

But in the spring of 1883, when my father was fourteen and Mischa sixteen, the brothers suffered an accident together. The snows were melting and the Tura was running high and fast, but boys, boys—they do seem determined to prove themselves idiots. Having hiked to a bend in the river not far upstream from the falls where the Tura joined the Tobol, the two set down their picnic of bread, onions, kvass, and white cheese. They were going to bathe in the river before they stuffed themselves with all they'd plundered from their mother's pantry. But Father hadn't even undressed before his brother went in and was caught by the current. Father waded in to save Mischa, but he couldn't. The water was so strong and held Mischa so fiercely that, once Father had an arm around his brother's neck, both boys were pulled downstream and nearly drowned. A man who happened to see—it was Arkhip Kaledin, the village blacksmith—fished them out before they reached the falls, but they took fevers, and in three days Mischa was dead.

After he lost his brother, my father's illness was made worse by his grief, and for weeks he went on being feverish and delirious and saying things no one could follow, until one day he woke up with voices in his ears. Sometimes they told him of things that had yet to come to pass; other times they revealed secrets or thoughts people hadn't voiced. He identified a man who had stolen a horse from a neighbor; he predicted the day, even the hour, of an uncle's death. The grass began talking to him, and the trees told him their secrets. When raindrops pocked the surface of still water, he could read the marks they made just as other men read a newspaper.

Worms under the dirt, they talked to him. If he lay down in a meadow, he couldn't sleep for all the noise beneath his head. The cries of trees feeling the woodsman's ax, the keening of sheep for their slain lambs, the scream of a rabbit with its leg in a snare. And the underwater screeching of the fish that swallowed a hook didn't drown out the shriek of the worm impaled on the hook. There was no voice he could refuse to hear, and this was frightening before it was tolerable, and tolerable before it was something he understood as a gift. Even when he was able to find joy in his unusual sympathies, still they exhausted him. To be at the mercy of all creation—because that was how it felt—sometimes this was a dreadful blight. Even if he clapped his hands over his ears, plugged them with his fingers, he couldn't escape the clamor. And what was he to do with such a gift? How was he to use it?

By the time I could sit up and take notice of who was around me, my father was no longer there. He'd left home to find his purpose in the world. On foot he tried to overtake it, his destiny, and he walked hundreds of miles, thousands of miles, before he at last arrived in St. Petersburg, and what he did along the way became a matter of curiosity and debate. The Mad Monk Rasputin had been, it was said, indoctrinated into a cult that preached sin as the means to redemption, and it was thus that he learned to be less a healer than a sexual outlaw, mesmerizing ladies of the court with the same hypnotic power he held over Alyosha and his disorderly blood. Somewhere along his path to the nation's capital, rumor had it, my father fell in with the Khlysty, whose members were thought to meet in the woods, where they lashed one another into a frenzy of lust, heightened by vodka and, ultimately, quenched by fornication.

It's possible. My father did enjoy the company of women. He wasn't much of a drinker, though, not before he came to St. Petersburg and found himself badgered day and night by countless petitioners eager to exploit his influence on the royal family.

. . .

AFTER MISCHA DIED, my grandfather Yefim told my father he expected him to assume ownership of the family farm, a thought that filled my father with dread. A daydreamer, Father took every opportunity to slip away from mending a fence or digging potatoes, from whatever my grandfather expected him to do, and wandered afield, called away from his chores by ants whispering in the grass or sent away by the protests of potatoes that didn't want to be pulled from their home in the soil. He could hear clouds gliding high overhead, and the singing of stones. He'd heard the Virgin calling him when he was ill. If he listened carefully, she told him, the world would reveal his vocation. Perhaps he'd be a hero of some kind. That would attract girls, with their soft skin, and their tight bodices that showed him just a little of their white bosoms, and their warm thighs that he tried to feel beneath their skirts.

I saw my father with countless women. In droves they came to the apartment at 64 Gorokhovaya Street, dressed in finery, silk buttons he undid with his unwashed hands, so I know of what I speak. Women threw themselves at my father. From dawn to dusk and late into the night, an endless line of them waited on the stairs to our apartment. They were always there, as familiar as the wallpaper. They wanted to be held and kissed and bedded by a man different from any they'd known. They wanted their hair mussed and the color on their lips smeared. They wanted the feel of his hot, callused hands on their smooth skin. They wanted to be healed, comforted, and even, some of them, scolded.

They wanted his blessing, or they wanted a more tangible favor: one of the notes I wrote and he signed. In order to preserve the secret of his illiteracy, I made up hundreds of these in advance and kept the desk in the sitting room well stocked with all he needed. *Dear Friend, As a favor to me, have pity on the bearer of this message and grant what she requests. Father Grigory.* There was another version for men, and I made far fewer of those.

"See, Father?" I said, pointing out that the ones for women were in the drawer on the right, those for men on the left. "And, look, I've tied a ribbon around the handle of the right drawer, just in case you forget." Not that he ever forgot anything.

A petition to have an officer husband moved away from the front? He could pack his kit that very day. An introduction to the creative director of the Ballets Russes? What could be easier? To avoid the censure of a man whose wishes were the tsarina's command, or so it was rumored, a madman who had power over life and death, Mr. Diaghilev would be happy to receive an unexpected guest.

I don't know that anyone else in my family—or anyone else who knew him, because the poor man had no friends, only those who intended to use his supposed influence over the tsarina—bore witness to the pressures heaped upon my father.

Varya and Dunia lived with us, of course, but I was the one who worried over things my sister never considered, and when Dunia wasn't out to market or cooking what she'd bought there or washing and ironing clothes or sitting at the kitchen table darning socks, or any of the countless tasks she performed each day, she kept to her room and her Sears, Roebuck catalogue. She couldn't read it—she couldn't read any language—and it was several years out of date, but it wasn't the idea of ordering anything that drew her back to it. She told me she just liked looking at pictures of machines used in the home, that was all. I've wondered since if Dunia imagined from the illustrations that there was, or would someday be, another life for wives and servants. I asked her once what she thought of such things as democracy and women's suffrage, but after I explained them she only shook her head, apparently mystified.

Mother asked me, one summer when I was home from school, about the women on the stairs. Did he love any of them, she wanted to know.

"I don't think he even knows their names," I told her.

AS A YOUNG MAN IN POKROVSKOYE, my father had liked to watch the girls in town, especially when they went to the river to bathe and afterward lay their bodies on their discarded clothing to dry in the sun, naked for anyone to see. And he liked taking his father's cart to the market in Kuban and meeting girls along the way. There were innkeepers' daughters who were happy to warm a young man's bed before he went to sleep. By the time my father found the woman who would become his wife, he was well practiced in kissing and probably much more.

In 1888, when the Dubrovins moved from Yekaterinburg to Pokrovskoye, my mother was twenty-three and my father was nineteen. They met during the May Festival, when the people of our village carried ikons down our one street to greet the spring, dragged tables from their houses into the sun, and piled them with food and drink, and there was no one too old or too young to resist the rhythm of the "Kalinka." My mother was beautiful, even by Petersburg standards, and she was voluptuous and blond and educated. My father could dance like a demon. From the ends of his too-long hair to the cracked leather of his peasant boots, he moved in a way that made people take notice, and once they'd looked they couldn't stop. He was tall and rawboned, and his long legs stamped and jigged so quickly it was hard to tell what steps they followed—a dance of his own devising, that much was clear.

Whatever my father did betrayed his carnal nature. Not that he made any vulgar movements; he didn't have to. No one could watch my father do anything physical in the company of a woman—walk, plow, sweep—without sensing lust and the intent to gratify it. Dancing, he took hold of a girl and led her firmly. One after another he took them, twirled them, wore them out, and left them breathless and clapping among the others in his spellbound audience. He spun my future mother until her cheeks blazed and her skirts flew out, twisting around his legs as well as her own. If I know my father, and I do, he spun every last thought out of her head and left it empty, ready to receive annunciation.

A Stately Pleasure Dome

· · · · ·

WHITE WITH WHITE. White with black. Black with black. Bay with bay. Dappled gray with silver. There never was a time when the Nevsky Prospekt wasn't crowded with long queues of fashionable sleighs, each pulled by a team of matching horses whose color complemented or reflected that of the sleigh, all of them moving slowly up and down the avenue and all the beautiful horses exhaling clouds of steaming warm breath. For there was never a temperature so low as to dissuade the vehicles' occupants from their daily promenade. They weren't going to wait for a party to show off new furs and jewels. Drivers drove and passengers poured champagne and spooned up caviar while taking in the sights—not architectural but human.

"Go on, Masha, don't stop now," Alyosha said. So I took him eavesdropping in our own sleigh.

"Make it black and give it a gold stripe and a lap robe made of monkey skins," Alyosha said.

"What good are monkey skins? You need a robe made from an animal that lives in the cold."

"All right, then. Make it a white sleigh with a lap robe made from the skins of white Siberian tigers."

"White tigers. How extravagant. Everyone who sees us will go green and faint with envy. All right, then, Alexei Nikolaevich, tuck our tiger-skin robe around your knees and here we go. We have to spy and eavesdrop on everyone, even if we have to stand on the seat of our new white sleigh. We have to see whose diamonds are newer, and whose are bigger. Who's just arrived in town, and who has departed and why. And you, Alyosha, it's your job to find out who that ridiculously fabulously blindingly beautiful woman is, the one over there in the carriage in front of the pastry shop. See her? Yes, she's the one. Have you ever seen eyes so big and so blue? Or diamonds so big and so new? Is she, could she be, unspoken for? Let's find out her name and invite her to Saturday's ball. She cannot be interested in that awful man. That one, over there, with those terrible teeth. Look, he's introducing himself, of all the cheek, he's practically crawling under her lap robe. You haven't met him, but I have, and I'm telling you that man is the most fantastic bore. His name is—oh, I don't know. Simon Someone. I was introduced to him at my cousin's and he talked and talked and would not shut up, and all about politics. Nothing, I tell you, nothing could stop him; you could have set his clothes on fire and he'd still have gone on about Mensheviks and Trudoviks and how was it no one had read the latest boring dreadful speech given by Kerensky. After all, it was published in three papers, and didn't everyone understand the necessity of higher taxes on foreign wines and shouldn't agrarian socialists be manipulated to do . . . something, I can't remember what, it had to do with serfs. No, no, not *serf* serfs, of course—I know we haven't any more of those—but farming people, illiterate country people. Was it necessary, Simon Someone demanded, to represent factions that didn't know what was best for them? And on and on—he ruined what might otherwise have been a lovely party, and my poor cousin, she can't say boo to a fly, she just stood there smiling sweetly, the little mouse. I was fit to be tied."

"Don't stop, Masha. Please."

I didn't. I was only catching my breath. Sitting next to him in the sunroom, where his bed had been moved to allow him more daylight, I told him how we circled together in our sleigh, one among many, a grand cotillion whirling slowly past pastry shops and haberdashers, past the French dressmaker's, and past jewelers and dealers in spirits and wines, the occasional swain bounding from his conveyance through a merchant's door to return with proofs of love, a bauble for his inamorata, another bottle of champagne, more costly than the last, or why not both? Flirtations began and engagements broke, love—infatuation, anyway—abandoning one sleigh to alight in another.

But if all this remained as it had been in years before, other things had changed. The last months of empire were as spectacular for deprivation as for giddy excess. As the Great War dragged on, the army had not only conscripted all the workers from the fields and factories but also consumed its lion's share of food and fuel. Crops went unharvested, and in St. Petersburg, breadlines tangled among sleigh runners. The shortage of coal halted one after another industry, leaving unemployed factory workers to discover new vocations: rioting, looting, sabotage. Once they'd got the tsar to abdicate, the Bolsheviks opened the locks of madhouses and prisons, for their occupants were hungry too, and it seemed less cruel to allow them to forage than to die in their cells. In any case, a man imprisoned by a tsar might be a hero to the revolution. Yes, people starved and people froze, and not just the poorest. The cost of an egg doubled and doubled and doubled again, until a dozen couldn't be had for less than a ruble. And as the citizens grew hungrier and hungrier, each day delivered them closer to revolution, something Alyosha seemed to understand better than his father did.

"Perhaps the women will march on Tsarskoe Selo, just as they marched on Versailles," he said. "Did you know it's the same distance between Paris and Versailles as it is between St. Petersburg and Tsarskoe Selo? All they wanted was bread, the French women. Their children were starving, just as they are in Petersburg. And because Louis the Sixteenth was hiding in his Hall of Mirrors, the 'Maenads'—Carlyle calls the women Maenads, isn't that funny?—anyway, they marched from Paris to Versailles, carrying swords and pulling cannons." Alyosha smiled. After he'd done with old Gibbon and his *Decline and Fall* (from which he edified me with epigrammatic pronouncements like *The possession and the enjoyment of property are the pledges which bind a civilized people to an improved country,* offered up in a stentorian, lecturing tone), he plunged into Thomas Carlyle's history of the French Revolution, which he used like an almanac, predicting storms to come. In defiance of the restrictions imposed on him by Botkin and the others, Alyosha had always been a precocious student. Having spent so many days in bed recovering from one or another mishap, he'd read more widely than most boys his age and liked demonstrating an intelligence that surprised anyone who assumed him to be incapacitated mentally as well as physically.

"There were twenty thousand of the king's guard and only seven thousand women, but they succeeded anyway. The king went back to the capital, where he belonged, and the National Assembly . . . Are you even listening, Masha?"

"Of course. Seven thousand women carrying swords. And pulling cannons. To Versailles."

In preparation for running an empire, Alyosha had studied history with his tutors. His health permitting, he'd been taken daily to the map room and taught how to wage war with more lead foot soldiers and cavalry than could be amassed from all the toy stores in Petersburg, Moscow, and Kazan put together. He could recite, in chronological order, the battles waged and won by Alexander the Great in Asia Minor, Syria, Egypt, Babylonia, Persia, and India, and he had given his first pony, barely twelve hands high, the name Bucephalus, without even the thinnest veneer of sarcasm. He'd memorized the military campaigns by which Julius Caesar had assembled his empire, from the crossing of the Rubicon through every last skirmish in Greece, Egypt, North Africa, and Spain. The tsarevich understood the destiny he was meant to fulfill, but the official history of Russia didn't include the lives of the tsar's subjects, and Alyosha had never been told the real story of his birthplace. Neither had I, for the Steblin–Kamensky Academy presented a curriculum intended for girls who would grow up to decorate the court rather than navigate the world beyond it. As my purpose had never been to seduce and capture a husband, once I stopped going to school I found that quite a few gaps remained in my education.

St. Petersburg began as a marsh. Every year for a dozen years, tens of thousands of serfs and criminals and prisoners of war were marched under order of Peter the Great to a cluster of sodden, scrub-covered little islands, where the forced laborers died as they arrived, by the thousands. Given no spades, they dug with bare hands, struggling to walk as the oozing sludge held tight to their bare heels, or their shoes if they had any. And their corpses sank in mass graves without so much as a prayer, their anonymous bones melting into the city's foundation. In a certain foggy light—just as the sun was setting, or before it rose—St. Petersburg could still appear no more substantial than a shimmering mirage, the conceit of a westward-gazing tsar floating above the confluence of the Neva and her handmaidens, the Fontanka and Moika tributaries. Long before the city was habitable, it had been washed away many times over.

Nearly every other fall, the Neva overflowed her pink-granite-lined banks and tried to scrub a layer or two of the city's populace off her dirty face. The previous October, having doused the streetlamps, she'd made off with all the shutters and awnings from the buildings on Galernaya Street. She washed, dried, and then buckled the floor of every street-level ballroom within a mile of her banks. She pushed open the front door of the Steblin–Kamensky Academy and made off with our desks and all their contents— notebooks and pencils and an assignment on the colonization of the Americas, over which I'd slaved for weeks and earned the highest marks for content, organization, spelling, and penmanship. I never had a chance to bring it home and collect my illiterate father's praises, God rest him.

Into the public library's main entry she surged and split into channels, spilling out the back and side doors, carrying off histories and dictionaries and novels whose authors' last names sentenced their titles to shelves below the high-water mark. B, F, K, M, P, S, and Y: all were lost.

"What was left?" I asked Alyosha.

"Well, Dostoevsky, for one. Dickens. Turgenev."

"Tolstoy," I said. "And Gogol."

"William. Makepeace. Thackeray," Alyosha produced with evident pleasure.

"Very good. Anthony Trollope."

"Do we have to give first names too now?"

"Don't ask me," I said. "You started it with Thackeray." It took a while for him to answer, and I couldn't be sure if he was suffering physically or just bored. By the time he said "William Shakespeare," I'd drifted away entirely and forgotten what game it was we were playing. The thaw had begun; what had been silence was filled with the sound of dripping coming from the park outside, the occasional thump as a heavy cake of snow slid from a bough to the ground below.

"That's S," I said after a moment. "S washed away. Anyway, Shakespeare wrote plays, not novels."

"Right, of course," Alyosha said, and then he smiled. "Nathaniel Hawthorne."

"Ooh, an American. Nice. Very nice."

IT HAD BEEN the demand for secrecy about Alyosha's illness that originally inspired his mother and father to remove the imperial family from St. Petersburg—where they might be scrutinized by aristocracy and proletariat alike—to Tsarskoe Selo. There, no one could note the comings and goings of doctors or watch the children taking their exercise, the tsarevich carried in a sailor's strong arms. Self-sufficient behind its walls, Tsarskoe Selo protected the family's privacy, kept its dreadful secret, and—though the Romanovs could not or would not acknowledge this—increased the scorn and even hatred of those citizens who blamed the tsar for remoteness, for avoiding the populace his coffers drained. As not one member of the court, let alone the rest of the citizenry, understood what had demanded the Romanovs' isolation, no one pitied or even suspected their plight. And, isolated in their enclave, the tsar and tsarina were granted an ignorance that proved fatal. Away from Petersburg in the early months of 1917, they heard stories of riots and looting in the capital, but they couldn't see, or understand, what was happening. Perhaps the tsar's ministers confined their observations to parts of the city that weren't under siege. Or maybe he didn't believe their reports.

Kubla Khan's Selo. That's what Alyosha and I called it. Kubla Khan's village. *A miracle of rare device, a sunny pleasure-dome with caves of ice!* Sometimes, when I was too tired to think up a story, I recited Coleridge. As a token of his grandiosity, Peter the Great had given his wife Catherine a village for her own amusement. Like the panorama inside a sugar Easter egg, her utopia was circumscribed, and its limits allowed her to create perfection, or the closest thing to it. St. Petersburg would have the ills of a city that existed in the real world, but Tsarskoe Selo, the arena in which her every wish was realized, would not. Her first desire was that a palace be built in her name, and so it was—a comparatively modest structure, compared to what it became. Catherine and Peter's extravagance, united in their offspring, continued unalloyed through generations—perhaps it even intensified—the original stone building rebuilt and remodeled until it was quadruple the size of the one in which we were held. With rooms of amber and of malachite, of lapis lazuli and mother-of-pearl, with gilded corridors and solid-gold sconces, it demanded a setting far grander than a Versailles, with its tedious vistas of topiary. *A stately pleasure dome,* decreed the Romanovs, more and more loudly as the centuries unfolded until, presto, so it was: a heaven made by human hands. Under a sky forbidden to cloud appeared concert halls and conservatories, stables—gorgeous stables, the likes of which I'd never seen or even imagined, with three tack rooms and hot and cold running water and polished brass hinges on every stable door—a pheasantry and hunting lodge, train and police stations, a slaughterhouse. Post office, cathedral, a parish school for girls, a block of shops, and a town hall. Two hospitals, a mountain named Parnassus, an obelisk and a Chinese village with a Chinese theater and an English garden. And a French garden. A lyceum, a pond and another pond and between them canals and a marble bridge. All of it as extravagant and fantastic as a poet's pipe dream, and Catherine, like Kubla Khan, decreed that all of it be walled, and Tsar Peter decreed it be protected by his own guard of hussars, housed in barracks within the royal compound.

> *And 'mid this tumult Kubla heard from far*
> *Ancestral voices prophesying war!*

. . .

As above, so below. Once the heavens hear of a prophecy, they do their utmost to fulfill it. Planets align, constellations spin; if need be, the sun can hold its golden self on the horizon for an extra eleven minutes.

The first to die were the tamed deer that roamed the tamed forest. It was over before we knew what had happened, a single volley of shots on the night Kornilov and his soldiers arrived at Tsarskoe Selo. Alyosha and I and our sisters ran to the window. The night was cloudless, the moon providing more than enough light for us to see how the snow-covered lawn was painted with the poplars' long blue shadows, and we watched as the band of soldiers of the new guard tramped back through them, singing and cursing. There had been a blizzard the previous week, and as soon as the skies cleared, Olga and Tatiana did as they'd always done during the winter. They set out hay for the deer, just as the younger girls, Maria and Anastasia, who worried the songbirds might starve before spring, hung pinecones spread with suet from the limbs of the park trees. I can't imagine what sport there can be in taking aim at a tame animal, but the soldiers had shot the deer nonetheless, all of them, leaving their bodies to bleed on the white snow.

The Romanov children were as unnaturally stoic about this as they would continue to be about all the cruelties to which they'd be subjected. Varya gave a little bleat, then covered her mouth and looked to Tatiana, but none of the Romanovs flinched. All five stared expressionless at the slaughter. Faces immobile, they bore witness to the murder of their pets, animals so used to the kindness of humans that they'd probably walked forward into the spray of bullets, expecting a caress or a treat. From the window we watched the soldiers make their way back to the palace, exhaling plumes of steam as they walked through the cold. Intoxicated, a few of them lurched and fell into the snow; one dropped to his hands and knees and vomited. The Romanov children turned from the windows, drew the curtains, and went back to their beds.

Ignored, for once, by OTMA, who tucked themselves tidily back under their covers, white nightgowns slipping between white sheets like letters into envelopes, Varya came to me as I brushed and braided my hair before bed. "What should we do?" she wanted to know.

"Nothing," I said. "There is nothing to be done for this."

Not without Father, anyway. From the day he died, things had spun more and more violently out of control. My sister and I were under arrest, not benefiting from our connection to the Romanovs, perhaps even tarred by the same brush that had painted them enemies of the state. Long after the others had fallen to sleep, I was awake and worrying. I think I didn't sleep at all. The next morning, I got up before dawn. I'd been waiting for enough light to look for the deer, hoping what I'd seen had been a nightmare, that all of the preceding day, month, year, had been a nightmare.

But when I put my lips to the windowpane and breathed on it until I'd melted a hole in the morning frost, there they were, as we'd seen them last, lying on the reddened snow. Behind them, in the woods, there was an orange light, and for a moment I stared through the hole I'd made, trying to imagine what could have caused the strange glow. Something was burning, I couldn't see what.

The Poplar Grove

· · · · ·

"WHAT IS THAT NOISE?" Alyosha asked, not on the first or even the second day we heard the sharp cracks that echoed so they seemed to come from all directions at once, but after it had gone on for more than a week.

"Don't move it," I said. For several hours a day, Alyosha's leg was forcibly straightened and strapped into a brace to keep the swelling from crippling his knee. It was on a Monday that he'd hurt it. April 2, 1917. I know because he recorded such events in a journal, which came into my possession after his death.

"I'm not moving."

"You are. I'm not blind, you know."

"What difference does it make? We'll all be dead in a month. I don't know why they don't kill us now. Shoot us all and confiscate every last trapping of decadent tsarist rule. Get it over with, why don't they?"

Either Alyosha—it must have been the nickname, Sunbeam, that led me to mistake him for an optimist, before fate threw us so continually together—was a secret cynic or his father's forced abdication had turned him into one. Preoccupied by a crisis no adult could manage, asking every day—when he wasn't too sick to care—for news of the provisional government's success in holding revolution at bay, Alyosha seemed far older than his years, and he spoke his mind without regard to what his audience might think. I liked his refusal to euphemize as the rest of his family did, pretending our incarceration in the Alexander Palace was something akin to a pause between acts. As if we were taking a break backstage, changing our costumes as the props were adjusted, practicing lines for an upcoming scene. The arrival of the White Army, for example.

"Matryona Grigorievna! What is making that noise?" Alyosha said. "You hear it, don't you? Yes, I see by your face that you hear it."

"Your father chopping, that's all."

"Father chopping what?"

"Wood, of course," I said. "What else?"

Tsar Nikolay was finishing what he'd started the day after Alyosha's fall and the bleeding it caused: cutting down a grove of poplars. Trees he'd planted himself, as a boy, on the periphery of the horse cemetery where Alyosha's pony, Bucephalus, had been laid to rest like all faithful servants of the Romanovs, under a proper headstone carved with his name and the dates of his birth and his death.

Tsar Nikolay—we were to call him "Colonel Romanov" now— wasn't felling trees wildly, as if in a rage. That would have been less unnerving. In this, as in all else, he was his methodical self. He used an ax to take down a single tree, directing its fall away from the grove and onto the adjacent park lawn, where he sawed off its branches, cut them and its trunk into logs of a uniform length, and split those whose circumference might prove unwieldy for whoever tended hearth the following winter. Dogged by two guards, he carried wood by the armload and stacked it neatly near one of the palace's sealed-off service entrances, and he gathered the smallest branches into tidy bundles of kindling, which he tied with twine. Only when he had dismantled all of one tree into firewood, delivered it to the woodpile, and raked away the remaining litter of twigs and leaves did he turn his attention to the next. He walked among the trees in the grove, took a cigarette from the case he carried in his right pocket, and lit it while looking at their boughs, peeling a bit of bark away from a trunk with his thumbnail, deciding which, after the cigarette was smoked away, would be the next to go under his ax.

All of us held at Tsarskoe Selo—everyone except for Alyosha and the tsarina, who had begun her months of prostration—had ventured outside, under guard, to learn what was causing the noise. The four Romanov girls; Dr. Botkin and Anna Vyrubova; Nagorny; my sister, Varya, and I; the two valets and six chambermaids, the footmen and the cooks, the butler and the laundress; the grooms and the stable boys; old Count Fredericks, who discomfited everyone with his silent weeping: eventually everyone found a discreet vantage from which to watch the former tsar of the Russian Empire work away at killing his trees with a deliberation that seemed to imply he anticipated a use for the wood they'd yield. Did he picture the fires it would afford those living there the following winter? Could he have imagined he and his family would remain in the Alexander Palace for that many more months? Guests of the Bolsheviks? Perhaps he thought we'd all be preserved as an exhibit, like the panorama of savages at Petersburg's Kunstkamera or, better yet, on the midway of a traveling circus, with a banner over our heads that proclaimed, *The Romanovs and their Two Wards, Matryona and Varvara Rasputin, Daughters of the Mad Monk Grigory Rasputin.* Newly minted Soviets would pass before us, thrilled and disgusted by the decadence of monarchists who extracted their lavish comforts from the suffering of the proletariat. Until the Soviets became not so newly minted and found themselves jealous, a credible response from a worker dressed in drab, with an apartment upholstered in drab, who ate drab food and rinsed it down with cheap vodka.

"Perhaps it is hard," I said to Olga, who was standing one afternoon with Varya and me, where her father couldn't see us if he happened to look up from his chopping and sawing. "Perhaps it is unsettling, not to have governing to do."

"He planted those trees with his brothers," Olga offered by way of an answer. "They are nearly forty years old."

Forty isn't old for a tree, but poplars grow quickly. These were taller than the Alexander Palace by now, spaced evenly and well apart, as if they'd been planted with an eye to felling them, the space required to swing an ax. After the tsar chose a tree, he stood beneath it for a moment, looking up into its branches. Then he pulled his ax from where he'd left it, the blade sunk into one of the fresh stumps, and paced out the direction of the fall he'd planned for the tree, starting with his back at the base of its trunk and setting the heel of one boot immediately before the toe of the other, close enough to touch, heel-to-toe, heel-to-toe, his eyes cast down as he walked, watching his feet.

"What is he doing?" I asked Olga.

"Thirty-five paces. I've been counting and it's always thirty-five."

"But for what?"

"For the stake." Olga stood with her arms crossed before her, frowning.

"The stake?"

"Yes, to test himself."

"What do you mean?" I asked, feeling dim-witted but no closer to understanding. We were far enough away that the precaution was unnecessary, but the two of us spoke in whispers. Something in the tsar's manner, in what appeared, even from a distance, to be an occupation demanding the focus of a surgeon, kept us standing at attention, absolutely still, our voices hushed.

"Watch," Olga said. "See, there, he's planting it." I nodded, still mystified, as he took a piece of wood from his pocket and drove its point into the ground with the ax head. "A skilled woodsman can fell a tree with precision enough to drive a stake into the earth. Each time, after Father picks a tree, he plants a stake he cut from the previous one."

"Did the tsar and his brothers grow up here, at Tsarskoe Selo?" I asked, wondering at the education such an expertise implied.

"No, at Gatchina Palace, where they were raised like little soldiers. They slept on camp beds and had no hot water for bathing and ate black bread without jam. I guess they must have spent a summer here."

The tsar made the first notch quickly, chopping with controlled ferocity. Each time the blade bit into the wood, the trunk shivered, the twigs and new pale leaves at the top shook. The second notch, opposite the first, required a more measured attack, as even a novice woodsman knows it is imperative to leave exactly the right width of wood for a hinge, that narrow bit of trunk that gives way with a crack as the tree starts to come down.

I'd forgotten how eerie and mournful are the keening sounds that come from a falling tree, the whining cries that follow the crack. Once, they had been familiar. My father said it was the grieving of the tree and her sisters, crying as her spirit was forced to separate from her wood. "Look," he said to me, when I was a little girl. "Do you see there, how her spirit remains with all her branches and just as tall as before?" And I would nod, believing I saw it too, even though such things were invisible to anyone who wasn't my father.

By the time the tree hit the ground with a jolt we felt through the soles of our shoes, Tsar Nikolay had stepped away from any chance of being struck by its butt, should it kick back. He buried the blade in a stump and pulled a handkerchief from his pocket to blot his red face before walking out to where the newly downed poplar lay on the lawn.

"He did it!" Varya said. She squeezed Olga's hand. "He hit the stake." And he had. I watched as he searched among the leaves and branches to check his accuracy.

Olga showed my sister more affection than I could, for if Varya's lies protected her from my prying into her soul, they made us more strangers than sisters. I felt sorry for my sister, orphaned and prevented from returning to our mother, as she may have felt for me, but we looked at each other now from a distance. I suppose her hiding herself from me inspired my hiding from her. The separation between us did allow me room to observe how our father's murder had diminished Varya, who looked slighter and younger than she had before and behaved more like a child than a young lady of sixteen. It was the opposite of Alyosha's response to the changes forced coincidentally upon him, as if my sister and the tsarevich were balanced on either side of a celestial fulcrum, allowing them a mysterious transference that gave him the years she'd lost. Under house arrest, my sister and I shared a bedroom with the four Romanov sisters, a bedroom far too small for six. Still, I saw little of Varya during the day, as she was always with Olga and the others, while together Alyosha and I killed the hours leading to what he anticipated would be our deaths.

"How do you think they'll do it?" I'd ask him when he was too morbid to be diverted from his imaginings—from the astute analysis and prediction I mistook for imaginings.

"Well, it isn't as if they've exhibited any originality, not with respect to violence, anyway. I guess they'll shoot us."

"It's fast," I said, "being shot to death." In the silence, Alyosha looked at me searchingly. Finally I added, "At least it is if you're not Grigory Rasputin."

"Yes. I imagine it will be. Fast, I mean, for the individual. I hope they have the decency to kill us all at once. It's the only thing I worry about, really, the idea of one of us having to watch while the others die."

"You think they'd save you for last?"

"Not necessarily. But I wouldn't want that for any of us."

"OF THE FOUR," Alyosha told me, after Tsar Nikolay had left his ax buried in a stump and come in for supper, "Father's brother George was the tallest. More physically imposing. More intelligent. Grandmother's favorite. 'Tall, handsome, and full of fun,' she always said. He died before I was born. In the arms of a peasant woman in Abbas-Tuman, where his physician sent him to take the waters." Given his own precarious health, Alyosha was understandably enthralled by the medical crises of others, especially those that involved bleeding.

"He was weary of being a prisoner of tuberculosis and so he took his motorcycle out for a ride, but then he collapsed on the road and the peasant woman saw and tried to help him. He coughed up blood all over her skirts."

"I suppose," I said, "the not-so-hidden message of the story is that Alexei Nikolaevich is tired of being a prisoner of hemophilia and looks forward to adventures of his own, even if they are to kill him."

Alyosha said nothing but looked, without expression, at the foot sticking out from the bottom of the leg brace. There were sounds other than those of trees being murdered he wanted drowned out.

We could hear the tsar in his study during the evenings, alone and laughing. For years he'd kept a little wood box in which he saved jokes his brother George had told him when they were boys. In his deliberate and meticulous hand, Nikolay copied each one out on a scrap of paper, perhaps planning to commit them to memory and then use them himself on an audience for whom the jokes would be unfamiliar. Or maybe Nikolay Alexandrovich preserved them as a solace he guessed he'd need: the voice of his brother encouraging him to laugh no matter how dire were his circumstances.

"I think he must ration out the pathetic old things," Alyosha said, "so they last him longer."

"You're hard on your father," I said.

"He's weak. Not like yours." Once again, Alyosha recited what had already—instantly—become the last act of my father's hagiography. His voice was steady but I thought his eyes looked bright. "Enough cyanide to finish off ten horses. A dozen bullets. An ax to the head. And still they had to drown him."

A Sunny Child

· · · · ·

"WHAT COULD HAVE PREPARED your mother for life with a family like the Romanovs?" I asked Alyosha, who, in compulsively sorting through the catalysts for his family's disgrace, had arrived at the tsarina's political naïveté and what his grandmother—the ever-disapproving dowager empress—had complained was her daughter-in-law's blind indifference to Russian society.

Although Alexandra Fyodorovna had embraced the faith of her adoptive nation to the point of transforming herself into a Russian Orthodox fanatic—just as she had previously been a fanatical Lutheran—this was the extent of her exploring her new homeland. (She'd read about it in books, of course. She'd read scores more Russian histories than had most literate Russians.) To the aristocrats she remained the aloof young woman she'd been when she and Nikolay Alexandrovich were betrothed, a girl who lived in an idea more than a place. One part obligations of royalty; one part romance; the rest that particular haze to which intellectuals are susceptible: it was an idea that allowed Alexandra Fyodorovna's life to unfold in a continuum of castles, from that of her birth, in Darmstadt, to those of her grandmother Victoria in England, and on to those she inherited by marriage, in Moscow and in Petersburg, in Kazan, Gatchina, and Livadia. Time stretched like a catwalk connecting one to the next; her feet never touched the ground. When she put on the uniform of a Red Cross nurse and attended to wounded soldiers, that, too, bore the mark of heraldry, the bosom of her bride-white dress emblazoned with a blood-red cross.

Perhaps nothing could have helped Alyosha's mother understand the Romanovs. Anti-intellectuals, they took what must have seemed to Alexandra Fyodorovna a perverse delight, even pride, in childish passions another family might have tried to squelch—tea-tray riding, for example—and that the Romanovs pursued as though they were sports closed to all but those of Romanov blood. The Meddlesome Four, as the tsarina called her husband's uncles, left toads tucked under pillows, filled bathtubs with carp, switched the sugar and the salt, reset clocks while the rest of the court was sleeping, glued coins to the floor in busy corridors. They sewed the legs of underwear closed, balanced cups of horse urine on top of doors they left ajar, tripped waiters carrying trays of glasses filled with champagne.

She'd seen that happen, not once but over and over, when her older sister Ella married Tsar Nikolay's Uncle Sergei. Because it was when twelve-year-old Alexandra Fyodorovna attended Ella's wedding to Sergei Alexandrovich that she met Nikolay. Sixteen, handsome, and athletic, the tsarevich was already an accomplished horseman and an enviably accurate shot.

"And, as you yourself know, your father was a wonderful dancer," I told Alyosha. "Not like my father—not inspired, intoxicated, spontaneous jigging about—but like . . . like a prince."

Nikolay had found his eyes drawn to his new aunt's sister. During the interminable Orthodox wedding ceremony, he occupied himself by watching her. Alexandra wore a simple white dress and a wreath of pink roses in her red-gold hair and sat unnaturally still for a child of twelve, for any living creature. All the cousins told him she'd been a sunny child, enough that she'd earned that term of endearment, Sunny, which, in turn, had inspired Alyosha's being called Sunbeam. But, as most sensible persons agree, this is just the kind of nickname to invite ill fortune, showing the gods a bright target to strike. When Alexandra was six, her mother died of diphtheria, and from that time forward, as anyone could see, a dark cloud held the girl captive.

Punishment enough to have lost one's mother. To that grave injury add this insult: every object from which the child might have drawn comfort, every doll, book, and toy, was taken from her room and burned for fear of contagion. Only one of these losses troubled Alexandra—for what toy can assuage the wound of being orphaned?—but it was a loss she regarded as tantamount to murder.

They told Alexandra it was for her own good. Her mother would have wanted them to burn Anne, they said, and that was how Alexandra knew they were wicked. Because Alexandra's mother had told Alexandra how important it was that nothing bad happen to Anne—the only relic of childhood her mother had cared to preserve—how Alexandra was never to drop Anne, because Anne's porcelain face could chip. Alexandra had been careful. She knew Anne was not a toy but a talisman, a holy object infused with her mother's love. If Anne wasn't human, she was better than human. Not alive, she would never die.

But then, as soon as Alexandra had no mother to protect her, they threw Anne in the incinerator.

IT WAS HARDER TO SEE IT INDOORS, especially in a church, given the way Orthodox priests swung their censers for a wedding, wafting great billows of frankincense over the crowd packed in the sanctuary—eyes and noses streaming from the tickle and sting of it, and incessant sneezing drowning out the liturgy—but it was there, all right, sometimes smaller, more often larger, and thank heavens Alexandra was born in an age that worshipped pallor, for outdoors in the light of day it was revealed as one of those very dense clouds, gray and purple and threatening to burst.

Cumulus fractus humilis, Nikolay found listed among the other cloud formations in *Brockhaus and Efron Encyclopedic Dictionary: Precipitated by a rising current of moist warm air that, having cooled to the dew point, condenses overhead.*

"When things are dire enough for a real crying jag—when, for example, it looks like you're dying sooner rather than later," I told Alyosha, "then it trends into *cumulus congestus.*" I pointed to the next drawing.

"A relatively flat base and rounded top, with a well-defined outline," Alyosha read from the caption below the illustration. "I don't imagine it's a common manifestation."

"Probably not. Completely psychosomatic, as I'm sure you understand. And, like any weather system, something of a vicious circle."

In either case, *cumulus fractus humilis* or *cumulus congestus,* when Alexandra was outside, the sun could not get through to her, not enough to provoke even one freckle or warm her cold cheeks and mauve lips, but at least she didn't have a governess running after her all day with a hat, as did her cloudless cousins.

Twelve was too young a girl for Nikolay to speak of his intentions—too young to properly inspire such thoughts—but surely there was no harm in declaring affection for his aunt's young sister. Before Alexandra went home to her grandmother's castle in England, the tsarevich had given her a gold brooch, which, as a properly brought-up princess who did not accept costly gifts from young men (flowers and sweets were allowed), she refused. But she wrote about Nikolay in her diary, as he did about her in his.

We love each other, he concluded after a week spent with the solemn girl. What would it be like to press his lips on hers, his big body against her smaller one? Her features were, as everyone said, beautiful, but truth to tell it was the cloud he found irresistible: the fact that he could burn a wisp of it away with a joke or lift her onto his horse and, after a good gallop, leave it looking more cirrus than cumulus, edges tattered, a bit of blue showing through here and there.

SEVENTEEN WHEN SHE RETURNED to Petersburg—not to visit Nikolay but to flee the awkwardness at court caused when she rejected the proposal of Prince Albert, heir to the British throne—Alexandra stayed with her sister Ella for the entire winter season. Night after night she attended balls, dinners, theater, and ballet, the kind of social flurry she despised—at least she did until the night she allowed herself to be persuaded to attend *La Traviata* and found herself seated in the imperial box, next to the tsarevich.

Alexandra had grown into an even more peculiar teenager than she had been a child. The unrelenting cloud remained, immune to capture in a bottle or incineration over a gas ring, and the girl under its shadow, always a rapacious, even gluttonous, reader, had finished with juvenile romances and moved on to tomes of history, philosophy, and theology. She held gossip in contempt and, raised by Queen Victoria the Prudish, shrank from all mention of the one topic that consumed Petersburg nobility, men and women alike. Sex. Alexandra's lovely face could have been chiseled from marble, its public expression so controlled and unreadable she impressed people as frigid. But Nikolay wasn't easily discouraged. Twenty-one, conversant in Italian, fluent in French (practically unavoidable, as it was the Russian aristocracy's chosen tongue), Tsarevich Nikolay spoke English as well as he did Russian.

"One happy, heavenly day, your image appeared before me," he breathed, whispering the lyrics' English translation as Alfredo declared his love for Violetta, who wrung her hands onstage and begged that he leave her, even as Alexandra shrank from the hot words the tsarevich poured in her ear's pale canal. "Since that trembling moment, I have secretly loved you," Nikolay whispered.

Alexandra moved her chair to the right, closer to the wall, and then Nikolay moved his closer to hers, and so it went, inch by inch. "If you were mine, I'd take care of you day and night," Nikolay said, his lips so close to her ear that she felt his breath wash over the damp curls on her neck.

"Stop. Please. Please, won't you please stop?"

"Why? Don't you want to know the translation?"

"No. I mean, I don't . . . I'm happy just listening to the music."

"Are you sure?" Nikolay said. "Wouldn't it make the opera more enjoyable, to know the meaning?"

"I'm fine as I am. Really I am." Alexandra fanned her cheeks with both hands, from nerves rather than heat. The habit was one her grandmother found worse than inelegant—outlandish!—and once, when she caught the girl "flapping," as she called it, during a state dinner, Victoria had kicked her smartly under the table, catching her on the shinbone and precipitating a cloud so dense that Alexandra had had to excuse herself and flee upstairs to her room.

"Are you too warm?" Nikolay asked. "There's champagne."

"No. No, thank you. It's very kind but . . ." Alexandra fell silent. In the minutes that had transpired between Act One's friendly rebuffs and Act Two's fatal passion, Nikolay had trapped her chair tight between his and the wall, and moved his body closer to hers until she felt the heat of his thigh through the fabric of her dress.

Was it the panic in her eyes that showed him? Was it her trembling fingers, or the shiver of her leg against his? Was it the hammer—not the race but the hungry throb—of her pulse under his lips when, while whispering, his mouth strayed from her ear to her throat? Something told Nikolay what other suitors hadn't drawn near enough to guess: virginal Alexandra was the prisoner of a secret, unslaked sexual thirst.

"Please, I want just this very little one," he said when the curtain fell after the final act. He reached forward and with his index finger caught one of the red-gold locks that had escaped her chignon during the chase of the chairs. Slowly, he twirled the trespassing finger until he had the hair coiled tightly around his knuckle. Her eyes remained on his and, not knowing how firmly he held the curl, she joined her hand with his and pulled, expecting to remove its too-familiar touch. But even had he wanted to, Nikolay didn't have time to loosen his hold, so together they yanked the hair hard, and, as it was growing from that most tender spot, at the nape of her neck, tears spilled from Alexandra's already brimming eyes.

"I'm sorry," they said, at the same instant. Still, neither let go of the curl. The remainder of the box's occupants—Ella and her husband, Sergei, Number Three of the Meddlesome Four—turned away when they saw that Alexandra was weeping, for, good heavens, the girl burst into tears at any provocation, or at no perceivable provocation, and when she cried, the cloud was sure to rain, causing that much more dampness and fuss, and the longer people stared, the longer it took her and the rain to stop.

"I have . . ." she said, brushing at her wet face when she'd regained her voice.

"Have what?" Nikolay asked, removing his coat to give it a shake. Did the girl never speak a full sentence? The wet curl, unwound, drooped over her shoulder.

"My grandmother gave me . . ." From her evening bag Alexandra withdrew a tiny red leather case, inside it a paper of needles, a twist each of white, black, red, blue, and yellow thread, and a pair of folding scissors that, unfolded, were no longer than her smallest finger. "For emergencies," she said, and she looked so solemn at the idea of an emergency that might be cured by a needle and thread that he laughed, and she smiled. "Here," she said. "Take all you want." Her sister and her brother-in-law had left; only the two of them remained in the box.

The scissors were too small. He couldn't get his thumb and finger into the holes. "I'm afraid you'll have to do it," he said, handing them back. "Just as well. I'd take too much." He watched as her hand found the pulled curl and separated it from the others. Another cascade of hair broke free of the pins, and then they, too, were falling. "Let me," he said, and he bent to retrieve them as she sawed at the lock of hair.

"Shall we trade?" he asked when she had finished, and he held out four platinum hairpins, each adorned with a flower of diamonds, in exchange for the one little curl. Once in possession of his prize, Nikolay lifted it to his mouth, feeling with his lower lip how silky it was. "At such a price only a king could afford all of you."

"I'm sorry?"

"So many diamonds in exchange for a bit of your hair," he explained, gesturing toward the profligate pins in her hand, and Alexandra blushed even more extravagantly than before, red blotches staining her white neck.

"I'm . . . Perhaps I will have something to drink. Water?" she said, and as the box offered only the sweating bucket of champagne, he took a glass and went in search of it. As soon as she saw her way cleared, Alexandra snatched up her fur and ran down the stairs leading to the grand foyer, to catch up with Ella and Sergei outside the opera house, the cloud following just as quickly, but a different color than ever before, almost pink, as if illuminated by a sliver of sun breaking over the horizon. Too high to fit in the carriage when the three of them climbed inside, it had no choice but to follow overhead.

What, what, what was I thinking, she asked herself all the way home, watching out the carriage window, staring at the houses they passed. So many windows, and each a square of golden light through which black silhouettes moved, some walking, others waltzing. Alexandra tried to keep her hands folded in her lap, but her fingers kept returning to the shorn place at the nape of her neck. What was I thinking, she asked herself. What have I done? And she answered.

I've fallen in love, she thought. Oh God, oh no, oh God have mercy on me, I've fallen in love. She stood and leaned out the window, leaned all the way out to look for the cloud, but, as she expected, it was gone. She caught the very last puff of pink as it vanished into the night.

"What's this?" her lady-in-waiting asked when she brushed out her hair for bed.

"What's what?" Seated, Alexandra looked into her lap. "Oh, that," she said. "Nothing. It was a snarl. I cut it out."

"Your hair got tangled at the opera?"

"It must have done. Or perhaps it happened when I leaned my head out of the carriage to get some air."

"Were you unwell?"

"Oh, no, not at all. Just . . . it was a bit stuffy, that's all." Alexandra pointed at her evening bag, lying discarded on the bed. "I used the scissors Granny gave me. The little sewing scissors I carry."

"And what about the . . . ?" The lady-in-waiting spun her finger in the air over Alexandra's head. "The . . . the you-know: it's disappeared."

"Has it?" Alexandra looked up, feigning surprise. "I'm tired, I suppose. I'm not feeling my usual self."

The Wayward Hand

· · · · ·

"IT'S PECULIARLY UNCOMFORTABLE," Alyosha said, "imagining Mother as a girl."

"What do you mean 'as a girl'?"

"You know what I mean. As the object of . . . of the attention of a suitor."

"Oh," I said, embarrassed enough that I glanced away, out the window. "I'm sorry, Alyosha. You can't imagine it was my intent to make you uncomfortable."

"No, but . . ." He waited, and when I said nothing, continued, "You told the story. I listened. That's all." As he was speaking, I noticed that Alyosha's hand was in my lap, having insinuated itself with exceptional delicacy, so lightly I didn't feel its arrival so much as I was aware, suddenly, of its intimate placement.

I looked at Alyosha, who opened his large eyes, showing me the thick fringes of his black lashes, black as the ring around each iris, which sparkled in complexity. Storm clouds; the breast feathers of a chimney swift; shadows fading into dusk; a rain of silver coins: every moody, moving, mutable gray was represented. His mother's eyes. I removed the hand from my lap and replaced it in his. We'd been playing rummy earlier, and a card fell from his lap to the floor. I can picture it still, the three of spades. I remember it as I might a title card between two scenes in a moving picture, announcing intrigue to follow. I bent to retrieve it and then popped back up too quickly, betraying my nervousness. But he hadn't moved.

"Father was supposed to marry Hélène," Alyosha said finally, offering me escape. "Wasn't he?"

"According to the Meddlesome Four."

NIKOLAY'S UNCLES COMPLAINED VEHEMENTLY when the tsarevich told them he hadn't any feelings for the daughter of Prince Philippe, Comte de Paris, pretender to the French throne.

"France is a republic," Nikolay Alexandrovich said. "It doesn't have anything but a pretend throne."

"That's not so," the Meddlesome Four corrected Nikolay Alexandrovich. "A throne can't be a pretender. Only a person of high birth can pretend. And Prince Philippe is Louis Philippe's grandson."

"And," Nikolay said, "an ardent democrat who fought for the Union Army in America's Civil War."

"That was under the Second Empire," the Meddlesome Four intoned. "That was under Napoleon the Third."

"Of course he went to America," Nikolay's mother said. "Anyone with the money to do so would have emigrated at a time like that. It doesn't mean a thing."

"Of course it does, Mother. The man is a democrat. It's only other monarchies that recognize him as a monarch."

"Nicky! We are a monarchy!" his mother said.

"But France is not."

"Nicky! Don't be illogical, don't be absurd, and don't try my patience."

The tsarevich's first obligation was to the empire, and, republic or not, France had a marriageable princess. As tsarina, Hélène would cement Russia's relationship with France, and, as Russia's sole ally, France needed cementing. But the future tsar was no wiser a statesman when choosing a bride than he would prove at placating revolutionaries. Having danced with clumsy, cloudy Alexandra, who had no inclination to make the kind of clever, carbonated conversation for which aristocrats had a thirst as intense as they did for Roederer champagne, he knew it was useless to try to love any of the other princesses, with their perfect manners and empty heads, their eagerness to nod and smile at whatever he might say. The little curl, folded inside his handkerchief and held together with a stolen bit of his mother's own embroidery floss, was safe in the pocket closest to his heart. Just knowing it was there bolstered his courage, and in a few weeks, as soon as Lent arrived and ended winter's revelry, he faced down his mother's disapproval.

"Nicky! The girl has nothing, not one single thing, to recommend her. Doesn't play cards. Can't speak French—"

"That's not fair, she—"

"Don't interrupt, Nicky. She can't speak it so anyone understands it. Her accent is absolutely and irredeemably abominable. What is it about the English? They simply can't, or won't, speak anything but English, not comprehensibly anyway. No matter how many far-flung colonies they claim, they remain provincial. They insist on seeing every acre as another opportunity to replicate their Englishness. You don't see the Dutch forcing Indonesians to wear clogs or the French tarting up the Congo in their national dress. But every last maharaja in India covers himself in epaulets and—"

"Mother. Alexandra isn't English."

"I know. It's worse than that! She's German, and living in England hasn't made her any less so. And she can't dance, not even to save her own life. The girl can't get through a waltz without tripping over her own feet, so we know she doesn't tango or polka or—"

"Mother."

"What?"

"Will you please stop calling her 'the girl'?"

"Why should I? She's seventeen, female. She's a girl."

"That's not why you're calling her 'the girl.'"

"Nicky! She can't dance, can't smile, can't make conversation. And she certainly can't preside over the Russian court with that . . . that . . . that preposterous emanation, or whatever you call it, over her head. I can't abide it when a person insists on making her unhappiness everyone else's burden. I know when a person has potential, and mark my words, Nicky, the girl has none."

"But—"

"And don't tell me she's beautiful. Beautiful girls are dropping out of the trees, or they might as well be, as there are so many of them. Beauty fades. Social skills improve."

"I wasn't going to say anything about her beauty."

"What, then?"

"I love her, that's all. I didn't decide to love her, I just do. I'm going to marry her. Anyway, Mother, you're the one who brings out the cloud. You frighten her. With me, it's hardly there at all."

"Oh, tosh! What will your father say? Who cares if you're in love!"

Unaccountably, his father did. Or if Alexander Alexandrovich didn't care about love, he did have a weakness for romance. He'd seen his strapping son take the pale girl in his arms. He'd seen him whisper in her ear. He'd seen the girl smile and put her silk-slippered feet on top of Nicky's. Away they'd waltzed, and the reigning tsar felt a catch in his throat, remembering when he was young and his worries confined to gestures of chivalry.

With his mostly irascible father's unexpected blessing, Nikolay followed Alexandra back to England, where he began his campaign for her to give up the one thing that prevented his marrying her: the Lutheran Church.

May the good Lord help any man who falls in love with a religious zealot. Days passed, days and weeks and months, and still Nikolay remained on his knees with a proposal that demanded Alexandra be thoroughly and indelibly catechized and converted to the Russian Orthodox faith, all of her private religious history, every last one of her prayers, invalidated. Or so it felt to Alexandra. The girl, and the woman she became, was devout to a fault—at least that was how the aristocracy judged anyone who wouldn't take up a religion until she'd read every last tome of theology it inspired—and acquiesced only after she and Nikolay had wept themselves blind, nearly, and after he'd chased her from Buckingham Palace to Windsor Castle and from Windsor Castle to Balmoral Castle and from Balmoral to Osborne on the Isle of Wight.

Rain, rain, rain, all spring long, so much it was impossible to judge where Alexandra's cloud ended and those of the more general weather system began. Russia might allow her princesses to stray unobserved, but Queen Victoria was of a different mind. Every meeting between the granddaughter she raised and the future tsar of Russia unfolded under the close watch of court chaperones, not one of whom approved the love match, because . . . well, because love matches are necessarily the kind to oppose. But the lovers were as they would always be: willfully if not blissfully oblivious to any opinion that didn't align with their own.

Once Alexandra had slogged through Macarius's *History of the Russian Church*, Levshin's *Exhortation of the Orthodox Eastern Catholic Church of Christ to her former Children, now on the Road to Schism*, Saint Innocent of Moscow's *Indication of the Way into the Kingdom of Heaven*, and every last word by Bishop Theophan the Recluse—she read most of his books twice and his *Manual of Spiritual Transformation* three times—she at last agreed to be stripped of her Protestant birthright and, in keeping with her nature, pursued her new religion to the point of hysteria, finding altogether too much in Orthodoxy to which she could cling. Over the years, the walls of her bedroom would become encrusted with ikons of one saint or another, some acquired during her years of desperate petitions for a son and heir, and more after those prayers were answered with an invalid.

But that was later. Newly wed, she and Alyosha's father were preoccupied by one thing only, and very frustrated. Immediately swallowed by their official roles, they had little time to themselves, impossibly little, it seemed to them. So impossibly and unendurably little that some nights, while the rest of the court was sleeping, Nikolay bundled his bride in furs and took her to the stables, where he harnessed horses to a sleigh and drove himself and Alexandra silently over the snow and out of the gates of the Anichkov Palace, where the newlyweds had been forced to make a temporary home with Nikolay's now permanently disappointed mother.

January, and the streetlamps stood at attention like soldiers buried to the knees in ice, every building frosted into anonymity, the signs for the jeweler, the baker, the butcher, the barrister—all of them hidden under layers of white. Once they were on the Nevsky Prospekt, Nikolay whipped the horses up and down the avenue. A city without color but splendid in its sparkle, austere in its silence, as if subzero temperatures had the power to stop not just trains and trolleys but sound itself from traveling. The sleigh's lamp cast its beams over the frozen path before them, and each ice crystal caught a needle-narrow ray of light and sent it arrowing back, one glint multiplied by infinity, the lovers gliding forward in a curtain of light. Already Alexandra was imagining their return to their suite, when Nikolay would have begun to shiver and she to burn under too many layers of furs. They would fall into bed then, flesh shocked by flesh, his cold, hers hot, each seeking the other.

Sometimes, while I was talking, Alyosha coughed or cleared his throat. But it was true what I said to him: when I told a story, I didn't steer so much as follow it.

When they tired of the city's streets, Nikolay took their sleigh onto the frozen Neva. East from the delta, toward Lake Ladoga, the river branched once and then three times more, each arm dull and dead and gray as lead until the April thaw. West was the Gulf of Finland, where the salt sea was frozen into stillness, where waves that had swelled and churned and beat restless, restless, against the shore were now motionless, as if sculpted.

West it was, toward the frozen sea. White horses, white sleigh, white ermine, and the pelts of polar bears: they'd broken through the veil of tedium that smothered each hour of the day, Nikolay trapped behind doors with the Meddlesome Four and the minister of this, the minister of that, and the minister of this and that as well—how could there be so many ministers? He was battered by lessons of statecraft he never wanted to learn, while Alexandra endured the dutiful, affectionless attentions of the Dowager Empress Marie. The apprentice tsarina's head began to ache and her cloud to gather after only a few minutes under the skewering eyes of her mother-in-law; she was as overwhelmed by the endless tedious rules of Russian court etiquette as was her husband by politics. Excellent student of history and of German and English literature though she was, and quick to memorize music for the piano—an instrument she played with a brilliance that could have elevated a commoner to fame—Alexandra couldn't tell a savory fork from the one meant for salad.

Seventeen pieces of silverware. How difficult could it be? Marie's own children could do it at the age of three. The dowager empress was at a loss. That her daughter-in-law had none of the graces or skills to preside over the highest of St. Petersburg's aristocratic circles was a scandal; that she didn't care to learn any, an inexplicable offense.

"What of it?" Marie snapped when Alexandra inquired about the style of Russian gowns. Was it true they were cut so drastically low to expose as much flesh as they could, to provide a backdrop for more diamonds (the Russian understanding of decency being quite different from the English)?

Marie had savored her reign over society's highest echelon. She loved jewels and the endless occasions offered to display them. For, as every imported princess quickly learned, the Russian court was like no other with respect to jewels. Diamonds especially, but also pearls, rubies, sapphires, and emeralds. Décolleté on top and, well, not much on the bottom. Sometimes nothing at all.

"Dear me," she'd say to anyone who took exception to the idea, "why do you think ball gowns are so long?"

Tiaras. Ermine. Taffeta. Champagne. Banter. Small talk. Sweet talk. Innuendo. Gossip. Scandal. Dancing and flirting and flaunting. Matchmaking and match breaking. Marie loved everything Alexandra disdained. She could tolerate Nikolay's marrying a woman she disliked—of course she could, she'd endured worse hardships. Back when she was Princess Dagmar of Denmark, her first Russian tsarevich had died and, it became clear, bequeathed her, pre-wooed, to his brother. She'd been a good sport about that, and she'd accepted the burdens of being a tsarina—a job at least as demanding as a tsar's, when done correctly. Having protected and refined the duties of her station, Marie found it hard to stomach a girl who refused to admit her responsibility to Petersburg society. She felt as if she'd spent the past thirty years building an elegant and seaworthy yacht, a perfect vessel, only to have it taken from her and given to a know-nothing who refused to learn to sail it.

"Without the firm hand of a tsarina at its helm," she told Alexandra, "court life will lose its focus. Guests will devolve into mere revelers. They will sink into debauchery, and political maneuvering will become impossible. Ab. So. Lute. Ly. Im. Poss. Ible. Don't you understand? You will be cutting off your nose to spite your face."

Marie stared at the girl. Why was it that intellectuals were always so stupid? If only Victoria, the old she-devil, had managed to pass even a fraction of her political canniness on to her granddaughter, but, no, here Marie was, stuck with a lost cause. Disgraceful how fat Victoria let herself get. Forty years of widow's weeds. And that was a disgrace as well, such an ostentatious display of grief. The single thing she'd imparted to her damp granddaughter, apparently. Forty years of black, and quite a lot of it, given the yardage required by a woman of her girth. Black silk organza. Black broadcloth. Black serge. Black challis. Black twill. Black vicuna. Black poplin. Black damask. Whatever it was, there'd have to be at least fifteen yards for the skirt, another eight for the bodice, and five for each sleeve.

What was the girl thinking in her stubborn silence? Marie's palms itched with the desire to slap her silly sullen face and send that farcical cloud straight to the stratosphere, where it would burn up like the pretentious puffery it was. So what if she was as well read as an Oxford don? Alexandra was too dense to understand that the glittering whirl had a purpose, and she a duty to perform. And it wasn't as if Marie hadn't approached the problem from every angle she could think of.

"You want to be liked, don't you?" she said. Growing desperate, running out of angles, she'd thrust a box of *marrons glacés* at Alexandra and was watching the girl chew the sweet behind her raised hand. What on earth was wrong with her? Did she fancy herself a geisha or some other ridiculous character from the backward kind of nation that told women to be as lifeless as statues? When at last the girl swallowed and spoke, Marie could barely hear her.

Of course Alexandra wanted to be liked. Or at least she didn't want to be disliked. But dancing made her back ache. She didn't remember what gossip she was told. She hadn't mastered even one of the repertoire of witticisms and risqué anecdotes Marie had suggested she apply as necessary to a halting conversation.

"There was a young lady from Thrace," Marie tried again, having explained that currently everyone was mad for limericks. She raised her voice and enunciated each syllable with hostile precision, as if speaking to a deaf person, or to a nitwit, or to a doubly afflicted deaf nitwit, and was determined to make her way past this and any other obstacle. "Whose corsets grew too tight to lace."

"Please. I've—I can't."

"Of course you can. The rhyme makes it easy to remember."

"Oh, dear. I just—"

"Alexandra Fyodorovna. If you won't think of Russia, think of yourself. You can't afford to make an unfortunate first impression. It's the courtiers whose favor will determine your political success. Or failure. And mark my words: they will make life very unpleasant for a woman they don't like, even if she is the tsarina."

"I'm . . . I'm afraid I'm a bit . . . Granny always says. I'm. The fact is. I see how inconvenient it is, but I'm afraid they say I'm shy."

"Shy! Shy is for little girls. Shy is for spinsters. Shy is . . . shy is . . . shy is not for the tsarina of Russia!"

BUT ALEXANDRA WAS SHY—not coyly shy but terror-struck by the demands of public life. She couldn't imagine sharing her cleavage with anyone save her husband, and as for using cocaine to overcome her reluctance to tango, as one successful ball-goer took her aside to suggest, she certainly wasn't going to do anything like that. Her heart fluttered and raced horribly enough as it was; its damaged valves leaked and its ventricles quivered. It mattered nothing to Alexandra that the tango was the newest rage and therefore de rigueur. All her happiness, and every smile, would be as private as those fragile hours before dawn, when she and Nicky streaked over the frozen river and past its banks and discovered a rent in the workaday shroud life casts over fairy tales.

White horses, white sleigh, white ermine, the pelts of polar bears, and water frozen white—they'd acted out an incantation. The sky was black above the snow-covered river, and the sleigh's runners moved as though on air, without the slightest bump or vibration. Along the banks, great snow-cloaked pines stood like sentinels. The Gulf of Finland should have terrified the driver, wind tearing over its surface and lifting fallen snow back into the air, crystalline flakes trembling in the strange northern sky, flakes like stars and stars like flakes, the sky twirling as if it meant to brighten. Did he hope to lose them in the snow before they were ensnared in what he knew they'd grow to abhor? He'd allowed himself to believe his father was immortal, behaved like a man who expected to avoid becoming tsar. He knew nothing of ruling the millions of people he'd inherited.

It's said freezing is a gentle way to die. Their lives would end right there, in happiness.

A Demon in Her Womb

· · • · ·

MY MOTHER TOLD ME the Holy Spirit appeared to her in the form of a raven. That's what she said, this cosmopolitan woman who scorned country superstitions. She was walking toward the church when she looked up and saw that one of the birds roosting on its cross had separated from the others and flapped down to stand in the road, just in her path. The raven told my mother she was to wed Grigory Yefimovich Rasputin, whom some would worship and others revile. In either case, no one would understand him. He would have enemies, the raven said, as holy men always do. He needed a wife to support him in his sorrow as well as his joy.

Well, being a girl who'd gone to school in Yekaterinburg and learned to ride a tram instead of a horse, my mother hardly knew what to think of birds giving people orders. And this Grigory, he didn't even know how to read or seem to care that he couldn't. He spent every minute outdoors, so that his skin was as brown as a walnut and his hair needed a good combing. Some people in town described him as a lunatic. But Father spun Mother around and around until every objection had flown out of her head. In a trice they had married, and, in keeping with tradition, my mother moved into the home of my father's parents, who were proud to have a refined, literate city girl for a daughter-in-law, especially as her education didn't seem to have inspired the same disobedience it awakened in so many other young women. But it wasn't a comfortable beginning for my parents' life together, as their love was physically passionate and they had little privacy. What choice was there, Mother told me, but to become adept at silent lovemaking?

It wasn't a year before they'd had their first child. But unwitting Father cursed the boy by giving him the name of his dead brother, and the baby, Mischa, died in the middle of his first winter, still a child in arms and unable to crawl when they lost him.

It was a terrible time for my parents, as it would have to have been, but for Father especially. Somehow he'd given himself the idea that the baby Mischa was the brother he'd lost six years earlier, the one whose life he'd failed to save, reincarnated and returned to him, and when the baby died Father fell into a despair that lasted many months. How could it be that God hadn't warned him of this tribulation? How could he have let him raise a goat from the dead and then failed to tell him his own child was sick and needed his help? As Mother told me, Father was unable to understand their son being taken from them as anything other than a punishment. The child had stopped living. That was it, no warning whatsoever. He'd been fine when Mother put him to bed, but by midnight, when she checked to see he hadn't kicked off his covers, he was cold.

Father raved, my mother told me, it was terrifying to see, and the neighbors heard him and came to the house to ask what was it that made Grigory howl like an animal and tear at his hair. He crawled on his hands and knees and beat his head on the floor and lay facedown on the ground and begged God to smite him. To restore his little boy's life or, if he wouldn't, take his own. But God wasn't listening, or he didn't care to change his mind.

"Your father didn't think that perhaps there wasn't any god at all, if such a thing could happen?" Alyosha asked.

"No. I can see what you mean, of course, and another person might have, but not Father."

Because the baby died in the night, Father had to wait for the sun to rise and give him light before he could collect wood for the bonfire required to thaw the earth for a burial. They were still talking about it when I was a girl—the size of that fire. It was a spectacle Pokrovskoye never forgot.

"Come away from the fire, Grigory," my grandfather said, as did everyone who witnessed it—Father Pavel, the village priest; neighbors; and Arkhip Kaledin, the smith who'd pulled my father and his brother from the river, for he was there as well. But they couldn't dissuade my father from making the blaze even higher. He threw whatever he could get his hands on into the flames: the chairs on which he and my mother had sat to eat their dinner, and the table as well, the few books on the shelf, along with the shelf, the churn and the dash—anything to keep it burning. Because when the fire died out, the grave-digging would begin; he'd have to put his son in the ground and cover him with earth. He seized a lamp and hurled it into the center of the bonfire, where the glass reservoir of kerosene broke, or exploded. Shards of glass sprayed the crowd, cutting people's faces, their arms and necks and chests—as some had stripped off their winter clothes in the heat from the blaze— and suddenly the roof of the barn was on fire, and then the neighbor's house, and soon three, four, five buildings were ablaze. And though my father atoned for the destructive nature of his grief and helped rebuild what had burned, still more punishment followed. My parents' second child, my brother Dimitri, born the year before me, in 1897, survived, but he was simpleminded, physically robust but unable to arrive at two by adding one to one. Only the girls—Varya and I—were sound in both mind and body.

My father tried to settle down and make himself into the husband and farmer he promised my mother he would become, but when he wasn't sunk in misery, he was tormented by restlessness. He'd lie in bed for weeks at a time, and no one could budge him. He'd make a trip to the market in Tobolsk, get sidetracked, and find his way home a month after he was expected. It got so my mother and grandparents no longer waited for him but went about their business and managed without his help.

As for Father, he was waiting for his destiny to announce itself to him. In Yarkovo, a town on the road to Tobolsk, he made the acquaintance of a nobleman who offered to pay him twenty-five gold rubles to take his son to the monastery in Verkhoturye, which lay just east of the Urals, on the left bank of the Tura. It was a long journey by wagon, more than four days, and en route my father and the young man argued about how to get to heaven, a topic that had consumed my father's attention since the loss of his brother. What existed on the other side of death? The young man, a novice, intended to seal himself away from the world and hide in a life of prayer. My father said enlightenment was to be found out in the world, in the midst of God's creation, not by running from it.

When they arrived in Verkhoturye, the novice introduced my father to the monastery's abbot, who invited him to stay as long as he wished. But after a few days spent cloistered behind the order's thick walls, Father left the monastery, bored by what he called endless "talk talk talk about nothing," and walked deep into the woods to seek the council of the *starets,* or holy man, Makary, whose name had surfaced in almost every conversation he'd had with the brothers. In his youth, Makary had been an officer in the tsar's army and had gained a reputation for dueling, drinking, and seducing the wives of other men. It was a lost wager that had sent him to live in a hut in the forest. Makary told my father it had been God's will that he lose the bet, to introduce him to the woods and his vocation as a hermit. Furthermore, Makary said, God had planned a singular fate for Grigory Yefimovich Rasputin as well.

The life of my father would be entwined with that of Russia's rulers, Makary prophesied. He would go to St. Petersburg and there he would die, a martyr.

Father returned to Pokrovskoye intoxicated by visions of his glorious future. He was twenty-nine, and although he had healed many animals—"Grigory has a way with the beasts" was how it was explained by those who brought him their lamed horses and moribund cows—he had yet to save a human life. That winter, he was given the opportunity by Timofei, the innkeeper's son, whose dog he had saved only a week earlier, when the animal was savaged by a wolf. Timofei was married to a girl who appeared mature for her fifteen years and physically strong, but, alas, things are not always as they seem. After the arrival of their baby girl, born dead after a labor that lasted three days, Timofei's wife succumbed to childbed fever, which killed many women in that part of the world, most of them so far from a physician's hand that a midwinter trip to the hospital would have finished them off faster than the plague. In the middle of a frigid January night, Timofei woke my father and mother, hammering with his fists on the door.

"Nadia is dying," he said, and it was true. Father followed the man home and stood over the young woman's bed. Her face was flushed and she moved her head from side to side, as people do when delirious. A basin of bile stood on the floor by the side of the bed, streaked red from the girl's retching.

"Why did you wait so long?" Father asked, and Timofei began to cry so that he couldn't make words to answer. Father nodded. "You didn't understand," he said. "That's all." He put his hand on Timofei's shoulder.

"Timofei," he said, when the man just stood there, "you must go into the other room now." But Timofei could not be persuaded to leave Nadia. "You won't like what you see, Timofei," Father said. Still the young man shook his head. "I cannot help your wife without putting my hand inside her."

Timofei nodded; Father rolled up his sleeves and asked for a basin of soap and water so as to make one hand slippery enough to ease its passage inside the girl. He pulled off Nadia's covers and pushed up her nightdress. Once he'd introduced the soapy hand into her burning flesh and found the entrance to her womb, he knew what to do. As he withdrew his hand, she labored again, straining and screaming as she hadn't when he put it inside her, screaming as if she were being murdered, until whatever had been inside her was delivered.

"What was it, Father?" I asked when he told the story, imagining a demon with a black lashing tail, or a few toads and snakes, as victims of fairy tales are made to vomit up.

But Father never told me what it was.

Father and Timofei bathed the girl and stripped the soiled linens off her bed. Timofei held her up and Father put a clean nightdress on her. They left a towel between her legs to catch whatever bleeding continued, and Father told Timofei to watch over her and to make sure she ate nothing and drank as much water as she could keep down.

Word spread, and by the time it had, the things Father had pulled out of that poor girl: imps and demons and lizards and slimy black eels, chains with links made of sin, and hobnails from a witch's boot. Soon everyone was coming to Father, asking him to cure whatever ailed them, from boils to broken bones, knocking at the door at all hours. And then Yuri Yurivich's mother came to Father. Yuri was spitting blood, she told him, not just a little. He was hemorrhaging, and Father had to hurry.

As Yuri's mother told everyone in our town and the next, Grigory Yefimovich had taken her son's face in his hands and, after what she assumed was a prayer (as Grigory's eyes were closed and his body motionless for some minutes), opened his mouth wide and sealed it over Yuri's nose and lips. He didn't even care that Yuri's face was covered in blood, that he was taking the contagion into his mouth. She watched Father blow his own breath into the child's tubercular lungs, and when Father took his mouth away, Yuri—who'd been half dead, barely conscious—began laughing, a sound his mother hadn't heard for months, because the child hadn't had breath to speak let alone laugh. Yuri's mother's relief was so great, as great as the fear that preceded it, that she began to weep, and she went down on her knees and kissed the hem of my father's tunic.

My father told me that when he healed he felt it physically: A rush of energy from deep within himself, as if he were exhaling his soul rather than a breath of mere air. A strange taste in his mouth, like iron and ash, as if he'd licked a pair of fire tongs. A disturbed sense of equilibrium that wasn't dizziness so much as the conviction that he was no longer standing on earth; he'd transcended gravity, atmosphere, mortality.

Yuri's mother was poor. She had nothing to offer my father in payment for restoring her son to life—only herself. What was Father to do? Without him, Yuri would have died, probably that very day, and it was as the woman said: she had only the one means of expressing her gratitude. Father's ability to cure bodily illness, the illustrious future predicted for him: did these not excuse him from conventions others felt they must obey? If a woman gave herself to him freely—and why shouldn't she, as healing required my father to use every power he had, all his faith, concentration, and physical vigor—was it wrong to take the recompense she suggested?

Neither of my parents believed it was. Mother knew from her own experience, when she was in the last months of pregnancy, that without the release of intercourse my father grew irritable and unable to concentrate. Later, when he first moved to Petersburg, she sent Dunia with him so that he should never be without a woman close at hand. If the tsar and tsarina depended on my father to preserve the life of the heir to three centuries of Romanov rule—if they needed him to preserve their hold over Russia—then who was Praskovia Fedorovna to stand in the way of the empire? Besides, she said to anyone impertinent enough to ask, he had "enough for everyone."

"YOU TOLD ME you wanted to know everything about him," I reminded Alyosha when he made a face. "You made me promise to share everything I knew."

Sometimes I imagined we'd get out of this together. We'd escape Tsarskoe Selo with a purse full of jewels and we'd bribe our way out of Russia. I'd help him as my father had done. I'd stop the bleeding and the fevers and the pain. He was young to be a husband, but then, so had my father been when he married my mother. He was four years younger than she.

If only I could have done what my father did. As it was, I worried I might become my father's daughter in the one way I dreaded. I was afraid to touch the body I couldn't mend, and when Alyosha touched me I was struck still, frozen. Too scared to move. Not of him, of myself. I wanted him to kiss me. I wanted him to put his tongue inside my mouth and make me forget what the guard had done, to put his hands on my body and make me forget every bad thing that had ever happened. But Alyosha was not yet fourteen. There had to be something wrong with me to feel what I did for a boy rather than a man, and I didn't have to give in to desire to fear it was something that would, were I to satisfy it once, make me its prisoner.

"Did he ever do it to you?" Alyosha asked.

"Of course he didn't! What are you talking about?"

"I want to know, did he ever heal you?"

"Oh, that. Yes. Naturally he did. What physician wouldn't help his own family? He did it for me and for my brother, sister, and mother."

"Tell me what it was like."

"You know what it's like."

"For me but not for you."

It was like heat, like thawing. As if illness were its opposite, a deep freezing chill, enough to slowly stop a heart or petrify a pair of lungs. My father's callused hands, a black crescent under each ragged fingernail, poured heat like a samovar. He kept his fingernails dirty on purpose, to show the aristocracy that cleanliness was not next to godliness. Though Varya and I were made to learn all the proper etiquette for life in a city like Petersburg, my father never relinquished any of his peasant ways. He ate with his hands and wiped them and his mouth on his hosts' tablecloths. He'd use his fingers to fish in his soup bowl for a morsel he wanted, or he'd take a picked-clean drumstick from his plate and bite the knob of cartilage off its end to reveal the marrow he'd then suck from inside the bone. He didn't care who watched—he was the man he was, and all his would-be worshippers should know that God cared nothing for pretty ways and pious behavior. Why would God squander his attention on tablecloths and finger bowls? God liked to appear in the guise of a beggar or leper or madman. Little point in emerging from the cultivated mind of a Schopenhauer or a Spinoza. Better to burst forth from a dull, asthmatic shepherdess, like Bernadette of Lourdes, or a ragged muzhik from Siberia, like my father.

"Grigory Yefimovich!" Dunia would say to Father, trying to block his way to the apartment door. "Comb your hair and put on a fresh tunic. See, I have one ready for you, washed and ironed." Dunia would point out the stains of wine and grease on Father's wrinkled clothes, in which he'd undoubtedly slept and for more than one night.

"Stop, Father! Don't you know what people are saying?" Varya always aligned herself with Dunia in disapproval.

"Let him be," I'd answer, wondering how it was they couldn't see that a clean shirt would alter something essential in the father I loved so well.

And Father would kiss my forehead. "Good night, little magpie," he'd whisper.

"IT FELT . . . ORANGE," I told Alyosha, "like the color of a flame. But it didn't burn. It displaced what was sick. Pushed it away. That's the best I can describe it."

"I'm always so hot when I'm ill," Alyosha said. "I think for me it's—it was—more cool than warm."

"So perhaps it is different for everyone, as you surmised."

"Did he tell you to think of something that made you happy?"

"Sometimes he did. I remember him sitting by my bed when I was a little girl. He told me he was carrying me on his shoulders, and he described the field through which he was walking."

He named all the flowers and every living thing we passed: the trees, the insects, the hares and birds and tiny shrews running through the grass at his feet. Where we lived there was no creature he hadn't heard calling him, none to whose beckoning he hadn't listened and taken the trouble to find and study. He described the wings of a dragonfly, how they were transparent and yet had color, a pale green paler even than new grass. He'd say I was growing sleepy on our walk and that I rested my chin on his head. The woods were filled with magic, he'd say. He kept talking until I fell asleep.

. . .

MY FATHER SAID all people were his friends, but really there were only two of us in St. Petersburg: Dunia and I. Everyone else wanted something from him. Dunia applied herself to caring for his physical needs. I paid attention to his singular life and its unfolding. No one, not Dunia, Varya, Mother, Dimitri—of course not Dimitri—and not Father himself: none of them seemed to have taken pause even once to consider the life of Grigory Yefimovich Rasputin. It was as if I alone among us understood that just the idea of a person such as Father—an illiterate, unwashed, and exultantly ill-mannered peasant, a bumpkin subject to what most people considered hallucinations—mingling with, and indeed holding more power than, aristocrats and royalty was fantastic, outside anything one might expect to happen in a life.

Once the excitement of moving to a new city wore off, Varya, fixed on our mother the way I was on Father, regarded her years in St. Petersburg as more exile than privilege. Her one effort at making the best of things was to convince Father a piano would assuage her loneliness for home, where our mother had promised to teach her on the one piano in town, in our tiny church, an instrument missing keys, like middle C, which had been struck one time too many. After he bought one for her, she paid attention to it and little else, so consumed by her lessons and hours of practice I never had to compete with her for Father's attention. I could make myself witness to all the selves my father commanded.

There was the Pokrovskoye peasant, whom my mother married, and the Petersburg mystic, who held the future of the Russian Empire in his hands. The louche merrymaker who stayed out all night, drinking and singing and carrying on until dawn in taverns where gypsy women danced. The satyr who could bed five women a day and another five that night, most often on the parlor couch. The one whose constitution was so strong he could fast for a month and walk thirty miles a day, day after day. The son of the steppes, for whom happiness lay far from cities and their woes. And under all these was Grigory Yefimovich, who once upon a time had fallen into a fever and woken changed—vulnerable to the anguished cries of every living thing, from the grass blades broken under his boots to the birds overhead, a man who would be visited by the Virgin, not once but several times.

All of life was dull and dark when measured against visionary ecstasy. It took only one exposure to this exaltation for it to become the god my father served. Whatever allowed him a connection to the divine, he knew it wasn't made as a gift to the virtuous—he was proof of that himself. Only a vain fool, a man who cared for the opinions of others, would cultivate virtue for virtue's sake. All my father wanted, all he sought, was the next of these rapturous episodes. I think they were the hooks on which he hung the rest of his life; they kept him from falling into despair, especially in a city like Petersburg, where there was so much ugliness and misery.

The medium didn't matter. Fornication, fasting, drunkenness, self-flagellation, holding his hand to a flame, losing himself in the woods, praying on his knees until he swooned: for him there was no distinction to be made among these or any other means that might return him, however briefly, to the Silver Forest or any of the other places in which he'd felt it.

These Things Can't Happen

· · • · ·

"ALYOSHA."

"What?"

"I want to ask you something."

"Well?" he asked, when I didn't continue. "What is it?"

"I'm—it's a thing I've been worrying about."

"What?"

"I have been from the start. Not since the day you did it, but soon after. When you were well enough for visiting and we started spending these afternoons together."

"Did what?" Alyosha said. "What are you talking about, Masha?"

"I'm just . . . I want . . . I don't want to believe . . ."

"Masha. Get on with it. You're torturing both of us."

"It's only that I . . . I've tried to come up with a way to explain why an intelligent person of uncertain health, whose injuries and illnesses have always distracted his family from—"

"What are you saying?"

"You know what I'm saying."

Alyosha flushed. "You think I did it on purpose? To injure myself?"

"To divert their attention. You said so yourself. You said at least you'd *distracted* them."

"I did not."

"Yes you did. That was the word you used."

"But you're ignoring the context. It was in retro—"

"Distracted them. That's what you said."

"I drove into the newel post on purpose? Is that what you're saying?"

"Yes. I mean, I'm afraid you—"

"For the sake of a father who has made one ruinous decision after another? Destroyed everything given him? No. Not given. Loaned. Loaned to him."

"For him, yes. And for your mother and sisters as well. Because you'd rather they worry over you than their own predicament."

"Well. Isn't that just like a girl to come up with so—"

"Anyway, it's easier to pretend you're angry with your father."

"Easier than what?"

"Than admitting you're hurt on his behalf. The fact that the political situation is no one person's fault makes it worse. Your father's being punished because he hasn't done what—"

"Stop it, Masha. You're being silly, sentimental. I did it, that's all. I was careless, stupid if you like, responding to the claustrophobia of arrest and of—of this illness. That doesn't mean I intended to make myself hemorrhage."

"And as you are—no, not *you* but your idea of yourself—too honorable to tell me an outright lie, you keep sidestepping the subject. You don't actually deny it, you only seem to."

"He allowed himself to be manipulated by his uncles."

"How can he oppose everyone? Your mother. His mother. His uncles. It's too much."

"It wasn't too much for his father."

"His father hadn't any uncles, and he wasn't threatened by revolution."

"His train car was blown up. In 1888, the imperial train was blown up near Kharkov by—"

"Wasn't it derailed? I don't remember anything about its being blown up."

"No, you wouldn't. It was blown up by an underground proto-Bolshevik group, which is not a fact you can find in a history book. It's considered the property of military intelligence. Most people don't know the truth, including Grandmother, who believed what Grandfather intended her to believe: that it was a simple derailment; there was no terrorist involvement. He withheld anything he could from her; he didn't want her to suffer the anxieties he was forced to bear.

"Granny told me the family was eating cake in the dining car, and Grandfather stood up from the head of the table and, with his shoulders, lifted the collapsed roof of his car, insisting his wife and children be rescued before anyone helped him. They estimated it weighed more than a thousand pounds."

"How could he have? That seems a—"

"The point is that's who Grandfather was, invincible not only because he was strong but also because he refused to believe in the possibility of defeat."

"That was his policy? To keep the truth from his wife? The truth about the nation she served as tsarina?"

"I think it was, yes."

"No wonder she was always so hard on your father," I said.

"Why?" Alyosha asked. "In any case, why shouldn't she have been?"

"Because she had no way of knowing that the people's unrest had been gathering force for decades. You've said as much yourself. Poverty and hunger creating a populace too desperate to consider the political consequences of their actions. The intelligentsia able to present the example of France to the only audience that would realize a similar revolution for Russia, a vast army of laborers whose children are starving. If your father is unfortunate enough to be the last tsar, it isn't so much character as timing. The die was cast long before he assumed the throne."

"That itself was a fiasco."

"What was?" I asked.

"The coronation."

"But not of his making."

"He made it worse," Alyosha said.

"He was given bad advice."

"Why do you insist on being his apologist!"

MOSCOW. MAY 26, 1896. A city freshly swept and scrubbed, painted and polished and hung with garlands. It was warm and pleasantly so, a perfect spring day under an aquamarine sky. Whatever the reason—the angle of the sun's rays? A fluctuation in the atmosphere overhead? A subtly different ratio of gases, as if the very molecules of which Russia and the air above Russia were made had aligned themselves to serve the Romanovs?—well, whatever the reason, on that day the blue over Moscow really was the blue of the pale, clear gem: a literally sparkling sky. Below it, a gentle breeze cooled the cheeks of the people crowding the city. The coronation of Nikolay II had been delayed the full and official eighteen months of national mourning for the death of his father and tsar, Alexander III, and, the ceremonies having been anticipated for so long, the plans for them had grown ever more extravagant: a performance staged not only for the urban aristocracy but for citizens who had traveled to Moscow from every corner of the empire. Moscow because Moscow always has been and always will be Russia's sacred city. Anyone could invent a Petersburg. All it was was bits and pieces taken from European capitals, the conceit of a tsar who turned his back on the Kremlin's fantastic landscape, embarrassed by the whimsy and excess of its blood-red walls and onion domes painted gold or, worse, striped and checked with riotous colors. Green, pink, blue. Yellow, orange. Peter had been determined to hide the Kremlin and its extravagance of Russianness, which made Versailles appear a model of restraint.

Nikolay entered Red Square alone, on a white horse, far in advance of the ranks of courtiers and foreign princes. He wore a military tunic, the same as an ordinary soldier would. His left hand held the reins; his right was frozen in salute. Far behind him, his mother, the Dowager Empress Marie, and his yet-to-be-crowned wife, Alexandra, rolled forward in separate gilded carriages, almost lost in the ubiquitous glitter.

Nine o'clock in the morning and already men were punching one another over nothing, women were fainting, children were crying, and two unattended urchins had fallen headfirst into a rain barrel and drowned, their thrashing and splashing unnoted. Barricades had been set up to separate the citizenry from the armed forces, as every Russian officer, soldier, and sailor had convened to parade under the eyes of their new commander-in-chief. For days they'd marched and galloped, rolled and sailed into Moscow.

Sailed? Yes, sailed. The Western Fleet cut east from Riga on the Baltic Sea through the marshy plains; the Northern Fleet headed south from Murmansk and Dudinka; the Far East Fleet came west from Port Arthur and Vladivostok: four thousand landlocked miles, and don't forget the Ural Mountains to cross. It was hardly fair to expect them at all, and yet the westbound ships were not delayed. In all, one hundred and seventy-seven ships dry-docked outside the city's walls.

How could such things be possible? They happened, Alyosha, that's all.

Hax pax max Deus adimax! A flash lit the sky and set the air ablaze. Across Red Square, St. Basil's shimmered. The Kremlin, too, and the Resurrection Gate, the Nikolskaya and Spasskaya Towers, the Imperial Museum, the market stalls—every wall and rooftop glittered and shone, as it would if seen across a burning lake. In the future, when people talked about that day, they'd tell their grandchildren their ears had popped as if they'd ascended a great height too quickly. And the smell! It was frangipani. It was vanilla. It was honeysuckle. Attar of roses. Jasmine. Ripe peaches. Rain on a summer day. Bread baking. Chocolate warming on the stove. Whatever it was—and no two people agreed—it was the best of all possible smells.

And that's not all—that was just the beginning. At eleven minutes past eleven—*hocus pocus, tontus talontus!*—every pendulum in every clock case in Moscow stopped, not gradually but right away, as if an invisible hand had reached inside to prevent its movement. A trumpet sounded with a blare so loud it left every ear ringing, and the great doors to the Kazan Cathedral swung open, and those of Saint Basil's and Iverskaya Chapel as well. And all the parents and grandparents swore to it—on the graves of their mothers and fathers, they swore. With their withered hands on the cover of the family Bible they swore it was the truth, so help them God: the ikons came to life. Unstuck their likenesses from altars and prayer chapels, peeled themselves off walls and ceilings, sprang from two to three dimensions, and headed immediately out of the doors and into the glory of sunlight. From the cathedrals they flowed into Red Square in gilded rivers, chattering excitedly among themselves, giddy with the delight of movement and of sunshine. Imagine, to have known only the inside of a stone cathedral, hundreds of years of dim, drowned light pocked only by candles and only during a service, and to walk out from the shadows into the daylight.

"Too much excitement," the tsar said to himself, and he took a deep breath and sat up that much straighter in his saddle, tensing his knees to steady the gait of his horse, which set the pace of all who followed. "Holy Mother of God," Alexandra whispered, and she made the sign of the cross, moved closer to the carriage window, and peered through her cloud to see if her mother-in-law, the Dowager Empress Marie, had noticed all the goings-on.

Russians, Russians, superstitious to a fault, so eager to find portents that we invent as many as we discern. From the moment the betrothal had been announced, aristocrats and peasants alike searched for ways to predict the success of the union of Nikolay Alexandrovich Romanov and Alexandra Victoria Helena Louise Beatrice, Princess of Hesse–Darmstadt, named for her mother, Princess Alice of England, the third of Queen Victoria's nine children.

"She has come to us behind a coffin," St. Petersburg observed of Alexandra, as the coach carrying Nikolay's future bride to his father's funeral had followed that of the dead tsar. Not that there had been any choice in the matter. The affianced hadn't had but six months—it seemed like fewer—to enjoy their engagement before Alexander's failing kidneys gave out. And just like that, from one moment to the next, on November 1, 1894, the tsarevich became the one thing he'd prayed he'd never be: tsar. His wedding to Alexandra, hurried forward by the political crisis, was celebrated immediately after the state funeral, which took place eighteen days—two and a half weeks!—after his father's death. The dead tsar's royal person lay in state long enough that maggots animated his features, and the stench drove away the same dignitaries whose lengthy pilgrimages to his wake had postponed his burial. But at least they were not, like his widowed wife and fatherless children—Nikolay and his betrothed included—required to kiss Tsar Alexander III's moldering lips each morning and evening.

She has come to us behind a coffin, St. Petersburg observed, and the meaning was clear. True, she'd been decent enough to muster up that mournful-looking shroud or whatever it was—a peculiar foreign custom, perhaps—that hovered over her head, but a coffin was a coffin, and a coffin was a bad beginning.

Our marriage, the twenty-two-year-old Alexandra wrote her sister Ella, *seemed to me a mere continuation of the masses for the dead.* Though she'd exchanged her black dress for one of silver brocade with an ermine-lined train of gold, and though the official mourning period was lifted for the occasion of the ceremony, their wedding, held in a chapel at the Winter Palace, had been attended by few, over in a trice, and followed by a modest—well, modest for royalty—reception.

Which, Alexandra now understood from her vantage on the coronation ceremonies, had been more of a blessing than a disappointment, given the frenzy with which her populace apparently greeted state celebrations. Safe inside her golden carriage, she reminded herself to breathe and keep her features arranged in the pleasant expression she'd practiced the night before. The cloud couldn't be depended on to hide her completely. And there was her poor darling Nicky, for whom she'd happily give all she had, her life included, looking even more alone than she felt, sitting up straight as straight on his white horse, as rigid as if he were wearing armor.

Twenty-nine monasteries and sixteen convents. Within the city walls were forty-five renditions of the fourteen Stations of the Cross. Think of it, Alyosha: 675 Jesuses who had taken a day off from the *Via Dolorosa,* of whom 225 were dragging crosses, 135 had fallen and were crawling on their hands and knees, 45 were naked and asking to borrow loincloths, 135 were bleeding from their wounds, and the last 135 were the walking dead. And those 630 weren't the only Saviors. Underfoot, swaddled, crawling, and tod-

dling baby Jesuses tripped up a score of angry Christs looking for
a temple full of money changers. One pair of Jesuses was dogged
by lepers, another by the siblings Mary, Martha, and Lazarus, all
twelve disciples in tow. The robes and feet of a baker's dozen were
wet from walking on the storm-swept Sea of Galilee. And then
there were the show-offs who stole the attention away from all the
rest: those seventeen transfigured Christs seeking higher ground
from which to sermonize, leaking enough light to confuse the
ikons around them, all of whom were forced to peer through their
fingers so as not to stumble as they poured forth from the dark
interiors of cathedrals and churches and into the already blinding
day.

Behind the Jesuses came corps of angels and saints, enough to
inundate the already crowded square. As vain as only the holy can
afford to be, and xenophobic through and through, each sought
the company of his or her replicas. Before anyone could draw even
one breath—for time had stopped, remember?—all the Gabriels
had organized into their own battalion, as had the Raphaels and
Michaels, their cumbersome wings taking down lampposts and
knocking hussars out of their saddles. And, as the mortal crowds
soon understood, it was better not to call attention to these mishaps, as every time an archangel turned around, there went someone's hat, or head.

"Separate!" one of the angry Jesuses said in that no-nonsense,
temple-cleansing tone he'd used to terrify the money changers in
the Gospels according to Matthew, Mark, Luke, and John. To prepare unenlightened, sin-soaked Moscow for so august an occasion
as the coronation of a tsar, Jesus said, speaking in parables that
went over the heads of all but his audience of spitting images, each
of his transfigured selves must find his own dark corner of the city
to illuminate.

And so all seventeen luminous, light-leaking Christs dispersed into the city, seeking out the most squalid and misery-filled locations. The regiment of Saint Georges, meanwhile, was making its own parade of the occasion, each seated on a rearing mount and followed by a dragon that, having been trampled under hoof, slithered along somewhat feebly, oozing black dragon blood. Through which limped all the Naked Blessed Basils, Fools for Christ, dragging chains in eternal rebuke to Ivan the Terrible, putting out fires with prayers just as easily as the rest of us do with water, Alyosha.

For the coronation, the Kremlin and its polychromed cathedrals had been lit with bulbs, not candles or gas, because even if all the other Naked Blessed Basils concentrated on keeping their minds on the procession, one was certain to let his prayers stray into the realm of combustion, and then out they'd all gutter. It had happened before—it happened dependably—and Naked Blessed Basil was always the last to be invited to a party.

Saints Barbara, Alban, Martha, Cisellus, Margaret, Aurea, John the Baptist: all the beheaded saints stayed together, using their hands to carry their unattached heads above their bloody necks, everyone trying to get a good look at everyone else. The Child Martyrs, more childish than they were saintly, ran and shrieked, discernibly different from mortal children only in that they cast no shadows.

Few among the saints levitate or develop stigmata, but as artists tend to prefer flamboyance to modesty in their subjects, for every demure little Monica there was a flock of Christina the Astonishings hovering overhead, high enough to avoid the effluvia of sin that emanated from the crowd. It was not an affectation to prove their delicacy! Really, they could not abide the smell. Anyone eaten by a lion was a guaranteed crowd-pleaser, and a few of the Ignatiuses of Antioch were followed by a predator whose sudden arrival in Red Square, 1,476 miles northeast of the familiar coliseum and nearly two thousand years past their prime, inspired anxious roars and even a few cowardly squeaks.

These things can't happen, Alyosha, and yet they did, in front of one million people. If you don't believe me, just ask anyone who was there. Moscow had invited all of Russia home to meet her new tsar, to see the plain man on the horse dismount, kneel before God, and by the will of God be made Tsar.

Ill Omens

· · · · ·

TURKS, TCHERNIGOVIANS. TARTARS. Tartaruchians. Caucasians. Estonians, Livonians. Kazans and Astrakhans. Azazelians. Abedonians. Semigalians, Samogitians, Siberians. Polodians. Georgians, Lithuanians. Yougourians. Yaroslavians. Bulgarians. Rostovians. Ukranians, Ukeleleans, Uzbekians. Karelians. Kabardinians. Oudourians, Obdorians. Oldenbourgians. Iverians. Lugubrians, Latvians, Leviathans. Condians and Cartalinians. Furfurs. Smolenskis. Belozeros. Samyazas, Sitris, Surgats. Haagenti. Beelzebubbians. Baraqielians. Eligosians. Valefarians. Belphegorians. Malphasians. Ziminiarians. Valacs and Valafars.

And Vulgarians, of course, who always turn out for a parade, not to mention free coronation souvenirs.

Every window was crammed with bodies. Balconies groaned under them. They lined the streets ten, twenty, thirty deep, necks craned so as not to miss even one detail, a sea of wide eyes and open mouths, and anyone who could climb on an ash can or fire escape had done so. Every so often one of these parasites fell, his eaves-hanging grip loosened by a competing spectator's fingers. So many people had climbed the equestrian statue of Field Marshal Kutuzov that both hero and horse had disappeared, replaced by what appeared to be a teeming larval nest, magnified as many times as it takes to grow a man from a maggot.

Maggots to men—a matter of proportion, that's all. Who's to say a maggot doesn't dream or pray? And its desires: why would they be different from yours or mine or any other creature's? To love and be loved. To eat, to sleep, to multiply. To build a home where it won't be swept away, flooded, or burned. To be spared the pain of what you cannot understand.

The God of maggots and of men turned Nikolay into a tsar, cloaked him in a robe and train of ermine so long and heavy it required the support of a dozen pages who walked behind his majesty, and crowned him with nineteen pounds of gold, silver, diamonds, rubies, and pearls, because only a tsar can hold his head up under such a weight of pricelessness. Then the priests blessed the tsar, and the tsar turned from the altar to his people and began the long processional around the square.

Most of the tsar's subjects believed he always dressed so richly and elaborately. Certainly they did not imagine Alyosha's father in the clothes he preferred: the unadorned military uniform issued to every Russian soldier, which was now hidden under layers of finery. No, once the populace had seen the tsar in his coronation finery, they couldn't call him to mind dressed in any other fashion. They imagined him filling palace corridors as he walked to breakfast—the vastness of the robe and train, and the addition of all the men required to carry it—and they assumed that when he sat down to eat, he did so in a formal dining hall, a cavernous room for entertaining as lavishly as would a . . . tsar. And as they watched Nikolay II, now seated next to Alexandra in her not-quite-but-almost-as-heavy robe and train and crown, the two of them presented on a gargantuan palanquin carried by a hundred soldiers, fifty on the left and fifty on the right, the people allowed themselves to dream of what they would never possess, wealth and splendor and fine foods, each imagining what he or she would have for breakfast and what it might be like to have such majesty that soldiers, sailors, angels, saints, and Christ himself, in multiples of forty-five, paid obeisance.

"Don't stop, Masha."

I didn't.

Tsar and populace. Angels and saints. Jesus. Who was missing? Not a one, for the Devil was too curious to stay away any longer. He arrived in Moscow more than fashionably late and dressed as he usually was, like a wealthy European in a Savile Row suit and shoes made by Bally—not ready-made but custom-fitted, because the Devil's feet are so exquisitely narrow that he can't wear the clodhoppers that come ready to wear. They're not cloven, his feet; they're not even hooves. In fact, it is that particular and infelicitous rumor that inspires the Devil to spend the outlandish sums he does for a mere pair of shoes. Shoes suit the Devil's vanity, which couldn't be more different from that of angels or saints, in their barefoot flamboyance. As for Jesus running all over the dusty desert in his contemptibly bohemian sandals filled up with his dirty, unpedicured toes, no matter where he went with his band of deluded disciples, at the end of the day there they were, washing one another's feet. Now, that was disgusting, and the Devil didn't care what point Jesus was trying to make. There was no reason to commune with another person's filthy, vile, and poorly shod feet.

It was in 1851 that the Devil commissioned his first pair of shoes from Carl Franz Bally of Schönenwerd. They'd met the previous year, in Paris. At least, the Devil considered their transaction to have been social in type. He'd been killing the hours blowing cocaine up the nose of a virgin (well, she had been a few hours earlier) who'd strayed from her maman's side—just for a moment, to talk to a novelist wearing Masonic medals on his watch fob, for that's what he said he was, a novelist, although his fingernails were too long for a gentleman's, and yet they weren't dirty, not at all, they were filed and buffed, and no sooner had she climbed into his carriage than she noticed—

No, no, the Devil wasn't obvious; that's one thing he never was. Obvious is something he left for earnest Jesus. Of course he didn't pose as a novelist; he made himself look like a respectable young man, his nails cut short and clean, otherwise Maman wouldn't have let the toothsome creature speak with him. In fact, the girl had hung back, tongue-tied, and her own maman had pushed her toward the young man with the straight part in his brown hair, the one who had a job with the city government as a vice inspector. Maman told her not to be shy, and so she wasn't. She allowed herself to be treated like a whore by the young man, because her mother had called him respectable and pushed her on him. Her maman had practically delivered her into his arms to be ruined. (Could that have been her maman's plan? To lure a potentially good-enough catch into a transgression that would end in matrimony?) As she curtsied to the vice inspector, the girl had no idea what her fate might be or what tragedies awaited her. She drank the champagne the Devil kept pushing on her, and she stayed out all night dancing, and then the Devil ravished her in his carriage and infected her with syphilis, which she didn't yet know. But she knew she'd been ruined and that, for the moment, was bad enough.

"Masha."

"Yes."

"As it turns out, it's worse when the girl is a stranger."

"What girl?"

"Whatever girl it is in the suggestive bits."

I put my hand on his, staying its progress.

"Masha. You said as long as I didn't unfasten any buttons, and I haven't. Not even one."

"Stop. I can't think when you do that."

"Well, what do you expect when you tell me a story about a devil in human form seducing an innocent—"

"It's not *a* devil, it's *the* Devil."

"Masha."

"Alyosha."

"Masha."

"I don't see how you can go on doing that, Alyosha, when he could turn around and see at any—"

"What do I care what he sees? Isn't he ruining enough of my life as it is?"

"And what if your mother or father were to find—"

"Do you honestly imagine they'd take the word of a Red Guard over mine?"

SO THERE THE POOR CHILD WAS, weeping at the Café Flore, imagining—*knowing*—her life was over, and she was only eighteen! She needed a bit of cheering up before she got maudlin, or else she'd be no fun and just as the Devil was blowing a little sparkle up the prettily formed nostril—such a pity, as all of her was formed for pleasure, and all of it over too quickly, but that's how the Devil is: wasteful. Prodigal, in fact. And distractible—anyway, just as his attention strayed from the pretty nostril, he spotted Monsieur Bally walking along the boulevard, looking preoccupied, but not so much that he didn't notice the mischievous breeze that teased open his coat and snatched one and then another hundred-franc note from the billfold in his breast pocket.

The breeze led Bally on a merry chase as the two notes landed on one paving stone and then another, remaining in sight and out of reach and traveling together in a way that was remarkable to

see. At last Monsieur Bally gave up, gasping for air so that he had
to bend over, his hands on his knees, for some minutes before he
caught his breath. When he stood up he saw he was on the rue du
Faubourg Saint-Honoré, outside a shoemaker's showroom. And
there it was that haberdashery history was made—you can look
it up in any biography of Bally or comprehensive history of foot-
wear. In the window of the shop on the rue du Faubourg Saint-
Honoré, Carl Franz Bally, the son of a weaver of silk ribbons, saw
a pair of slippers that would make a perfect gift to bring home to
his wife. But the colors they came in were all so pretty, how could
he choose one over the others? He bought five pair, one in each
color available, and, *spit spot,* just like that, he forgot silk ribbons
and went mad for slippers and shoes. He went to bed dreaming of
vamps and insoles and calf-hide uppers, of tongues and laces and
enameled brass grommets.

By the time the Devil arrived at Bally's atelier in Switzerland,
Carl Franz had contracted with a German shoemaker, installed
him in his basement workshop, and was taking orders.

"Hummingbirds, but only their breasts, and only from Panama."

Bally bowed deeply. What exactly was a hummingbird? Living
as he did in the old world, he knew nothing of the birds of America. Could he interest the Devil in peacock-blue patent leather?
Touch the stuff; see how unusually supple.

Never mind, the Devil said, he'd have the skins delivered himself. And so he did, packed in snow, because that's the only way
to ship them—you can't cure the skin of a hummingbird with salt.

And you don't walk on muddy parade grounds in shoes that cost
a fortune, not even if you are the Devil. Who, by the way, had not
arrived for the coronation itself, as he found pomp insufferably tedious. Instead, he waited until just before dawn the next day, when
the newly crowned tsar was to give the traditional coronation

party for the hoi polloi. The thing about the Devil is this: he enjoys manipulating private citizens, little people without rank or power. The bigwigs who come out to participate in state affairs, mortal and immortal both, don't need the Devil to lead them astray. By the time the sun rose for the open-air feast for all one million four hundred thousand of Moscow's citizens, the holy hierarchies were no longer paying attention to the event for which they'd convened.

Levitation, stigmata, speaking in tongues, healing incurables, appearing in more than one place at once: all night the ikons had been arguing over proofs of holiness. What was more to be worshipped—perfect virtue from birth, or turning away from sin? And how could angels lord it over saints when Christ himself had willingly gone slumming not only among but also *as* one of them? No one dreamed of knocking the Trinity from off the top of heaven's pyramid, but as God is everyone's witness, and as Dante Alighieri tried to explain, the nine circles of hell are mirrored by concentric celestial spheres. It isn't a simple hierarchy—how could it be? Wisdom, justice, courage, and temperance. Faith, hope, and charity. All of these and more are weighed.

And then, Lord have mercy, there went the Jesuses with all their perplexing blather about first being last and the meek inheriting the earth and little mustard seeds that sprouted versus those that fell by the wayside. They made it just about impossible to decide who was holier.

"But that's the point!" all the Jesuses cried, except for the baby Jesuses, who were notable for never crying.

While the heavenly host argued and complained, the Devil and his entourage surveyed Khodynka Meadow, a vast training ground for Moscow's troops, complete with trenches. At the sight of so much mud, the Devil's cat, Behemoth, black as a rook, tall as a man, and standing upright on his hind legs, washed his whiskers furiously. Azazel, holding tight to the red string he'd tied to his scapegoat's horns, let out a high-pitched giggle, joining Thanatos and his sisters, the Keres, in mirth. Suddenly all of them understood what high jinks the Devil had planned. A queue of tumbrels on the eastern border of the grounds held hundreds of barrels of beer, and at the opposite, western border were the tables on which the souvenirs had been displayed—enameled commemorative cups bearing the imperial crest. The sun was yet below the horizon, and hundreds of thousands of those intent on making merry lay sleeping between the cups and the beer, each having arrived the previous day to claim a choice spot in the meadow. The crowds who squandered their time watching the coronation would have to squeeze in where they could.

"That one," Behemoth said to the Devil, and, still busy with his whiskers, he used the tip of his unusually long and prehensile tail to point to a man with sand-colored hair and a doughy face. The man looked innocuous, perhaps because he was sleeping on his back with his mouth open.

"Are you sure?" the Devil asked.

"Positive," Behemoth said. He'd chosen Vlodya—that was his name—because Vlodya's wife had demanded he go without beer for a week to prove he could, and he'd gone three days so far. And today was a holiday.

"All right, then." The Devil snapped his fingers and Azazel gave his little black goat's red string to one of the Keres to hold. He fell on his knees and fastened the Devil's galoshes over his hummingbird brogues, careful not to muss their double-knotted silk laces. With the one outlandish part of the Devil's attire covered, his looks weren't the kind to attract attention—for the most part. The pupils of his yellow eyes were the rectangular kind found in goats—while, curiously, Azazel's scapegoat had the round ones of a human—so he had no choice but to hide them behind dark glasses. He carried a long walking stick and poked it gingerly into ruts and holes, picking his way carefully across the field, as if he were blind.

"Bloody fucking cunt, watch what you're doing," Vlodya yelled, woken by a stab in the groin, not so shy of his left testicle that the Devil's stick hadn't grazed its tender skin.

"I'm terribly sorry," the Devil said. "I'm afraid I can't . . ." He trailed off and made an abbreviated bow.

"Vlodya!" the wife said to the husband, sitting up and collecting her long hair in her hands. She twisted it into a knot, through which she drove a twig to secure it, stood, and brushed at the chaff clinging to her skirts.

"Listen," the Devil said. "I heard it said there wasn't enough beer ordered."

"Just as well," the wife said, now shaking her skirts vigorously to rid them of the last bits of dry grass still clinging to the fabric.

"What's that?" Vlodya said. "What'd you say?"

"I don't know that it's true," the Devil said, "as I can't see for myself. But there's talk of only enough beer for the first in line." *And look at the size of this crowd,* he whispered directly into Vlodya's addled brain. *This isn't loaves and fishes, Vlodya. This isn't Jesus's party, it's the tsar's.*

Just like that it was done: the sun popped above the horizon, everyone woke up stiff and cranky, and the Devil moved out of the way to watch the fun from where his entourage waited, having made themselves comfortable on a red-and-purple Turkish rug Azazel pinched from one of the Kremlin's guest rooms and spread on a current of air a hundred or so feet above the crowd. They might have caused their own stampede, had anyone looked up and seen anything as astonishing as a man-sized black cat jigging with delight on a floating carpet. But no one did look up.

"Am I not the shit!" Behemoth crowed. "Christ on a cracker, will you look at them go!"

The Devil smiled as Azazel removed the galoshes, and his smile wasn't terrible; it was the kind of smile that said everything was going to be fine. Below the Devil's narrow, narrow, three times narrow, elegant feather-shod feet, Vlodya was leading the stampede, which had progressed already too far to control or even limit its destruction. From on high he looked like a whirligig beetle moving swiftly over the surface of a pond, his charging head the point of a great V drawn in the crowd. Behemoth smiled, and his smile was filled with sharp teeth and said everything was going to turn out badly.

Between the tables holding the souvenir cups and the tumbrels with their barrels of beer, hundreds died, trampled and suffocated in muddy trenches, and thousands were wounded. By afternoon, hospitals overflowed with bodies crushed by the wild headlong rush of men, women, and children, limbs and ribs broken by the press of countless running feet.

Shocked and sickened by a tragedy that had strangled any celebratory impulse he and Alexandra might have gratified, Nikolay told his mother he planned to forgo the evening's festivities, but the Meddlesome Four advised against it. Nikolay had chosen a bride who wasn't French, and still France was sufficiently gracious to host a grand fête for the newly anointed tsar and tsarina. To decorate the ambassador's ballroom, her government had stripped Versailles of its silver and tapestries. How could he think of making so infelicitous a statement?

"Nicky!" the Meddlesome Four cried. "Our only ally!"

So they went, the two of them doomed to always do wrong no matter how pure their intent. They danced a quadrille, and their guests were offended at how stricken they looked. The tsar was pale and drawn; the tsarina's eyes were red with weeping.

A thousand rubles to each victim's family, and a coffin for every corpse. The tsar paid for these condolences out of his own private pocket, and he and the tsarina visited the wounded, personally, every last one of them. But no sum of tears and rubles and bedside apologies could undo this most dreadful omen of all. From behind one coffin to the purchase of hundreds: the reign of Nikolay II would not be a happy one.

Holy Rollers

. . . . .

"Do you know what my father loves?" Alyosha said one afternoon. "Do you, Masha? Passing, by train, through a town where all the people turn out to see him—*the tsar*—so near their humble homes. Like an apparition. As if Christ himself had deigned to walk among them, his vassals.

"Great-grandfather Alexander may have freed them fifty—more than fifty—years ago, but they don't care, or they don't know it. They regard themselves no differently than they did when they were serfs. There are no revolutionaries outside of Moscow and Petersburg. The people who suffer and starve blame Father's ministers, who they assume must be incompetent or venal. Who somehow pervert Father's will. Not one of them believes the tsar makes mistakes."

"Don't you think he wants—"

"As long as he can glide through those towns like a god in his chariot, the train moving very slowly, so as to give the populace a good look at him, as long as he can greet every single citizen—for of course no one is too busy, or too sick, no one turns away uninterested—then he's satisfied. Everyone waves at him standing in his car's open window, they bend to kiss the earth where his shadow falls, the earth that is Russia, that is the Romanovs, that is the tsar, all of them implicitly kissing his hand when they kiss the earth. Then Father can believe in the myth of his own making, that all the tsar's people love him and believe in his goodness as they do their own fathers'.

"Even now he imagines his loyal subjects have united on his account and will storm the palace and rescue him, restore him to his proper throne. He'd trade his flesh-and-blood children for that . . . that kind of fatherhood."

"Alyosha. You know that's untrue. You're conflating two worlds: the world of your father's obligation to a role he was born to—not one he chose but one he had no choice but to accept—with the world that is his family. You know it's unfair to complain he doesn't care for one as he does the other. He inhabits parallel universes, that's all. It's his fate, his misfortune."

"Masha. I'm not talking about that. I'm talking about what makes my father look happy. That's how to tell what he cares about. It's the idea of his being the beloved and all-powerful tsar."

"No, it's only how to tell what gives him pleasure. You don't suppose love makes people happy, do you?"

"Sometimes it does."

"And more often it doesn't. If all he cared about was his crown, one would think he'd be very unhappy now, deprived of his exalted position, separated from any agency he had, reduced from a tsar to a colonel. And yet he doesn't look it. He seems almost unburdened. Have you ever seen him like this before? He laughs, enjoys his meals, though they are nothing as rich as they once were. Enjoys his gardens—"

"Don't you find it maddening how he poses himself by his window?"

"What do you mean?"

"I think he hears a knock at his study's door, jumps up from his chair, and arranges himself on the windowsill, focusing his eyes on a distant leaf or twig or something, and only then does he ask you in.

Before you've had a chance to open your mouth, you've gotten the idea that no matter what it was you'd come to speak about, it's of no importance compared to what preoccupies the tsar. In the end you give up and leave with the impression he's heard nothing you've said and thus has no responsibility to respond to whatever it was."

"I've never knocked on his door," I said, thinking that if Alyosha was correct then it made little difference that I'd always gone running to the stables rather than petitioning the tsar to arrange for Varya and me to be evacuated from Tsarskoe Selo. Even were the tsar able to help us now, the addled tsarina might forbid it—she would if she still believed I had any ability to heal Alyosha. My company did provide him entertainment, and even a measure of solace, and Dr. Botkin had told her Alyosha was improving steadily. I didn't know what to hope for: exile or imprisonment. What I felt for Alyosha . . . the only person who wouldn't have thought it wrong, who wouldn't have thought anything of it at all, was dead. Anyone else would judge me to be as immoral as my father had been; in me they'd see his flaws, unmitigated by his gifts.

Alyosha's arms were rigid at his sides, his fingers curled into fists. Emotion chiseled angles into his ordinarily smooth countenance, and I could see the man who would have emerged from under youth's softer contours.

"I know things you don't," Alyosha said before I could assemble a response to his anger, an emotion he betrayed so seldom I had little practice at placating it. The tyrannical temper-tantrum-thrower had grown up into something more like a yet-to-be-lobbed grenade, its fuse burning. He sat up on his elbows to look me in the eye. "I know about my father, about my mother, about everything. Things other people don't. You know why? It's because I'm always listening—I'm never so sick I can't hear—and even when I'm not out of my head or unconscious or whatever it is they think I am, people say anything in front of me. It's the greatest proof I have that everyone expects me to die. Not to be assassinated but to expire. There's never been a reason to keep state secrets from me. And because Mother's apartments have always been so close to my own, I know secrets that aren't about the state."

"Such as?"

"About your father and my mother."

"What about them?"

"The joke is, after all the poisonous gossip, your father was innocent. With respect to my mother, he was. She offered herself to him. She knew the sort of . . . of . . . of currency he could expect to receive outside Tsarskoe Selo, and she didn't want to take any chances. She still believes your father was a direct connection to God, like a human telephone wire. She prostituted herself for me."

"Don't be ridiculous."

"And your father, the most talked-about lothario in the history of the empire, he bowed and kissed her hand. He said he was unworthy."

"You heard this?"

"I saw it."

"This . . . this scene played out before your eyes?"

"I told you, anyone who notices me assumes I am witless from pain, and the rest of them don't see me at all. From the time I was aware of the world around me, I've observed that I manage to be both invisible and the focus of all attention. Remarkable, really. It must be a talent of some kind. Oh, Masha, don't look at me like that. You know your father."

"Yes," I said. "I do." I'd never known Alyosha to lie—he was too proud for that—and yet there was something in his face or his voice, something that suggested he wasn't telling the truth. Or perhaps I just couldn't imagine such a thing as Alexandra Fyodorovna, at least the version of her I'd invented, offering herself to any man other than her husband, not even Grigory Rasputin.

. . .

HOME IN POKROVSKOYE, my young father had suffered periods of despondency. He loved my mother, but he wanted to leave home and take up the life of an itinerant healer. Every day that he didn't go, he paced, he raged, he broke down and cried with his head in Mother's lap. If his vocation was genuine, why was he torn by such guilt? Why such anguish at the idea of leaving his wife and children? He spent hours in prayer, remaining on his knees long enough to cause a man to faint, and at last he received the answer he sought. The problem was one of identity. When he was doing God's will, healing the sick, he was no longer Grigory Yefimovich but the force that moved through Grigory, the force that claimed him as its servant. Grigory was no more and no less than the conduit of God's will. Grigory's hopes and fears, his woes—none of these mattered. Grigory, the individual, was beside the point. Had the prophet Isaiah not proclaimed it? More than once, more than ten, twenty times, he'd quoted the passage for me:

"All flesh is grass and all its beauty like the flower of the field. The grass withers, the flower fades, when the breath of the Lord blows upon it. Surely the people are grass. The grass withers, the flower fades, but the word of our God will stand forever."

As my mother understood Father's vocation as absolute, an expression of unalterable divine will, she told Father there was no choice in the matter, that was that, they would embark on a life of separation, and we, their children, would soon learn not to expect to see our father. He'd come and he'd go according to his own lights. He was en route from here to there. He was stopping at a house where lived an ailing child. Having healed the child, he was overwhelmed, intoxicated, by the gratitude he received from his or her parents. From one sickbed to the next he went, restoring happiness—that thing we recognize in retrospect, after we've lost it—carried forward on a warm tide of goodwill. Never staying anywhere longer than a night or two, unattached to any one human being, he was free and he was flooded with love. I think that must have been a form of rapture too.

It was then, after years of being received as a holy man, of having people prostrate themselves before him, kiss his fingers, his feet, the hem of his blouse, I think it must have been then that my father began to imagine himself as having become one with God, and therefore a god himself.

He forgot the man who had discarded the idea of a particular individual named Grigory Yefimovich.

And something else happened, something equally dangerous. The heightened assurance he projected in the aftermath of a healing changed the way women responded to him. No longer did he need to pursue them. Women were drawn to him now, as they hadn't been before. He had always possessed sexual magnetism; now it had intensified. He told himself women were no different from children, who were to be loved and who were to receive proof of his love's impartiality. And how does a man demonstrate love to a woman, other than with his body?

Dressed in the simple clothes of a monk, Father walked from one town to the next. He carried few provisions, ate fish if he caught any, went hungry when he didn't, and grew as thin as an El Greco. In those days, when I was five or six, he looked like a man without home or hearth, a mendicant, holy. People began to speak of a new *starets*, a messianic healer who had walked out of the wilderness, a mysterious Father Grigory, of humble origins yet possessed of a transcendent force that allowed him to heal the sick.

When he came upon a town, he'd go first to the church to pray, lying on the stone floor, facedown and arms spread like a crucified Christ before the iconostasis. Exhausted by his endless pilgrimage, or immobilized by a force no one could see, he was able to remain motionless, his breathing imperceptible, for as long as a day. By the time he'd resurrected himself, enough of the town's inhabitants had seen and spoken of his saintly prostration that when he appeared in the marketplace a throng had gathered, eager to feed him in recompense for his healing touch.

"He could walk and walk from morning until night, day after day?" Alyosha asked, his face tight with pain. I hated seeing evidence of his suffering—hated both the fact of it and that I couldn't banish it. Too, it returned me to my preoccupation with the accident that caused so dangerous an injury. The topic was one Alyosha refused to revisit, sullen and silent at any mention of tea trays or staircases or newel posts.

"Let's loosen the brace, just for a bit."

"No, no. Botkin will come running. He has some preternatural connection to the beastly thing. As soon as I touch it, he appears."

"Well, let me, then. I'll take the blame if he catches us." I was as gentle as possible, but still Alyosha panted through his nostrils, teeth clenched behind his closed lips, for as long as it took me to unbuckle the straps. Even in his suffering he had to be careful not to bite his lip or his knuckle or do any of the thoughtless little things another person might do to distract himself. "Did I tell you what happened in Kazan?" I asked when I'd finished adjusting the brace.

"No." Alyosha, who had been sitting up on his elbows, dropped back onto the pillows behind him. "Will you?" he asked.

"Of course." I pulled my chair closer to his bed, slipped my hand in his.

IN THE CITY OF KAZAN a merchant named Katkoff invited the increasingly acclaimed Father Grigory to dine and sleep in his home, if only the *starets* would try to cure his wife of the arthritis that no doctor had been able to alleviate. Madame Katkoff was "crumpled up like a discarded piece of paper," Father said, so that she couldn't even rise from her chair. Her knuckles had swollen to the point that her hands were unrecognizably deformed and, as her chin was frozen to her breastbone, he had to go down on his knees to look into her eyes.

He closed his own in prayer before reaching out and touching her chin, which he lifted as easily as if her neck were as sound as any other woman's. From there he went on, down her spine and then onto her crippled limbs. One by one he unlocked every joint, and when he was finished he held out his hand and pulled her to her feet. It wasn't just that Madame Katkoff could bend her elbows and knees, hips and fingers. Each place he had touched returned to its former appearance, not only her health but also her beauty restored.

"Come," my father said, and he showed her the mirror.

Rich enough to own a telephone, and so dedicated a gossip that when she was no longer able to hold the receiver herself she had hired a girl to keep it pressed to her ear, Madame Katkoff called everyone she could think of and told them Father Grigory worked miracles. Anyone who doubted her word could come to her home and see for herself.

As for her husband, the rich merchant's gratitude was such that he presented my father his brand-new motorcar. My father didn't want to accept so extravagant a gift, but Katkoff insisted. He told Father he'd be insulted if he refused. "At least try it," he said. "Anyone who sees you on wheels, without a horse to pull them, will know to pay attention, that a healer approaches!" For in those days, in Siberia, who hadn't seen threadbare holy men wandering the land? But a motorcar—that was a vision of unprecedented power, more mysterious and inspiring of awe than an antiquated old *starets*.

Father refused. "Perhaps they'll think I'm the devil," he said.

"It's nothing to be afraid of," Katkoff answered, pricking Father's vanity.

"Because, little magpie," Father said when he told me the story, "you know your papa is not afraid of anything.

"Panhard et Levassor was the maker," he'd begin when speaking of it. "The upholstery was green leather."

As there were no other cars on the roads he traveled, no one had the misfortune to encounter him as he taught himself to drive. Like a small child who has just learned to run and therefore never walks, not even to cross a room, Father drove so fast that when he arrived in a town he was followed, like an Old Testament prophet, by a pillar of cloud—funnels of dust twirling heavenward in his wake. By the time he'd parked at a local inn, he'd already caused such a commotion that a queue of supplicants formed immediately, and news of his arrival spread beyond the town's borders to outlying farms.

"What about praying in the church for a day?" Alyosha wanted to know.

"I asked him the same thing. He said no one needed a church to pray and that the way he drove inspired all who saw him to fall on their knees." Katkoff had given Father a lot of extra habiliments— pairs of goggles, a long green coat Katkoff called a duster and insisted Father button over his ragged brown robe, green driving gloves the size of gauntlets, a green cap, and green gaiters.

"To match the upholstery," Father would say, laughing uproariously.

"And then?" I would prompt. "Tell what happened then, Father."

"Well, the machine came with a windscreen, but that was gone before a month was out. I was so delighted by the speed of the thing, not like a train, nor like horse and buggy, but a different kind of speed, a thing I'd never felt before. Like a fool I tore through fields of frozen potatoes that bounced up and hit the glass." Sometimes the bough of a tree hit the windscreen. Sometimes the frozen potatoes were rocks left in a poorly tilled field. The leather covering the seats was so slippery that many times, when he took a sharp turn, anyone unfortunate enough to be his passenger slid out of the vehicle and onto the road.

"Who were they, Masha?" Alyosha asked.

"Who were who?"

"Who were the passengers?"

"Well, let's see," I said. "The usual sorts of disciples and clingers-on. Anyone who asked him for a ride along the roads he traveled. Damsels in distress, of course, and damsels who were happy to trade their favors for the excitement of a motorcar ride. Quite a lot of those, you know, Magdalene types who were willing to mend their ways after a celebratory farewell to carnal pleasures."

"Ah, yes." Alyosha smiled. "There would be a few of those, Masha. Tell me what they looked like."

"Well it's not as if I was in the automobile with them, you know."

"Still, you can tell me."

"Well, one of them was an Arabian princess. But that was later, when he was driving around in the Holy Land."

The miracle of the motorcar, I told Alyosha, was that it provided my father passage to the Holy Land. A proper *starets* must visit the birthplace of Christ, and, as Father had a car and could drive, more or less, off he went. Around the Black Sea he tore. Odessa to Varna, he sped southward in a cloud of dragonflies the size of hawks. The sky was red, the earth was yellow: three hundred miles without a flat tire. Varna to Istanbul, the Blue Mosque's swordlike minarets scratching at the heavens: he'd gone another two hundred miles and still he hadn't stopped to fill the tank with gasoline. Istanbul to Ankara—

"Conquered by Caesar Augustus in 25 B.C. He—"

"Don't interrupt. This has nothing to do with your old war-mongers."

Ankara to Adana, not a drop of gasoline to be had, not for any price. He floated on fumes, and thank heavens for goggles, as the Turkish sand blew without cease. Aleppo, Alexandria, Tripoli, Damascus—

"That's the Silk Road."

"Alyosha."

"I'm—"

"You must be feeling better," I said. "It's not as if I haven't read a history book, Mister Know-It-All."

Aleppo to Damascus, Father flew along the Silk Road, and nothing, nothing could stop the motor built by Panhard et Levassor.

"The will of God carried me to Jerusalem," Father would say. "Not Panhard et Levassor. When God the Father appointed Solomon king over every living thing, he gave him a green silk carpet, and on it Solomon sat on his throne, and with him were the four princes: Berechiah, the prince of men. Ramirat, the prince of demons. The lion, prince of beasts, and the eagle, prince of birds. Even when Solomon carried an army of four hundred thousand men, his green silk carpet sailed so quickly on the wind's back that they breakfasted in Damascus and supped in Medina. Now, if such things are commonplace in the Holy Land," Father said, "who was I to question a car that runs without gasoline?"

No matter what transpired in the Holy Land, Father found it mysterious and wonderful: sandstorms; spitting camels; fruit falling from the date palms; women dancing barefoot, their faces covered and their middles exposed; his hosts, whoever they were, eating with their hands, as Father liked to tell the Petersburg aristocrats.

It meant something to him that he'd seen Gethsemane and

kneeled where Christ prayed on the eve of his crucifixion and that he'd visited the room of the Last Supper, in which God changed wine to blood and bread to flesh. That was as big a trick as walking on water or sermonizing after you'd been crucified.

Jerusalem, Damascus, Tripoli, Alexandria, Aleppo, Adana, Ankara, Istanbul, Varna, Odessa. Back home to Mother Russia, past minarets with pointed hats and skies filled with falling stars, fields of purple thistles rippling under the wind's invisible touch. No Arabian prince ever got more pleasure from his carpet than my father received from his Panhard et Levassor.

"Alyosha." I tried to pull my hand out of his but he caught me by the wrist, showing me how strong he could be when he wanted.

"Kiss me." He pulled me toward him. "You're such a pretty little thing, Masha. Did you know that?"

"Little? I'm almost five years older than you. Besides, pretty is as pretty does, they said at school."

"Not yet five. And if your schoolmistress was right, the more you kiss me, the prettier you will become."

"Very funny." I stopped resisting and let him pull me onto the couch next to him. "Am I not pretty enough, then?"

"Of course you are. Nothing is prettier than blue eyes and black hair, and your mouth is . . ." He put his finger on my lips, as if to part them. "We could pretend you're one of those Magdalene types."

"Alyosha—" But that was as far as I got before his mouth was on mine and I was feeling things I'd only heard described, feeling them exactly, my pulse throbbing even in my—

No I didn't feel any of that. Having wondered and worried over what it might be like, being kissed by someone I wanted to kiss me, I was clumsy with nerves, and in my attempt to keep clear of his bad knee I fell forward into the kiss, knocking our front teeth together. Sure that I'd cut his lip and killed him, I pulled away, ducked out of his arms, and burst into tears.

"What is it?" Alyosha said, after what must have been the longest and most awkward silence in the whole history of love. "What's wrong?"

"Nothing," I said.

"Something."

"I'm afraid," I told him.

"Of what?"

"I don't know." I think he knew I was lying. But the truth—that it wasn't only my anxiety about being touched but that his illness had stolen something else from him—seemed worse.

"Didn't you . . . didn't you like it?"

"It doesn't matter if I liked it."

"Of course it does. It's the only thing that does matter, whether or not you liked it."

"To you."

"What are you talking about, Masha?"

"Just that there are other things to think about."

"What other things?"

But I didn't answer. Instead, like a child I covered my face with my hands, and I remained like that, blind as well as mute, until he let the matter go.

The Wild West Show

· · • • ·

"**T**HAT'S WHAT WE NEED," Alyosha said, once I'd finally taken my hands away from my face.

"What?"

"A magic carpet. Woven of all dark colors, blue and purple and black. We'll ride it only at night, so if anyone were to look up, all he'd see was the dark sky; we'd blend right in. No one could apprehend us."

"Where will we go?" I asked, praying he wouldn't return us to the midnight sleigh rides over the Neva. Not that I didn't deserve it, teasing him by telling stories that implied I might like to be ravished like the heroine of a romance and then behaving as I had.

"Australia," he said, and then shook his head. "No, America."

"Do you think it's wise to take a flying carpet that far, over an ocean?"

"Of course, Masha. It's the safest way to go. It can't sink or run aground or collide with an iceberg."

"I suppose not. Where in America?"

"Chicago."

"Why Chicago?"

"It's the only American city I know anything about. Do you remember Joseph?"

"The Abyssinian guard?"

Before the tsar abdicated, two tall men with shining black skin had guarded the family's private apartments in the Alexander Palace. Their scarlet uniform jackets were trimmed with gold braid and epaulets and buttoned over voluminous blue silk trousers that looked like those in the color plates accompanying Alyosha's edition of *The Arabian Nights*. Whoever had designed the uniform must have considered Arabia close enough to Abyssinia to excuse poetic license, or ignorance. Turbans, scimitars, jeweled slippers with upturned toes—having been imported as objects of curiosity from an exotic land, the pair of Abyssinian guards appeared more ridiculous than imposing, just as did, to my mind, gondoliers with striped shirts and red-ribbonned hats on the canal or Mandarins in the Chinese theater, dressed in coats of stiff, quilted silk, with red pom-poms on their heads and extravagantly long mustaches dropping from their jowls . . .

"One was from Addis Ababa," Alyosha said. "The other, Joseph, came here from Chicago. He said the city had a river going right through it, like Petersburg, and that the winters were cold, with a lot of snow. He told me about the World's Fair in 1893. He'd been an Abyssinian there too, in one of the exhibits. Only they called it by another name. Ethiopian, I think it was."

"What, for an anthropology exhibit, you mean?"

"Yes."

"I don't understand. Is he an Abyssinian, then, or not?"

"He isn't. There were also Esquimau and Argentinean vaqueros and a replica of a Viking ship that sailed to America from Norway. Japanese geishas. It was all in a great hall constructed for the purpose. You know, to edify onlookers."

"How horrible that must be, to be put on display like an animal at the zoo."

Alyosha smiled. "You haven't spent much time at court, have you? Anyway, he said he didn't mind, as they paid him quite well and all he had to do was stand there in a costume."

"Ah," I said. "Good training for the Alexander Palace."

Alyosha nodded. "He said as much. Although in Chicago, for the exposition, he had a whole native diorama in which to pose, with vegetation that was genuinely from Abyssinia, as were the clothes they dressed him in and the furnishings in his hut. Joseph was the only part that was false. The scholar who presented the exhibit had acquired a real Abyssinian but something happened to him at the last minute, Joseph didn't know what, and they needed a particular-looking individual, with attributes that Joseph had—his height and the shade of his skin. The anthropologist picked Joseph out of a park. He'd been walking to work—he was a bricklayer— and the man accosted him, inquired what his wages were, and offered him three times that to stand or squat in his little Abyssinia and pretend he spoke no English. All he wore was a striped loincloth, white paint, and a lot of necklaces made of bone."

I laughed. "People tell you such curious things about themselves, Alyosha. I can't imagine Joseph telling your sisters that."

"My English is better than theirs."

"That's not it, though."

"No," Alyosha agreed. "I've wondered if perhaps they don't feel sorry for me and go out of their way to be friendly and produce a tribulation or two of their own."

"What will we do in Chicago?" I asked, as Alyosha had fallen silent.

"I'm trying to think."

"Once we arrive," I said, "we'll have to find employment."

"Right," Alyosha agreed. "Do you have any skills, Masha? I mean aside from . . ."

"From what?"

"From whatever ones I already know about."

"I can perform tricks on horseback," I said.

"No you can't."

"I can."

"How would a girl learn *dzhigitovka?*"

"A *girl?*" I said.

"I didn't mean it like that."

"Yes you did. That's exactly how you meant it. Lying only makes it worse."

"All right. I'm sorry—I am, Masha. Please accept my apologies."

"I suppose you think I should apply for a position as chambermaid just because I know how to make a bed."

"Masha. Stop it. Tell me about the tricks."

"They aren't anything to do with *dzhigitovka,*" I told him. *Dzhigitovka* refers to fancy Cossack cavalry exercises requiring saddles and stirrups. A master of the art can gallop into battle invisibly, hanging from one side of his mount, completely hidden by his horse's body.

"What are they, then?"

"Stunts I taught myself, that's all."

"But how?"

"Well, I did grow up with horses. And you'll laugh, but my childhood dream was to go to America to become a cowboy. There was an American horseman—they call them cowboys there—who assembled what he called a 'Congress of Rough Riders.' He got them from all over the—"

"Buffalo Bill Cody," Alyosha said. "The Wild West Show. I saw it. Nagorny took me. And Derevenko. They'd cordoned off the Nevsky Prospekt to turn it into a theater for the performance."

"Yes, that's the man I'm talking about. He died this past January. I saw it in the paper. January tenth. He died of the same thing that killed your grandfather—kidney failure."

"I didn't know he'd died."

"He did, two weeks after Father."

The first time Cody came to Europe was for the American exposition, and Edward, the Prince of Wales, took his children to see the show; they all liked it so much Edward asked his mother, Queen Victoria, to see it. "Victoria invited the Congress of Rough Riders for a command performance," I told Alyosha, "as part of her Golden Jubilee festival. It was 1887. And there were kings and princes and princesses invited from all over, as it was her fiftieth year as empress and she was related to half the kings and queens of Europe. Kaiser Wilhelm was there. He'd just been crowned."

"Right," Alyosha said, making a face. "The man at the other end of the wire to Mother's boudoir. Can you imagine my mother as a German spy? It would be funny if it weren't so . . . so . . ."

"Ludicrous. Poor woman," I said. "She'd suffer a nervous collapse before she could relay any information whatsoever."

Everyone loved the Rough Riders. It was the spectacle everyone had to see. Annie Oakley was there too, and she had so many medals she couldn't pin them to the front of her dress; they went all the way around the back. Wilhelm challenged her to shoot the ash off the end of his cigarette, and she did. The show was invited from one palace to the next, all over the continent.

"Was it—did it go to Moscow or St. Petersburg?" Alyosha wanted to know.

"It didn't come to Russia, not for that first tour. Just to Rome, Paris, Brussels, Madrid, and Berlin. They stayed for months at the Hohenzollern Castle, and before they went back to America, Cody went looking for Cossacks to add to the show—he'd got the idea from the kaiser, who'd turned cowboys and Indians into a national craze. Cody had come to Europe with ninety-seven red Indians, aside from the white Americans in the show, and nearly two hundred horses. When he went back he had a dozen Cossacks and their horses as well, and all of them sailed together on a single steamship. I was a little girl, five or six, when Mother told me about it. She knew about it because two of her cousins, two brothers, went back to America with Cody.

"This is silly, I know, but I'd never seen a modern sailing vessel before I come to Petersburg, and I imagined the ship the way Noah's ark was illustrated in the children's Bible Mother used to teach me to read—one of those cutaway pictures that show the interior of a thing. Only instead of all different animals in the stalls, my ark was filled with nothing but horses. Every night I fell asleep looking at that picture in my head. Imagining myself going from one stall to the next, saying good night to each horse.

"My poor mother. Once I learned about her cousins, she couldn't budge me from the idea that I was going to join the Wild West Show too. The brothers' names were Pyotr and Arkady, and every night when she put me to bed I'd ask her to tell me about them. I wasn't interested in saying my prayers, only in her Cossack cousins. She soon ran out of things to tell me, so I made up stories for myself and determined to become a trick rider. I was good with horses, and I loved them. The thing they used to say about Father—that he had a way with the beasts—that, anyway, was true of me as well. Long before you were dreaming of Caesar's Egyptian campaign, I was planning my glorious reign as the queen of Buffalo Bill's Wild West Show."

"So. Tell me, Masha. Tell me the tricks."

"I'm going to."

We had five horses at home in Pokrovskoye and I tried, as a child, to love them democratically, but my favorite was Valentine. He was half Yakut—the only horse that can survive Siberian winters—and half something else, a bigger animal, with longer legs. Father said the man from whom he'd bought Valentine told him all sorts of rubbish, that he'd been sired by a Cossack cavalry horse, that he'd been gelded twice and both times everything had grown back. Had revolutionary soldiers attempted to conscript him, they would have discovered his temper, and I liked imagining his big teeth sinking into the meat of a soldier's arm or buttock. Whatever it was it would go on hurting long after the man pulled away from his bite. Because Valentine bit everyone who came near him. Except for me. He had a wide, smooth, sleek back, with the Yakut's insulation of fat covered by thick hair. Almost before I could talk, I'd figured out how to climb onto him, using his mane and grabbing the tufts of his chinchilla-colored hair. Anyone who mistook him for a plain animal would change his mind once he pushed his forelock out from before his eyes, which were so dark it was hard to find where pupil stopped and iris began. The shorter hair on his face was more silver than gray, and his black eyes were ringed with black, and his mane, tail, ears, and socks were black too.

"Once I'd resolved to make myself a trick rider, I used pinesap to make Valentine's back sticky, and I began by teaching myself to stand on his back while he walked, and then while he cantered. Trotting was harder. Valentine almost bounced when he trotted, as if he had springs instead of legs, and I fell and I fell, I can't tell you how many times. Mother would try to wash the sap and grass and dirt from my hair, and I was so tired after spending all day pursuing my brilliant equestrienne destiny that I'd fall asleep almost as soon as she dipped my head in the warm water."

"Why did you never tell me about it before?" Alyosha said. "The trick riding?"

"Oh, I don't know. You knew I went to the stable as often as I was allowed."

"But I didn't know you did anything but ride."

"That's the silly thing, actually. I don't know how. I mean, not as your father or sisters do. I'm sure I could teach myself to ride with a saddle and reins, but I don't like the idea of having anything between my body and the horse's. Tack always seems an encumbrance. Something to inhibit rather than aid communication. And I'd never consider using a bit—that's just stupid. When a horse and I are used to each other it doesn't take any steering, only a shift of balance or the touch of an ankle. And if for some reason the horse doesn't feel like listening, it's enough to use his mane. But mostly I like doing tricks—somersaults, handsprings, that kind of thing."

"On the horse's back, you mean?"

"Or on two at once, when I can match up a pair that are willing to work with each other. Usually it's enough to hold our three heads together until our breath aligns. Then we're a team and I can guide them with my feet. I can stand with a foot on either horse. Stand while they run."

"No you can't," Alyosha said. "That's ridiculous."

"Of course I can."

"No. You can't."

"What, do you think I'm lying to you?" I looked at Alyosha to read his expression. Usually I did my best to sidestep whatever his health prevented him from doing, and when I mentioned the trick riding I'd intended to speak of it as a fantasy, not admitting it was something I actually did. It was his saying "a girl" in that supercilious way that made me lose my temper.

Buffalo Bill Cody. The obituary was published when I was ill in bed, but Varya saved it for me—I have the notice still. I remember being ashamed to have cried as I did when I learned of his death, to have cried for a stranger as I couldn't for my own father, facedown on my bed in the palace to smother the sound of that awful, hot, wet, hiccupping, disheveled, childish sobbing. After, when I looked in the mirror, I saw that my nose was as red and swollen as a new potato.

"I suppose I'm to be the ticket-taker?" Alyosha said.

"Don't be stupid. Once the audience sees your act, they'll forget about me. We'll begin by making a big show of carrying our carpet onstage, unrolling it before the crowd, and flapping it about to exhibit its ordinary appearance. We'll let people in the audience touch it. Then I'll set it on the center of the stage and you will sit in the middle, cross-legged, like a swami or yogi or whatever they're called, and I will ask for silence, as levitation requires absolute concentration. You'll make terrible faces, so it's obvious the strain of what you're doing is nearly unendurable, and slowly slowly slowly the carpet will rise from the stage. You'll let it go up only a few inches, no more than a foot, and you'll keep up with the awful faces—you want it to look as if the effort to stay up in the air is practically exterminating you. I'll pass a cane under—no, I'll invite people from the audience to come up and investigate. And all along you'll be gritting your teeth and keeping your eyes shut—I hear it's quite hot under stage lights, so you'll be perspiring too—and whoever comes up will see it's real, there's no hidden strings or anything like that. At the end, you'll act as if you have to stop out of exhaustion. You'll just . . . I don't know, go limp or collapse on the floating carpet, and it will drift gently down to the ground. It will be a sensation, much better than any horse nonsense could ever be. Much safer too. You'll have a career that can't possibly harm you. We can charge extra to the people who want to come up close and try to figure out how you do it."

"Why can't I fly around on the carpet?"

"Because no one would believe that. They'd call it an optical illusion or something. It's better if they can see it up close. And for it to look as if it's you who's keeping the carpet up, rather than the other way around. If they thought it could really fly, it would just frighten them."

Russian Roulette

· · · · ·

SEPTEMBER 23, 1904. The autumnal equinox. Day and night equal, and in balance. From that day forward the days would grow shorter and the nights longer. The planet had tipped, a degree, no more, but still, harmony was undone, darkness had gained the upper hand.

Alyosha, six weeks old, began bleeding from his navel. No need to try to picture the baby he was, for his father and mother and sisters and grandmother, aunts and great-uncles—yes, even the Meddlesome Four—took photograph after photograph of his gummy wet smile and button nose. They immortalized the fine golden hair that grew on his perfectly formed head, the dimples in his plump arms, and the lashes that curled around his gray eyes—his mother's eyes, they all said as soon as they saw them. This child, received by his family as its messiah, upon whose life the fate of Russia rested, the answer to countless fervent petitions—

. . . to Saint Agatha, who protected the tsarina against sterility, to Saint Felicity, who granted her conceiving a boy, to Saint Catherine of Siena, who hadn't allowed her to suffer a miscarriage, to Ulric, who watched over her labor lest there be a complication, to Giles the Hermit, who summoned her milk to flow, to all the Holy Innocents murdered by Herod who stood guard around his cradle, to Margaret of Antioch, who used her crucifix to prick the insides of the dragon that had swallowed her, forcing it to vomit her up so she could take her position at the nursery door, still armed with that crucifix, and of course to the Virgin, the Mother of God, whose mercy is without limit: was there a saint Alexandra hadn't begged, an ikon under whose gilded glassy gaze she hadn't knelt?

I wonder if, at the first sight of blood, in that moment when the tsarina saw the future and the trouble it would bring, she contemplated her happiness, if she held it tight and looked at it, the way one does before letting go of a treasured possession. Six weeks without so much as a wisp of a cloud over her head. Just the previous evening she and Nicky were laughing together. Tsar Nikolay had come to the nursery knowing he'd find his wife there, for she could hardly stand to let the baby out of her sight, and, yes, there she was with Alyosha just out of the bath, lying on his back on a towel as she knelt over him.

"Look," Alexandra said, and she smiled as no one but her family ever saw her smile, her expression so radiant and unguarded he couldn't help but take her hand to pull her up into his arms. "See how strong he is!" she said, ducking out from under Nicky's kiss. The two of them laughed with joy, watching as Alyosha kicked his sturdy legs.

A dot of red, that was all. She tried to brush it away from his blanket. Jam, perhaps, from when his sisters were cooing over him at breakfast. Yes, oh, please let it be, please God, please let it be jam. But it wasn't the right color, she could see that as it spread, and it wasn't quite sticky enough, and oh God help me, please God no. But it kept on growing. Not sticky like jam, and getting bigger. Alyosha gurgled as she put him on his back. He waved his fat fists as his mother pulled away the blanket and dress, pushed up the little vest, pulled down the diaper. The violent shock of it, so red, so, so very red, seeping slowly out from the umbilicus, which had healed—she thought it had. She had to put her head down so she didn't faint, and still all the world went inside out and black and white as if she was looking at a photographic negative.

For nearly a decade Alexandra had been in a state of constant anxiety, knowing happiness would disappear, knowing it was the nature of happiness to depart, tormenting herself with questions of when and how. But she hadn't anticipated this. No person was perverse enough, wicked and profane and mean enough, to imagine what she was seeing now, her perfect child, a baby only six weeks old, with blood welling up from his middle. She hadn't understood the risk she carried. How could she, when no one had ever spoken of its existence?

Yes, there had been rumors about the deaths of young men in Victoria's family, some of them little boys, some of them babies, but no one knew what had really killed them. Victoria's son Leopold died after a fall, as did her grandson Leopold. And Alexandra's own brother, Friedrich, fell on his head when he was three, knocked himself out, and never woke up. To hear people talk, Victoria's male descendants were afflicted by a terrible clumsiness, a flair for operatic tumbles down stairs and out windows and, when they were old enough to drive, for running off the road straight into the afterlife. But no one ever mentioned anyone bleeding to death. Court physicians were discreet, in caution for their positions and their lives. And so what if the Battenberg branch of the family bundled their princes in padded suits before they were let out to play in a padded park, every tree trunk wrapped in layers of cotton batting, every ball deflated to a disappointing lack of bounce? Who knew what they did in far-off lands or why?

An attenuated and especially deadly game of Russian roulette, played with a pistol bearing only two chambers, one for each X chromosome a mother can bequeath to a child—as a boy receives only one of these, he has half a chance of living a normal life, half of getting the wrong X.

The fault lay within that fearsome fat queen, Victoria. It had to have, because whatever caused Alyosha's hemophilia was unknown before Victoria's reign. Unknown before her cloistered childhood, with no companion save her little spaniel. Unknown before her father died and left her prey to her selfish-monster-of-a-mother's tyrannies, before her mother seized the regency and plotted with a lover to prevent Victoria's ascending England's throne. Unknown before Victoria, at last wearing her rightful crown, exiled her cruel mother to a remote tower, though not nearly remote enough to forget her.

Some misfortune, or the sum of her misfortunes: whatever it was, it reached inside Victoria and twisted the stalks of her ovaries, poked at the clabbered pink jelly of her still-sleeping eggs, pinched and popped some and did the rest grave damage.

But no one saw this portent. How could they, hidden as it was deep within her lament?

IT WENT ON AND ON, that first slow hemorrhage, almost too slow to call a hemorrhage, had it not continued from one day to the next and the one after that. Alexandra Fyodorovna held Alyosha. She refused to relinquish him to another woman's arms, not even the steadfast arms of an Experienced, Bonded, and Insured Imperial Baby Nurse, but rocked and paced, and hushed and shushed, all the while weeping silently onto his head, her tears plastering the golden floss to his scalp. And when she saw, in the morning light that streamed through the nursery windows, his heartbeat flicker in that tender dangerous place where the bones of his skull had yet to close over his brain, she cried harder. His first smile inspired a fresh cascade of tears—although it was difficult to tell where one left off and another began—as would his first tooth and first steps and first words.

Once the tsarevich began to bleed, Alexandra wouldn't let anyone see or touch the umbilicus—no one other than Botkin, sworn
to secrecy—and she dressed the wound herself, a wound that
wasn't a wound so much as slow seep of blood that saturated the
pad of gauze held in place by a long strip of the stuff she tied gently
around his middle. Alyosha didn't complain. He was the kind of
baby mothers call easy. He never cried for long. He wouldn't, not
once he discovered that when he cried he couldn't hear what he
wanted to hear—the sound of his mother's heart beating on the
other side of her skin, on the inside of her, where he'd swum and
turned like a fish to the tune of that throb, woke to it and slept to
it. What sound did Alyosha know as he did the thumping of his
mother's heart, which had quickened and slowed, quickened and
slowed, lapped and tapped at his ears' tender drums? The sound
he'd felt in his fingertips and his spine, the one that animated the
walls of the womb in which he'd made himself up out of nothing,
inventing two eyes and two ears and two feet with five toes and,
when he was done, thought his first thought. A thought that was,
more or less, *lub dub, lub dub.* But now, as he heard with his ear
pressed to the warm skin of his mother's chest, the beating of her
heart was too fast, much too fast, and because it was too fast it held
his attention. So Alyosha rarely cried, as he always had to listen.

Listen past the hundreds of prayers, thousands of prayers, the
Lord's Prayer, the Hail Mary, the Acts of Contrition, and, squeezed
among the formal words of the Church, her own increasingly frantic, sometimes nearly incoherent begging, endless help-me-dear-
Lords, please-please-pleases, and reflexive bargaining. My life for
his, my blood for his, my umbilicus for his, please please please, another blight, anything, gangrene, lightning strikes, burn down the
Alexander Palace, the Alexander and the Catherine and the Winter
Palaces, burn them all down, Anchikov, Gatchina, the Kremlin,
even Livadia with its sunny white walls and hills of flowers, burn

up all seven of the wretched things, cut off my hands, blind me and take my books away, every last one of them, the icons, too; take them, I don't want them, give me cancer, poison my blood, make me bald, make me stupid—make me anything, my mother-in-law if You like—just punish me, punish me, punish me please and not him. Or take a different child, God forgive me, but please won't you take one of the girls, not the boy, not the boy, take Olga, she's sulky and stubborn and intellectually arrogant, or take Tatiana, she broods, forgive me, God, but it's the truth, take one of the girls, any of the girls, God help me, take two of them but not him, not him, please don't let him die, don't, dear God, don't.

Chicanery

. . . . .

"IF YOU REFUSE, we'll die not knowing what all the fuss is about."

"You're not even fourteen, Alyosha."

"I am, almost. And you're just eighteen."

"That's what I'm saying. I haven't had any experience either."

"But that's what I'm saying, Masha. We don't have time to waste."

On the afternoon of the day the Romanovs learned they were to be exiled east, over and beyond the Urals, Alyosha and I began an argument we wouldn't resolve before we were separated. It was about sex, of course.

Alyosha put my hand on the "ache in his lap" so I could feel how hard was the torment I caused him. "It doesn't matter if it's wrong under ordinary circumstances," he said. "As we're going to be murdered, we're excused from conventional morality."

"You think virtue is relative? That it isn't absolute?"

"Naturally I do. There are no virtues other than those we invent and manipulate to suit our needs." He was sitting up in bed, his leg free from its brace, and he had his arms crossed and wore his most patronizing expression. "An obvious example," he went on, "is our executing murderers at home while we decorate those soldiers who are the most prolific murderers when we wage war.

How can you reconcile those two facts without a moral code that's relative?"

It was the end of July. Alyosha was well enough to be allowed out of bed for most of the day, and we were sitting together in one of the few rooms allotted the imperial family, under the guard of two humorless soldiers in gray woolen uniforms, bayonets at the ready. The announcement of imminent exile was accompanied by a doubling of our "protective" security, whose drabness made it hard to remember the tall glossy Abyssinians dressed in red and gold as anything other than a quaint decoration. I couldn't imagine how or where Alyosha thought we could be alone with each other, and I said so.

"Outdoors, in the Chinese theater, or one of the hothouses."

"Nagorny," I said. "You can't go outside without him."

"I can get rid of Nagorny."

"How?"

"He does anything I say, as long as I don't run about and risk falling down. Haven't I managed to banish him almost entirely from our afternoons together? I'll tell him we're reading and that he's to leave us alone. He can sit on a bench. Smoke. Drink tea. It doesn't matter what."

"I don't think Nagorny likes me," I said, changing the subject.

"He's jealous, that's all."

"What does he have to be jealous of?"

"The time we spend together. Remember, he stayed when Dina left. He chose me over his freedom. Come on, Masha," he said, when I was silent. "We'll be careful. We'll bring our books and sit and read and they'll get bored and fall asleep just as they always do."

As grim as they looked, the new guard of revolutionary soldiers had turned out to be as lax in discipline when sober as they were when drunk. After all, as any of them would happily tell you, there was no incentive to behave any better than they did. Guarding that Bastard Decadent Tsar and his Shamelessly Corrupt Family wasn't the appointment they wanted—not if they weren't allowed to maim and murder them—so what were they to do but smoke, drink, play cards, and break things? No excitement whatsoever, as the fools weren't going to try to escape. To hear the family members talk, they didn't even know they were going to be assassinated—a thing as simple as that, a thing anyone could have guessed. If that didn't prove they were fools, what did?

And what hoity-toity toplofty fools, too good to fight back, too polite to object to being mistreated. Really, they didn't seem to be proper adults, even. Why, hadn't Nikolay Alexandrovich celebrated the thaw by pedaling out of his castle on a bicycle? Consider a thing like that, a tsar on a bicycle. No wonder Russia had come upon such dire times, when tsars went around on bicycles. Just like a little boy he was, in his cap and coat, following the path, when one of the guards thrust his bayonet forward.

It could just as well have been a branch, because all the man did was stick it through the spokes of the back wheel. The bicycle came to a sudden halt, and the tsar in his little-boy cap flew over the handlebars and landed on the path.

He wasn't tall, the tsar, so perhaps that was some of it, but God have mercy—well, there's no God anymore, there's only the Soviet, so mercy upon him, whatever the source of that mercy. Although perhaps it was a thing of the past: mercy. Certainly it was in short supply. Anyway, mercy on us, the tsar looked about ten years old. Even a mustache and beard couldn't disguise the friendly innocence in his eyes.

But wait, surely that was the affectation of a clever manipulator. All the world knew he was a bloodthirsty savage who cared nothing for the suffering of his people. The savage picked up his cap, dusted it off, picked up his bicycle, dusted it off, and he smiled.

Perhaps he intended this to be disarming, but it wasn't as if smiling proved his forbearance, or his virtue, or even his manners. It didn't admit to any of the countless crimes he had perpetrated against the proletariat. All it proved was deceit. Either that or weakness. That turning-the-other-cheek shit, it was exactly that: shit. A fairy tale the moneyed class fed the workers to make them humble, to make them believe there was a world-to-come after they'd been trodden down, broken, and exploited in this one.

The tsar got back on his bicycle, tried to ride off to the left, and, when the guards closed ranks before him, tried to go right. But the guards opposed him at every turn, and he dismounted and wheeled the bicycle back to the Alexander Palace. The tsar could do nothing without half a dozen guards following him. When he did, at long last, receive permission to ride on his bicycle, the sound of armed soldiers running behind him, jackboots crunching on the path, killed whatever pleasure he might have taken in the excursion, and he didn't ride it again.

THE REST OF US were not so unfortunate. We were watched, but by fewer guards and from a greater distance. So Alyosha could assume the guards wouldn't pose a problem. But what of ignorance? It's always a problem.

"What then?" I said to Alyosha. "Neither of us knows . . . knows how."

"I do. I mean, I think I know enough."

Perhaps he did. The kiss he gave me before we parted, the one that turned out to be our last, was unexpectedly adult, as if I were kissing a man rather than a boy. And, while we did not sacrifice our innocence, over the next weeks I allowed Alyosha's hands into my blouse, as I might not have had he not begun to convince me that what he feared was true: he and his family, and perhaps the rest of us as well, would be killed. It was a matter of time, that was all.

"Don't you see?" he said. "It's the first step. Removing us from the capital, sending us out of sight and out of the public's mind."

"They'll probably take us too," I said. "Technically, as wards of your father, we are part of the family."

"Technically, your blood isn't Romanov. It isn't flowing through decadent tsarist veins."

"Technically, I'm the daughter of a man assassinated for his alleged deviltry."

"Assassinated by monarchists determined to save the faltering empire. As it's generally assumed your father helped topple centuries of depraved Romanov rule, the revolutionaries may ask you to accept a medal in his stead. Have you asked what will happen to you and Varya?"

"No. If there was anything—any definitive thing, like a decision one way or another—I'm sure your mother would tell me."

"Unless she had a choice in the matter and could have let you go but didn't, on my account. Then she might feel guilty and avoid telling you."

"But, Alyosha, there's nothing I've done to help you. Just seeing me makes her cry."

"Oh, she cries all the time anyway, Masha, you know that. I wonder if it isn't a nervous affliction. Really I do, don't look at me that way. Besides, you've been my friend, kept me company."

"Well, yes, but—"

"You're the first I've ever had, Masha. Don't you know that?"

"No, I . . ." With all of us locked up together as Russia descended into anarchy, no one had seen any friends. Not that this was an excuse, and I didn't offer it as one. "I should have," I said.

"Because," he went on, "the secret had to be kept. And even if it could have been told, Mother thought it was asking for me to be injured, there being no way to prevent boys from being boys. Oh, Masha, don't look like that. There were adults who befriended me. Nagorny. And Derevenko. I considered him my friend before he . . . before he left. But, other than my sisters, there's never been anyone remotely near my age. That's why you seem not so much older than I. That and your height."

"You mean my lack of height." I was small enough that by the time Varya was twelve, she got the new dresses and handed them up to me. "Anyway, Alyosha, you know what's to happen if we are left behind. I'm to be foisted on that charlatan." And at that we both fell silent.

I DID MARRY THE CHARLATAN Boris Soloviev, as my father told me I would. Boris had made a career of conducting séances in St. Petersburg, bilking women of their jewels in return for messages from their departed.

"Oh, Father, honestly!" I'd said when he told me, and I laughed, thinking he was teasing. I jumped up from where I was sitting and dropped into his lap, tweaking his beard to tell him what a fine joke he'd made, even if it was at my expense. But he took my hand away from his face and held it.

"Masha. He is a wealthy man. Tsar Nikolay will make sure that—"

"He's a fraud! How can you suggest something so . . . so . . . so obscene as to shackle me to such a person!"

Father's grasp tightened, so that I had to pull my hand away, he held it so tightly. "I am telling you, Masha—"

"I know what you're doing. I know very well. You're making sure I understand there is no other Grigory Yefimovich by foisting me off on the adult equivalent of a conjurer hired for a child's birthday. You think I don't know a shameless mountebank when I see one? You think I don't know there is no other like you?"

"Masha," Father said again. I closed my eyes; Father took my face in his hands. I covered my ears; he pulled my hands away from them. He wouldn't allow me to avoid hearing what he had to say and what I always denied because I couldn't bear to listen.

"Masha, child. My death is foretold. I am dead already. I won't live to see the coming year. And Russia will descend into civil war, brothers killing brothers, women fighting like men, bearing arms. You'll need help if you are to escape. "

Seventeen is too old to stamp your feet and bury your head in your father's chest and cry the way little girls do. But he waited until I'd stopped, until I'd gone to the sink and washed my face and smoothed my hair, before he asked me to write a letter for him, one he would give Tsar Nikolay to be opened on the occasion of his death.

"Thank you," he said when I handed him the page to sign. He pulled me into a hug and kissed the top of my head. "Don't fret, Masha," Father said. "He won't live to be thirty."

"How old is he now?" I asked, and he laughed and I tried to laugh. But to leave my father's home and make one with Boris—it didn't seem possible to endure such a punishment. I never could decide whether or not to mention the letter to the tsar; that was one reason I'd avoided inquiring about my fate. For Varya to go home to Siberia in the care of a chaperone while I was to be traded away like chattel didn't seem any fairer now than it had when I wrote out my father's wishes.

"Why can't I go home with Varya?" I asked Father.

"Because," he said.

"Because what? I'm not a child, to be given an answer like that."

"Because your destiny is not in Russia."

"Not if I'm to be dragged off by . . . by that . . . that . . . illu-sionist!"

"Masha."

"What?"

"Don't you trust me?"

"You know I do. But it isn't so easy for those of us who can't see into the future."

"Is that what you think?" he said. I shook my head. His was, of course, the harder vision, including, as it must have, the ends of all of us, his son and daughters and the wife he loved, the homeland for which he died.

"Isn't there something, please?" I asked. "Any little thing you might tell me? A tiny hint?" Father was strict about his ability to prophesy. He wasn't, he'd tell anyone who asked, a fortune-teller. The heavens would close before his eyes, he'd say, refuse to reveal another thing to a man who squandered a gift of the Spirit, and if anyone argued he'd quote First Corinthians straight on to Second until that person gave up and went away.

"No hints. Only this: you will, like your father, use the talents the Good Lord gave you."

"What talents? I don't have any talents!"

"Of course you do."

"No I don't. Tricks on horses, that's all. Somersaults. Riding backward. What's the use of that?"

But Father had said all he would say.

YEARS LATER, during one of our fiercer fights, Boris asked me why I hadn't written my own intentions into the letter, if I'd been opposed to the idea of marrying him. It took me a minute to understand so preposterous a question. What answer did I have for my husband, other than the truth?

"If you imagine I'd consider such a thing," I told him, "you have no idea who I am or who my father was to me. Even now, years after his death and married to you, my allegiance is to him, not you. He told me what I was to do and, trusting in his wisdom, I am doing it."

Aside from that, only a stupid person would try to deceive someone who could hear her thinking.

I guessed Boris was a bona fide fake the moment Father introduced me to him. The next moment I knew it. Too proud of his chicanery to keep the details of its accomplishment secret from the woman he expected to become his wife and whose pedigree—the daughter of Rasputin!—would enhance his ridiculous enterprise, Boris gave me a tour of his tricks. The switch on which he stepped to produce rapping noises across the parlor from where he sat receiving news from the beyond. The darkroom where he made the "documentary" photographs cherished by his bereaved patrons, the ones he took of them sitting alone on a velvet-upholstered love seat, unaware of the proximity of a ghost—the evocative white blur Boris added when making the prints.

"See how simple!" he said. He showed me what looked like a tiny flyswatter, demonstrating how he waved it between the negative and the photographic paper, preventing light from darkening part of the paper's coating of emulsion. The print this produced revealed a "ghost" sitting or hovering next to the widow. She might not feel his presence, but her husband was there at her side just as he had always been. Though she was lonely without him, missed his physical being, she need not feel bereft—for he hadn't left her after all. Whoever she was, when she left Boris's séance parlor and "World Famous Photography Studio," she felt an emanation, an ectoplasmic hovering, a cold draft or a phantom hand at her waist, even a cool kiss upon her lips as she fell to sleep that night.

"I'm giving them what they want, Masha," Boris said when I asked if he wasn't troubled by being dishonest about so serious a matter. "I'm providing solace. Proofs of the afterlife. Even the

Christ hasn't done that—not for nearly two thousand years, anyway. Ha!"

What point was there in arguing with such an egoist? Crystal balls were for women, Boris thought. He had his monocle, his cape, and carried a cane with Anubis, Egyptian god of the dead, for a handle. The top half of Anubis was a jackal and the bottom half a man, and before the dead could enter the underworld he weighed their hearts to determine their worthiness.

In the years before the Bolsheviks seized the city, St. Petersburg was a playground in the throes of the kind of decadence—determined, desperate—that presages collapse. As if the aristocracy knew apocalypse was imminent and, also knowing there was nothing to prevent its arrival, stayed up drinking and dancing and inhaling cocaine when they could get their hands on any, distracting themselves by whatever means they found. Spending money in a frenzy on champagne, caviar, jewels, gowns. On parties with full orchestras, themed costume balls excusing all manner of ostentation: hostesses riding through ballrooms on gilded elephants, servants dressed up like gondoliers or Vikings or pharaohs. Spiritualism was the fiercest rage, with a choice of séances to attend on any given night, but only Boris happily took advantage of mothers who'd lost sons at war or stripped a widow of her savings in trade for a message from her dead husband.

I didn't like the idea of being joined until death divided us to a man whose métier was equal parts deception and self-importance. But by the time an Orthodox priest had muttered his shibboleths over our heads, splashed us with holy water, and ordered us to kiss, Russia was dying, my father had been murdered, my mother, sister, and brother were lost, and Alyosha and his family were a few thousand miles closer to their deaths. Petersburg had been looted and burned. As Father foresaw, the jewels Boris had amassed proved useful for bribing border-control agents and all the other opportunists and thieves lying in wait at the countless stumbling blocks en route to freedom. As the gods in heaven could see from on high, we left a glittering trail behind us, and I thanked him— Father, I mean—each time Boris handed over another bracelet or earring he'd earned with his lies.

Travel by Combustion

. . . . .

*U*PON HIS ARRIVAL back in Russia—because he did truly go to the Holy Land—my father discovered how hard it was to attend to one sick person after another, how physically and mentally exhausting it was to be the instrument of a power outside himself. After a morning spent with supplicants, he spent the afternoon lying flat on his back, not asleep but blank with weariness.

His ability to heal had grown stronger, but it had nothing to do with his pilgrimage. That was something he regarded as akin to a diploma, a thing he'd needed to validate his vocation. Or perhaps it did have to do with the pilgrimage, just not directly. As if he had fulfilled a celestial requirement, within a week of his return Father saw the Virgin. He'd seen her before, back home, but never with the heightened, almost hallucinatory detail with which he did on this day.

"It was before he saw her in the snowy woods?" Alyosha asked.

"Seven years before."

"Tell me," he said. "Tell me what she looked like this time."

"I can tell you only what he told me."

Father saw something in the road as he was driving home to Pokrovskoye from Jerusalem. He pulled over, turned the engine off, and left the car behind, as he wanted to walk. To approach her on the feet God gave him, as a man, not a foolish creature on wheels.

She stood on a cloud of butterflies, he said. In winter, a cloud of butterflies. Butterflies of all kinds, and of every color. And she wore a dress made of animals—not of the skins of animals but of animals themselves. A cloak of buffalo and tigers and monkeys and zebras, birds and tortoises and more, all of them alive and, as with the story of Noah and his ark, every creature represented. A vast and rippling many-colored cape of white, red, brown, orange, silver, black. Thick, glossy pelts stirring and twisting, an orgy of fur and feathers—held together by what force? What could it be other than the power of the being whose cloak they formed? When I wondered aloud at how huge a woman he must have seen there, standing in the road, he laughed and said, no, she was no taller or wider than he. But how then, I wanted to know, could she have worn a cloak of countless animals, each of which Father could see down to its last whisker?

"No, Masha," he said. He hadn't been *looking* at the Virgin. The apparition overcame him, forced itself inside his head, where it was revealed in more, or other, than the three dimensions mortals see. After all, why would the Holy Mother of God himself be limited to three? She had infinite dimensions.

Her face was as it is always described, at once radiant and sorrowful. And she was, as she always is, crowned. But not with jewels. Nor with stars. Flowers of all kinds circled her head—flowers whose beauty transcended that of jewels. From them, light sprayed into the chilly air like errant sunbeams. She took a step toward my father, and her cape parted to show her sparkling dress, blue like water. The reverse of the story of Moses and his rod, as Father described it, because Moses parted the waters whereas the Virgin's cloak of land creatures opened to show him the sea. The gown of blue was alive with silver swimming creatures of all kinds—porpoise and tuna and swordfish, even whales. She could contain them all.

"How . . . singular," Alyosha said, his brow creased. Someone who didn't know the tsarevich might mistake his frown for evidence of anger, but it was thinking that made him look cross. When he was angry his face had no expression at all, and if you knew him you understood he had composed it carefully because he didn't trust his anger, not enough to betray it.

"When he talked about it," I said, "I could tell it was something he'd experienced. He wasn't making it up, because if he had been he couldn't have spoken of it in the way he did."

"How did he?"

"He was sad, disillusioned. He'd expected different revelations from those he received. He waited on his knees for the Mother of us all to show him the city—a city—of enlightenment." A city of pure gold yet clear as glass and lit by the light of God, not by the sun, who hid her face at the end of each day. A city in which there was no night, only brightness. But that city, the one he used to describe to me at bedtime, was inspired by descriptions in the Book of Revelation, and the Virgin had something else she wanted to show Father.

The Virgin didn't speak but handed my father a message written on a scroll only he could see. "He could see it," I told Alyosha, "but he didn't know how to read. To learn what it said he had to transcribe the message onto a piece of paper and take it to someone who could read, and that someone was me, because Mother had taught me."

"What did it say?"

"It doesn't matter what it said. What matters is that he returned to the car, retrieved a pencil and a piece of paper, neither clean nor whole, and walked back to the same place in the road, an ordinary patch of trampled dirt as far as any other mortal eye could tell. Father went down on his hands and knees to labor over the message, squinting up at the sky and then down at the paper, copying from what no one else could have seen even were he squinting there with him. Eyes other than my father's would have seen only a few loose flakes of snow turning in the sky and settling onto the barren ground. Father couldn't do anything but copy, because he didn't know how to write. He could never have done that if it hadn't come from a source outside himself."

"But what did it say?"

"That he was to go to Omsk and there buy a ticket to St. Petersburg. It would be a journey of eight days by train. It was time for him to come to the aid of his country."

"Like Joan of Arc," Alyosha said. "Her voices told her the same thing. Except in France, of course. Joan was beatified in 1909," he added.

In 1920, two years after Alyosha was murdered, Joan would be canonized. She'd be declared a saint—a girl who had been called mad and a heretic possessed by demons. They burned her once, and twice more after that, burned her up until there was nothing left of her but a handful of ashes to throw in the Seine. Burned her lifeless body as they did my father's, although his ashes were left for the wind to scatter.

Staggering toward the end of the Hundred Years War, about to succumb to what seemed like the inevitability of English rule, Charles VII, of the House of Valois, had been in straits direr than those in which Tsar Nikolay found himself. But Charles VII reigned during the fifteenth century. There was no proletariat to threaten—or even question—the idea of monarchy. Only citizens who, having escaped the previous century's Black Death, were eager to believe their king ruled by divine right.

Had Tsar Nikolay kept the throne, I might be the daughter of a saint rather than a madman. Russia would have had no choice but to have the Church declare my father a martyr, as France did Joan of Arc, retried *in absentia,* twenty years after her murder. After all, what king can afford to be associated with madness? A man prone to hallucinations and yet allowed access to the tsarina and her children: that man had to be declared holy, a saint rather than a scheming impostor. Otherwise it would reflect badly on the ruling dynasty.

FATHER LEFT HOME almost as soon as he'd arrived. He got back in the ruined automobile and drove it as far as Kazan, where the thing broke down and Father told its previous owner that its service was done, he'd been called to the capital. Katkoff looked at what had once been his pride and joy, green paint dulled by desert sandstorms, no windscreen, no doors, no spare tire, not much upholstery, one headlamp gone, the other hanging by its cord like an enucleated eyeball.

"Keep it, my good man," he said. "I never expected you to give it back—it was a gift. You can drive it to Petersburg."

No, the Virgin had said Father was to take a train from Omsk.

"Drive it to Omsk, then."

But Father had been galvanized by his encounter with the Virgin. The automobile—it had been revealed to him as a toy, nothing more. "*When I was a child, I spoke as a child, I thought as a child, I understood as a child,*" he quoted 1 Corinthians, Chapter 13, Verse 11. "*But when I became a man, I put away childish things.*"

Katkoff understood there was little point in arguing with a man who answered back in Bible verses. He bid Father Grigory farewell and gave the wreck to one of his tenants, Oblomov, who hitched a pair of mules to the thing and took it to town each market day, well pleased with his windfall.

The train from Omsk to St. Petersburg did take eight days, as the Virgin had said it would. The speed at which it traveled—the engineer told him it was harnessed to the power of 2,000 horses.

"How can that be?" Father asked, perhaps picturing, as I did when he told me, a great herd of animals running before the locomotive.

"Combustion," the engineer said.

And if that wasn't wickedness—to burn up even one horse to produce such a scream of iron wheels on their iron track, clouds of black smoke issuing from the locomotive and the black ash, all that was left of the poor beasts, on the white snow. For a peasant raised in Pokrovskoye, the train was a figment inspiring more fear than a visit from the Virgin.

My father arrived in St. Petersburg in March, during a snowstorm, unnerved every time he turned a corner and came upon another clot of freezing beggars and drunkards and prostitutes. A man who dreamed of a harmonious city upon which God's light shone without interruption, he'd imagined the tsar's city would exhibit some lesser degree of holiness, but a palpable holiness nonetheless. Certainly he'd never anticipated a world in which a millworker might choose to sleep on the floor by his or her loom because it was more comfortable, clean, and safe than a doss-house. The sole lodging factory hands could afford, doss-houses offered the one advantage of an invitation to drink oneself to death, as one couldn't in a textile factory. So, it was mostly women who slept by their looms, and had their babies there, too, as mill foremen didn't give a woman even one day off to bring a child into the world. How could Father have predicted that workers at the tanning factories were hungry enough to eat the rotten bits of meat they scraped from the hides? He had no more idea than Alyosha that destitution claimed most of the populace, no idea how desperate were the lives of most of the city's poor.

Even if Father dressed like a beggar, we had never been poor in Pokrovskoye, and we weren't poor in St. Petersburg. Our apartment was spacious, five rooms as well as a kitchen and a private toilet and bath, in the safe and not-unfashionable neighborhood my mother had insisted on for Varya and me. Third floor, with a private entrance. No filthy stairwell reeking of cabbage and cluttered with unclaimed bills and broken-down boots. Equidistant from the Nikolaev and Tsarskoe Selo stations, a short walk from the Maly and Alexandra theaters, not even half a mile from the Winter Palace. Within shouting distance of the Hotel de l'Europe, and five blocks from the Astoria.

When I, and later Varya, arrived in St. Petersburg, we couldn't believe our eyes. Such opulence, and so many buildings and electric lights and things we'd never seen before, things we never knew existed. Water that came out of shining taps, shops with doors made of glass, hospitals and restaurants, streets crowded with more people than we imagined existing in all of Russia, let alone one city, buildings twenty stories high and cathedrals so grand we could have fit a hundred of our humble little church inside and still have room for more, trams and trains, and every month more automobiles: there was no end of things to astonish us.

When good fortune greeted my father, when unexpected gifts arrived and doors opened—doors to affordable lodgings in the good part of town—he interpreted these as further evidence that the Virgin's prophecy, as well as Makary's from years before, would be fulfilled. All would unfold as he had been told. He had no idea Duchess Militsa, who initiated the craze in spiritualism, was a close friend of Madame Katkoff. Militsa had made such a success of séances that they were no longer avant-garde, and before they became as tired as the next parlor game, she replaced them with Father. Within a month of his arrival in the city, he'd become a fixture in her sitting room, with its walls covered in green silk, its heavy sterling sconces and samovar. It required a Militsa, married to Tsar Nikolay's cousin and intent on continuing her reign as the hostess whose invitations were prized above all others, to make an unwashed, uncouth, sexually incontinent peasant with an un-barbered beard into the most sought-after sensation in Petersburg. The aristocracy had never seen a man like my father. They looked into his blue eyes, eyes he fixed on theirs with a relentlessness they'd have called rude in one of their own set, and concluded he was authentic in a way they were not. A member of the true *Rus*.

A holy man named Father Grigory—perhaps she should bring him to the palace? That was the question Militsa asked Alexandra Fyodorovna, who practically advertised herself as a religious ma-niac. The one she asked herself was: what better way to secure her fortunes than to inspire firmly and forever the tsarina's gratitude?

A Prophecy

· · · · ·

"YOU MIGHT JUST WANT to wash your hands before we go," Militsa suggested to my father a few hours before they were expected at the palace. Hand-washing was the least of it. It was her intention to make him thoroughly presentable. She was starting modestly, so as not to alarm him.

"For Mamochka? The mother of all Russians should know how dirty are her children's hands! Take those away."

Militsa had come to Father carrying new clothes for him to wear to his audience with the tsarina. Shoes, trousers, and a long black cassock.

"What do you think?" Father said to her. "You think I want to be confused with a priest who serves the worldly Church? I have nothing to do with those thieves and liars!"

"Of course, Father Grigory. Forgive me, please. It was stupid of me. I suppose I was trying to be helpful," Militsa said. Inside, below the carefully applied veneer of polite self-deprecation, she silently cursed my father for his pigheadedness. How was she to bring a person like him to a palace? It was one thing to allow him to lounge about her house with his filthy boots on her silk cushions—actually, it made quite a favorable impression on her guests when they saw how their once acquisitive hostess's attention had moved on from worldly to spiritual inquiries—and another to bring a genuinely filthy person, a person who smelled as if he didn't bathe, to meet the tsarina, the most high of the highest echelon of society. Even if she was a completely hopeless, holier-than-thou, stick-in-the-mud killjoy.

Now if she, Militsa, were Alexandra Fyodorovna, she would have turned that silly cloud to an advantage! Everyone wants what the tsarina has, everyone always does; she's the *tsarina*. It's a law of physics almost—a force like gravity. Why, after Louis Quatorze had surgery on his rectum to cure a fistula, half the French nobility went clamoring after their physicians to arrange to have their perfectly healthy derrières cut apart with a scalpel, and this was before anesthesia. But in a case like that of the cloud, every woman would be stuck pining for what only the tsarina could have. Other women, rich enough women, could afford jewels as extravagant as a queen's—after all, Militsa shopped at Fabergé too—and they could wear prim, fusty gowns like hers if they liked, made by the tsarina's very own dressmaker, whom she happily shared, should anyone want him, which they did not. Fashion had taken a blow when Alexandra Fyodorovna ascended the throne and ushered in the age of dowdy frumpitude.

But who could pull off the trick of her own private weather? If Alexandra Fyodorovna went to balls and enjoyed herself, if she did as she was supposed to do, which was to preside like a fairy godmother over all of society, then she'd be out and about, pulling her cloud behind her up and down the Nevsky Prospekt, in and out of the most recherché shops. She'd dance a quadrille and it would whirl along with her, tango and it would dip daintily, nodding like a flower on a stalk.

Imagine if the Dowager Empress Marie had been the one to arrive in Petersburg with a cloud. Of course, Marie's would have been a fetching little thing, frothy and bubbly, without that awful, looming, dank, and sodden look of Alexandra Fyodorovna's.

Within a season of Marie's arrival in Petersburg as Princess Dagmar of Denmark, affianced to Alexander III, every duchess and grand duchess in the city would have been wearing a cloud-shaped hat. Everywhere one looked there would have been fantastic piles of ostrich or egret dyed a lovely mauve-gray. That sort of hat would require a chassis of wire and tulle to support the feathers; otherwise, it couldn't be built high enough. But tulle and feathers weren't even the slightest bit heavy, and that fantastic genius of a modiste, that mad hatter in the shop on the southeast corner of Gostiny Dvor—whatever that man designed was nothing less than exquisite. He'd put diamonds here and there to sparkle like drops of rain. That might even be attractive. Well, of course it would! It didn't matter if it didn't flatter your face. A hat like that wasn't about your face. It was about the *tsarina*.

And now here Militsa was, the one duchess in the history of the Russian Empire unfortunate enough to have to bring a person who didn't bathe for an audience with a fussbudget of a tsarina! And it was Militsa's own fault—this was the worst of it. Hadn't someone once told her it was a lack of hygiene that inspired the creation of perfume, not bathing being the mother of that particular necessity all those centuries ago, when people made a practice of avoiding water? The great unwashed might get used to their own stink, but the stink of others would still be intolerable. It would have to be eclipsed by a better, stronger smell. And here this Father Grigory person was, looking like a thirteenth-century peasant, a man literally from the Dark Ages. Because that was what Siberia was. That was practically its official definition. Dark Ages.

Father smiled at Militsa. He knew her thoughts. And he knew that in this instance, sophisticated as she might be in the ways of society, she was wrong. Father was beyond and apart from society. His value to the tsarina would be the same as it had been for Militsa: that he was an outsider, unapologetically.

"Come," Father said, and he stood up from the couch and opened his arms. "Come, little one, don't cry."

Militsa put down the clothing and walked toward the open arms. Through his stained and unwashed blouse, his armpits smelled like onions, and like onions they made her eyes water. "Look at me, child," he said, and she tipped her face up and he tipped his down and then she was looking into his eyes. Or he was looking into hers. In either case, the result was the same. Militsa breathed through her mouth while she unbuttoned her dress. It was possible to will yourself not to smell something unpleasant. No doubt doctors had to do it all the time. In a minute he would be on her, and in her, and he'd make her cry out.

Oh, she'd cried plenty of times with other lovers, but this wouldn't be crying. This would be crying out.

"I TAKE IT YOU'VE FORGIVEN ME," Militsa said in the carriage on the way to the palace.

"I take it you've forgiven me," Father answered.

The decorative Abyssinian guards at the door to the royal apartments stood aside and bowed. My father looked the one on the left up, and he looked him down.

"Heavens above," he said. "You're as black as my boot."

"Ssssst!" Militsa spat like a cat, trying to hush him.

"Yes," the man agreed.

"Where are you from?"

"Chicago."

"What's that?"

"It's in Illinois. The United States. Of America."

"America! Heavens be praised!" Father clapped his hands together and whistled with appreciation. By the time he was introduced to the tsarina, he was laughing raucously, jigging down the halls, pinching the fabric of the servants' uniforms with his dirty fingers, touching all the bibelots and weighing them in his hands to know their value.

"Alexandra Fyodorovna, may I present to you Father Grigory, about whom you've heard so many wondrous things." Militsa curtsied deeply, and Father went down on his knees like a child, bowing his head.

"Mamochka," Father said.

When he didn't get up, Alexandra looked at Militsa, who shrugged and made a face that said, as clearly as if she'd uttered the words, *That man is beyond anyone's ken.*

"Father Grigory?" Alexandra said.

"Mamochka."

"Wouldn't you like to . . . I mean, it would be lovely if . . . I do hope you don't think you ought to remain kneeling."

AFTER THE AUDIENCE, the tsarina went to her mauve boudoir and wrote something on a slip of paper that she folded and slipped between the Old and New Testaments of her Bible. Then she took it out and gently kissed it and put it at the feet of her largest Virgin, the one that had no baby in her arms. But that wasn't right, perhaps. She tried one of the ones holding the Christ Child and then put it back between the Testaments. She felt breathless; her heart was beating too quickly.

She wasn't going to share the date with Nicky or even tell him about the meeting with Father Grigory. Not that Nicky would doubt Father Grigory, not after he met him. There wasn't a person on earth who could meet that man and doubt his goodness. But Nicky would worry about the strain on her nerves that hope represented. He'd start watching her that way he did, peering up under his eyebrows with a diagnostic intent he could never disguise. After he'd done it enough times, she'd feel as if there really was something wrong with her, and then it would all begin again; she'd end up having to lie down for a month.

So she kept it hidden until September 23, 1904. And when Alyosha began to bleed and no doctor could stop it, she showed the paper to Nikolay Alexandrovich.

"Alyosha's birthday," the tsar said when he saw it. "You can't think I've forgotten that."

"No no. Of course not. It's just that . . . Nicky, listen to me. I wanted you to see the paper because I wrote that date down more than a year ago. The *starets* Militsa brought to see me, Father Grigory—"

"Someone else was telling me about a Father Grigory. A sort of peasant madman. He's taken over my cousin's house entirely. He's—"

"Nicky."

"What?"

"Listen to me, Nicky."

"I am, dearest. Tell me."

"Father Grigory gave me the date. He asked God, and God told him we would have a son on that date. And we did. Alyosha was born on the day Father Grigory said he would be." Alexandra held the paper out to her husband, who looked at it again without taking it from her hand. It was hard to read his expression under his beard. "You don't think I'm imagining things, do you, Nicky?" she asked.

"Of course not. Why would I? Some people do have . . . what do you call them? Premonitions. He had a premonition, and because he's a simple sort of person he calls it God, but it's—"

"Nicky. You have to have him brought here, for the baby. Please, Nicky, I beg you, please—please do it for me. Indulge me, Nicky. Please."

"My poor dear girl," he said. "Let me hold you."

"Nicky, Nicky, please. Please, Nicky. What harm could it do? If you don't believe in Father Grigory, or in the idea of a person like him, that doesn't matter. It doesn't. I don't care."

"Alex—"

"I'm suffering so terribly. Please, Nicky. I think he's dying. He will if the bleeding doesn't stop, and it doesn't. It just goes on and—"

"Darling girl, my poor darling girl. Alex, you haven't slept. You'll soon be ill if you don't sleep. You have to leave him with the nurse for at least a few hours a night."

"Are you even listening to me, Nicky? Our son is going to die. He will bleed to death. *Our son*. Father Grigory can help him. Please, he's—Nicky, he isn't even two months old."

"Alex!"

"Nicky!"

"Masha!" Alyosha patted the cushion on the divan. "We've got another hour before dinner," he said, lying back, pulling me on top of him. "And, look, the guard is at it again, his finger in his ear."

"There must be something stuck in there, the way it commands his attention."

"I hope it's poisonous, whatever it is. I hope it's a venomous spider, and that it's made its—"

"Stop. You promised, Alyosha."

"Promised what?"

"You know. Nothing below the waist."

"Ah, yes. The Marchioness of Queensberry strikes again."

"Who?"

" 'That no person is to hit his adversary when he is down,' " he recited. " 'Or seize him by the ham, the breeches, or any part below the waist.' It's one of the rules governing boxing matches only it was established by the Marquess, not the Marchioness, of Queensberry. Well, actually, before the marquess revised the rules they were called the London Prize—"

"I'm not your adversary, Alyosha."

"You are when you refuse me what I want." I pulled my hand away, and he took it back. "Just your hand, Masha. Only your hand. Please." I pulled it away again.

"Oh, fine. Tell me a story about someone else. I'm sick of hearing about myself."

"I can't. You've driven them all out of my head with your . . . your . . ."

"Well, tell me something. I'm so bored. I know, tell me the first thing you remember."

"A horse," I said without hesitation. I don't think I have any childhood memories that don't include horses.

"Really? Not your mother or father?"

"I suppose the horses made a bigger impression."

"Whatever do you mean?"

"They would have to have, right there in the house." Alyosha looked so astonished I began to laugh. "Where I come from, all but the wealthiest landowners live with their animals. For most of the year we need the heat of their bodies near our own. Why would we live separately and less comfortably than we could when we slept in the same room with the livestock?"

"You're serious? You're not teasing me?"

"I swear it," I said.

"Why didn't you tell me before?"

"I don't know—probably because it seems so natural to me. It would have felt like announcing we had mice in the woodpile or icicles hanging from the eaves in the winter."

My life began with horses as much as with humans. As soon as I could stand, I was walking under their great bellies and between their stamping feet. I don't remember ever being afraid of their size. Money changed things, though. Once Father had become an established celebrity, half of Petersburg had paid him for one favor or another. Almost all of it he gave away, to those who were destitute, to the nuns who cared for the indigent, and, really, to anyone who asked for it. He didn't like to have to use it or even to touch it, muttering about God and mammon and serving the right master. Still, each time he arrived home after a spell away, he'd take off his overcoat and the rubles—paper money and coins as well—would pour out of his pockets, all of it jumbled up and most of the bills crumpled together into wads that Dimitri took great delight in smoothing out. Dimitri didn't understand much about money, but something inspired him to handle each bill with a care approaching reverence, and he was especially pleased—so much that he had to run in circles around the ironing board—if Mother would allow him to watch as she ironed the bills flat before putting them away. She was saving them for something: a second story on the house, and a stone chimney with hearths on both floors.

I didn't care for the new story on the house. I saw no reason our mother shouldn't make herself happy, but I missed the horses when I came home in the summer. I wouldn't have wanted them with me in an apartment in St. Petersburg, but in Pokrovskoye it felt unnatural to be separated. Especially at night, after I had gone to bed and could hear them whickering and sighing a floor below and out of reach.

I rode every day I could when I was home, in all but the most inclement weather. At the prospect of returning to Siberia, I thought of the horses before I did my mother, who regretted having encouraged what she considered my unnatural fixation on them. Often during the winter when I was a child, even one as young as four or five, Father found me lying on Valentine's back, my face buried in his mane, my legs hanging limp—asleep. He didn't think to lift me off. I was a little girl, but he knew I was safe there. Mother didn't believe that, though. She hated Valentine, especially after I lost my front teeth, a good year ahead of time, by falling off and hitting my face when he tore across a field. But it was never that he'd thrown me, and he always came back to where I'd fallen, standing guard over me like a warhorse. If I was still lying on the ground catching my breath, he'd push my shoulder with his nose until I got myself up. I was never frightened, and there was never any reason to be. It just didn't occur to me.

I rode in St. Petersburg, without a saddle or a bridle—much to the astonishment of other riders in Dubki Park. There was a stable there, and horses for hire, and I spent as many as I wanted of the rubles Father kept stuffed in a chamber pot under his desk, much to Dunia and Varya's disgust. He'd laugh whenever either of them tried to move the bills to a drawer. "No," he'd say, "that's the place for it. The root of all evil, with a smell worse than shit."

Spiderweb

. . . . .

THE POLICE CAME to the apartment on Gorokhovaya Street. It was the first day of the New Year, 1917. They took Varya and me to the Petrovsky Bridge to show us where they'd dragged a body out from under the ice. We hadn't seen Father for three days—no one had. The night he went out and didn't return, Varya and I had hidden his boots. It was an old game with us. From the time we came to live in Petersburg, we hid Father's boots when we wanted him to stay home with us instead of disappearing for hours to dine with his important friends, few of whom genuinely cared for his welfare. That night, it had been Yusupov's palace to which he'd been headed, and rather than laugh, as he usually did at our childish game—for it was one of those things between a father and his grown daughters, preserved from childhood, a gesture of affection—he grew unexpectedly angry and shouted and cursed us for making him late for a host who might consider tardiness rude. He kicked over the little side table on which Dunia had left her mending basket, scattering pins and spools and scraps of fabric, and we hurried to fetch his boots from where we'd hidden them. He wouldn't allow me to help him but pulled the boots on by himself, taking the service stairs into the alley to avoid the police stationed in front of the building. I thought to stop him, to alert the police (who were there for his own safety, under orders from the tsarina) as to where he was headed, but I didn't. I remember thinking how useless it would be to try to sway my father from his pigheaded course, but I should have tried. I don't know why I didn't. I was tired, probably. It was exhausting living with my father. He had no idea how we fretted over him and his recklessness.

Before the collapse of the empire, Felix Yusupov was the richest man in all of Russia, heir to uncountable fortunes made on her fur trade and her mines. Married to Princess Irina, a niece of Tsar Nikolay, he was an eccentric man, by all accounts, with a face of surprising beauty, and he had a passion for dressing in his mother's gowns and jewels and finding men to tease, rough men he found in places aristocrats generally didn't visit. Because of this habit and his delicate features, it was said he preferred men to women, sexually. Many times he came to our apartment under the pretense of soliciting help from Father. He complained of headaches and ringing in his ears, and if Father was out he'd wait for him in our parlor, lying on the couch in ladies' underclothes. When he came home, Father ignored Yusupov's peculiar attire and took him at his word, holding Yusupov's head in his hands and praying over it— as if it were the head of an honorable man, even though for months it had been rumored that Yusupov was conspiring to put an end to Father's influence over the tsarina.

One look at Yusupov was all most people needed to see he was the type who'd rather murder a man than lose his social position. But Father, who could not conceive of killing, not even in the context of war, never understood he had enemies who would resort to murder. His martyrdom had been predicted, he foresaw he would be killed, but for Father this knowledge wasn't attached to a particular person or persons. Once he'd met a man, he couldn't imagine that man as a murderer, much less his murderer. He knew Yusupov's intentions, he always knew what people tried to hide, so he must have trusted he could overcome these by force of will, naïve enough to believe love could disarm an assassin, that he could rely on summoning that power from on high. Or he was ready for it, perhaps, ready for the end. What I do know is this: my father wasn't afraid on the night he walked into the trap laid by his enemies. He was angry with us for hiding his boots, but he wasn't afraid. He never expected to escape his fate. God's will would, necessarily, be done.

The tsarina, however, was not willing for the prophecy of his martyrdom to be fulfilled. For months we'd lived under police watch. Every time we left the apartment, there they were, in their black automobile. Meant to protect him, all they did was take notes on his comings and goings, fueling rumors. There was no way to prove he hadn't ravished the tsarina, a mother of five, and neither would there be a means to establish that Father hadn't had sexual intercourse with her daughters—not after the way their bodies were handled following the execution, thrown into the back of a military truck and taken, before dawn, to an abandoned mine where they were hacked to pieces, doused with gasoline and lit on fire. Whatever wouldn't burn was thrown down a shaft. But once the Bolsheviks had seized control from the provisional government, their investigation into my father's influence on the tsar and tsarina forced Anna Vyrubova to go before a physician, who examined her and found her hymen intact. She was a virgin.

My father had intercourse with many women, hundreds of women who threw themselves at him, who, given the chance, searched our apartment for his nail parings or hairs that had fallen from his head, who stole tea glasses bearing smudges in the shape of his lips. But he wouldn't have touched the tsarina or the Romanov girls or Anna Vyrubova. Often, Anna was the one sent to fetch Father to Tsarskoe Selo, where he would tend to Alyosha and then come to Alexandra Fyodorovna's private apartments to pray with her before her ikons. That's why it was rumored he was

Anna's lover as well as the tsarina's and her daughters'. Servants knew not to talk about Alyosha's illness, but they didn't extend that discretion to my father's comings and goings.

The empire was crumbling, and a few monarchists decided there was no hope of saving it without first removing my father from what they mistook as a position of political power. Yusupov and his accomplices—three other aristocrats who dreamed of the glory that would be theirs once they snuffed out the pernicious influence of the sinister Father Grigory—lured my father to a late supper at Yusupov's palace on the Fontanka Canal. There, they promised, he would at last meet Yusupov's wife, the beautiful Irina, who was hosting a private party and would come for an audience with the famous *starets* as soon as her guests departed. In fact, Irina was far away, at the Yusupov's villa in the Crimea, the party nothing more than a cranked-up Victrola playing at top volume. While Father waited downstairs for Irina, his assassins fed him cakes poisoned with cyanide and glass after glass of wine with more cyanide. It was enough, the coroner said, to kill a team of horses, but it had no effects on Father. Yusupov and his accomplices shot him in the head and in the back, and still he escaped. They chased him, still upright and lurching forward into the snowy night, to shoot him once more, bind his wrists and ankles with rope, and drop him through a hole in the frozen river.

THE DIVER WHO FOUND FATHER was still there when Varya and I arrived. He was a huge man, his furred chest caked with white grease—it looked like lard—to keep the cold water from killing him. He'd swum under the ice, breathing air through a tube, until he encountered the body of a man drifting slowly toward the frozen sea, his sleeve caught on a set of springs from a bed or couch someone had dropped in the Neva. Or maybe it had fallen in from the back of a truck passing over the Petrovsky Bridge. The drowned man wore a wool coat and boots and had a long beard and long hair that floated up from his skull. The diver tied a rope around the man's chest, high up under his armpits, tore his sleeve away from the wire that held it, and then climbed up out of the hole and gave the other end of the rope to the police. Wrapped in a bearskin, the diver drank from a steaming glass of tea while the police pulled on the rope. He'd never searched for a corpse before, only for lost objects, and his encounter with Father under the ice seemed to have unnerved him. He kept shaking his head from side to side, slowly, as if registering a mute refusal.

It was snowing when they brought us to the river, nine in the morning and still dark. Already a circle of onlookers had gathered—nothing like what was to come, but a crowd nonetheless, growing bigger. Father's body had been carried to a small wooden structure on the bank, a shed of some kind, where he'd been stripped naked and laid out on a bench. A physician was present, inspecting his wounds and dictating to an assistant.

"Do you know this person?" the police inspector asked. Poor Varya: for all her pretensions at adulthood, she was only sixteen and seeing what no child at any age should ever be forced to see, her father dead and wearing nothing more than his wounds. They had a brazier going and his frozen body was thawing. The water that ran from his hair was stained with blood and dripped red on the floor; little rivulets ran toward our feet. Varya kept backing up to avoid the blood touching her shoes, but I left my feet where they were. I kept those shoes and wore them with their stains until they fell into pieces, and then I kept the pieces. I have them with me even now.

There was a hole where a bullet had entered the very center of Father's forehead. I remember noting how perfectly placed was the hole and thinking, of course, Yusupov would shoot a gun that way, as straight as the nose he looked down when he was aiming. He was incapable of untidiness or asymmetry. Aside from the bullet hole, Father's skull had been broken with an ax or a boot, his poor head with its beautiful thoughts. No one understood what was in him. The intelligentsia, they were too stupid to recognize simplicity. I signed a paper of some sort, testifying to the body being that of my father, and Varya and I were taken back to Gorokhovaya Street. We didn't imagine we'd ever return to the apartment, so we gathered our belongings.

I kept a few drawings my father had made, any I could lay my hands on: the one of the Virgin in the silver forest, and a few of animals and birds. We divided the photographs. A few included Father with a member of the imperial family, as the Romanovs, every one of them, were camera mad. Even under arrest, they took pleasure in posing and photographing one another. I packed my clothes, an ikon my mother had given me when I first left home for Petersburg, a shirt belonging to Father, the cross he always wore and that the police had allowed me to take from around his neck, his Bible, which he knew by heart but couldn't read. I'd unpack and repack those few things a half dozen times before Boris and I reached Paris.

Belgrade. Budapest. Prague. Berlin. Frankfurt. Though I know it can't have been so, my memories of each of the cities, of two years spent in a succession of cities, all take place in the same one-room apartment, unheated and unplumbed, a dirty communal toilet and sink at the end of a long, drafty corridor paved with broken tiles. One window, its cracks stuffed with rags and paper, admitting the cold. At night, in bed, Boris and I were forced to lie so as to align as much flesh as possible and thus hold on to the warmth of our bodies.

. . .

"Who will tell Mother?" I asked Dunia, whom we found sitting on a stool before the fire, chewing on her apron strings.

"I cannot," she said, shaking and shaking her head after she'd spat out the strings. "Please, Masha, I cannot."

So it was I who called Anna Vyrubova to ask her assistance in sending a telegram to Pokrovskoye. She was the only one I could think to ask for help. Assuming such a thing as a telegram was even possible in January, when the town lay unconscious as a bear during winter's deepest cold. Mother and poor dull-witted Dimitri in their chairs before the hearth, eating and sleeping there as well, as the rest of the rooms were sealed off until the April thaw made them habitable once again. In winter we kept the samovar in the middle of the one upstairs room, opposite the fire, and if you put yourself between samovar and hearth, it was warm enough to remove your coat, and your fingers were not too numb and stiff to mend clothes or turn the pages of a book.

January 1, 1917. Pokrovskoye would have been invisible from both road and river. After a blizzard or two, not only roofs but also walls were coated with snow, fences buried in drifts. Often the wind was so fierce it snatched away your footprint as soon as you lifted your foot from the ground beneath you. The only evidence of life seemed to suggest arachnid rather than human occupation, as the town was covered by a weblike collection of ropes crisscrossing every which way, from each house to its woodpile and its barn, to the church, the store, the post office. The custom had been adopted generations before, when one of our town's citizens lost himself on his way to fetch the midwife. Turned around and around by a blinding whirlwind of snow, he must have walked with one hand before his face, protecting his eyes, while the other felt for any recognizable thing, a trough or a gatepost, the side of a barn. But he never found anything. Tragedy on all fronts: the mother died; the baby died inside her; when the skies cleared, the husband was found kneeling with his forehead frozen to the trunk of a tree not even fifty yards from the midwife's cottage.

After this, by October all the people of Pokrovskoye had lines tied from their houses to anyplace they were likely to go. Because the church stood in the middle of town, ropes like the radial filaments of a colossal web connected that central structure to each house, as there wasn't anyone who didn't go to Mass, not even the village idiot (who was not my brother but a man we called Major General Sweeper, as sweeping was his one consuming vocation. He wore a uniform left him by an uncle who died fighting Napoleon at Smolensk, and he carried his broom like a weapon when he wasn't furiously chasing dust). The rest of the ropes sprawled out like the spiral produced by an especially untidy race of spider.

"Wait," Alyosha asked when I told him about the custom, which spread to other towns in the area. "Aren't all spiders' webs alike?"

"Of course not. Every spider spins a web particular to its . . . to its . . . you know, particular species. Imagine not knowing a thing like that." That was what happened to people who grew up in cities, I supposed.

Who would deliver a telegram in Pokrovskoye on January 1? There were winter weeks when the postmaster didn't bother coming to work. But that was before Father, by virtue of his connection to the tsar, puffed up the vanity of our town. I sent word of Father's death, prepared to receive no reply, and got twenty within an hour, pious wishes, many of them, from those who had openly mocked Father when he was among the living.

Travel impossible, the one from Mother began. *By the will of God the duties are yours, Masha. Dunia and Varya will help.*

"What is she saying?" Anna Vyrubova asked, when I showed her the message. "What does she mean?"

"She's talking about the body. Father's body. It must be prepared for burial. As it's winter there's no barge to bring her to the train in Tobolsk, supposing the trains are even running. She cannot come here, and I can't get Father home to her."

"But what is she saying? What does she mean?"

"He will have to be brought to me. The police cannot keep my father's body." I looked at Anna. She had one of those fleshy faces that are never immobile but always quivering with some unarticulated emotion, whatever it might be.

"What do you mean?" she said again.

"I'm saying it is for us to do. His family must prepare him for burial."

"Here?" Anna squeaked. "Here at Tsarskoe Selo?" For already my sister and I had been moved to the Alexander Palace, wards of the tsar.

"Yes. If this is where we are to stay. I must—my mother has asked it.

"Although," I said, seeing Anna's face crumple at the idea of such an imperative, "perhaps it might be arranged for us to wash and dress Father at home, back on Gorokhovaya Street? His body is in the hands of the Petersburg police, so it is close to the apartment, where his clothes and other things I need are. And Dunia—she's there as well. She can help."

Stitches Large and Small

. . . . .

TWO OFFICERS CARRIED Father up the building's back stairs, like a delivery of coal or potatoes. He was frozen again, his body as stiff as rigor mortis could have made it, but by now almost a week had passed since his murder. Once they thawed, his limbs would move; his fingers and his spine as well. He was wrapped in layers of coarse cloth, and the officers, breathing heavily from the climb, set him on end and leaned him against the doorjamb. "Where do—"one said, and I interrupted him, impatient to have them lay his body down.

"There." I pointed at the table at which Varya, Dunia, Father, and I had gathered most evenings to eat. We had a bathtub, but Father was at least six feet tall. Even had his limbs been pliable, we'd have had to fold him into it, and once we had it would have been a trial to get him out. The table was long enough to seat four to a side, but when the officers laid him down on it, his feet stuck out over the end.

"Thank you," Dunia said, and she curtsied as she bid the officers a good day, reflexively polite under even such peculiar circumstances as these. They left through the apartment's front door, the shorter of the two wiping his palms against the seat of his trousers, as if to rid them of the memory of so distasteful an errand. Whoever had tied Father up in his winding sheet was a professor of knots, but Dunia, who hated to cut a good length of twine, waved my scissors away and went on picking at them with her fingers. Perhaps it did take, as she said, only minutes to untie them all, but the last of the gray winter daylight was seeping away and it was dusk and time to light the lamps when she coiled the unbroken length of it around her fingers. She put the looped twine in her apron pocket and gave it a pat. I could see it was something she would keep, something she held valuable, whether it was Father who made it so or what she considered the inherent value of a long piece of twine. Dunia's passions, like her reverence for Singer sewing machines, tended to the pragmatic. Or maybe I wanted to think of her as lacking in romantic attachments. I wanted to believe that her having provided my father sexual relief had been a chore like any other, washing the sheets no more involving than what she'd done while lying on them.

Unwrapping the body was a clumsy operation. To give us enough room to work, Dunia and I pushed all the chairs back from the table and against the wall. I had insisted Varya return with me to the apartment, but as soon as we began she ran away and hid herself in Father's bedroom. Dunia took hold of the crude winding cloth and pulled, while I made sure Father's slowly turning body didn't roll from table to floor. Under the layers of sackcloth was one of linen, stained yellow in places, a long, rust-colored line where the fabric had pressed against the autopsy incision. From the base of his neck down to his groin, he had been cut open and sewn shut with large, clumsy stitches. The incision was a straight line, neatly centered except for the interruption of one small semicircle: a detour around the umbilicus. A coroner, perhaps the same one we saw examining Father after he was pulled from the river, had opened him just as he would his Gladstone bag. He'd cut into his stomach, looking for his last meal of poisoned cakes and wine. For that's what all the newspapers had reported, how much cyanide my father had swallowed without its having any effect on him. Dunia took the piece of linen with the long rusty stain, folded it once and then again, until she had pressed it into a small square she set on the shelf where we kept our bowls and dinner plates. To whom did that belong, I wondered? Mother? Me?

The bed where Dunia slept was in an alcove adjoining the kitchen, and off its mattress Dunia pulled a sheet and handed it to me. "Do it as you would if we were changing linen on a sickbed," she said. She took hold of Father's arm and cold flank and pulled him onto his side, hauling his body toward her so I could spread the sheet over the part of the table that wasn't under him. When she let the body go, it rolled back to where it had been. Then we traded sides of the table and repeated the motions, and when we were done he was lying on Dunia's bedding.

"Won't it get soiled?" I said stupidly.

"We'll need it to turn him. After we wash the front, we'll have to wash the back."

I nodded. The two of us stood, each on one side of the table, and looked at the body between us. The scar on my father's flank gave me a turn. I knew what it was, but I hadn't remembered its size. June 28, 1914. The Romanovs were on holiday, in the Crimea; Alyosha was in good health; Father, Varya, and I had gone home to Pokrovskoye, unaware we'd been followed by a woman from Petersburg. Spring was short that year, and the summer days were long and already uncomfortably hot. The horses slept fitfully downstairs, swishing their tails in the heat. Fruit on the trees ripened early and fell before it could be picked. As I lay in my bed at night, I'd hear the thud of plums dropping from their branches onto the ground below. Used to the bustle of the city, I found it too quiet to sleep after dusk and had fallen into the habit of reading all night and sleeping during days that were too hot to enjoy on the prickly back of a sweating, lethargic horse. That's what I was doing when Father was attacked—sleeping. Having received a telegram from an acquaintance asking his help in securing a political appointment, he was walking to the post office to send his reply. But the telegram had been a ruse; the conspirator who followed us home was lying in wait for Father and accosted him in the street outside the door to the post office. No sooner had Father put a coin in the left hand of what appeared to be a beggar than Khionya Gusyeva—for that was the name of the wicked woman who was said to have been a prostitute back in Petersburg—stabbed him with the right, dragging her knife upward and nearly disemboweling him on the street. He walked, staggered, back home, holding his intestines so they wouldn't spill out from his side, and I woke during the ensuing commotion, one neighbor screaming for a doctor, others running in and out the front door, my brother covering his eyes and bellowing the way he did when frightened, Varya whimpering and wringing her hands.

Mother and the doctor laid Father on the kitchen table, cut off his blood-soaked trousers, and found a wound the length of his forearm, from it protruding wet pink bubbles of flesh. Surgeries, one and then another and another, were required to prevent peritonitis. It took many months for Father to improve, and he never recovered completely. He was in pain for the remaining two and a half years of his life; he slept poorly and grew to depend on tinctures of opium or chloral hydrate added to his glass of Madeira for the few hours of oblivion they promised.

"Come, light the stove," Dunia said as she filled a kettle.

"Varya," I called down the corridor, and, noting how it hurt my throat to raise my voice, "find his cloak and prayer rope." No answer. "Varya!" I said, louder. I knew I was coming down with something worse than a cold.

"Shouldn't he . . . don't you think he might want to wear his better clothes?" Varya answered after a silence, referring to the chest filled with blouses he had been given over the past years, gifts he never wore, in every color of silk, with collars, cuffs, and hems embroidered by his admirers, a few by the tsarina herself, whose needle produced work as subtle as an artist's brush, motifs of flowers, vines, birds.

"No," I said. "It has to be the cloak." For I intended to return Father to the days when he had no enemies, before he ever set foot in Petersburg. To a time when none of us could have imagined that anyone would ever bear him malice, much less find reason to kill him. "On the top shelf, Varya. You'll need a step stool. It's all there—the cloak, his plain blouse, the old tunic and trousers." With tattered hems and holes at the knees. Everything washed and folded and set carefully aside and out of reach, as if he'd planned for the day when he would once again put them on and leave this city. At last it had arrived.

Varya came back with the clothing and stopped at the kitchen door, her face averted.

"What are you waiting for?" I said, annoyed by her hesitating, her tendency to do any chore in twice the time it would have taken me.

"His eyes," she said.

"What about them?"

"Are they closed?"

"What does it matter?" I said. "He can't see you, you know."

"I won't come in unless they're closed. I won't, Masha. You can't make me."

I pushed the hair up off his brow, where it was matted, half-stuck there with blood. I swallowed. "The left is swollen shut and the right is half open, no more," I told her.

Varya began to cry. It wasn't the sound to which I objected but the way she tried to stop it, holding her breath and then, when she couldn't hold it any longer, letting it out with a rush and the bleat of an inadequately swallowed sob. "All right," I said, "all right." I tried to gently force the parted eyelids together, but as soon as I took my fingers away, the lids returned to where they had been, revealing a sliver of pupil and a bit of blue. The white was red, completely shot with blood.

I don't know that there is anything more unsettling than the open dead eyes of a person you love, eyes that can no longer return your gaze. Back home, in Siberia, it was said that if you were to look into the eyes of a corpse, you would see your own death reflected back at you. Looking at Father, the only thing I understood was why people covered the dead's faces, blindfolded them, weighed their eyelids down with coins—whatever it took to stop the devil from speaking through their silence, from telling you you were look-ing at yourself. Although I don't know why people said it was the devil talking. God would say the same thing, I think. "Never mind, Varya," I said. "This isn't—don't do anything you don't want."

Now that I'd released her, Varya stepped into the room, her face averted from the table and its occupant. She laid Father's clothes on the seat of one of the chairs pushed against the wall and crept away. I almost went after her, but there was no way to pity my sister without pitying myself, and that—that wasn't possible, not now. Dunia said nothing. Standing at the head of the table, one foot braced against its trestle, she took hold of the sheet and pulled Father's body toward her until his feet slid up onto the table's other end.

"All right, then," she said, "water must be hot by now, hot enough."

He was still frozen, enough that his heavy head didn't fall back when it was no longer supported by the table, but it looked so un-natural that I couldn't help but put my hands under it while Dunia placed a basin on the floor below, took the kettle from the gas ring, and poured water over his hair. Saturated with blood, it spilled down into the basin in steaming red streams. We traded places. She held his head and I unwrapped a cake of imported soap, a gift I'd saved for a special occasion. This wasn't the one I'd imagined, of course, but I was glad to have something a little ceremonial. I lathered Father's hair, and then Dunia rinsed away the suds, stained brown, and I soaped the hair again and still once again until, after the third washing, the tinge of blood faded away, the soap foamed up white. There was a long gash in his scalp, and each time Dunia poured water from the kettle's spout, it lifted the flap of skin, showing me the crushed bone beneath. He'd cheated death so often I'd come to believe he'd never die. But he was mortal after all, my father, made of flesh and bone that could be crushed.

"I think . . . I think we had better . . ." I said, staring at the gash and feeling so sick at the sight of it that I failed to say what I meant: that the wound had to be closed somehow, his body made whole, to the degree we could. But when I looked up, I saw that already Dunia had fetched her mending basket and was searching in it for thread the same color as his hair. I pulled the sheet so that once again his head rested on the table and his feet hung off, and Dunia set a lamp next to his head. With her needle and thread she sewed the wound closed with tiny stitches. When she'd finished she bit the thread off and, with her lips so close to the place she'd sewn, kissed Father's wet head.

I was surprised I could see that and not cry—a measure of my shock. Dunia had done so good a job that even when his hair was combed back from his face, the gash was no longer visible. The soap, made with oil from the laurel plant, had a delicate, astringent smell, and I turned the bar over and over in my wet hands to make the lather to wash his face, his ears, his throat. So strange to push my fingers through his beard and feel lifeless cold skin beneath, strange to feel his nose and his brow, to wash the crease beside each nostril and wipe the foam away from his lips, as if it mattered. As if he would taste and find it bitter.

Neck, shoulders, chest: we took turns soaping a cloth, running it over his torso, rinsing it, wringing it, washing the skin again. At first Dunia tried to follow and catch the dripping water with her basin, then gave up and set bowls and saucepans on the floor under the table's edge. But it didn't matter; everything was wet, slippery with suds.

"Towels," I said, going to fetch them from the closet.

We worked on, in silence, as night pressed against the windows, and there was peace in the room, a calm that, like the warm soapy water, washed over and over me. Though I'd never before readied a body for burial, it was as if I had rehearsed all these unfamiliar motions, accomplished them so many times I required no direction, and Dunia and I spoke little as we worked.

"Varya?" I called every so often, wanting her with us, not for her help but because I saw how she was hiding from the one thing that could bring her any solace.

The body, doused over and over with hot water, eventually thawed in the warm kitchen, whose walls had begun to sweat and drip. Soon it was possible to flex the elbows, pull his arms far enough from his sides to soap his armpits. I looked at his ragged fingernails, which were unusually clean—from his three days in the river, I guessed. For some time I considered them, then I took Dunia's sewing scissors from the basket and, careful not to nick the damp, wrinkled tips of his fingers, cut each nail. So many years of city life. My father's arms were not strong and sunburned as they had been when I was small. The black hairs stood out against skin that was pale, white. Clean and manicured, my father's graceful hands now looked like a saint's or a nobleman's. They looked as if they'd been fashioned to hold a chalice. The only thing to mar their beauty was the one fingernail that had remained black for years now.

"What happened?" Varya and I had asked, curious to know what an exorcism was, when he came home the night the finger was injured.

"Nothing," Father said. "She fell asleep and stayed asleep for many hours, and when she woke up she'd forgotten why she'd been put to bed.

"There's only this. " He showed us the index finger of his right hand, the flesh under the nail bruised.

"What is it?" we asked.

"The devil," he said, smiling. "He nipped me on the way out."

I never forgot the girl's name; it was Elizavetta, and she'd lived in the Convent of the Holy Trinity. The prioress had summoned Father. She said Elizavetta had been visited on eleven consecutive nights by a demon with which she'd had intercourse, and now she was suffering convulsions and vomiting up pins and feathers, buttons, bottle caps. She blasphemed and made lascivious gestures. Her personality changed abruptly from that of a sweetly selfless, shy young woman to a coarsened whore who alluded to sexual behaviors assuredly unknown to a virginal nun in a convent. She told of a fantastic past life in which she had been a temple prostitute who performed intercourse with strangers. She'd lived in ancient Babylon, she said, and to ensure the fertility of crops, she had to open her thighs to anyone who came to worship Astarte.

"Hush, child," my father had said. He sent the prioress away, pulled the blankets off the girl, bathed her, dressed her in fresh nightclothes, fed her broth, and sat for two days with his hand on her forehead. He allowed her to get up and urinate in a chamber pot, but that was all. If she tried to leave her bed, he held her down. Finally, he told us, the fever broke, and then she had no memory of what had happened to her.

If only someone could have done that for Father, I couldn't help thinking, if only I had been able to keep him home, safe, until the devil had passed him by. I went from fingers to toes, washing between them, cutting their nails as well, and Dunia, seeing I had skirted my father's private parts, washed these without comment. She soaped his thighs and I his shins; each of us took the knee closer to her own side of the table. We turned him then, and that was difficult. Even with both of us on one side, pulling and lifting the sheet, it was no easy thing to turn Father onto his front so we could soap his back. And no easy thing to discover there were another two bullet holes in the poor man, one just inside his left shoulder blade and another a few inches below it. By the time we had finished washing his body and had turned him back over so he was again faceup, we needed baths ourselves, soaked as we were with perspiration and dirty water. I used my own comb to part his wet hair as he used to do, down the center. My hands were raw and waterlogged, my fingers stung, and my knees shook. I sat in one of the chairs we'd pushed against the wall.

"We'll take a break?" I said, and Dunia nodded. She looked at me with her hands on her hips.

"You have a fever," she said. "I can see it in your eyes." I shrugged. Dunia confirmed her observation by feeling my forehead and declared she was going to brew tea. I tried not to think about what might be in it. Dunia kept a lot of poisonous-looking dried plants in the pantry.

THE OPEN EYE made no difference once Father was dressed, as it is the custom, when preparing a holy man for burial, to put his cloak on backward and cover his face with the hood. Around his head we placed a crown of paper, upon which I had written the proper words: *Holy God, Holy and Mighty, Holy Immortal one, have mercy on your servant.* In his right hand went his crucifix, in his left a prayer rope with its knots and beads. We tore two strips from the bottom of his cloak and bound them around his body in the customary manner, crossing over his chest, hips, and legs, and then it was done. We mopped and dried the floor and moved him to his bed by dragging the table through the door of his bedroom, first sliding a carpet beneath the legs of the table so it would travel more easily.

"He is ready, Varya," I said to my sister, once Dunia and I had moved the body to the bed and returned the dining table to its place, and she came to sit with us beside him, one of his daughters on each side of the bed, Dunia at its foot.

Dunia had forced her foul-tasting medicinal draft on me and, after I vomited in the sink, told me not to complain, because that had been the result she intended. In the hours remaining until morning, when Sergei Gavriilovich, the coffin-maker, would come to measure Father and build him a box, it was our duty to stay with his body, reading from the Psalter, and we did this, taking turns, passing the book back and forth over his corpse.

Hothouse

.....

"MASHA CAN STAY," Alyosha said to Dr. Botkin, and so I sat in silence, pretending to look out the window while the doctor examined the tsarevich, who answered questions only of a medical nature, and even those with barely a syllable. To sound Alyosha's lungs, Botkin pulled the tsarevich's shirt up over his back, showing me its fair, smooth skin, without a single freckle. Hemophilia hadn't made Alyosha into a boy who looked sickly, and the attitude he maintained when he wasn't in pain suggested that whatever was wrong with him was nothing serious, nothing that wouldn't soon go away. Looking at him attended by his physician, I saw no evidence of April's agonies, when he'd screamed for someone to help him, crying with his head in the tsarina's lap for however long Dr. Botkin allowed Alexandra Fyodorovna, another ailing patient under his care, to sit with her son.

Alyosha's suggesting I forget what he refused to talk about had, of course, only fixed my determination to learn whether he'd ridden the tea tray into the newel post on purpose. Over the past months I'd gone out of my way to pass by the service stairway whenever possible. Half the time it wasn't even conscious, I just found myself there, in the spot from which Alyosha had gone down the stairs, trying to conceive the trajectory that ended in the post. The steps were steep, their treads polished with wear, and they terminated in a cramped landing that, before it was closed off by the Red Guard, had given onto a corridor immediately to the left. I couldn't see how, even if he'd missed the post, the tray wouldn't have carried Alyosha into the wall opposite the last stair. It was only five feet away. One day, I went so far as to reconstruct the accident, with the same tray weighted down with two andirons. But the results weren't consistent, or conclusive. If the irons stayed on the tray, they sometimes hit the wall with it, and sometimes they didn't. Was I being an idiot, as Alyosha said, in imagining he'd harm himself to distract his family from their predicament?

Everything in Alyosha's manner communicated his impatience with Botkin's ministrations. His lips were drawn tight around the thermometer, his arms were crossed; he tapped one foot against the floor. Still somewhat lame, he looked otherwise well. It had been possible for the Romanovs to hide his illness for as long as they did—and preserve the nation's faith in the strength of the dynasty, with its single male heir—because the tsarevich was never seen or photographed unless he was well. Should he require his leg brace, it was concealed.

We remained in silence for a few minutes after Botkin's departure, each of us absorbed in his or her own thoughts, Alyosha imagining exile, no doubt, and the empire's downfall, and I—what did I think about? As long as I devoted myself to distracting Alyosha, I avoided worrying about my future.

"I'll tell you what's mad," Alyosha said, a few minutes later. Though he limped, he could walk now without crutch or brace, and we were approaching the upper garden and the hothouses. "What's mad is that your father gave mine sound political advice. He knew a war against the Central Powers, especially Germany and Austria, was foolish, and he told Father not to declare it. But the

Meddlesomes and the ministers insisted Russia had to protect her borders. Without a single munitions plant east of Moscow, without troop transports. All we have are bodies, hundreds of thousands of soldiers to march into Allied fire, with all their factories and their artillery. Before it's over they'll bring in their armored fighting vehicles and just roll forward over the Russian infantry. They call the armored cars 'tanks.' They pretend they carry water."

"I'm sure Father didn't know any of that." We were in one of the hothouses by now, the door closed behind us, Nagorny in the park outside, the Red Guard uninterested, as it was clear we weren't going to escape by going for a stroll among the plants.

"No. But he had the sense to want to protect the people from being slaughtered. And to see that the rioting had more to do with people starving than with political impulse. I heard him tell my father he should fill the troop cars with grain and send them west to the starving cities, rather than east to pour legions of ill-equipped men into battle. You don't have to be educated to understand that if industry is confined to Moscow and Petersburg and the rest of the country remains as it was in the Dark Ages, Russia will be destroyed. It's common sense, that's all."

"I suppose."

"Are you going to kiss me, Masha?"

"Yes."

"And let me undress you?" He began undoing buttons before I had a chance to answer.

"Stop." My buttoning couldn't catch up with his unbuttoning, and I turned away, annoyed at his presumption.

"What is it?" he asked.

"It's your being imperious. So certain that no one can refuse Tsarevich Alexei Nikolaevich—"

Whatever he demands, I was going to say, but Alyosha had

pinned me, without warning, against the glass wall and his tongue was in my mouth, silencing mine. His hand wasn't in my blouse but under the waistband of my skirt, and my underclothes were as compliant as a prince might expect. The drawstring I thought I'd double-knotted gave way immediately to his seeking hand, as good as inviting it between my legs. The air within the hothouse was so humid on that August morning that enough moisture had condensed on the glass's surface to prevent anyone seeing through with any clarity. Except that he'd forced me right against the wall.

"Someone will see," I said, feeling the wet through my blouse and picturing what it must look like from the outside, my silhouette pressed against the glass. "Alyosha, stop."

But he didn't, not until he was ready, and when he let me go he brought his hand to his mouth, tasting his fingers that had been between my legs, a gesture I found so outrageous—I did then, at eighteen—I couldn't speak. I tied what had come undone, buttoned what had been unbuttoned, straightened my blouse, tucked it back into my skirt, and went outside. It was a cool day for August, heralding the approach of fall, and I was glad for the air on my face. Confused as I was by his touching me the way he had, I could still feel his fingers, where they had been and how they'd moved inside me. He'd put his fingers where I'd never even thought to put my own, and I didn't know which of us to be surprised at—him, for doing such a thing, or me. Was I so innocent, then, to be shocked by what he'd done, and was it shock I felt, or was I running away from what I was afraid I wanted? I was walking—marching—so quickly that by the time I heard Alyosha call my name I was passing the grove of poplar stumps and wondering, as I did whenever I saw them, who would burn the logs that had been cut and stacked by the last tsar of Russia. And then, as I burst though the door, pursued by two guards, I was looking right at him.

"Matryona Grigorievna! Just who I wanted to talk to." The tsar smiled. "You're out of breath," he said. The guards stood, waiting, silent. By now I thought of them as something closer to furniture than people, as they were always there, in uniform, looking bored and rarely initiating eye contact.

"Oh. A little. I was walking outside." I hoped my face betrayed none of what I felt, because I thought he gave me a look of pointed concern, and I had never before seen any but his habitual expression of hearty, avuncular good spirits. It was Tsar Nikolay's innate courtesy, I think, and not pride, which inspired his manufacturing an optimism so clearly counterfeit that it had the effect of conveying his misery better than tears might have done.

"Well, then, Masha, catch it, catch it. I'm not in such a hurry that I can't wait for you to catch your breath." Hands clasped behind his back, he rocked on his military heels and smiled at me under his mustache. It was uncanny how closely Tsar Nikolay resembled his cousin George V, whose refusal of asylum would end in the murder of the tsar, the tsarina, and the five children she bore him. I'd heard it said that whenever the tsar visited England, friends of King George singled him out to talk intimately to a man they assumed was George but was in fact Nikolay. When they were young, the two went so far as to trade clothes and play the kind of pranks for which identical twins are infamous. I thought of that when I bumped into the tsar in the corridor.

"I wanted to tell you as soon as I knew," he said. "We—I—have argued successfully for your release."

"You . . . I mean, we . . . Varya and I? We're to be released? When?"

"Immediately."

"Today?"

"Yes. We will all leave today, as soon as we are packed."

"All of us?" I said, momentarily astonished by what I hoped I'd heard. "We're all to be released, all of us together?"

"No," Tsar Nikolay said. "My family and I are going east. Comrade Kerensky has generously provided for our safety by offering us transport to Tobolsk."

"Tobolsk! Good heavens, that's Siberia," I said, like a simpleton, and I burst into tears.

"Oh, no, Masha." The tsar pulled me into an awkward embrace, which only made me cry harder. "There's no need to worry. You'll see. Everything is going to be fine for us once we're out of the capital. Why, as Alex said, the people of Siberia are your father's people and will be more friendly to . . . to the idea of us."

"But where will you live?" I asked. "How?"

"I'm told the governor's mansion has been barricaded, and some of its grounds as well. We'll be able to plant things there. Vegetables." He said this with a wondering tone, as if surprised by his good fortune. And I nodded, struck dumb at the thought that the tsar had—or imagined he had—been given what he'd wanted all along: a little farm.

I wanted to talk to Alyosha before I told Varya, but I couldn't find him.

"I don't know what you're crying for, Masha," she said as we packed. "We're going to get out of here."

"You won't miss OTMA? Tatiana? All of them?"

"Well, yes, of course. But all the worry is over—they're not going to be harmed, only exiled. And only for as long as the war goes on. Once the Reds are defeated, OTMA and everyone will come back home, here."

"Don't tell me you believe that."

"Why wouldn't I?"

"Because it's a lie."

. . .

By the time Alyosha and his family, along with Botkin and Nagorny, were ready to leave for Tsarskoe Selo's station, we still hadn't had a chance to exchange any words in private.

Alyosha was dressed for the trip east in his military uniform, as was his father. Both were of green wool and included a line of medals pinned under the collar. He put his hand out as if to shake mine, and his sisters laughed. Wasn't he going to kiss me? they wanted to know.

But he didn't, he just stood, and we held hands in front of everyone, looking into each other's eyes for a long moment, enough that I sensed restlessness on the periphery of our locked gaze. I gave him the gift I'd been saving for the goodbye I'd been dreading. It was a pocket-sized sailor doll that I'd found among the children's old toys. I'd replaced his uniform with one I'd made from the same fabric as Alyosha's, and I gave him a little sword, which I bound to his hand with thread. *For Handsome Alyosha,* I'd written on the box I'd put it in and tied with ribbon.

"Don't open it now," I said, "please," and he nodded. Neither of us cried, not then or there, in front of so many eyes.

That night, Alyosha and the rest of his family boarded a train disguised as a Red Cross foreign-aid vehicle bristling with Japanese flags. They went with two valets, six chambermaids, ten footmen, three cooks, four assistant cooks, a butler, a sommelier, a nurse, a clerk, and their two spaniels, Joy and Jimmy. Within a year they'd all be dead, all except one of the dogs, the one named Joy, of all things. I'd never see any of them again. Not in my waking life.

Anna Vyrubova escorted Varya and me to 24 Nikolaevskaya Street, the villa of the tsar's brother Michael, but we saw neither the prince nor his family, only servants. Michael, in whose favor Nikolay had abdicated, was tsar for only one day before abdicating in hope of saving his life. Later, I'd learn he'd been exiled to Siberia as well, but to Perm, where he was executed, alone, on June 12, 1918. Nathalie, his wife, and their son, George, escaped to Paris.

Long before she was murdered, the tsarina's sister Ella (at whose wedding Alexandra met Nikolay) had been widowed, her beloved Sergei dispatched in 1905 by an assassin's bomb. Ella, who crawled over the snow on her hands and knees to collect what bleeding bits she could of her dead husband—a foot still in its boot, a piece of skull, one arm, half a torso—never remarried but abandoned court life for that of a nun and, ultimately, an abbess. She and a handful of other Romanovs were transported to Alapayevsk, Siberia, where, on July 18, 1918, they were blindfolded and ordered to walk the length of a log placed over an abandoned mine shaft, sixty feet deep. Anyone who refused was shot, and the rest all fell off the log before they reached the other side. According to the officer in charge of the massacre, Ella was still singing Orthodox hymns after he'd thrown two grenades down after her; he'd had no choice but to fill the shaft with brush and debris, which, just to be safe, he doused with gasoline and set on fire.

As for Vladimir, Alexei, and Paul, the remaining three of the Meddlesome Four, they were held in the Peter and Paul Fortress in Petersburg, where they lived off rats and rainwater until January 28, 1919, a Tuesday. Ordered to strip to the waist before being taken out to the frozen courtyard, they waited, chained and shivering, for nearly an hour before a firing squad arrived and put a stop to their chattering teeth.

City of Light

· · • ·

I T WAS 1926, Boris had died, and I had left Paris, by the time
I learned that Varya's train, the one she had taken home to
Pokrovskoye under the care of a paid chaperone, was shunted off
the rails just west of Kazan. Soldiers boarded the cars to requisition
anything of value. They were Bolsheviks, or they were base persons, rapacious and villainous, who called themselves Bolsheviks
to excuse their wickedness—for such things were commonplace
during those years of spreading anarchy—and they took jewels,
billfolds, firearms. They raped whom they pleased, who pleased
them, I suppose, and murdered anyone who didn't escape.

I didn't learn all the details at once. A letter was passed from
hand to hand until, at last, the hand it reached was mine. Varya had
never arrived in Pokrovskoye, it said, in my mother's painstaking
script. It had been more than five years since I'd seen or heard from
her, and the sight of those carefully formed letters was enough of
a shock that I stared at them for a few moments before opening the
envelope. They summoned a clear vision of my mother sitting at
the table, the lamp to her left, and the inkwell to her right, her head
bent in concentration.

Writing a letter was not a casual undertaking for my mother.
Always, she prepared for it as if for a sacred project. If her hair had
grown untidy while she did chores, she'd comb it out and put it up

again. She'd clear the table and run a damp rag over its surface, wash and dry her hands, before opening the drawer that held her pen and paper.

From 1926 to 1929 I wrote hundreds of letters to dozens of people, to anyone who might know anything and whose address I had. Somehow, until the day I saw my mother's handwriting, I'd managed to keep my face set forward, away from the past, focused on the future. But the letter acted on me like a spell. Consumed by my need to know what had happened to my family, I wrote whomever I could think of, and I asked each person I wrote to make inquiries on my behalf; I asked for the address of anyone who might have information or be able to help me in some other way. Hundreds of messages that never found their way to their intended recipients. I'd lie in bed at night and try to imagine the fate of those letters. Did the Soviets seize and destroy them? Did they keep them in a growing file labeled *Matryona Grigorievna Rasputina*? Did they use them as a justification—not that they seemed to require such a thing—to investigate the persons to whom they were addressed? I had no idea and, really, I didn't care. I knew I should care if my inquiries brought harm to anyone, but I didn't. After years of determined avoidance, a kind of protective carapace that shattered at the sight of my mother's letter, I was so fixed on finding out what had happened to my family that I couldn't care about anything else.

BY 1919, EVERYONE KNEW the Romanovs had been executed— everyone except my husband. We hadn't lived in Paris for even a year before Boris had organized a secret ragtag society of rabid anti-revolutionaries plotting from afar to restore the tsar to his throne.

"Clever Papa has hidden himself," Boris would say as he paced the apartment, referring to Nikolay Alexandrovich, what little was left of him jumbled among the remains of his wife and children at the bottom of a mine shaft—not the one in which Ella sang her last hymn but another of the countless deep graves left conveniently open after the miners had exhausted the earth's ore and moved on to dig other holes in which to drop the bodies of other enemies of the revolution.

As reported by Yakov Yurovsky, the commanding Bolshevik officer and chief executioner, Alyosha had been the last to die, just as he'd feared he would be. A detailed account of the family's last minutes was made public two years after their murder. Yurovsky woke the Romanovs just after midnight on July 17, 1918. They were being moved, he told them, to a new location, and they were to dress and gather their belongings immediately, which they did. For weeks all the women had been sewing jewels into Alyosha's sisters' underclothes. Still hoping for rescue on the night they were shot, the family had decided the girls would carry their remaining fortune secreted under their clothing, and each night the girls took the precaution of wearing their corsets to bed, under their nightdresses, in case of just such a contretemps as this. Forced to dress in front of four armed guards, they didn't remove any clothing, only added more layers. Once the family had packed, the guards escorted them to the basement, where Yurovsky waited, along with their few retainers: Dr. Botkin, the tsarina's lady-in-waiting, the cook, and the footman.

"Nikolay Alexandrovich, your friends have tried to save you but they did not succeed."

Yurovsky read the execution order aloud to the eleven people assembled before him. A few miles away, concealed in the woods, a battalion of White Army soldiers slept, prepared to storm the house at dawn and rescue the tsar and his family. Two officers had been given the express assignment of carrying Alyosha, again bedridden, as he recovered from one injury only to tumble into the next.

"The executive committee of the Ural Soviet has placed its authority in me."

A line of militia formed behind Yurovsky as he spoke. Eleven targets against one wall of the room, nine rifles pointed from the other. Yurovsky, being in charge, had claimed the privilege of dispatching both the deposed tsar and his son and heir. In his right hand he carried a Nagant M1895 double-action revolver, the standard-issue sidearm for the tsar's army; his left held the handwritten execution order.

"*Your life is ended,*" he told the deposed tsar.

"What?" Nikolay Alexandrovich asked, rising from the chair in which he'd been sitting, his arm around Alyosha. Yurovsky raised his revolver and shot him between the eyes, and then Nikolay Alexandrovich Romanov, the last of the tsars of the Russian Empire, was dead.

Alexandra Fyodorovna made the first three motions of the sign of the cross, right hand moving quickly from head to heart to right shoulder, and then she, too, was dead, along with Botkin, the cook, and the footman. The gunman responsible for eliminating the former tsarina's lady-in-waiting missed his target. With the militia between her and the door there was no escape possible, and she ran back and forth against the wall, screaming, until the nine executioners advanced, forced her into a corner, and stabbed her with their bayonets, each delivering half a dozen thrusts, many more than necessary to kill the woman.

Olga, Tatiana, Maria, and Anastasia were shot and bayoneted repeatedly before succumbing to blood loss. What was later estimated to have been nearly twenty pounds of jewels sewn into the linings of their underclothes transformed the sisters' corsets into what were, in effect, bulletproof vests, protecting their vital organs and prolonging their suffering.

Alyosha: Yurovsky somehow missed.

. . .

IN PARIS, THERE hadn't been much work for a penniless spiritual-
ist separated from the tricks of a trade that was all tricks. Boris
got his identity card and a job with Renault—which turned out
not to be the good luck we first imagined, as most of the Parisians
who worked at Renault were socialists, their sympathies aligned
with the Bolsheviks. Meanwhile, the Russians in Paris, almost exclusively toppled aristocrats forced into menial labor, as only the
wealthiest had been able to command the funds necessary to get
out, were vengefully opposed to the regime they'd been forced
to flee. Every other week, it seemed, the French workers went on
strike for one reason or another and the Russian refugees, who
would rather pluck out their eyes with sugar tongs than join forces
with the Socialist Workers Party, showed up for work on the other
side of the line drawn by the trade union. Often Boris came home
with stories of altercations, and although he swore he never provoked any attacks, he was beaten himself a few times, once badly
enough that he couldn't work for two weeks.

It made no difference to show him newspaper articles or any of
the things a reasonable person might receive as evidence of the Romanovs' deaths. All of these resulted, Boris said, from Bolshevik
control of the press. It was misinformation intended to demoral-
ize the White Army. I admit there were times I cursed my father
during the last year of Boris's life. What was the point of escaping
Russia only to make myself the prisoner of a madman?

Because Boris truly had lost his reason. I knew this after the
night I bought the chest of drawers from a family down the hall.
Desperate to seize on a chance to emigrate to America, they were
selling off everything they couldn't carry, and the bureau cost so
little I could tell myself honestly that were I to give up even some-

thing so insignificant as the bread I ate with my tea in the morning, I could pay for it in a matter of months.

"See!" I said to Boris, when he came home. "Drawers!" I slid open the top one so he could see his nightshirt, neatly folded, and next to it my own nightclothes.

Boris didn't smile, didn't nod, didn't say a word—not immediately, anyway. Instead, he held his hands to his head, clutching the hair on either side. His hat fell on the floor behind him and rolled under the table. "What have you done!" he shrieked. "What! What have you done!" He looked around the room, frantic. "Where is it? Where is it?"

"Where is what?" I was looking around too, trying to see what had upset him, but everything was in its place. We had so little it was easy to see that nothing was missing. "It's all here," I told him. "Nothing is wrong."

"My suitcase! Where is my suitcase? What have you done with my suitcase?"

"It's . . . it's with mine, under the bed. Why? What's the matter, Boris?"

But now he was on his knees before the bed, pulling out the suitcase and opening it on the floor by the new chest of drawers.

"Boris?"

He stood up and yanked the drawers from the bureau one by one, jerking each so violently that they came all the way out and their few contents fell to the floor. Each hung from his hand like a valise, opened and emptied. Once he'd torn all the drawers out and thrown them to one side, he picked furiously among what had been in them, separated his clothing and few possessions from mine, and replaced them in the open suitcase—his razor and strop, a pair of diamond studs and a stopped pocket watch that had once belonged to his grandfather, an Orthodox prayer book, also his grandfather's, a short dagger with an engraved silver scabbard. He slipped the prayer book, studs, and watch into the left side pocket, the razor, strop, and dagger into the right. Then he took his Cross of St. George and the two photographs of his parents and brothers from the top of the empty bureau, where I'd arranged them among my photographs, and laid them in the suitcase under the folded nightshirt. He sat back on his heels, looking at the repacked case.

"Boris?" I said after a minute.

But he remained silent, sitting with his back to me. It wasn't until I picked up one of the drawers and replaced it in the bureau that he spoke.

"Unpacking suggests we intend to remain here, in Paris. And that isn't true, is it, Masha?"

"I . . . I don't understand you, Boris."

"No," he said after another pause, one so long I understood its purpose was to punish me. "We can agree on that much, anyway."

I was still trying to decide if I should speak—if there was something I could say that would not provoke him—when he closed the suitcase and stood up and looked at me. "Boris?" I raised my hand to touch him, to put my hand on his chest, to calm him down, but he pushed it away. Grabbed me by the shoulders.

"It isn't over!" He said the words so loudly I felt ashamed for the neighbors to hear. And he shook me, hard. Hard enough that my head snapped back and forth with each syllable—*it-is-n't-o-ver, it-is-n't-o-ver, it-is-n't-o-ver*. Finally, he pushed me so hard that I fell backward, tripping over one of the drawers that remained on the floor.

"But—"

He was on me before I could finish a sentence or even assemble the thoughts in my head—too late for that; they were as jumbled as the contents of the bureau, those that belonged to me, strewn underfoot. He picked me up with a hand under each armpit and threw me onto the bed.

"It is not over!" he screamed, his face inches from mine. "It won't be over until Russia is liberated!" He had me pinned to the mattress, and his weight held me down in the same hollow that received the thrusts of his forcing intercourse on me. His face was so near to mine and his breath so hot that I closed my eyes. I knew shutting my eyes to his rage would make him that much angrier, but I couldn't make myself look at him. Not when he was like that, his lips pulled back over his teeth like a dog's.

"Don't you understand!" He lifted me from the mattress by my shoulders and held them so tight I cried out.

"Are you so witless that you don't know we are planning our revenge even now! We will liberate our people from the occupation! Yes! And return to the throne the anointed tsar! The lawful and righteous tsar!"

"Take your hands away." I could speak calmly from behind my closed eyelids. "Take them off me."

But he didn't. He stopped shaking me, but he did not let me go. Instead, he straddled my legs and held me in the position into which he'd pulled me, half lying, half sitting on the sagging bed. "Let go of me," I told him for a third time, bracing myself for what I expected, that he'd force himself on me in anger, bruise and subjugate me to remind me who was boss. But he didn't. He dropped me. Backed off my body and off the bed where I lay with my eyes still closed, listening as he moved about the room.

The door slammed and I waited for his footfalls to reach the landing and for the slam of the second door, the door to the street. Then, when I was sure he was out of the building, I got up to retrieve my trampled nightgown and shawl, the few keepsakes I'd saved from the apartment on Gorokhovaya Street, and put them back in my suitcase. I didn't feel afraid. I felt, perhaps, a little sorry for Boris, knowing how he would loathe himself for losing control, for behaving like the kind of man he said he despised. On the other hand, it served him right. I loathed him too. I put on my shoes and went out, leaving the bureau as he'd left it, drawers empty and lying on the floor, their contents reclaimed.

I walked. Walked, walked, walked. Was this the glorious future you saw for me, Father? I was asking him the question—talking to him in my head, as I sometimes found myself doing—when I came upon the advertisement. It was plastered to a corner kiosk, just near the entrance to the Bois de Boulogne. *Acrobatic Champions on Horseback—A Startling Divertissement of Difficult Drills in Galloping Unison.* The words appeared below an illustration in the style of Lautrec, a line of dancers performing on the backs of horses, one girl per horse. I pulled the bill off the kiosk to which it had been tacked, folded it, and put it in my pocket. The following day, after Boris had left for work, I dressed to ride and went straight to the address printed on the bottom of the bill.

The manager of the *Startling Divertissement* wasn't looking to hire another performer. "I'll watch," he said when I asked to audition. "But I got all the girls I need.

"When can you start?" he said after I dismounted. He'd put me through every test and discovered the only thing I didn't have was the vocabulary to go with the tricks. "Feet jump-in!" he barked when he wanted me to jump from what he called a "teeterboard" onto the back of a running horse. Roman riding. Flag. Half-flag. Vault. Milling. It was a good thing he had that board, as it was balanced over a spring so that it took less effort to jump up from it onto the animal. Unused to vigorous exercise, I was out of breath by the time I'd run through all I knew.

But God in heaven, it felt so good I nearly hugged the manager and kissed his pockmarked cheek after I dismounted. Every inch of my skin was tingling with gooseflesh—just the feel of a horse's back, warm and alive, under my feet, and the smell of the animal, the sting of his mane flicking against my shins when he cantered. How was it that I'd left this behind? Why had I settled as long as I had for a life that didn't include any of what I loved? My body in harmony with an animal as it would never be with a human being. It might have been, with Alyosha, had we been given more time. Although it is difficult to know how much of our heat was created by circumstance. As it's turned out, I've chosen animals over people. Falling in love with a man—if I'd had the knack, I'd lost it. But it wasn't only me. No one escaped Russia with his or her heart intact.

"Can you start next week?" the manager pressed.

"Yes, yes—as soon as I get my identification card. I'll go right away."

On the way home, I ran into a few Russian women from the neighborhood, one of whom observed that I had a bit of hay in my hair. "Look at that," I said, running my fingers through the rest of it to check for more. "I go to the market for tea and come home with straw on my head!"

As soon as I asked for news of home, they forgot me and shared what they'd received from family in Kiev and Petersburg and Moscow and Minsk. In St. Petersburg, it was said, the lines for bread, for meat, for anything edible, were so long that it was possible to wait all day and not reach the front of the queue. The poor people slept in the street to hold their places. The rich sent servants to sleep in line.

BORIS'S DELUSIONS DIDN'T FADE. He nursed them with vodka and they grew stronger and more florid. After months of his feverish rants and nights spent trying to get him to sleep rather than carry on banging his fists on the walls, I resolved to leave him. But on the eve of the very day I'd decided to walk out, Boris announced he had tuberculosis. Perhaps he'd experienced his first genuine moment of telepathy and guessed my intentions, for, as he admitted, he'd known he was ill for some time, hiding his bloody handkerchiefs from me and complaining that fumes from the plant had brought on a respiratory catarrh.

It's said consumptives become libidinous toward the end, and I mistook Boris's lust as a harbinger of his death. How much longer until he succumbed, I asked myself each time he used one knee to force my two apart? I owed him my escape from the Bolsheviks. The honorable thing was to stay with him until the very end. Which had to come sooner rather than later, didn't it? His thirtieth birthday would be upon us in less than two years.

"You like it."

"So you say." If I resisted, he pushed himself that much more insistently on me.

"You want it," he said.

"And then I say don't and you do it again."

"You can't refuse a dying man his last pleasures."

"Why not?"

"A black mark on your soul."

"Who says I have one?" I felt my husband as hard as a pointing finger, but blind, missing the mark. "Stop. I don't want to. Whether you're living or dying, I don't want to."

"Masha." He reached down to guide himself between my legs.

"Don't."

"Masha."

"Don't say my name like that."

"Like what?"

"You know."

"Masha."

"Like that."

Easier to give in than to refuse. Easier and over and done with more quickly.

Exile

· · • · ·

As SOON AS you cross over the Urals, I told Alyosha, the temperature drops and the world appears unlike any you've seen. Sky and earth: each holding a mirror to the other, stretching without limit in every direction. The wind moves over the steppes as it does over water; the grasses ripple at its passing, they lean this way and that. Sometimes it looks as if the land under your feet is racing toward the horizon, and then the wind dies, it eddies back. If you think you don't have time to waste on watching, the wind will show you otherwise. You feel it in your chest the first time you understand, as you never have before, how wide is the world and how small a creature you are. That's what the steppes teach you: how finite is a human life. Like a struck match, it burns and goes out, and the knowledge doesn't inspire what you might imagine. It isn't fearsome; it's reassuring. It's terrible to live believing everything you do is of the utmost importance.

The first thing Father always said when asked about Siberia was how beautiful it was, how vast and empty the land, how little touched by industry. A village like Pokrovskoye had only the one street, and it was unpaved. We walked on ice in January, mud in May, and by August dust boiled up from under the wheels of a passing wagon. As there were no lumber mills within a hundred miles, each home was hand-hewn, as was our tiny general store, our post office, and our church with its Orthodox cross on top. The cross's three bars offered the highest vantage in town and drew ravens and jackdaws by the score, as if they were perches designed expressly for the birds' pleasure. Were an errand to take you by our church, you might catch the village priest as he tore out of his lodgings next door, his cassock tangling around his ankles as he crashed pot lids together like cymbals. Up flapped the birds, cawing and raucous and black as black, but as soon as priest and pot lids went back inside, down they dropped, just as many if not more than before. And all the while, from noon until its setting, the sun pushed the cross's lengthening shadow over the graveyard, so we could see how it scraped the tombstones and the pretty blank-faced Madonnas. Some years there was talk of buying the church a bell, but bells were costly and the congregants poor. A village like Pokrovskoye, it could dry up like a scab and crumble away, and who would take note? The deer would trample what was left of our gardens, the snow cock roost among the tumbled chimney stones.

The sky we saw when we looked up was bluer than the one over St. Petersburg, smudged as it was with factory smoke, and our clouds were more beautiful too. They rode high in the sky like ships with gray hulls, bright sails lined with silver. Winters, our snow-covered fields remained as white as a swan's back. Then came the thaw, pale grasses poking through the melting drifts and rivers running like mercury, they were that silver and quick. And our woods: so dark, alive with unfamiliar sounds, the restless air whispering to the pine tree and shaking her needles. Every so often someone walked into the forest and didn't walk out. For if you heard the wood folk summon you, you couldn't not obey their song, as powerful as that of the sirens, and then no one could help you.

Each fall came a night when the wind grew so impatient it stripped every last golden leaf from every last birch tree. I'd lie in my bed and listen as they skittered over the roof, watch them fly fast past the window as if some great being—the Christ himself perhaps, a thousand feet tall in his cape of sweeping black sky— hurled fistfuls of yellow coins into the night. In the morning the whole village looked dull and that much more impoverished, nothing left but ghost-gray trunks, their branches clacking and chattering together. Evergreens kept their needles, of course, when all the other trees were bare, and then the forest looked black and forbidding, as if the pines had closed ranks and pinched off every path we'd worn through them.

While I was learning the secrets of married life, Alyosha was with his family in Tobolsk, living in the governor's mansion. The Romanovs were to stay there for the better part of a year, long enough to plant a garden on the grounds but not to harvest the fruits of their labor. Not a happy time, but neither was it as unhappy as I imagined before reading Alyosha's account of those days, nearly twenty years ago. Should he have lived, Alyosha would be a man of thirty-one years. But that's unlikely, I tell myself, as thirty-one would be something of a record for a hemophiliac.

In Tobolsk the family was together longer than it had ever been before. As tsar, Nikolay Alexandrovich had been away from Tsarskoe Selo more often than not. Now husband and father was present week after week, and this was an unknown luxury for Alexandra and their children, who found a good deal of contentment in these circumstances, which they believed to be a temporary interruption of their real lives. Only Alyosha expected the worst, and he kept his apprehensions to himself. On those nights that he lay awake, alone with his thoughts, he crept from his bed to the table that served as his desk and, wrapped in his blanket, wrote until he grew tired enough to return to bed and sleep.

Kerensky had been honorable and had done what he'd said he would do. He'd evacuated the Romanovs for their own safety, but

Kerensky was no longer in power. In October, the provisional government had collapsed in less than twenty hours, and then Russia belonged to the Bolsheviks. More blood would be shed, but most of the aristocracy had already abandoned their homes; the contest was over, the story as well, with this farcical epilogue: Felix Yusupov became the proprietor of a salon in Paris where ladies went to get their nails varnished. The women he employed there had been princesses in Russia. Better to paint women's fingernails than to be shot for the crime of possessing too much power and too many jewels. Even if individual Bolsheviks didn't necessarily want the former tsar and tsarina and their blameless children murdered, the Soviet had declared God's death and its own apotheosis, and the Romanovs were the sacrifice it demanded.

But Alyosha's parents and sisters continued to speak to one another of their imminent rescue by loyal monarchists conspiring to free them. If Nikolay Alexandrovich's supporters couldn't reinstate him on the throne, they'd manage to arrange for his and his family's safe passage out of Russia. True, George V had refused them asylum, but the Hesses were not the only rulers to whom the Romanovs were related. The Schleswig-Holstein-Sonderburg-Augustenburg branch of the family might be extinct, but Schleswig-Holstein-Sonderburg-Glücksburgs occupied the thrones of Denmark, Norway, and Greece.

It was a matter of arranging safe passage, that was all, and how difficult could that be?

It was impossible. Kerensky and his ministers had been too naïve—too civilized—to imagine it was necessary to hide the deposed tsar and his family. They'd had no choice but to set the Romanovs out of the way of harm until they could safely export them, and as Tobolsk was a backwater—far from Moscow and Petersburg, where radical elements might plot to harm the former royal family— it seemed an ideal place. But after October 1917, Kerensky himself had been forced to escape to Paris and Bolsheviks had surrounded Tobolsk. There were no roads on which the Romanovs wouldn't be ambushed, no train that would transport them to any destination other than Yekaterinburg, the city chosen for their execution.

Confined to the governor's mansion and its cramped garden, around which a high wall of logs had been hurriedly hammered together both to protect the family from voyeurs' hungry eyes and to discourage misguided monarchists from making a Quixotic rescue attempt, the Romanovs continued on as they always had, according to rigid schedule. Raised by British governesses, themselves governed by Routine, highest among the nursery gods, and by now steeped—thoroughly pickled—in the tradition of the Orthodox Church, Alexandra Fyodorovna applied the punctiliousness of a mother superior to her family, which convened according to her version of the Divine Office: breakfast at eight; coffee at ten; luncheon at one; tea at five; dinner at eight. Every day, no matter where or under what circumstances, celebratory, mundane, or dire, Nikolay Alexandrovich, Alexandra Fyodorovna, Olga, Tatiana, Maria, Anastasia, and Alyosha, assuming he was well enough to join them, gathered around a table, ate, drank, and prayed together.

Perhaps there wasn't so much to do in Tobolsk besides eat and pray. Alexandra Fyodorovna and the four girls read and knitted. Nikolay Alexandrovich persuaded the guard to give him work to do—chopping firewood. Alyosha wrote that the members of the family had devoted themselves to simple tasks they'd never performed before, tending their vegetable garden, for example. They discovered there was pleasure in digging on their hands and knees, feeling the spring sun on their backs as they dropped seeds in the soil they'd prepared. Each member of the family had his or her own row of beets or cabbages or carrots, and every morning each hurried to inspect its progress. To see how sunlight passed through the tiny red-veined leaves of new beets and set them aglow, like jewels, in colors no jewels possess, to thin the seedlings, to sacrifice one life and not another, to weed and water—for the Romanovs these represented a whole new arena of entertainment. *Better than theater,* Alyosha wrote.

Old enough to dream of future husbands, and young enough to remain in the thrall of romance, thrilled at the idea of being so poor and unknown they'd have to learn to cook, Tatiana and Olga asked permission to help the kitchen staff prepare meals. It was only Alyosha who suffered from terrible restlessness, to judge from the complaints that filled his journal. He did until the day he made himself a promise and wrote it down. He would die a young man with a sexual history, no matter how truncated. He set to work searching for what he called a *paramour,* a girl he could possess by the divine right of princes. Not that he believed in that right, he wrote, but if other people did, it would be useful in his quest.

When I came across the word "paramour," I recognized it. It wasn't borrowed from an adventure novel—Alyosha didn't read those. It was taken from one of our games, the one about the Neva overflowing. With each retelling, the story of the flood and what it had carried off grew that much longer, until it had become a kind of memory game, P representing "pocketknives, pencils, presumptuous politicians, parboiled potatoes, pachyderms, pots, pans, partridge pie, pickles, plums, peaches, pork, porridge, pale princes, and persistent paramours." Afterward, neither of us could say the word "paramour" without falling into a laughing fit. It must have been my having put the word after "prince," and Alyosha's being a prince, and the fact that he'd had to ask me the definition. I knew he couldn't have written that word, "paramour," without thinking of me, and I tried to remember where I was on that date, December 8, 1917. Having the breath squeezed out of me by Boris in Budapest, perhaps, or Berlin, one of the cities we tried before Paris.

My father and mother had been physically passionate—this wasn't something that could be hidden in a house with as few rooms as ours—and had I grown up in Siberia I might have become a woman like my mother, a woman who never worried over what she did or didn't do with a man. Intercourse wasn't painful, it didn't disgust me, and I fulfilled the obligations of marriage, in my case to a husband who took his pleasure from me without considering mine. Not that I complained. I was sitting across the room from Boris when, in reading, I came across the word and looked up its meaning. *La nymphomanie.* So it had a name. If such a fixation lay dormant within me, might not its expression be provoked by a man's touch, like a seed germinating after being watered?

I set myself against it. Avoided any touch that might awaken what I was determined to keep at bay and asleep.

For Alyosha it was different. At his age, he didn't need to discover his sexual nature; it owned him. Alyosha could arouse himself, of course, but he wanted more than the company of his hands. He wanted a girl's hands, and he wanted her mouth and all the rest of her. He wanted to touch her and put himself inside her. Until he figured out a way to satisfy it, his journal was filled with that hunger, the one I, out of fear, had frustrated.

He approached a boy with whom he was allowed to socialize to ask a question. It was Kolya, the son of his new physician, for of course wherever Alyosha went, there had to be doctors at hand; old Botkin wasn't enough. "Didn't you tell me you had an older sister?" Alyosha asked the boy.

He had said so. Her name was Katya.

KATYA WAS DARK and very small for seventeen. She'd been having intercourse with men for more than a year. Not for money, but for its own sake. She liked it, but only with patients of her physician father. This quirk in her nature placed Alyosha in the pool of acceptable partners, even if his youth was less than ideal. But, as Alyosha was to discover, the real inducement was that he was the son of the former tsar.

"Where can we do it?" Alyosha asked Kolya.

"It will have to be at our house. She won't come to you."

"When?"

"After Mass on Sunday. Father and Mother will be away from home, dining with my grandfather, and Katya and I will be left behind, with the servant. The servant always sleeps after Sunday dinner. She'll have a skin full of kvass and won't wake up, not even if Christ himself shakes her shoulder."

"How do I get there?"

"Well, it's not me that's going to fetch you."

No matter how long he thought, Alyosha couldn't conceive of a way to leave the house alone. It was impossible. He was allowed off the grounds under Nagorny's supervision, and that was it. He'd have to convince Nagorny.

"I want to go on an outing with you," he said. "On Sunday."

"What outing is that?"

"To Kolya's. It's a party. A party for a birthday."

"Kolya's?"

"Kolya's sister."

"You don't know Kolya's sister."

"I know Kolya."

Nagorny looked at Alyosha. "All right," he said, after holding the boy with his eyes, trying to penetrate him, find the truth he wasn't telling. "What time on Sunday?"

"Two. Two in the afternoon."

Katya

. . . . .

THE DAY WAS DARK, a moody sky, a sharp wind. Nagorny buttoned "Handsome Alyosha"'s coat as if he were a child, and "Handsome Alyosha" pushed his big kind hands away.

I wanted to believe that Alyosha's referring to himself in the third person, as Handsome Alyosha, was proof he'd intended the journal to find its way into my possession, or at least imagined it might. Perhaps, though, he was comforting himself by telling stories in the manner I had told them, and in this one way I remained with him until the end, just as he has remained with me.

"You have a gift for the young lady?" Nagorny asked him.

"Thank you for reminding me," Alyosha called over his shoulder as he ran back into the house. "I'll go fetch it." He went directly to the room his sisters shared. Hairbrushes, ribbons, books. Tatiana's glass horse. Was there anything they wouldn't miss? He picked up one object after another: handkerchief, brooch, bottle of toilet water. A tiny rose tree planted in a porcelain pot with matching saucer. That would be missed, but not like a glass animal, and it didn't require wrapping, like other gifts, which weren't alive. He took a red grosgrain ribbon—it matched the one tiny bud on the tree—and tied it under the lip of the pot. He hid it inside his jacket, pulling the lapel over it, and ran back downstairs and out into the wind. "Silly to forget the present," he said, avoiding Nagorny's eyes. "Let's go, shall we?"

The sky was unsettled. The wind pushed the clouds so quickly past the sun that as soon as Alyosha got used to the brightness, it vanished, leaving him in shadows. As the two walked to the home of Katya's father, Alyosha rehearsed what was to happen. Now that he had a gift, a gift for a birthday that was a lie, he would present it to Katya as a little polite something he'd thought to bring her, the way a young man should when arriving for, say, tea. The little tree would be something to talk about. He'd hand it to her, and she would take it from him and say thank you. She'd notice the ribbon and the bud, how they were the same color, because girls did notice those sorts of peculiar, not-worth-noticing things, and then he'd ask what her favorite color was. And she'd answer and ask him his favorite color, because it was that kind of silly tit-for-tat question that demands a matching one. And by then she'd be looking for the perfect place to put the flower, and the ice would have been broken. They would already be talking with each other.

The walk was too short for Alyosha to perfect the scenario. He'd run through it only twice in his head and made a few improvements, but there they were, walking toward the house; he didn't have time to change the script now. Nagorny rang the bell, and for some time no one answered. And when someone did answer, it was not a servant but Kolya.

"Goodbye, Nagorny," Alyosha said, and he slipped into the house and closed the door before Nagorny could follow or even object. Nagorny rang the bell again, and when at last someone answered, it wasn't Kolya but Alyosha, who poked his head out the second-story window and said the party would last only until four, and Nagorny could come back then to collect him.

Inside, Alyosha followed Kolya, walking mindfully, with his eyes cast down, as he always did when in a new environment, alert to things over which he might stumble. It was almost as chilly inside the house as it was out, but Kolya was barefoot, the soles of his feet black.

"Katya!" Kolya said when he reached the landing, and Alyosha withdrew the rose in its pot from under his jacket and adjusted the red ribbon. He heard a response that sounded like *mudak*, but that was impossible. It was a word he'd learned only the previous week, when, having heard one of the guards use it, he'd asked Nagorny what it meant until the man blushed and then wrote on piece of paper *asshole*.

"What? You mean the part of the body?"

Nagorny nodded. "It's not a word used by nice people," he said.

Kolya rolled his eyes and kicked at the closed door through which the unladylike word had slipped, and Alyosha ran through the conversation he had planned. There was the sound of feet striking the floor as if the person to whom they belonged had been dropped from a height, and then, after a second or two, the door opened. Alyosha stepped forward and immediately forgot what he'd rehearsed. The girl was only partly dressed, wearing a chemise that ought to have been in the care of a laundress and what Alyosha assumed was a petticoat. The skirtlike thing was trimmed in lace that dangled in places where the hem had come unstitched. Her expression wasn't so much friendly as it was hungry, and she ran her tongue over her front teeth, the top two of which were separated by a gap. After a moment of what appeared to be deliberation, her black eyebrows drawn together, she executed a sulky little curtsy that conveyed more insolence than respect. Watching her, Alyosha felt himself grow immediately aroused, enough to dismiss the awkwardness of the encounter. It was clear to him that nothing he'd learned from observing his mother and sisters applied to this girl. He looked at Kolya, who dipped his head in a tiny bow that echoed his sister's mocking curtsy.

"I'll be downstairs," he said, and he left Alyosha there, on the threshold to Katya's room.

Alyosha was grateful the girl was so petite. It made him feel less of a boy, less reprehensibly young, to be able to look down on her a little, as he could do with me. Her long hair was dark, almost black—*like Masha's,* he wrote, *wavy and thick*—and her eyes reminded him of mine also, a greeny blue. Except her left eye had a flare of brown, which gave it a look more knowing than the right's. She wasn't pretty—her features were too sharp for prettiness—but it didn't matter. He wanted to touch her.

"I brought you this," he said, holding out the flower in its pot, and she took it silently. Without noting the bud, or the ribbon, or anything about the gift, Katya ran a finger lightly along one of its slender stems, skimming its tip over the tiny thorns, and then set it down on a table far from the window. "I expect you should put it nearer the light," Alyosha said, and she looked at him and crossed her arms. It was a contest of some kind, who would move or speak next, and he wasn't going to back down. Nor was he going to allow her to touch his face and discover how smooth was his skin.

"If you step in, I can close the door," Katya said, already bored with what he'd assumed was a standoff. Alyosha stepped forward, just enough to get out of her way, and she closed the door. Her room was tidy, but really there wasn't much to get out of place, no books, no china dogs or bottles of scent or lacy table coverings. No brush, no mirror, no tortoiseshell hair combs. Nothing at all to suggest the room belonged to a female person. Perhaps it wasn't even her room but a servant's or a place for guests. The bed was unmade, and she sat on it, swinging her bare feet, also with dirty black soles.

"So," she said, "what is it like to be the tsarevich?"

"I'm not the tsarevich. There is no tsarevich anymore."

The girl laughed, although he hadn't been making a joke. "Well, then," she said, "what was it like to be the tsarevich when there was a tsarevich and it was you?"

"I'm not sure if you're asking me a question or teasing me," Alyosha said, and Katya, perhaps unused to sincerity, made no answer to this.

"I did want to know," she said after a moment, frowning at the rose. The bud drooped on its slender green neck. Alyosha wondered if perhaps he'd squashed it on the walk over or if the cold air had gotten to it. Perhaps it wouldn't open before it fell from its stem.

"It's a question with a long answer," he told her.

She nodded.

"Maybe even a disappointing answer, as there's nothing very surprising in it. A lot of strictures more than any other thing."

"Strictures?"

"Do's and don't's."

She nodded, and then, after looking at him, his clothes as much as his face, smiled. "I suppose that's why you're here," she said, and she lifted her camisole over her head and pulled off her petticoat. Naked, she sat on her bed without any indication of shame. "No?"

"And you?" Alyosha said.

"Me?" She laughed, and her small breasts moved up and down with her shoulders. "I live here, remember?"

"I meant why you agreed to . . . to this."

"Curious. And even if you think you're not, you are still the tsarevich, you know." Alyosha didn't answer. "The future tsar of Russia. I'll always have that to remember."

"Don't you know . . ."

"Don't I know what?"

"There isn't going to be another tsar of Russia."

"Of course there will," Katya said. "There always has been before."

It would help her get to heaven, a thing like that. That's what she told Alyosha she believed. She would be forgiven for her lack of modesty with other men. The two would cancel each other out.

"Come here," Katya said. She patted the bed as if she were calling a dog to her side, and he obeyed. He sat next to her, left his arms limp at his sides while she undid the same buttons Nagorny had done up. Once she had his coat off, she sat in his lap, facing him. "What's this?" she asked, pulling on the fine gold chain she found inside his collar. On it was a miraculous medal stamped with a likeness of the Virgin, as well as medals for Saints Paul, John the Baptist, and Basil Fool for Christ.

"Something my mother likes me to wear. She thinks it can protect me." Alyosha could tell by the way Katya touched him, carelessly, as she would anyone else, that she had no idea he was ill, and it was this as much as the sight and feel of her that excited him.

"Oh," she said, noting immediately that he had grown hard. "What do I feel?" She put her hot little hand over his groin, rubbing him through the fabric of his trousers, and just like that it was over. His erection subsided under her touch. He'd taken less time than a field rabbit. Alyosha felt his face burning as Katya withdrew her hand and climbed off his thighs. He told himself to look at her, to pick up his head and not stare down as if he felt ashamed. But he did feel ashamed, and he couldn't look at her face.

Her skin was dusky in comparison to his sisters', at whom he had peeped when he got a chance, now that they were all thrown together, and she had a birthmark, a port-wine stain, splashed across her stomach. It wasn't so large, but its outline was sufficiently irregular that it looked almost topographical, like a body of water on a map. As Alyosha couldn't lift his eyes above it, he stared at the birthmark.

"Lake Baikal," he said, when the silence had grown long enough that saying something silly seemed better than saying nothing at all. "Only on its side."

"What?"

"The mark, the one over your navel. Its outline reminds me of the . . . of how water looks on a map. And it's . . . it's long and it looks like the outline of a particular body of water. Lake Baikal."

"I was born with a cowl," Katya said.

"What's a cowl?"

"It's when a baby arrives inside the birth sack. It's very lucky. It means I can't be drowned, not even if I fall overboard. That must be why the Good Lord put a picture of a lake on me." She looked down at her own bare body as if she hadn't seen the stain before. While she inspected it, stretching the skin under her fingers, he managed to lift his head and his red cheeks.

"It doesn't matter what happened," she said, seeing his mortification. She stood up and retrieved her camisole from the floor, bending over and lifting her bottom so he could see *everything that was there,* as he described it. She dropped it over her head.

"I bet you could do it again," she said, looking at him as her hands tied the camisole's grimy ribbon.

Alyosha said nothing.

"I can make it happen again, if you like."

"I . . ."

"Just tell me if you want me to."

Alyosha nodded.

"All right then, Tsarevich," she said. "Lie down. On your back. And close your eyes."

Katya unbuttoned Alyosha's trousers and pulled them down

around his ankles and right off him entirely, and when his eyes popped open she closed them with her hand. "No," she said. She climbed on top of him and started kissing him, putting her tongue in his mouth. *The way I wanted Masha to do,* wrote Alyosha, Katya's *hot, slippery little tongue* exploring his while her hand was on his penis, stroking it.

It appeared the word "penis" was one Alyosha had settled on after much deliberation, as there were other words that had preceded it and had been scratched out so thoroughly I couldn't read a single letter.

"See," she said as it lifted under her fingers. "I told you." She kissed his neck and moved down, kissing his chest, his stomach. At first he couldn't imagine why she'd left off kissing his mouth— he'd never imagined a girl might kiss him down there. But her lips were on his penis; her tongue licked his testicles (another word on which he had settled after a long inky deliberation). He was so hard, as hard as before, but now he didn't ejaculate, not yet; he could just lie there and let her do this astonishing thing to him.

Alyosha had died and gone to heaven. They could do anything to him they liked, the Bolsheviks, because there was nothing left on earth that felt better than—or even a fraction as good as—this. Katya had climbed on him and put his penis inside her, and she was moving up and down, very slowly. She seemed to know whenever he began to worry that it would happen again, and it would be over, and then she'd stop moving. She'd wait. She even got back off him, and she put her mouth on his penis again, and with his eyes closed and Katya doing what she was doing, Alyosha had gone to a place he'd never visited before, a landscape pulsing black and red and—

"You can open your eyes now," she said when it was over. She was wiping her mouth with the back of her hand, and Alyosha hadn't any idea what was proper to say in an improper situation like this. He couldn't just say thank you, could he? Thank you for . . . for what? For allowing me to—

"Won't you tell me one little thing about it?" Katya said, interrupting his thoughts. "About being a tsarevich. A thing I couldn't guess for myself."

Relieved, Alyosha tried to imagine what she might find surprising. "The guards were a different color than you are," he said, after thinking for a moment. "The ones that stood at the door to the palace."

"A different color? What do you mean, a different color?"

"Their skin was black."

"Really black?"

"As black as your hair."

"Not painted black?"

"Not painted."

"Are there other colors of people there, in St. Petersburg?"

"No. There are people like you and me, and people who are black, like the palace guards."

"Were their parents black?"

"I'm sure they must have been."

"Would they have black babies?"

"Of course."

Katya lay on the bed pondering this, her eyes closed. "I like that," she said finally. "That was good. I'll tell you what, Tsarevich. You can come back, and I'll do it again, what I just did. But each time you'll have to tell me a bit more." She bounced off the bed and pulled on her petticoat. "Kolya will tell you when." Having buttoned her underclothes, she called her brother's name.

"I . . . I'm afraid I told Nagorny not to return until four," Alyosha said, when the boy stepped into the room.

Kolya shrugged. "Doesn't matter," he said. "He didn't go anywhere. He's asleep outside, on the ground."

"All right, then." Alyosha stood and quickly drew the sides of his coat together and began buttoning them, not allowing himself to make things even worse by checking the front of his trousers to see if it looked as it felt. Awkwardly, he put his hand out to Katya to bid her goodbye, and when she put her hand in his, he did as he had seen his father do so many times before: he bent his head and kissed her hand.

"You can come back," she said again. "Kolya will tell you."

"OVER SOONER THAN YOU EXPECTED," Nagorny observed when Alyosha shook him awake. He got to his feet and brushed a few leaves off his coat.

"Yes."

"I didn't see any other guests arrive."

"No. It was a small party."

"So that's it, then?" Nagorny said, his tone suspicious.

"Yes."

After this unusually terse exchange, Alyosha and Nagorny walked together in silence.

Last Rites

· · · · ·

IT WAS THE TSARINA'S WISH that Father be laid to rest near her family, at Tsarskoe Selo. It had been my father's wish to be placed in a simple coffin, a six-sided box made of pine, without ornament.

Sergei Gavriilovich, the coffin-maker, arrived at nine in the morning to measure Father and, made even greedier by the unusual length of Father's body, tried to convince me to pay for mahogany.

"No," I said. "Pine."

"Cherry is nice." He showed me a varnished sample.

"It is pretty. But I do want pine."

"Walnut is not so expensive and also a rich grain."

In a temper by the time he'd forced me to refuse every species of tree he suggested, Sergei banged the rough yellow boards together so hard that each strike of his hammer made the tea glasses jump on the shelf above his head.

"Gentle," Dunia said to him as we lifted Father into the box, and Sergei Gavriilovich dropped the shoulder he was supporting too soon. "There's no need to hurry."

"Please," I said. "He has been beaten enough, as you see."

Dunia, Varya, and I followed after Father in a hired droshky, his plain pine box bouncing on the back of a cart from 64 Gorokhovaya

Street to the station, where all three of us boarded a train to Tsar-skoe Selo. Two black carriages bearing the Romanov crest were waiting there to take us to the Sophia Cathedral, which marked the center of the tsar's village, just next door to the police station. It was a pretty church, remarkable for the restraint of its decoration, a place Father had often stopped to pray.

In accordance with Orthodox tradition, all of us gathered before his coffin and held a lighted candle throughout the Mass. The priest recited the requiem liturgy, and a deacon walked around and around the open casket, all the time swinging his censer until we could barely make out my father's face through the clouds of smoke, the cowl of his backward cloak pulled down by the priest so he could peer out of the slit in his eye and not miss any of the exequies. Mass over, we followed the coffin, without its lid, and Father's face still uncovered, out of the cathedral. To ensure no one fell, boards had been laid over the snow. They formed a long yellow path from the cathedral to the spot the tsarina had chosen for Father to be buried.

Just as Father had had to build a bonfire to thaw the earth to bury his firstborn, so had the imperial park gardeners had to thaw the ground before any of them could force the blade of a shovel into it. While Dunia and I were preparing my father's body, the gardeners were building a fire and feeding the flames until they had done their work and a man could dig.

As we walked behind the priest and the coffin to the open grave, the traditional bells were tolled. Slowly, from the smallest to the largest, from highest to lowest in pitch, each bell was struck, each given its voice. I'd heard them before—who hadn't?—but it wasn't until I heard them while walking behind my father's coffin that I understood what they were saying. The first rang out with the high clear tone of a very young child, as did the second, only a little lower than the first, the voice of a slightly older child. The third was older still, and so the bells went, on through the chapters of a human life, until the lowest one, with the deepest voice, called out so forcefully it shook the loose snow from the pine boughs. I felt it reverberate through my chest, as if I had opened my own mouth to speak its message: a human life, how brief it was, over and done with as quickly as a handful of notes.

When we reached the hole in the ground, all the bells rang out together, and as they did the priest stepped forward. "By the grace of the risen Lord, which has been transmitted to me, Grigory Ye-fimovich Rasputin, your sins, whether they be word or deed or thought, are all absolved."

Varya and I stood still, our backs straight and our eyes forward, practicing the good posture and silent poise the Steblin–Kamensky Academy had taught us to maintain at events, such as funerals, that would have summoned wailing and wild keening and even falling on the ground were we home in Pokrovskoye. By now Dunia's potion, which had at least held my fever at bay, had worn off, and I had to clench my teeth to keep them from chattering. Only Alex-andra Fyodorovna wept, but her grief was soundless. Already, at forty-four, she looked far older than her years, her red-gold hair faded and her face etched with worry. I watched her, wondering at the conversation, now three days past, in which she'd charged me to guard the health of her son, who stood beside her, his face pinched and white. Alyosha had been trained, I saw immediately, in the behavior befitting a tsarevich. His back was straight, his shoulders squared, and he offered his arm to his mother, so she could lean on him as well as on her husband, but his stoicism con-veyed misery nonetheless and I felt, with a sudden jolt, not only the weight of his mother's expectations but also his own attach-ment to—indeed, dependence upon—my father.

The priest rolled up the paper from which he had been reading and placed it in Father's right hand: a ticket for the boatman who ferried souls across the River Styx. Charon in his loincloth. I'd always been able to picture him so clearly, his scrawny shoulders bent as he hunched over the river pole, naked except for the loincloth. He didn't speak. You gave him either your absolution ticket or the coins that had closed your dead eyes, whatever currency he would accept, or he left you on the riverbank. And there you sat until the living you left behind on earth paid for enough novenas and did enough acts of charity for the repose of your soul, depending on how many sins you needed absolved when you died. You might never escape purgatory. Most people don't.

THE TSAR AND TSARINA and all their children came one by one to the side of the coffin, leaned in, and kissed Father's forehead, his rolled-up absolution, and his crucifix. Then it was Anna Vyrubova's turn, and then Dunia's, Varya's, and last of all mine. When I looked into the coffin, I saw that the rolled-up absolution had pushed aside Father's prayer rope, and I reached in and took the rope for myself. The priest looked disapproving, but poor dead Father would have been happy for me to have it. Then all of us around the coffin took hold of the hem of his cowl and pulled it up over his face, and the priest took a handful from the mound of black earth and with it made a cross on my father's chest. At last the pine box could be closed, its lid nailed on.

"Open wide," we sang to the silent earth as the gardeners used ropes to lower the coffin into the hole they'd dug. "Open," we sang, "for he returneth again unto thee that gave him birth."

The priest took a shovelful of dirt and made another sign of the cross, this time on the lid of the coffin, and then he passed the spade to me, and after I dropped a shovelful on the coffin, everyone else took a turn. It was over. I watched the family, as well as Anna and Varya, walk up the hill to the palace, out of the cold. They went silently, in single file, along a second path of yellow boards laid over white snow. Their breath rose over their heads as they walked, and for a moment it appeared that each of them, not only the tsarina, moved under his or her own cloud.

Even through the yellow boards the cold penetrated the soles of my shoes, and my feet and ankles ached, but I stayed with Dunia, who pulled me into her fur coat and encouraged me to lean against her as we watched the gardeners fill the grave. We didn't say anything to each other, but I knew that she, like me, wouldn't leave until the job had been completed. The men worked in unconscious harmony, each of their spades entering the mound of dirt with a scrape and then dropping the cold clods on the pine lid. The four sets of the two sounds aligned and then diverged, over and over, and I thought of how farmers mowed a field together, each swinging a scythe, the arcs of their curved blades synchronizing and then diverging. Once the lid was no longer visible, the falling clods made less and less noise, and finally all I could hear was the scraping of the four spades and the call of an owl, already hunting on a day when the sun set by three in the afternoon.

Though I well knew the difference between sleep and death, covering my father's body with a blanket of dirt, of the soil he loved, felt like pulling up the bedclothes, tucking him in tight. Standing by the grave, watching the progress of the gardeners, seeing the hole as it was filled in, I found relief under my misery. For months I'd worried for the safety of my father, who refused to take even the simple precaution of telling the tsarina's police where he was headed and whom he planned to see when he left the apartment. He'd predicted his death and left me no choice but to wait for it. Now it was done, his prophecy fulfilled, his body washed and dressed and laid to rest. We watched the gardeners tramp back and forth over the dirt, packing it down with their boots, and then we, too, went back to the palace, where Dunia put me to bed as she had when I was a little girl. Varya said Dunia stayed only the one night before heading back to Petersburg and from there home to Siberia. Apparently she and Botkin had very different ideas about patients with fevers.

Father remained in his grave for only two and a half months. After midnight on the day Kornilov came to Tsarskoe Selo to inform the tsarina of the Romanovs' house arrest, the Red Guard smashed Father's gravestone and dug up his coffin. This must have happened after the Romanov children, Varya, and I had watched the drunken soldiers stumble back to the Alexander Palace after slaughtering the deer, after we went to our beds if not to sleep. It was a gardener perhaps, maybe even one of those who had helped to dig the grave, or some other disgruntled servant who'd abandoned his or her post when Kornilov released the palace staff: whoever it was must have told one of the new guards where the infamous Grigory Rasputin had been buried, and they hadn't been able to wait until daybreak to dig up his coffin and pry off its lid.

They uncovered his face and body and spread a rumor that he had not decayed—which was possible, of course, and hardly outside the laws of nature, as he'd been buried in ground that quickly refroze. But no one mentioned that fact. Months after his murder he looked and smelled as he had when he was buried, perfumed with laurel, the men who exhumed him said, his flesh as incorruptible as a saint's. Except he had a mouthful of blood, they said, and other marks of possession by unclean spirits, and they'd had to stake him through the heart. They'd had to drag him into the woods and lay him on a pyre and pour gasoline on him. They'd had to light him on fire, and when they did, they said, he sat up to accuse them, sat up on fire with a stake through his heart.

When I found out what had caused the strange orange glow I'd seen when I got up to see the dead deer in the daylight, I was grateful Dunia had left Petersburg and was safe at home in Pokrovskoye, with my mother. She would never learn what happened to the body she'd prepared so meticulously—lovingly—for the afterlife. I didn't care what the soldiers had done so much as that they'd done it without my being there to mark the flight of his ashes on the wind. Someone who loved Father should have been there, with him.

Still, the soldiers had served their purpose. Now all of it had happened as Father had said it would in the letter he dictated before he died. *Bury my body,* he wrote. *It will not be left in peace. My dust, returned to dust, shall be scattered to the winds.*

A Bureaucratic Adventure

· · · · ·

"LIKE BANGING A CORPSE," Boris said, rolling off.

"At least it was a warm corpse."

"You don't pretend otherwise."

"Why should I? I told you I didn't want to."

"Fair enough."

He got up, pulled on his trousers, took the tin pot from off the gas ring, and went out the door to the sink at the end of the hall. He came back with it filled with water.

"We don't have any tea, do we?" he asked, as he did each morning, never looking for himself and implying by his tone that I was deficient in my housekeeping.

"On the sill there, next to the bread."

He pinched what was left of the loaf. "Hard," he said.

I shrugged, he shrugged, he broke the bread in half, pushed his finger into the center. I sat up and waited for what he left in me to seep out, onto the sheets, before drawing on my underclothes. Intercourse was a concession to pragmatism, not sentiment, especially on a morning when I was going yet again—this would be my fourth attempt—to apply for an identity card, without which I risked being deported. It had taken me two years to collect all the documents I needed, and if submitting to Boris was yet one more block over which to stumble, so be it.

"Hard all the way through." He bit off a piece. "Oh, well," he said, chewing while rereading the previous week's edition of *Le Canard Enchaîné,* through which, he was convinced, General Pyotr Nikolayevich Wrangel was sending him encrypted messages from his outpost in Belgrade. The paper was satirical and targeted the French government. I don't think the leader of the evacuated White Army had ever been mentioned in one of its articles, but this made no difference to Boris. Nights, after he came home from work, he pored over it, circling characters according to a pattern of prime numbers between one and one hundred—first, second, third, fifth, seventh, eleventh, and so forth, on up to the ninety-seventh, at which point he began again with one. Then, as he tried to make me understand, the circled letters and the blanks between words (for he circled those too whenever a prime number landed on them) from the first, second, third, fifth, and so on articles could be arranged by applying a different mathematical code—one I didn't even try to comprehend—into directives Wrangel sent to Boris to share with his secret squadron of monarchist soldiers.

I washed myself as well as I could in a sink, dressed, and prepared to present myself once again at the préfecture de police. I'd lost my way and as much as an hour on my first pilgrimage to the Île de la Cité, so, although there were more direct routes to the heart of the city, I followed the Seine all the way to the Pont Neuf, keeping the river on my left. That way I didn't have to pay attention to street signs and the time passed more quickly.

The Pont Neuf crouched over the water in a series of squat arches with crenellations above. Each pier rose out of the Seine like a small bastion, a fitting enough passage to the island and its grim government buildings. The office to which refugees were to apply for identity cards was on the third floor, at the end of a long, ill-lit corridor against whose walls leaned what appeared to be the same hushed queue of foreigners as were there the previous month, and the one before that. They looked to be almost exclusively Russian and spoke to one another in whispers, like children who had been scolded and warned not to make any more noise. All the snatches of conversation I heard concerned matters of employment: who had gotten a job doing what and for how much and how many hours a week.

Eavesdropping in the corridor of the préfecture had already afforded me a wealth of necessary information. The ubiquitous handbills announcing, in Russian, free medical care at Salpêtrière, des Invalides, Val-de-Grâce, even the Institut Pasteur, were not the charitable offers they appeared but purposefully misleading solicitations designed to lure refugees into medical experiments. All the trade unions that might protect a refugee from employers eager to underpay or otherwise exploit him or her were avowedly pro-Bolshevik and therefore closed to any White Russian who, after all, had arrived in Paris because of his monarchist sympathies. Gendarmes were eager to arrest Russians on any pretext, especially insolence, and were particularly vindictive to readers of *Zveno,* for its suspected ties to Bulgarian anarchists. Really, it was best to never carry any Russian language publication at all. For those unfortunate enough to be arrested, political asylum would be withdrawn. It was a one-way ticket to the Soviet Union and execution for defecting in the first place. In such a world, taxi driving was considered a plum career, as was carpentry, hairdressing, waiting tables, and laundering hotel sheets. Anyone who had been a physician or professor or lawyer back home couldn't work in France without French citizenship, and he would be required to pass French exams and obtain French diplomas.

The building was unheated; I kept my coat pulled tight around me. Each time I'd come to the préfecture I brought a book with me, but the light was poor and the atmosphere so permeated by anxiety and discomfort that, even when I wasn't actively gathering information from other people's conversations, I read the same paragraph over and over without noticing. There were no placards announcing that eating and smoking were forbidden, but whenever a uniformed official walked past, anyone with a crust or a cigarette hastily hid or extinguished it. The place conveyed the pessimism and hopelessness of an internment camp.

I waited, that morning, two hours and fifty minutes for my turn before the prefect. There was a different one each time, so I hadn't seen this one before, wearing a stole of white fur to complement his black robe. He held out his hand, the flesh of its smallest finger squeezed by a signet ring.

"Are they in order?" he demanded in French, speaking quickly as if he hoped to force me to ask him to repeat the question, giving him license for intensified impatience and further impoliteness. "Your papers—are they in order?"

The authentication from the Office of Russian Refugee Affairs. A letter promising employment as an equestrienne. A letter of permission from the labor ministry. A permit from the Billancourt police station. I put them all on the high desk, all they'd asked for the last time, when I'd come without the letter promising employment. "I wondered why you didn't ask for one," the manager said when I returned, "but not until after you left."

The prefect looked at the documents slowly, squinting at each as if it were in a foreign language, and then returned to the authentication from the refugee office. "Matryona Grigorievna Rasputina. Praskovia Fedorovna Rasputina. Grigory Yefimovich Rasputin, deceased. Which are you?"

"Matryona Grigorievna."

"Born 1898. Pokrovskoye. Is that right?"

"Yes."

"Where is Pok—Pokrovskey—sko? Where is it?"

"Siberia. The closest large city is Tobolsk. But before Paris I lived in St. Petersburg."

"For how long?"

"From 1908 until 1917."

"Paskrovia, this is your mother?"

"Yes. *Praskovia*."

"And this . . . this deceased Grigory Rasputin, he is your father?"

"Yes."

"You are the child of Grigory Rasputin?"

"Yes."

"*The* Grigory Rasputin? The infamous monk Rasputin?"

"Yes."

The prefect gathered my papers together, placed them on his desk, and folded his plump hands on them.

"I have other documents," I told him after his silence grew pointed. "If you wish to see them."

"What are they?"

"A letter. Two photographs. One of my father, my sister, Varvara, and myself, standing before a fountain at Tsarskoe Selo. And one of my father and myself in the company of the late Alexandra Romanov. This is me, here." I pointed to the girl in the picture, the one seated to the right of the tsarina. The prefect held out his hand and I gave him the envelope containing the letter.

"The letter was written by the late tsar to my father. You can see"—I showed him the crest on the paper—"it is official."

For what seemed a long while the prefect gazed at the photographs and the letter. He removed a magnifying glass from a drawer and held it to his eye. "Michel," he called, "come look at this." A thin man with a tic in his right cheek came out from behind a screen where he'd been typing, and the prefect handed him the forms, the photographs, and the letter.

"You speak French fluently," the prefect observed.

"Yes. My sister, Varvara, and I attended Steblin–Kamensky Academy in St. Petersburg."

"Steblin–Kamensky Academy?"

"Yes, my father—"

"Your father."

"Yes."

"Your father, Grigory Rasputin, the same Rasputin who brought down the Russian Empire."

"My father, Grigory Yefimovich Rasputin, who was a devout man and a healer. A person misunderstood. Not a person of . . . of official status. It was our mother's wish that her daughters be educated in the European style, like the young ladies Father encountered in the city, girls who had gone to finishing schools. Educated, as the simple people in our village were not. In 1908 I traveled west by rail to live with my father and attend school in St. Petersburg. I learned the usual things—languages, history, elocution, and deportment."

The man the prefect called Michel looked up from the documents. "Extraordinary," he said.

"Indeed," said the prefect.

"But there isn't any . . . There's nothing irregular." The secretary handed the papers back to the prefect.

"Nothing irregular!" The prefect pushed his thumb and forefinger under the lenses of his glasses and rubbed his eyes. Mouth closed, he laughed, expelling little gusts of air through his nostrils, which were very narrow, as if pinched by invisible fingers.

"Not in as far as the papers—the necessary papers—are concerned."

The prefect settled his eyeglasses back on the bridge of his nose. "Nothing irregular," he said once more, still shaking with inaudible laughter.

"In any case," I said, "my papers—they are in order, no?'

"Yes." The prefect lowered his chin into his hand. "You can go," he said to the secretary, waving him away without taking his eyes off me.

"So I may be issued an identity card?"

"What employment does the daughter of Grigory Rasputin expect to find here in Paris?"

"You can see for yourself." I pointed to the letter from the manager of the equestrian troupe. "I am promised a job where I live, in Billancourt, with my husband."

"Why, if you have a husband, are you known by your father's surname?"

"Our marriage document was lost when we fled and, hoping to avoid further confusion, I am using the name on the papers I have."

The prefect nodded. "And what will you do for a . . . what is it, an equestrian troupe? Clean stables? Sell cigarettes and confections? Summon the devil?"

"No."

"What, then?"

"Ride."

"You will ride?"

"Yes."

The prefect smiled. "So, you are a horsewoman?"

"Yes."

"You are the star of the show, perhaps?"

"I haven't begun performing yet. How could I have without a permit?"

"But you have a position?"

"Yes."

"A position for which you auditioned?"

"That's correct. May I—"

"And how did it go, your audition for the . . . um, troupe?"

"It went well, thank you. I—excuse me, but I don't under—"

"You're talented, are you?"

"I am good with horses. I grew up with them."

"How so?" The prefect lifted his shoulders and his eyebrows, both at once, as if those parts of him shared a single marionette string.

"Why are you making sport of me!" I said before I could prevent myself from ruining my appeal. "Why must I be . . . be persecuted to get my card! This is the fourth time I've come here to this office. I am just—all I want is the means to work legally, without being arrested. I am trying to comply with—"

"Who is persecuting you?"

"You. You are, yes. All of you. You make this as difficult as possible. Some of us with our families missing." I snatched up the authorization paper from the refugee office.

"And my father, my father whom you disrespect with your insinuations—you know nothing of my father. Nothing of what, of who he was. You make judgments without any right. You're no better than the murderers who put him in the river. Because you kill him also with your slander, your falsifying rumors, and, and . . ." I was on my toes now, my hands on the desk, my chin thrust over it. The prefect pushed his glasses back up his nose. He looked at me, no longer laughing, and not smiling either.

"I want my papers, my photographs," I told the prefect.

"And your identity card. You want that as well. It is why you are here, no?"

I nodded, unsure if he was taunting me. But, no, he called to Michel, who crept forward with a card—orange rather than blue, as Boris had been given for industrial labor. On it was typed my name, Matryona Rasputin, and Billancourt as the subdivision in which I was allowed to seek employment, as well as an expiration date, December 15, 1925—five rather than the standard three years hence. The prefect drew a large envelope out from a drawer. I watched him gather my papers and the new card together, slip them into the envelope, and then, without looking at me, he pushed the envelope toward me and called for the next petitioner to come forward.

After I had walked along the river for some minutes, after I was calm, I realized something. The prefect's response to my surname, more impertinent than what I'd come to expect, underscored what others' reactions had tried to teach me since my arrival in Paris. I'd just been too stupid to understand.

The sole thing of value I possessed was my father's history. His history and his name. Before another year passed I'd be performing as the Daughter of the Mad Monk Rasputin.

That Hollywood Bear

· · · · ·

ONCE I JOINED, I knew I'd never leave, never make a home and live in it. I wouldn't—nothing could induce me to—step away from what I'd discovered.

In the circus I was no longer part of the strictly mortal world, gray and workaday, the dispiriting, dull, humbling slog of one day into the next that I'd grown to expect living in Paris. Not that it was all luck, all pleasure, all reward. I went to bed exhausted, and my time in front of an audience was a small fraction of the day. Performing before a crowd, I didn't need to try to synchronize the horses' movements with my own, it just happened. I felt their legs beneath them as if they were my own, felt the impact of each hoof as it struck the ground. I entered the ring barefoot and bare-legged, on two white horses. Together we appeared as if by magic out of the black night and into the ring's circle of light. I never rode but stood on the horses' backs, my left foot planted on the horse to the left, my right foot on the right, as we moved into a canter.

Before the equestrian troupe signed with Barnum, I didn't wear so vulgar a costume, but circus performers are expected to sparkle, and sparkle I did in a short, spangled red leotard that ended in something like a gash between my legs. The horses' reins were red and sequined and glittered like my costume. I held them in both hands, slack. They were the same as an aerialist's net, for use only when something went wrong. All our communication was through my bare feet, balanced where a saddle would sit, on the horses' rosined backs. For me it was just our twelve white limbs, the horses' and mine, moving in a rhythm practice couldn't deliver. They asked, I answered. I asked, they answered. That was it.

Around, around. Flurries of yellow-white sawdust rising around the blurred hooves, tails rippling like flags in a light wind. Dream-like, the sound of hooves striking in concert, over and over, incantatory. The orchestra played, but I didn't hear their music. We went in counterclockwise circles, most of my weight resting on my left leg, flexed as I leaned into the curve. Three loops around the ring and then, before anyone had a chance to see how I'd done it, I was standing backward, looking over the horses' tails and holding the reins behind my back, and we made another three loops that way. A jump was carried into the ring, a jump four feet in height, and I took it; I took it standing on two horses, I took it facing forward, I took it facing backward. When I got stronger—it took months of training with the floor acrobats—I could do a backbend from one moving horse's back to the other's and take a jump with my hands on one horse, my feet on the other, back bowed.

AFTER BORIS DIED (before he'd turned thirty, just as Father promised), there was nothing to hold me in Paris, and from that point forward I closed every letter asking for information about my family with the request that I be contacted care of whatever show I was traveling with. It made me feel safe, as if the circus were a kind of magic kingdom, impenetrable by outside forces, even Soviet spies eager to punish anyone so cavalier as to ignore an iron curtain.

Months would go by without any answer, but I didn't stop asking until, bit by bit, I received enough information from enough people to piece together what had happened to my family after I'd left. Whoever contacted me didn't do so in writing—that wasn't safe—but they carried messages, one to another. After the show's finale, which gathered all of us—aerialists; equestriennes; dancers; clowns; dogs wearing tutus and walking upright; monkeys capering; elephants swaying under sequined headdresses, toenails painted gold; gymnasts doing handsprings; and I in my sparkling tunic and, later, jodhpurs and tailcoat—after we'd taken a final sweeping bow and the orchestra had screeched its goodbye crescendo, the lights would go up and, every few months, a man or woman would break away from the audience and hurry to accost me as I made my way back to my car. Whoever it was had information, a message to whisper in my ear, old news that was, perhaps, no longer true. But by the time I left Europe for the United States, I was able to confirm that Varya and her chaperone had escaped the soldiers who commandeered the train, only to fall prey to another band of predators. She was buried in a communal grave in the city of Perm. Dimitri was conscripted by the Red Army and became something of a legend for what his superiors called valor. I suspect it was the obedience of a hugely strong and stupid boy that made his military career. My mother was still living in her two-story home, alone except for Dunia and the livestock.

Of course, I didn't have to ask for news of the Romanovs, as their deaths were genuine news, printed in papers all over the world. After the news reports stopped, I never expected to learn any more of Alyosha, but I did. Working for Barnum & Bailey, I toured in Europe until 1935, when I auditioned for a smaller, American company. I imagined I'd be happier in a new world that didn't hold so many memories, forgetting of course that it isn't places but people who hold memories. Too, performing in America satisfied a little of my childhood dream, even if I was no longer on horseback but working with cats and bears and had joined the Forepaugh–Sells circus rather than Buffalo Bill Cody's Wild West Show.

. . .

"TOO BIG FOR YOUR BRITCHES." That's an American expression for hubris. I hadn't been traveling with Barnum for long before I'd been seduced, thoroughly and indelibly, by the cats. The horses were my friends, old friends. I knew them inside and out. But the cats—I couldn't stop looking at them. I wanted to be closer to them, wanted to be the one they watched, the one on whom their eyes remained fixed. It got so that I felt I needed them to recognize me, acknowledge me. I dreamed of touching their faces, made myself a nuisance hanging around their cages. Then I discovered there weren't any women who tamed lions—not after Claire Heliot retired—and I couldn't let go of the idea that I could be the next. Either that or it didn't let go of me.

I knew every minute working with cats would be like that gap in the air between two trapezes, when the aerialist has let go of the first bar and is flying, falling, yet to grab the next bar or catch a partner's hand. The only thing that gave me any rest from my fantasies of being a lion tamer was becoming one, but it took two years to find someone willing to take on a female apprentice, and the only reason he did was as a parting blow to his rivals. Seventy-five years old, Nero Highgate—Master Nero—was retiring from show business, and leaving all he knew to a woman whose father was an infamous madman: that seemed to him enough like a final triumph over other tamers, in their prime.

It began, like any art, with watching. And it began not with lions but tigers. For a fortnight all I did—all I was allowed to do— was sit outside a tiger's cage, hour after hour, focusing my every thought on the beast within.

"Banish from your mind," Master Nero said, punctuating his instructions with snaps of his whip, which I rarely saw out of his hand, "whatever thought does not concern the animal. The animal has powers of perception you cannot understand. While you will never learn its thoughts, it will always know yours."

What I'd loved about horses was our shared, silent, almost sacred partnership—we understood one another. It looked hard, but it was easy. Now the inequality, the challenge, the shift of power—all of it was exhilarating. Master Nero brought me a battered red stool and placed it on the ground outside the bars of the tiger's cage. If I found my attention wavering, I was told I should stop, walk away, take a break. The cage was one of six in the circus's winter quarters, a run-down compound in a run-down port city in the south of Italy—Brindisi, where the breeze off the water smelled of motor oil and rotting seaweed. My apprenticeship, all said and done, was six months of tedium punctuated by moments of panic.

"Although you will never see into a cat's head," Master Nero said day after day after day, "you can memorize its behavior. A cat isn't like a person, hard to predict. It always responds the same way it responded the time before." And there was this, his parting caution:

"I've seen you on horseback," he said, "enough that I can guess your weakness with cats."

"What is it?" I asked him, when he didn't continue. He'd given me my own whip—never to be used on a cat, only as a visual cue to direct its movements. I'd spent enough time with him that I hadn't expected a purely celebratory gesture.

"No matter what I tell you, you believe you will establish a sympathy with the cats you train. You're vain. You think your heritage, your father's gift, whatever it was, *if* it was, will exempt you from the rules. But mark my words: if you try to push your friendship on the animal, then, *pffft,* you will be done for." He smiled at the idea. He was a small man with a very large smile filled with tobacco-stained teeth. We shook hands. A year later I heard he'd married for the seventh time, this time to a pretty gymnast half his age. Apparently he hadn't been so astute in his estimation of human behavior, because she did to him as she'd done to her first two husbands: run off to Argentina with all his money. She picked men who were old enough that chasing a wayward wife around the globe seemed, in the wake of her departure, not quite worth the trouble.

I never lied about my abilities. I was a competent trainer of lions, tigers, and leopards, and professed no unusual talents. Whoever hired me lied in my stead, advertising a performer with the power to hypnotize animals, an occult ability illustrated on the midway as blue electricity zigzagging from my eyes. I could almost hear Father laughing. As for me, I found the portrait a little too similar to the cartoons of him and the tsarina plastered over every blank wall in St. Petersburg.

AN AMERICAN AUDIENCE wasn't going to be satisfied as easily as those back home—that was clear from the start. The expectation of spectacle added to a name like Rasputin: I couldn't claim such a heritage without doing something that seemed impossible. As impossible as laying hands on a hemorrhaging hemophiliac and stopping the blood from flowing. Anything less and I'd disappoint. In Europe, people wanted to see me perform because I was a Rasputin. They didn't care about my proving my expertise. They accorded it to me as a birthright. But Mr. Forepaugh—every time I proposed an act he asked for one more element, one more twist. Lions, tigers, leopards, pumas—I wanted to keep it to cats. I had experience with cats. Two lions, two tigers, two leopards, and two pumas. Not enough.

"A bear," Mr. Forepaugh said. "A bear maybe could shake things up."

I agreed: a bear. How different could a bear be from a lion?

"Can't have just one."

I said we'd add another. Mr. Forepaugh frowned. "There's something . . . Something's missing."

Ten animals. What could be missing?

"I know what's missing—that Hollywood bear," he said. "That Hannibal bear."

Hannibal tipped the balance because he had a history, like I did, the kind that seizes hold of people's imaginations and inspires morbid curiosity. We weren't even halfway through the off-season before they'd drawn up a new program that included his biography, ginned up to make him seem that much more dangerous, and hired a publicist to plant articles in the papers in Chicago, Detroit, Omaha, St. Louis, Indianapolis, Cincinnati—anywhere Forepaugh–Sells was scheduled to perform—pitting the Daughter of the Mad Monk against the Man-Eating Hollywood Bear. Which might have been fine, if there hadn't been ten other animals in the ring. If bears, like cats, had good eyesight and responded to visual cues.

They'd scrapped the jungle picture. It had been one of those blighted ventures, the kind in which everything went wrong—sets flooded, people got sick, the female lead broke her ankle, props burned up in a fire. A biblical onslaught of plagues, one after another, and then Hannibal, without provocation, tore a piece out of an actor's shoulder, and the general disaster that the project became excused the bear any responsibility for his attack. It was interpreted as a spell of bad behavior generated by the picture's unbeatable bad luck, something that hadn't had anything to do with any particular bear; that would have happened no matter what bear, because that was the kind of bad luck it was—pervasive. Circus people are as superstitious as Russians.

. . .

NERO. HANNIBAL. THE names seemed taken from an invocation. I never looked at Hannibal without thinking of Alyosha memorizing the Caesars as part of his ill-fated training for leadership—not after Alyosha suddenly returned to me, returned to life, it felt like, in his journal.

The under-trainer, Jim Nelson, and I were blocking out my ridiculous, stunt-packed "exotic extravaganza" on the day I received a thick envelope, much creased and smudged, addressed to Matryona Grigorievna Rasputina, with a series of crossed-out addresses. The idea had been to have two bears doing somersaults while I waltzed with a third, Hannibal, and an assortment of lions, pumas, leopards, and tigers sat on their haunches, looking at us and bringing their front paws together in clumsy, nearly silent applause. Hannibal learned the simple box step quickly. As soon as we played the recording, up he'd go on his hind legs. He couldn't lead, but he did move in time with the music, and none of us had hoped for that much. It was enough to have a waltzing bear. For the Daughter of the Mad Monk to waltz with a bear to Strauss while a dozen potentially murderous animals watched was enough, even for Americans. He kept his front paws in the right attitude. As long as I did my part, his left paw looked as if it were guiding me at the waist, and he held the right one up for me to hold.

That afternoon, I had my hand on the arm of the phonograph and was about to set the needle on the record when a little man whistled from outside the fenced ring to catch my attention. He seemed to have appeared out of nowhere, and he looked like a Rumpelstiltskin with his huge ears and nose, his hunched back, and his peculiar black coat with its enormous pockets, out of one of which he drew the thick envelope.

"What is this?" I asked him as he pressed it into my hands.

"A gift from a friend," he said in Russian.

"Who is this friend?"

"A friend in the old country," he said, and he gave a deep bow.

The handwriting on the envelope was crabbed. Inside, an unsigned typewritten letter was tucked between the pages of a small black leather-bound book—a journal, written in a hand I knew well, as sometimes when Alyosha wanted me to come to him and tell a story, he sent me a note, usually through Nagorny. The letter explained that the journal had been smuggled out of the house where the family had been executed. As a kind of introductory remark—or perhaps a warning—the note's author explained that the book contained the tsarevich's account of his family's exile, from August 1917, when they left Tsarskoe Selo, until July 17, 1918. I looked up from the letter to ask how the bearer of the envelope had come into its possession, but he had vanished.

THREE BEARS, TWO LIONS, two tigers, two leopards, and two pumas.

"Asking for it," Jim Nelson said of the act. "Too big for your britches," he said. But it wasn't that. I was distracted; I'd lost focus. Having read Alyosha's journal once, I read it again and again, I don't know how many times. I had trouble sleeping and couldn't keep my mind on work. We were rehearsing when Hannibal escaped my control.

Jim shook his head when he visited. He stared morosely at the sheet tented over my leg. I hadn't seen it. The expression on the face of whoever was unlucky enough to change the dressing told me all I needed to know. At night, with the door to my room open, light entered from the hall, and instead of the sheet I'd see a luminous white blur above my weeping, sutured thigh. What with morphine and fever dreams, I took this to be the ghost of my leg hovering over its mangled flesh, uncertain as to whether it was to go on to the next world or remain with me in this one.

According to the calendar hung on the wall opposite my bed—"To help orient you," the nurse explained—it was nearly May. I'd slept through half of April. Well, not slept exactly. The last thing I remembered, Hannibal was on my chest. He'd pinned my shoulders to the ground and was licking my temple. I was laughing. I thought he was kissing me.

"How many stitches?" I asked the nurse unwrapping my thigh.

"Do you have any idea what lives in the mouth of a bear?" she answered, as if to imply I'd been careless in choosing a means of injuring myself. I did know, actually, as the pathology report was clipped under the fever chart at the foot of my bed and I'd got the night nurse to show it to me. *Staphylococcus epidermidis, Streptococcus, Escherichia coli, Serratia fonticola, Serratia marcescens, Aeromonas hydrophila, Bacillus cereus, Enterococcus durans.*

Jim visited with a photographer from a local paper and two panther cubs. "Borrowed from the zoo," he said. "Mr. Forepaugh wants a little good publicity."

"We see a lot of circus people," the nurse told the photographer. "And there are accidents. There are always accidents. Rasputin," she said, shaking her head. "Can you imagine?" She talked about me as if I weren't there or couldn't understand English, and I was reminded of Alyosha's telling me that was how he knew he wasn't expected to live, the way no one ever bothered to keep anything from him.

She cranked up the bed so the photographer could pose me with the under-trainer and the cubs. *Miss Rasputin being comforted by her lifesaver, Jim Nelson, who brought the cheerful cubs to her bedside at the Dukes Co. Hospital.* The whole thing couldn't have taken more than ten minutes, but it exhausted me. All the articles I saw lauded

Jim for his courage in pulling the bear off me. A lot of telegrams, mostly from people I didn't know.

I waited until the nurse left the room to ask if Hannibal had been put down.

"I'm sorry," Jim said. And then the nurse came back in; he slipped away. Poor Hannibal.

I had the most peculiar dreams. Even when I thought I was awake. I'd look up and there Alyosha would be, sitting not just on the bed but on my injured leg. "Well," he'd say, "this is unexpected—you bleeding to death for a change," and he'd laugh as if it were a fine joke on me. Apparently I very nearly had. Bled to death, I mean.

It Was Magic

· · • • ·

ALREADY AS HE WALKED HOME with Nagorny, Alyosha
was beset by images of Katya's naked body—plagued
by suggestive and even outright wanton visions, which would be
enjoyable to a degree, but that was just it. There was no degree,
no gradual anything. All he could think of was her nakedness, the
dusky pink and brown of her nipples. And her thinness, her ribs
and her collarbones—so different from the women he was used to
seeing. She looked that much more naked, sharpened by leanness.
The hair between her legs was thick, dark. It was curly and silky at
the same time. He'd imagined it would be coarse in texture. How
could he think about anything else when he was vulnerable to visions like that? Katya's body, the slightly acrid smell of her hair,
the birthmark—these eclipsed every other thing. He couldn't even
see Lake Baikal represented on a map without becoming aroused.

Aware that Katya was doing something illicit, that she should
not, at seventeen, sit astride him and rub him so confidently, betraying this as something she'd done many times before, Alyosha
knew he should feel disgusted by her. He'd been raised to find
such gestures too vulgar to succeed in exciting his attention. Instead, he itched with lust. No sooner had he ejaculated than he
wanted to be doing whatever would lead to that feeling again. And
if Katya's knowingness about intercourse made her a wicked girl,

it also made her a powerful kind of goddess; the two coexisted. Not a deity he'd been raised to worship, that was true, but he was learning the world was big, so very big, and filled with many different kinds of women to admire, to want to see naked and hold in one's arms. Anyway, he hadn't time to waste on waiting for the right kind.

He had to see her again, as many times as possible. And Nagorny would have to help him. Nagorny would have to understand that this was not the kind of thing that should be denied to a person. Especially not to a person whose days were numbered—it might be all right to deny it to another boy, under other circumstances, but Alyosha wasn't that other, theoretical boy. He was the one being shipped off to his death, one way or another. He was the one who deserved Katya.

"Nagorny," he said. "I'd like it very much if we could do this again."

"Visit Kolya?"

"I want to go to Kolya's house. I want to go as often as I can. But I want . . . Here's what I'm asking you, Nagy. I'm asking you to tell Father and Mother that we are going out for walks. Say it's for strengthening my leg. I want to go whenever the weather permits."

Nagorny looked at him.

"Please, Nagy," he said, and Nagorny, knowing what he was being asked, agreed.

IT WAS MAGIC. The skies remained a clear sparkling blue; the temperature never dipped uncomfortably low. Reason suggested it would be difficult if not impossible to arrange even a few meetings between Alyosha and Katya, what with the presence of Katya's family in the house as well as her father's medical practice. But one opportunity after another presented itself. The mother had gone to the market in Medyanki Tatarskie; the father was at an old man's deathbed; the maid, asleep. The maid had woken up and gone to help her seamstress sister, who had fallen behind in filling orders; the father had been summoned to attend to a birth in Savina; the mother, having eaten some bad meat, was ill and confined to her room. The mother had recovered and was in her garden, pulling all the weeds that had sprung up while she was ill; the father was closeted in his examining room with a difficult case; the maid had taken the carpet down to the river to wash, as it was too large to wash at home.

Handsome Alyosha, he wrote in his journal, was astonished by his good luck—it was even better than winning a bicycle race against Hermes and Chronos. He was able to be with Katya almost as often as he cared to be.

At night, lying in bed, he sorted through the details of "being a tsarevich," as she called it, to come up with the most amusing among them.

Servants having to walk out of rooms backward so as to never turn their backs on the tsarevich.

Having a heated indoor saltwater swimming pool, so you could bathe in a summer ocean while a blizzard raged outside.

Almost anything about Tsarskoe Selo fascinated Katya, from the Chinese theater—the whole Chinese village!—to the elephant house to the pyramid and the Turkish bath. Alyosha soon learned that his part of the bargain didn't have to be any harder than his imagining himself back at home, walking or being pushed along one of the many paths through the grounds, and narrating what he saw as he continued from one marvel to the next. She didn't even care if they visited a place twice. In fact, she soon developed a preference for some destinations over others.

"Take me back to the Chinese village," she'd say. "Tell me again what it looks like."

So he'd begin with a pagoda's roof, explaining how it was different from the roof over her head, how it wasn't just one but one, two, three roofs stacked on top of one another, or more if you liked—as many as you liked—and the higher up the smaller they were and each had a little pointed corner, like the shoes worn by Ali Baba. And then of course he'd have to tell Katya the story of "Ali Baba and the Forty Thieves," because the most interesting thing about Ali Baba was not how the tips of his Arabian slippers curled upward from the ground. This was how Alyosha made the walks through Tsarskoe Selo last so long, because he always digressed off the path and into a story, and at some point he realized he didn't have to be strictly truthful. Even were Katya to grow up and marry an aristocrat—an outcome that was impossible, as aristocrats had been outlawed—she'd never visit Tsarskoe Selo. The Bolsheviks were probably burning it down even as Alyosha and Katya lay together in her bed.

But in Kubla Khan Selo, as narrated from the smallest bedroom of a physician's house in Tobolsk, the zookeeper had just taken shipment of a team of pachyderms, and the elephant house was being rehabilitated for its new occupants. Their names were Flora and Belle, and Flora was thirty and Belle was thirty-three, and when the tsarevich came to greet them, they bowed their heads down, then laid their trunks on the ground, each asking to be the first on whom the tsarevich would tread, walking up the trunk and over the huge gray skull and into the howdah.

"What's a howdah?"

"It's the saddle an elephant wears, only it's not a saddle, really, as that would look like a button on anything as enormous as an elephant. It's a chair for as many as four people. Two face frontward and two face backward, and there's a canopy above, to keep the heat off their heads. You can get brain fever in the jungle, if you don't wear a hat and keep out of the sun."

"Father said you were sick. What's the matter with you?"

"What did he say was the matter?"

"He didn't."

"It's more that I'm . . . that I have been ill and now am better, but my mother is a nervous woman; she likes to have physicians look in on me."

"What was it that was the matter?" Katya asked.

"They don't know."

"Well, what did it feel like? Did it have a rash?"

"No. You can't always see it. I get injured easily, that's all."

"Do you fall down?"

"Katya."

"Do you?"

"Not more than anyone else. Tell me where you want to go, Katya."

"Where were we?"

"On the roof of the pagoda."

"Then let's go back there, Tsarevich."

" 'Let the lion dog be small,' " Alyosha quoted. " 'Let its face be black, its eyes be large and luminous, its ears like the sails of a war junk. Let it learn to bite the foreign devils instantly. Let—' "

"What foreign devils? What are they?"

"It's how the Chinese refer to people who are not Chinese. Empress Dowager Cixi—she was the one who ruled until 1908— made up a sort of poem about the dogs that guard the temple." Alyosha closed his eyes while he spoke. Imagining: he could do it, but it wasn't second nature.

The Window in the Egg

. . . . .

*I*F I WASN'T UNCONSCIOUS in the weeks following the bear's mauling me, I wasn't more aware of my surroundings than a high fever and a great deal of morphine allowed. The wound in my thigh was reopened and drained three times, infection carrying me off to landscapes both familiar and strange. Often I found myself at Tsarskoe Selo, in the company of the Romanovs. Sometimes it was 1917, and Father was dead. Sometimes it was earlier, and he was still living. Always it was a wrench to be returned to my hospital bed, for when I fell under the influence of morphine, I heard my father's voice and saw his face as I no longer could in my sober, waking life. Alyosha, too, and all the rest of them—so real, so alive, and I wasn't dreaming but remembering what I couldn't, or hadn't, for many years. Many of these memories evaporated once I recovered, but one remained with me; it continued to preoccupy my thoughts. A memory, not a dream.

It was April of 1909. I'd turned eleven in March. Alyosha was recovering nicely from an injury, and Father and I had been invited to tea at the Alexander Palace. My first real visit, as I thought of it, in which people seemed to actually see me, as they hadn't on those occasions when I'd accompanied Father to an emergency because he hadn't had time to take me home to Dunia. It was a new experience for me, being corporeal in the palace.

The Romanov girls, given the chore of entertaining me while my father and their mother were with Alyosha, asked would I like to see the imperial Easter eggs?

"Oh, thank you," I said, and I said, "Yes, please," as I would have to any suggestion made by a quartet of princesses. Tatiana took my hand and led me down a shining marble-floored corridor that seemed, as I walked with the sisters, to stretch longer and longer. At last we reached the end of it, a door to a room filled with glass cabinets lit from within by concealed electrical lights. Inside them were the imperial Easter eggs.

Many of the eggs were clocks, which I found surprising and even sinister, perhaps because they were all wound, and ticking. One wasn't an egg at all but a tree with a songbird made of sapphires, which burst out from under emerald leaves to mark each hour with a song. Another had a serpent's tongue pointing to the time. An egg with a white top and gold bottom balanced on the spires of the Kremlin. And—Tatiana pointed to each in turn—there were the tsar's gold-coronation-coach egg, and the Romanov yacht, *Standart,* floating on an egg-shaped crystal sea, and a tourmaline egg containing an easel bearing miniature framed portraits of all the members of the family.

"The pelican is a symbol for Christ," Tatiana said. She reached into one of the cabinets and touched a white bird with an unusually large and pendulous beak, perched with its young in a golden nest on top of a golden egg. "The children of the pelican won't ever starve. When there are no fish, their mother or father tears open its own breast to feed them with its blood."

I couldn't think of what to say to this, so I was silent as Tatiana moved on to the next egg, a deep-purple one that opened to show me a swan. "Look," she said. She showed me that under the bird's wing was a little key. She turned it and the swan moved its head and spread its wings, separating its feathers. They were no longer than matchsticks and so intricately wrought I could see the barbs that made up each one. When she took my hand and unfolded its fingers to set the swan on my palm, my hand dropped under its surprising weight.

"Don't you like it?" she asked. I nodded and returned it to her.

"Here we are praying, all four of us girls, at a little temple of love. And here, on top, that's Alyosha. He's made to look like Cupid, but you can see it's him. And it's a clock too, so the twig he's holding—see there—that's what points to the hour.

"Do you want to see my favorite?" Tatiana said. Only a year older than I, she betrayed no strain at having to make conversation with a child too overwhelmed to speak. From a new cabinet she withdrew a large egg cut from translucent pink jade and decorated on the outside with a lattice of diamonds. When she set it on a table, I saw that the narrow end of the egg held a tiny window.

"Look inside," Tatiana told me, and I hesitated, and again she said, "Look."

I knelt before the table, my eye level with a circle of glass about the size of a monocle. Inside the egg was a park and trees and a white-and-yellow palace so detailed I almost had to believe I was seeing a real building, only through the wrong end of a telescope. There were balustrades and balconies, patios, windows, arched porticoes, a man-made pond and grotto, a Chinese village, a marble bridge, and an elephant house. The longer I looked, the longer I had to go on looking.

It was Tsarskoe Selo. It was where we had been walking, the Romanov girls and I, before we were called in for tea. I saw the path we'd taken from the greenhouses to the palace.

"It magnifies. The little window does," Tatiana said, and, as if she had uttered a spell, something happened to me while I was on my knees, my left eye closed and my right pressed close to the circle of glass. I no longer knew which side of the window I was on. I remained there, kneeling, my eye to the window in the egg, for what must have seemed a peculiarly long time to my hostesses, because, the next thing I knew, Father was coming to fetch me, and when I felt his hand on my shoulder I jumped right up, turned around, and hid my face in his coat.

"Why, Masha," Father said, and he went down on his knees too. I felt his coat moving against my face as he descended, and I kept my eyes tightly shut; I put my hands over them. "Did something frighten you?"

I shook my head no, but I didn't take my hands away from my face, and when he asked would I please open my eyes, I shook my head again to tell him I could not.

"Why?" Father said, but I had no answer to give him. "All right, then," he said. "Masha will have to agree that her papa can carry her."

I nodded. He picked me up. He carried me back to the room where he had been drinking tea with Tsarina Alexandra Fyodorovna and sat down with me in his lap. I listened to them talk on the outside of my closed eyelids.

"Is everything all right, Father Grigory?" the tsarina said. "Would you like to take Matryona Grigorievna home?" And he said, no, no, Masha is fine, only a bit tired, and they went on talking and talking of things that bored me and, my head resting against my father, I fell asleep.

Later, at home with Dunia, Father asked what had frightened me. "Were the princesses unkind?"

"Oh, no. They were friendly."

"What, then?"

But I couldn't explain it even to myself. I tried all night to come up with a way to make it make sense. I saw into the egg, all the way in, and not only did I see the tiny palace's rooms but I entered them, and there were people inside, not people made of jewels but real people, and the people were us. I was in the palace in the egg and in the palace the egg was in, and one was the same as the other, and I didn't know who was the real me—the one who sparkled inside the egg, or the one kneeling to watch her. I didn't want to let go of either one of us, and what would happen if I were to close my eyes? Perhaps we might both disappear.

"Fever," Dunia said, putting her hand on my forehead. "It's too much for her, that place. Remember last time? I had her in bed for three days. Three days of fancy school wasted."

TWENTY YEARS LATER, 1929, in Vienna, I made my debut with the big cats: *The Daughter of the Mad Monk Whose Feats in Russia Astonished the World in an Unparalleled Risk to Life and Limb Against Jungle Claw and Fang!*

I wasn't frightened once I entered the ring. I had been nervous; all winter, as I rehearsed, I was consumed by equal measures of excitement and panic. I slept poorly, dreamed my horses had died and I was washing and preparing them for burial. I dreamed of Orthodox priests and tolling bells and of having to thaw the frozen earth to dig their huge graves in Tsarskoe Selo's equine cemetery. I never imagined it would go badly—I was sure I would succeed—so the panic had nothing to do with that. I knew I was waiting for something, expecting some tremendous something, but I didn't know what it was until the show began and it fell on me.

The beam of light from above. How was it I'd never before seen that under it everyone was beautiful? The acrobats, the trapeze artists, the ringmaster in his top hat and tails, the clowns in their fantastic makeup and ridiculous clothes, even the boy who followed the elephants and picked up their dung. Each fragment of sawdust sparkled. The center pole, the aerialists' platforms, the nets, the bleachers, the buckets, the bales of hay, the rope ladders and the clown car and the cats' bloody meat as bright as garnets, the coarse hair on the elephant's head standing up straight in a luminous corona, and all around me diamonds the size of pinpricks falling through the air.

I'd been returned to the window in the egg, but I was no longer a child and I wasn't frightened. I saw the world I inhabited transfigured, as if it were on the other side of the egg's glass portal, a lens that magnified by bending light. Dust motes on one side of the window, and diamonds on the other. Colors I'd never known existed, colors for which I had no names. I was as close as I could be to the threshold of the world as God must see it, as my father had sometimes seen it—not every blight erased, not even one erased, only revealed by a different light, a light that bestowed beauty on withered leaves and broken twigs, on lepers, drunks, and criminals, on people who were sick and those who were well. A convergence of light and love.

Released from their holding cages, the tigers surged through the chutes that delivered them to the fenced center ring. The ripple of muscle under fur, the effortless grace of their leaping onto their platforms. Even their faces—to look at one required something like endurance if I was not to be overwhelmed by its beauty, which, like the tolling of Father's last funeral bell, reached under my skin and found that place where I couldn't defend myself, couldn't withhold what it demanded.

I didn't see their faces so much as their faces sprang toward my eyes. Their capacity for violence infused their beauty with terror, intensifying it to the point that I felt intoxicated—by color, and by form and depth, by all that creates the image of a thing. I lacked a volume knob, a means of turning myself down; my heart was wrung by love. Each white whisker shimmered. Together they radiated outward from the center of the animal's face like a spray of spangled sterling wands. The wide nose wrinkled in a snarl of perfect symmetry, and out from it twirled a living pinwheel of black and orange stripes, the animals' eyes lost in the pattern of their coats. Their hot breath came at me in waves, rank and moist on my skin, when I gave the audience what it wanted most: my head in the cat's open mouth.

Each choreographed movement, each flick of the whip and twitch of a tail, each snarl and raised paw with its scimitar claws and black pads creased like the palm of a man but infinitely more complex, not just the animal's but the whole world's destiny fore-told. In every living thing, in every cell of our beings, was the world's destiny foretold. I could hear, at last, the tremendous voices in what had once been silence.

Anyone who saw me in the ring assumed my crying was a symptom of stage fright, but that wasn't it, not at all. I was so alive in those moments it was as if I were burning all over, every nerve awakened, and in that state I couldn't help but feel my mortality with an equal force. I cried, caught between the knowledge of my life and that of my death—to think I'd one day lose myself, myself and all this splendor, everything I loved. How would I bear it?

With the cats, under the spotlight, I understood what—whom— I'd been waiting my whole life to understand, what I once imagined I'd felt with horses but now knew I never had. I knew what my father felt when he healed. Ecstasy. Of course it had to have been. I'd known that, but I hadn't yet felt it.

Tickets to an Execution

· · · ·

MAY 29, 1918, YEKATERINBURG

I've been here almost a week. (Father, Mother, Maria, and a few servants arrived on April 30, in the vanguard. Olga, Tatiana, Anastasia, Nagorny, Botkin, and I followed three weeks later, as I'd bumped my knee on Katya's bed frame and Botkin wouldn't allow me to travel before he was certain there would be no further "complications," as he calls them.)

They've painted all the upper story's windows white so we can't see beyond the high wood fence around the property. I noted the fence as we were taken to the house from the train station. Clearly they'd only just built it, anticipating our incarceration on the premises, as the lumber was new and yellow. There are few excursions outside for us, who are locked on the second floor, the guards directly below us. Sometimes one will bang the butt of his rifle on the ceiling, just to give us a start. Each day from three until four in the afternoon we are escorted outside to a "garden," where we may walk and breathe fresh air, Mother and I both in our wheeled invalid chairs. There is no vegetation that hasn't been trampled underfoot by the guards, a dozen or more of them, each carrying a revolver as well as rifle and bayonet. They enter our quarters whenever they please, without knocking. Already they've seen

Olga undressed. There are two machine guns, two that we have seen, one on the balcony outside the room I share with Mother and Father and another on the roof. Across the street is a barrack with one hundred and fifty men inside.

The official name of our lodgings is "The House of Special Purpose." Rather grand, isn't it? I wonder if all totalitarian regimes don't share a fondness for euphemism. A man named Ipatiev used to own the building. I asked our footman, Trupp, what kind of man Ipatiev was, and he said he was a military engineer. I asked again and he said he was a rich Jewish burgher, whatever that means. It wasn't what I was asking, and I suppose it doesn't matter, only that a White Army engineer might not like to have his house used for such a "special purpose" as this.

Although, judging from our reception at the train station, Yekaterinburg is thoroughly Red. Not one of the ten thousand revolutionary soldiers stationed here (that is the number reported by the Reds themselves) made any effort to subdue the mob.

"Show us the Romanovs!" people kept shouting, which, as Mother pointed out, is arguably better than their asking that we be handed over to them to do with what they would, but it made me feel that much more a criminal and a freak to hear people screaming for a look at us. It wasn't any different from the way crowds flocked to the Kunstkamera's Cabinet of Curiosities when the Fiji Mermaid came to St. Petersburg. Everyone wanted to see her, even if all she was was the top half of a dead monkey and the bottom half of a dead fish sewn together into a creature that never existed.

That's exactly what they are, *the Romanovs*: a false family at which to peer and shudder. *The Romanovs* resemble us physically. In fact, they look just like us. But they have nothing to do with us, with the human beings we are. They're made up—made up by other people, people who don't know us, who've never met us—and the parts they've sewn together are worse than dead monkeys and dead fish. *The Romanovs* are a family about whom horrors are written and illustrated. Drawings of women who look like my mother and sisters fornicating with a satanic rendering of Father Grigory, who drinks blood from a wine bottle he extends to my mother's lips, and drawings of a man supposed to be my father without any clothes, which doesn't matter as he hasn't any private parts to cover. Those are in my mother's hand; she holds them as if making a toast, blood running down her white wrist.

He's a good person, Trupp, you can tell from his face. He's old enough for the lines to have set in their habitual expression, which is one of patience, benign. He reminds me of a squirrel. It's partly those funny ears, with the reddish hair growing up off them in pointed tufts, but his eyes have a quizzical look, and he moves with sudden energy. He seems unaffected by the situation in which he finds himself, the officers always insulting and high-handed, punishing him for what he can't help. Ordering him around for the fun of it. When it seems imminent I'll give him this volume. A shot in the dark, Nagorny would call it, but if anyone can figure out how to smuggle it out, Trupp can.

JUNE 4

I don't know why I told Masha that Mother had prostituted herself to Father Grigory. It was disgusting of me. And of course there's no way to apologize now.

After Dina took my things—as if I cared to keep my toys— I found copies of handbills with dirty pictures in my room. He'd thrown them all over, dozens of them. It's taken me some time to understand myself (it's more than fourteen months since Dina left), but it was those pictures that provoked my bad behavior. Saying what I did to Masha—perhaps I was frightened it might be true, perhaps I was testing her. Or maybe I was just being an idiot out of boredom. Whatever the reason, I am ashamed of myself.

Here in the "House of Special Purpose," no one escapes humiliation. The guards have drawn pictures of Mother and Father Grigory on the wall inside the water closet we are to use. No one's allowed to relieve him or herself without accompaniment to the lavatory door. Once whoever it is has gone in, the guard stands outside and waits. "Have a good long look," he says each time he takes one of my sisters, and he sings lewd songs outside the door or comments on any noise he might hear through the door. He made sure all of us heard his telling Tatiana he'd love to give her "the ride on his pole" she'd "begged for"—speaking in his version of a stage whisper, guttural and almost wet, as if to suggest drooling— but he was "under orders not to fornicate with the prisoners."

It didn't matter that the idea was preposterous, that whatever he said reflected only his vice and not hers, as we all knew Tatiana was innocent. Suddenly her ability to perceive every torment as a sacrifice, a thing she could endure for the sake of her faith, for Christ, collapsed, and for two days now she has refused to get out of bed. She pretends she doesn't hear Father's cajoling or Mother praying for her. Unless she really doesn't hear anything. It's odd to see her, of all my sisters, sinking into apathy. If I'd ever anticipated such a passage as the one we are enduring, I'd have guessed Anastasia would be the first to succumb to despair, but she just goes on reading or sewing or, unaccountably, conjugating Latin verbs.

"What are you doing that for?" I asked.

"Be quiet, Alyosha," she said. "Now I have to start over."

As for Tatiana, she remains curled on her side, her face averted from the doorway, from anyone who speaks to her, and her eyes fixed on one of the painted windows, staring at the white square. She will end in making herself ill by refusing to ask when she needs to go to the water closet. It's just a matter of time.

At dinner, soldiers walk around the table and spear what they want from off our plates. Especially Father's. Every time he tries to lift his fork to his mouth, Avadyev—he's the commanding officer—intercepts it with his dirty-looking pocketknife.

"Haven't you had enough of the Soviet's generosity, bloodsucker?" he says, and he laughs as Father replaces his cutlery on his plate and leans back in his chair, tells the man to please help himself.

JUNE 12

Nagorny has been executed. A guard tried to take my chain with the saints' medals. I'd left it looped around the bedpost—that rule Mother has about never wearing anything around my neck when I'm sleeping—and had forgotten to put it back on. Nagorny stopped the guard, told him it belonged to me, and took it out of the man's hands. Within minutes he'd been arrested and taken away in an automobile. The next day Avadyev brought the chain back, its gold links and medals crusted over with blood. "Here," he said. "Your nanny has paid for your trinkets."

I didn't imagine revolutions advanced by subtleties, but I thought it would just be us they shot, not Nagy or anyone who wasn't a Romanov. Now I'm grateful Masha isn't here. I like to imagine she's somewhere wonderful, America perhaps, and that she's happy and has enough to eat and beautiful dresses to wear and a stable full of horses. Now it's I who lie in bed at night and imagine her saying good night to them one by one, just the way she used to dream of doing in the ship that carried the Wild West Show. I hope Soloviev isn't ever unkind to her, but I can't hope she's grown to love him.

Their killing Nagorny so unreasonably, for protecting me, for the crime of caring for me, has made me feel that much more friendly to the idea of being dead myself.

The happiest I ever saw Nagorny was on those occasions my health took a turn for the better. When I could walk after a period of lameness, when I could play outside with the dogs, when he was at last allowed to take me into the park—a few times I caught him crying on such occasions. "Why, Nagy," I'd say, "Nagy! For whom are those tears?" And he would brush me off. "They are nothing," he'd say, "a bit of soot in my eye." And I was young enough and ignorant enough to believe him when he told me sailors didn't cry.

I feel sorry for the rest of us—Father, Mother, my poor pale sisters who sit grimly sewing and sewing, hiding jewels in their corsets. Poor Botkin and Trupp. They aren't even guilty of being Romanovs. I've known I was about to expire ever since I was conscious—really, I have no memory of being without the looming threat of extinction—so this situation, this particular punishment for the rest of the family, is simply more of the same for me. Before Nagorny was killed, the only thing to cause me true unhappiness had been separation from Masha. Even Katya, much as I still long to feel her touching me, was just a pastime.

I think I understand something. If complete enlightenment demands relinquishing the self, then complete enlightenment implies the acceptance of mortality. Not that there isn't more to being enlightened than accepting that our lives are brief and end when we die. But I do think it's a requirement. Whether by temperament or circumstance, I am more Buddhist than Orthodox, not that I'd let on to Mother. I admit I felt a flare of hatred for Mother and her religiosity when the chain and medals were returned to me. "Trinkets." It was the right word for them. I never believed Father Grigory's gift had anything to do with God. Not her God anyway. And she doesn't believe in anything that doesn't belong to her God. It's funny—I think I loved my mother better when Masha was with me, when she turned everything into stories. She made all of us more sympathetic. She made us out to be braver and kinder, with flaws that were delightful. Like Mother's cloud.

I was so eager to discover everything I could about lovemaking, and I liked it as much as I expected I would, but now, here, I'd trade all my afternoons with Katya for one of Masha's stories.

JUNE 21

It's suffocating in this house—at least it is on the second story, because they won't allow us to open the windows, not even a crack, and the nights have been as hot as the days. We move around the rooms taking care not to brush against one another, that's how humid and sticky it is. Inasmuch as we move at all. I can't tell how much of our apathy is in response to the heat, how much a symptom of our waiting for what everyone still refuses to talk about. The condition that used to apply only to me, the tacit agreement that none of us would speak of my dying, has grown to include all of us.

A man named Yacov Yurovsky has replaced Avadyev. Trupp says Yurovsky is a member of the secret police. The courier who brings our meals from the barrack across the street told him so. There's no kitchen here. There used to be, when Ipatiev lived here, but they've turned the entire ground floor into offices, a headquarters of some kind. We all preferred Avadyev. He was not a professional, and this reassured us. He was cruel, but in fits, and seemed incapable of organized action. Spearing meat with his knife, singing dirty limericks—these demonstrated the caliber of his talents. Yurovsky is different. He is a man who makes his living murdering people. Just as others do plowing fields or mining coal. A job, nothing more, nothing less. He stopped once and stroked my hair, patted my shoulder, and told me he had a boy my age. The unnerving thing is, it wasn't an act of cruelty. He didn't do it to remind me that there were other boys in the world who were going to go on living, boys whose fathers could protect them. In order to be cruel you have to possess emotions. What he said—it was something that crossed his mind, that's all, and he saw no reason not to say it aloud.

Yurovsky has replaced Avadyev's guards, to whose particular nastiness we had grown accustomed, with a new lot of men, Hungarian prisoners of war. Apparently the Commission for Combating Counter-Revolution determined that Russian guards were too likely to feel a vestigial sympathy for the former tsar and his family. I'm sure the commission considers the replacements ideal. One of them spits at Father.

Be ready was the message written on a slip of paper rolled up and hidden inside a tube whittled out of a cork. It arrived with supper, stoppering a bottle of milk. When Anastasia found it, I saw a spark of light flicker around the room, through everyone's eyes, and then go out.

Once rescue was announced, how fine a treat to watch us as we begin, with each hour that passes, to lose hope. Like pulling wings from an insect, or chasing ants with a magnifying glass's concentrated beam of sunlight, seeing them try to outrun the burning white dot. Little experiments in inhumanity. There is no means of escape, and they know this better than we do, afflicted as we are with hope. So why not have a bit of fun and slip a note inside a milk bottle's cork, see how the message affects the prisoners' morale?

JULY 14

Bastille Day. Masha took me by surprise, asking if I'd taken the tea tray down the stairs to injure myself on purpose. I might have talked about it with her—I wish I had, maybe it would have helped me understand myself better—but I felt suddenly so naked and read like a book. I'm not sure I convinced Masha it was an accident. More likely, she grew as sick of the topic as I and gave up asking. Once she did, I put it out of my mind. It's only during the past weeks here in Yekaterinburg, imprisoned and insulted and ordered about as we hadn't been before, that I've found myself puzzling over it.

I didn't plan to do it, I know that much. I was walking with Nagorny, up and down the corridor, both of us dutifully taking exercise for the benefit of my health. We were talking about the Red Guard. Only hours before, one of them had deliberately knocked my father off his bicycle.

"What happened?" Olga asked when Father came in, but he didn't answer her; he went straight to his dressing room to change his clothes. I suppose none of us children might have learned the truth had I not badgered poor Nagorny to tell me why Father was upset, why his clothes were torn and dirty. But I did. I always could get him to do as I asked, and on our walk up and down and back and forth I chipped away at his refusal. "Nagy," I said. "Why should you know something about my father that I don't? He is my father, after all." For the first few laps he remained obdurate, his mouth shut tight in a line, shaking his head no. But I wouldn't leave off until he told me what had happened.

"You're . . . you're not upset, then?" he said, once he had told. I don't know what he expected. Tears, perhaps.

"I don't know what I am," I said, and I didn't, at least not then.

We had stopped at the service stairs. Nagy asked me to wait there, as he had to use the water closet. "I'll be back straightaway," he said, and I nodded. I saw that someone had left a tray on the table near the landing, and as soon as Nagy was out of sight—as soon as I was out of his sight—I picked up the tray, set it on the top stair, sat on it, pushed off, and rode down.

It was just like Masha to believe I'd martyred myself for the rest of the family. She couldn't help subscribing to the conceit that suffering had ennobled me rather than making me that much more spoiled. I can't think why else she might conclude I'd hurt myself.

I've interrogated myself until I'm dizzy trying to remember what I was thinking. I know it wasn't that I came up with the idea to shift everyone's attention off our hopeless situation by creating a new crisis. Nagorny went to the toilet, I picked up the tea tray and rode it down the stairs. I didn't steer it into the newel post. It was going too fast for that and, anyway, I just—I don't know, it seemed more that the tray took me than I took it.

I behaved like the stupid child I was, and then Masha made it out to be something noble and manly like she did when I didn't protest Dina's mistreating me. Had the tray not been there, had I not grown up begging to join in whenever Father took OTMA tray-riding, I might not have done anything at all. But there it was, a moment's solace, and I took it without thinking about anything but that. Masha was right about its being a distraction, but I'm afraid it was for myself, not the others.

July 15

I'm of two minds about having pushed myself on Masha the day we said goodbye. I was glad to have had that little bit more of her, but it's hardly the parting I would have chosen. She told me she liked our kissing, and she did allow me to take liberties with her, but she was capable of lying out of generosity.

Although maybe it was better to be spared that kind of thing—a private goodbye fraught with worry and grief. I couldn't stand to see her cry, and I know she hated it when I did. And what if she didn't cry? What if I cried and she didn't and we both learned that I didn't have the kind of hold over Masha that she did on me?

The Four Brothers
and the Four Sisters

· · • · ·

YUROVSKY HAD RETURNED his Nagant M1895 revolver to its holster when he saw Alyosha's hand stir among the tangle of dead limbs, reaching for his mother. His executioners were rolling the family's bodies up in sheets pulled from their still-warm beds. He pulled the revolver back out as he walked toward the former tsarevich, put its barrel to Alyosha's left ear, and, as he reported to his superiors, discharged it twice.

THE EXECUTIONERS STACKED the corpses like logs on the back of a truck and drove them to the place chosen for their dismemberment. Weeks before Yurovsky was given the order for execution, he and his militia had anticipated needing a discreet spot in which to hack up bodies, and they'd scoured the woods around Yekaterinburg for a safe place to hide evidence of any murder they might be called on to commit. They found an abandoned mine shaft near a village fourteen miles outside of Yekaterinburg. On maps the village was called Koptyaki, but no local people used that name. They called the place the Four Brothers, as the shaft opened in the shadows cast by four immense and ancient pines that had stood and witnessed the folly of mankind for a thousand or more years.

One hundred and fifty gallons of gasoline. Four hundred pounds of sulfuric acid. Totalitarian regimes do have a fondness for euphemism, as Alyosha observed, and for keeping exact records of their crimes.

Yurovsky's crew threw the larger bones and anything else that had withstood the fire down the shaft to be melted away with acid. "The world will never know what we did to them," the guard who bought the gasoline assured whomever it was Lenin sent to inquire.

Six months later, in January of 1919, an investigation undertaken by the White Army in Siberia, yet to fall to the Red, searched every inch within fifty miles of the House of Special Purpose and found the Four Brothers and the mine shaft they protected. At the bottom, under a foot of ice, were Alyosha's belt buckle and fragments of the military caps he and Tsar Nikolay had been wearing when they died, as well as a pearl earring and an emerald cross recognized as having belonged to Alexandra Fyodorovna, buckles from all four sisters' shoes, 119 blobs of lead—revolver bullets that had melted in the pyre, which burned for three days—and a few ambiguous bits and pieces.

As it happened, Alyosha was mistaken. Letters were found—not forgeries but genuine letters written by people who admitted authorship—promising rescue and asking for details about the House of Special Purpose. Were any windows ever left open or unlocked? Was it possible for Nikolay Alexandrovich or one of his family to unlock a window? How well armed were the guards and how many were there altogether? Could Nikolay Alexandrovich provide a plan of the floor on which he and his family were being held? Either these were intercepted or the Bolsheviks got wind of the number of White Army soldiers hidden in the woods and decided to shoot the whole family all right away. They'd kill them when the townsfolk were sleeping, dispose of the bodies, and get the place cleaned up before dawn.

. . .

I HAD A DREAM LAST NIGHT. Remarkable for its persuasiveness, it returned me to Tsarskoe Selo and to the company of those who live only in memory and dreams. I was sorry to wake up.

Once again, I'd accompanied my father to tea at the Alexander Palace, but the Romanov girls were no longer children. They were grown women now and had already been murdered. I could see holes in their heads, their bodices, their necks—everywhere—and yet they weren't bleeding; they didn't seem to be suffering in any way. When they moved, jewels fell from their sides to the floor, spilling from where their gowns had been rent by bayonets.

"Come," Tatiana said to me. She took my hand and all five of us entered the wide marble corridor, walking abreast until we arrived at the door to the room of glass cabinets, inside which were the imperial Easter eggs. "I want to show you my favorite," she said, taking the lead and pulling me into the room behind her. "The one with the window.

"Come," Tatiana said again, when I balked.

"I'm not sure," I said. "I don't think I want to."

"But you must," she pressed.

Though I was no longer a child, and though I had lived so intimately with them for so many months, in my dream to disobey one of the tsar's daughters required fortitude, and Tatiana had always been the most imperious among the Romanov girls. More beautiful than the others, she was tall and slender and carried herself in a manner that was genuinely queenly. It was apparent that her determination had not been diminished by her new circumstances.

"But I know what's inside," I said. "I don't need to see it again." At this, Tatiana and her sisters looked at one another and began laughing, so overcome by mirth they couldn't speak.

"Of course you don't know what's inside!" Tatiana said when she'd recovered her breath.

"But I do. I remember it in detail."

"You can't know," she said. "No one can. It's never the same twice."

"But how can that be?" I asked.

She turned up her empty palms. "It is," she said, "that's all."

Behind Tatiana, her sisters nodded, and I understood that the situation offered me no choice. We would stand there for eternity, Tatiana and I, disagreeing, until I gave in.

"All right," I said.

Again—as she had when I was a child—Tatiana opened the glass door to one of the cabinets lining the walls of the room. The egg cut from pink jade was larger than I'd remembered, and Tatiana struggled to lift it from the shelf. Once she had, she held it in her arms like a real burden, pressed close to her breast. When she placed it on the table, I saw, as I hadn't before, that it was a pink so luminous it appeared that light emanated from within its jade shell rather than from without.

"You can't delay looking forever," Tatiana told me when I was slow to move, and I nodded, then kneeled before it. "Remember," she said as I put my eye to the glass. "It magnifies."

For a moment I couldn't see anything, it was so bright within the egg, everything shining like sunlight reflected on water's surface. I had to squint to make anything out.

Spring, richly green. Even as my eyes were dazzled, every other sense was sharpened. I could smell the grass and feel sun on my skin. There was a riot of birds in every tree. It was the park outside the Alexander Palace, and the poplar grove had been restored to life. A bicycle, painted red with chrome mudguards, leaned against one of them. Handsome Alyosha's. I recognized it as the one I'd given him, and Alyosha was there too, with the most mischievous look on his face. I'd caught him doing something, and he put his finger to his lips, as if asking me not to tell on him. He'd disabled the sundial—not dismantled it completely but taken away the part that casts the shadow around the dial of Roman numerals. I could see he was very pleased with the prank. His smile was so radiant I couldn't help but smile back at him.

But at just that moment, when Alyosha had stopped time's shadow within the egg, one of the imperial eggs that contained a clock began to chime, startling me.

Tatiana put her hand on my shoulder, and I turned away from the window to look at her. "Say goodbye," she said.

"Oh, no," I said, stricken at the idea of leaving. "Please, no."

"I'm sorry," Tatiana said, and now all the clocks were chiming. "It's time."

"May I come back?" I asked, taking the hand she offered to help me up from my knees.

"Of course, as often as you like."

"But the egg—the window—it won't be the same next time?" As I spoke the words, I understood I'd already lost him. I dropped to my knees, and Tatiana moved between me and the egg, covering the little window.

"No," she said. "It won't be the same."

Acknowledgments

. . .

THANK YOU Millicent Bennett, Dylan Brock, Nicole Bufanio, Janet Gibbs, Joan Gould, Julia Harrison, Courtney Hodell, Jynne Martin, Kate Medina, Sara Nelson, Kate Norris, Beth Pearson, Lindsey Schwoeri, and Amanda Urban—all of you, each of you, for your support, which extends beyond any single book.

When I first arrived in prerevolutionary Russia, my guide to that world was *Nicholas and Alexandra* by Robert K. Massie. It was an odd book for an eleven-year-old to fasten on; yet I reread it several times as a teenager. Massie, whose son suffered from hemophilia, gave the tsarevich's illness center stage where other historians might not, and it was this particular narrative thread of the Romanov tragedy that caught the attention of a girl (and, later, a woman) who sought out stories of violent martyrdom, stigmata, vampires—anything that presented bleeding as a vehicle of transformation. Once I was introduced to Russia, there was much to hold that girl's (that woman's) attention, and I lingered, reading novels and history books.

Upon discovering, in middle age, that Grigory Rasputin had a daughter whose career as a lion tamer ended in 1935 in Peru, Indiana, where she was mauled by a black bear and nearly bled to death, my excitement didn't fade but began, slowly, to eclipse other interests.

The Devil and his entourage, who appear in the chapter "Coronation," will be familiar to readers of *The Master and Margarita*, a novel that no amount of rereading has diminished for me. As it is Mikhail Bulgakov's characterization of devilish high jinks to which I turn as one of the few reliable remedies for a great number of existential complaints, I take this opportunity to express my gratitude to the author of that inimitable work.